THE CENTER
BOOK 2

RECOVERY

THE CENTER
BOOK 2

RECOVERY

Denise Coulson

www.blkdogpublishing.com

Also by Denise Coulson for your consideration:

The Center

The Center revolves around nine young scientists and friends, working together to save the human race in the not too distant future.

Our main character, Dr. Ben Logan PHD, has been visited by a woman, in his dreams, since he was five years old. Over the years she has shown him events that will begin happening to his planet, Earth. Natural disasters, and manmade ones. Uncontrollable Global Warming, Political unrest, corruption, and War. Events that will eventually lead to the end of life on Earth.

She has tasked him with building a team and finding a way to lead that team and a handful of other Earthlings, to her, in the Center of the Universe. The Center holds nine planets surrounding a sun. Each planet has a creator living on it. Nine sisters who are responsible for creating and maintaining a section of the universe and all the galaxies within their sections.

This is their story, and their journey.

This one is for you, Mama
For sharing your love of books, stories and magic
Thank You!
I love you

CHAPTER 1

Kenji Tanaka was thirty-six years old. He was a pilot, an engineer and had been alive nearly four thousand years. He was a member of a team that made the trek from a dying planet called Earth, to the Center of the Universe, to save humanity and rebuild a human society.

Kenji was the elder of two children. Born into privilege to a wealthy, successful businessman and his wife, a medical research biologist, he was five years older than his little sister, Akemi. And was eleven years old, when his mother was killed. She was Christmas shopping in Tokyo with her sister and got caught in a gang shootout. His father moved his children out of Japan and ran his business in London then Dubai and then moved them to the United States where they became citizens. His father and sister never returned to Japan. Kenji visited a few times in secret. They still had family there and he felt an obligation to keep his mother alive by being a part of her family there. But an earthquake triggered three tsunamis and his beloved Japan and all the remaining family he had were wiped off the face of the Earth. Kenji became a pilot and joined the US Air Force. He flew planes and helicopters while his sister flew through high school and college, graduating with her PhD before her 18th birthday. Their father had her tested when she was 7 and again when she was 13 – her IQ was beyond anything previously measured.

That's how he ended up here. Akemi became a part of a team building a ship and a self-sustaining engine for long term space exploration. At least that was what he was told. It was years later, after Kenji left the Air Force and took his place at his father's side, to learn and prepare himself to take over the family business. He learned the truth. Earth was becoming unstable. The abuse man had inflicted on her had become too much and in a matter of years all life would become extinct, when all the volcanos on the planet erupted as one and covered everything with ash and would block out the sun for generations.

Kenji's father negotiated a place for him on the team. He was welcomed and tasked with finding pilots to fly the ships they were building, off the planet and to the Center of the Universe.

He learned that Ben Logan, the leader of the team had been visited in dreams, since he was five years old, by a woman called Gaia. She was one of nine sisters who were creators of galaxies and worlds. She came to him and told him of things to come and showed him the way to The Center.

Kenji had been a little skeptical in the beginning, but every prediction from Gaia came true at the exact date and time Ben told them they would. From natural disasters, presidential assassinations and the New World Order taking over the planet and creating a global police force.

So, when the time came, Kenji flew the lead ship, *The Destiny* away from Earth and toward The Center, followed by ten other ships including two occupied by the US military, men and women that refused to follow the New World Order and wanted to find a new planet to inhabit and continue their lives upon.

The journey took close to four thousand years, most of which was spent in cryofreeze. Each member of the team woke every fifty years, to make sure they were on course and that there had been no malfunctions.

He saw nine ships safely to The Center, but two went down following him through an asteroid field. The ship *Stonehenge* was hit and damaged by a large asteroid and *The Rapture* escorted that ship to the nearest planet to ensure its survival. There were 250 souls on those two ships, and 300 frozen embryos. The last thing Kenji told them was that he would come back for them. So here he was, 500 years later, navigating once again through the same asteroid field toward that tiny little blue and green planet to see if they were there. He knew that the original teams would be gone, long ago dead, but they may have family, descendants there. Gaia told him that they had lived and built a thriving community. He needed to see for himself what had become of his friends and the people he felt responsible for.

He remembered what Ben Logan had told him when he asked if he could take a ship and return to this place. Ben told him to take *The Destiny* and follow his. So, he had loaded the ship with things he thought might be needed. Clothing, seeds, medical supplies, and some of the universal translators Gaia had provided, just in case.

He had twenty-seven other passengers on board all in cryofreeze, just waiting for him to hit the button to wake them up. He had a doctor and two nurses, a contractor, an agriculturist, and six members of the military, who lay down their weapons and agreed to a life of peace instead of war. One of them was Josh Cole, whose father led an attack on The Center and attempted to murder Gaia. There were twelve security team members, that helped all of them escape from Earth, while the New World Order tried to stop them. One other pilot, Shawn Brooks. Mateo Delgado, Zander Delgado's brother. Zander had led their security team on Earth. He was also married to Akemi, and father to Kenji's nephew, Kai. And there was Sarah Lindsey. Nuclear Physicist, PhD, genius, ballerina, and the woman he was pretty sure he was falling in love with. A gorgeous blonde with green eyes, built like a cover girl model. She had style, wit, and just to top it all off, was one of the smartest people Kenji had ever known.

Kenji shook his head a little, He was in the heart of the asteroid field, and those rocks were getting bigger and closer together. He needed to get his mind off the hot little doctor, frozen in her cryotube, behind him and pay attention to the path and get to the planet his people landed on.

He considered waking Shawn, just for another pilot's eyes on the path, or waking Sarah to have her brain helping him navigate, but decided, if something should happen, better for them to sleep through it.

He started seeing the planet more clearly, as he steered through the asteroids. It was tiny. All blue and green. It looked like it had two continents, one a little larger in the north, and the other smaller one in the south. The northern land was facing toward the sun. He had to assume that his pilots would head there. It was sure to be warmer than the southern side which was further away from it. It had one moon on the far side of the planet. It was grey, and reminded Kenji of Earth's moon, but much smaller.

A large asteroid appeared in front of the ship and Kenji had to maneuver quickly to get below it. Once he was under it, his path opened up, and he smiled. It looked like smooth sailing the rest of the way.

He hit the remote on his console to disengage Sarah's cryofreeze and start her warming program. He wanted her to see it as they approached the tiny little planet at the edge of the asteroid field.

He heard her tube open, then her husky English accent. "Good morning, Captain," she said. She came up front and sat next to him in the other captain's chair in the cockpit. "We made it?"

"Almost," Kenji told her. "Just another thirty or forty minutes."

"It's beautiful. It looks so small and clean. And all that blue water. I think we're going to find something special here, Kenji.

He nodded. "Gaia said it was created 320 years before *The Rapture* and *Stonehenge* landed. It took us 250 years after that to get to the Center and another 250 to get back here. So, it's only 820 years old. It's barely old enough to start evolving."

"I can't wait to see what our fellow Earthlings have done with it," she stood and kissed his cheek. "I'm going to get dressed and wake the rest of our passengers."

He nodded and kept looking ahead at the planet they were approaching.

When all of the people on board *The Destiny* were awake, dressed and fed their dry rations, they all stood looking out the windows as Kenji made his final approach.

He entered the orbit and began looking for somewhere to land. The really cool thing about the ships was they were made like airplanes, so they could land on and take off from the ground. The atmosphere surrounding the planet was very thin, which was a concern, but Kenji continued through it and began searching the northern continent. He made his way down to about 11,000 feet, and they could see lush green grass, forests with tall thick green trees, rock formations, lakes and waterfalls. There was a mountain range, again all green. There were no other colors. All green land, some grey rocks, green trees and foliage and blue water. There were very few clouds in the sky, but what was there had a purple tinge to them. And the sky was clear and blue.

"I don't think I've seen so much green in my life," Sarah said with awe in her voice. "It's breathtaking."

Shawn was sitting in the co-pilot's chair and monitoring the console, checking for signs of life. "I've got something, Kenji. Looks like a settlement on the southeast part of the continent."

Kenji nodded and turned the ship south. They saw the coastline. Green grass, filling all the space until it met with the crystal clear blue ocean. He followed the coast east.

"Umm, Kenji," Sarah started.

"Yeah, I see them."

Suddenly they were surrounded by what could only be described as dragons. Probably fifty or more in various sizes and colors.

"Holy crap!" Sarah said. "Be careful you don't hit one, Kenji!"

Kenji reduced speed as the dragons flew all around the ship, one came up to the window on the side of the ship and seemed to look in at the passengers, then flew on. None of them came close enough to cause any damage or be injured. It seemed like they were just curious to see something else flying through the sky with them.

"They're gorgeous," Mateo said.

"Yeah," Josh agreed. "Let's just hope they're not fire breathing, and decide we look tasty."

Suddenly they began lining up around the ship, some in front, others on each side, and some behind like they were escorting it – or herding them. Kenji dropped down a little as their escort moved lower, about 6,000 feet. Then, as if they were doing an elaborate dance, they started moving aside. One to the right, and the next to the left until they were all flying on either side of *The Destiny*. They saw another group of dragons heading toward them, and they started doing the same thing. Moving to the left and right, so they had a clear path. Then they saw an enormous golden dragon coming directly toward them. Kenji could still see the other dragons on each side of the ship, so he couldn't go to the right or left to avoid the oncoming one. As it got closer, they saw a man riding on its back. He had his hands in the air and was waving and smiling. Then he and his dragon veered off to the north and waved for them to follow him.

Kenji looked at Sarah and Shawn and shrugged his shoulders, then turned the ship to follow the dragon rider.

Ian had been edgy all morning. He felt off, like there was something he needed to do, but couldn't quite remember what it was. His work was completed, and he had nothing more to do. But he couldn't shake the feeling that he needed to be ready. For something. His dragon, Darcy, must have been feeling the same, because she wouldn't leave his side and kept nudging him toward the sea. He had raised Darcy since the day her egg hatched in his hands on his 10th birthday. They were truly joined and bonded.

"Shall we go fish and swim, my girl? Maybe that's what we both need to relax today."

She nudged him again and pushed him with her huge head. He laughed and kissed her on her snout. Ian grabbed his pole and spear, and they headed toward the sea.

After about an hour, he decided his heart wasn't really in it, he put his pole down and just floated in the water as Darcy circled and dove in. tossing her catch in the air before swallowing it whole.

He heard the trumpets of the herd seconds before he heard the wings flapping. He saw what looked to be the entire herd of riderless dragons flying quickly in formation heading west. He had only seen them do this once before, when he was a child, and he felt a gnawing in his belly start to stir. He could feel Darcy's need to go with her herd mates but called her to him. "Let's ride, girl," he said and jumped onto her back.

Before he joined the herd, he circled the city and saw people coming out of their homes to see what was going on. He flew low when he saw his mother. "Keep everyone close," he hollered down to her. "Darcy and I will see what's happening." He rode up fast, before she could say anything and headed after the herd.

They stayed to the back of the others. He could feel Darcy's dilemma. She wanted to fly in front, as was her place, as alpha, but her need to protect him was stronger. Suddenly they saw the western herd escorting a ship toward them and Ian let out a big joyous laugh. He recognized it immediately; it was an exact replica of *The Rapture* and *Stonehenge*, the two ships that had brought his ancestors here. The elders had always said that someday, they would send a ship back for them. It was the last thing they heard from their lead pilot, Kenji Tanaka.

"Tell them, Darcy! Tell them they are friends and mean them no harm."

A few moments later, the Western herd started breaking off to fly to the side, and his Eastern herd followed suit, until he was directly in front of the ship. He began waving his arms in greeting and told Darcy to fly to the landing area. He gestured for the ship to follow, then he and Darcy pulled to the right, he turned and saw the ship following, and when they turned he saw the words on the side of the ship. "The *Destiny*," he whispered. The flag ship for the expedition from Earth, led by Ben Logan, and flown by Kenji Tanaka. The ship that held the nine.

As they followed the golden dragon, they could just make out a small city to the south of where they were flying along the shore. There were hundreds of buildings and roads. There were parks and pavilions. Up on higher ground he saw acre upon acre of crops. Kenji could make out wheat and corn fields. A little further out it looked like groves of apple and lemon trees and more buildings. Some looked like houses, and some like they were possibly greenhouses for growing. As they traveled north of the city, Kenji could see a wide and long, cleared pathway. It looked like they had made a runway for him to land on.

The dragon went lower and flew close to the ground showing Kenji the way and indicating that he should set down on the runway.

"Ok, everyone. We're touching down. Hold on to something or take a seat," Kenji told them. "It might be a little bumpy."

Kenji dropped his landing gear and pulled back on the thrusters. As soon as the wheels were on the ground, he pulled the brake. They taxied along the runway for about 500 yards, then the path curved back toward the city. Kenji came to a stop at the end of the runway and depressurized the cabin before opening the hatch. They saw what looked like thousands of people standing around the ship. Young and old, children, and babies in the arms of their parents. Some were waving, all were smiling. In the distance there were dragons grazing in the field, some flying around in the sky. There were red ones, blue, green, silver, grey, and any other color you could imagine. Some were huge, the size of a small jet plane, others were smaller and some just the size of large birds. Kenji wasn't sure what he had expected, but this definitely wasn't it.

"Ok, guys, let's go meet our hosts," he said. He moved toward the hatch and headed down the stairs, with Sarah close behind him.

Sarah could feel the difference in the air. It had a lightness. She could breathe just fine, but also felt like if she really wanted to, she could just float away. She had to make a concentrated effort to keep her feet on the ground. She looked at Kenji and he was taking deep breaths, and when he looked at her, she knew he felt it too.

A woman that looked to be in her mid-thirties stood next to the young dragon rider that had led them in. Both of them were standing in front of what had to be every member of the community. There was a strong family resemblance between them. Both looked mixed race, with light brown skin, dark eyes and hair. Hers was long and pulled back in braids and beads, his wild and also long, brushing his shoulders and standing up all over his head. Not quite an afro, it was longer and crazier.

The woman stepped forward and extended her hand to Kenji. "Welcome to Asteria," she said. "I am Charlie." Kenji took her hand and shook it.

The young man stepped forward and held his hand out as well. "You're Kenji Tanaka," he said with a bit of wonder in his voice.

Kenji shook his hand. "Yes," he said.

The woman, Charlie smiled. "This is my son, and your guide, Ian," she told them. "He's a bit of a fan Mr.

Tanaka. He learned all about the expedition of the nine, in his AROE classes."

"Please, call me Kenji. It's nice to meet you Ian," Kenji said and smiled at him. "Thanks for the lead in. It was pretty extraordinary." Then he turned to Charlie. "Your son? I would have thought maybe brother."

Charlie smiled. "You flatter me."

"Not at all. You look very young to have a full-grown son."

"I'm 54 years old. And Ian is 27," she told them. "My grandmother is Abby, daughter of Ali and Kendra, who I believe were friends of yours, Sarah."

Sarah's jaw dropped. "You are their great granddaughter? Yes, Ali and Kendra were both very dear friends of mine." Sarah stepped forward and embraced Charlie. "We have so many questions."

"As do we," Charlie said. "You made it to the Center?"

"We did," Sarah said. "We stayed three days, then came back for you."

Charlie nodded. "We've been expecting you. My mother went to wake the elders. They always said you'd come, and here you are. Please, follow me."

She linked her arm through Sarah's and began leading them away from the runway. The people cleared a path for them, then fell in behind. As they walked across the field, Sarah had the sensation again that if she wanted to, she could just fly across the ground.

"I have something you may find interesting," Charlie told her.

As they walked they realized they were in a meadow, and it came to an abrupt end with a steep grass overed cliff overlooking the outskirts of the city nestled by the sea. At the far end sat *The Rapture* and *Stonehenge*. Sarah's breath caught in her throat. "The ships!"

The tops were covered with green moss, which explained why Kenji didn't see them from the air. "They look like they're in good shape," Kenji said.

"They are," Ian told him. "We keep them maintained. They were stripped for their resources, but they provide most of the power that keeps the city going."

"So how do we get down there?" Sarah asked.

Charlie smiled at her. "Do you trust me?"

Sarah nodded. Charlie grasped her hand. "Just jump."

"Jump?" Sarah asked.

She heard Ian laugh, and then he leapt into the air. He floated down, touching once on the side of the slope, then leaping back up into the air and turning a somersault before coming to a landing on the surface below. He turned and looked up. "Come on down," he shouted up at them.

Suddenly the townspeople started doing the same. Jumping into the air and floating down to the bottom.

All that remained on the top were Charlie and the team from the *Destiny*.

"You may have noticed that the air here is very light. We have a much higher gravity level than you are used to. We can't fly like the dragons, but we can jump long distances and run faster and longer than you could on Earth. When our children are young, we have to tether them, to keep them on the ground." She laughed a little at that, remembering Ian as a baby. Always wanting to float away from her.

Sarah took a deep breath. She was still holding hands with Charlie and reached her other one out for Kenji's. "Ok," she said. "Let's do this."

Together they jumped into the air and out into the open space, floating down and landing softly on the ground below. "Oh, wow," she said and laughed holding her stomach. "That's going to take some getting used to." The rest of the team, after seeing them land safely, jumped down as well.

"That's just crazy!" Josh said. "This place is gonna be fun!"

Charlie and Ian led them through the city, to the site where the ships were. As they approached, they saw another woman climb down from *The* Rap*ture* and walk toward them. Sarah could see the resemblance to Ali in this woman.

"My mother, Lena," Charlie said and extended her hand to take the other woman's hand in hers. Kenji and Sarah just looked at each other. This woman looked no more than ten years older than Charlie.

"Did you guys discover the fountain of youth here?" Kenji asked them.

"Clean living, Mr. Tanaka," Lena said with a laugh. "Literally. There are no toxins here on Asteria. We eat only what we grow, with no pesticides or added ingredients in the soil. And for protein, we have fish from the ocean. All water here is fresh. No salt or pollution in the air or water. We work the fields and walk or run to get where we need to go. So, we have a much longer life than you did on Earth."

"Please, call me Kenji. Mr. Tanaka is my father."

She nodded. "Kenji. It's so good to meet you. And you, Sarah. My grandparents talked of you so much, I feel like I already know you both. And I'm very much looking forward to meeting the rest of your team. And hear all about the others at the Center."

As she spoke, they noticed a group of people exiting *The Ra*pture. They looked much, much older than the rest. But Sarah recognized Ali and Kendra as they stepped to the ground. And Kenji saw his pilots, Jason and Brad behind them.

"Oh, my God," Sarah whispered. "How is this possible?"

"Go," Charlie told her. "They'll explain everything you need to know."

Sarah broke into a run and went to greet her old friends. When she reached them, she threw her arms around both of them and held on. "I can't believe you're here!"

Kenji and Shawn followed and went to Brad and Jason. They exchanged handshakes and quick hugs.

There were twelve of the original crew. A couple of the medicals, and one from each of the other groups. scientist, contractor, agriculturist, two of Zander's security team and an engineer.

A little later they sat in one of the pavilions and told them of the Center and meeting Gaia and her sisters. They described what it looked like, the nine planets surrounding a large sun. They talked briefly about the military trying to take over and being banished to the moon Kajax. Then started learning all they could about Asteria.

They learned that Kenda had named the planet after a Greek legend. Asteria was a Titan deity. During the fall of the Titans, Zues chased Asteria who took the form of a bird, then fell from the sky like a shooting star. Kendra shrugged. "It seemed appropriate," she said, "as we fell from the sky like a shooting star."

Once they landed and got a little acclimated, they started planting and building.

"We knew you'd come back for us," Jason told Kenji. "But we also knew you had several hundred years to go before you reached The Center, and it would take several hundred more before you could return."

"We knew Asteria was a very young planet, but the soil was rich, and our seeds took root and grew very quickly. There are no ground bugs here," Ali said, "so, we had no pests to worry about."

"No bugs?" Sarah asked. "It's sounding more and more like paradise to me!"

"How do things pollinate?" Kenji asked.

"Well, no *ground* bugs," Kendra corrected with a little laugh. "We do have buzzers. Each ship was stocked with seeds, and pollinators. Several thousand honeybee eggs. Over the decades, they have mutated into what we call buzzers. They're mostly nocturnal, and resemble fireflies, but they do the job. "How was Jewel when you left the Center? The baby?" she asked.

Sarah smiled. "We left three days after we landed. But Gaia told her that her baby was healthy and would be a girl. I think she and Hank were going to name her Eve. She asked me to give you, her love. Both of you," she said to Kendra and Ali.

"So, no bugs," Paul, one of the nurses who traveled with them said. "Any other life forms when you arrived?"

"There are many species of fish. And the dragons, of course," Ali said.

They learned that there were two species of dragons. One came from the sea and the other born on land. Both could swim or fly, it was just preference as to where they lived as far as they could tell. When they first arrived, they found four eggs in a stream by a waterfall after they had been there for a few months and were scouting the area. They had no idea what kind of eggs they were, so they kept watch over them to see what hatched. When they did, they were tiny little dragons.

"A few months later, I was sitting by the sea, just watching the fish jump, and the sun set," Kendra told them, "And a very large red dragon came out of the sea. My first instinct was to run for my life, but I figured it could easily overtake me, so I just sat very still and hoped it wouldn't notice me." She laughed and reached for Ali's hand. "When she reached the shore, she looked right at me and dropped three eggs out of her mouth. She rolled them toward me, then backed away toward the water again. It was like she was giving them to me. I stood and slowly approached the eggs, and I swear she smiled at me. I could almost hear her thoughts. She was entrusting me with her children and asking me to care for them. I know that sounds a little crazy but it's true. When I picked up the eggs, she bowed to me and returned to the sea."

"They're lovely and loving creatures," Ali said. "We care for them, nurture them, and when they come of age, they choose a rider. Or most do. Some choose to remain riderless." She looked at Ian and smiled. "And I hear, my darling grandson, that your Darcy has become Alpha of the eastern herd."

"She has, Grandma. And we are growing in numbers each year. We have over seventy riders now."

"So, they're not the fire breathing monsters of our stories and legends?" Sarah asked.

"No. They are gentle and kind. Some are a little mischievous, but not one of them would hurt a fly. If we had flies," Kendra laughed.

They continued talking into the night. Most of the others went to their homes, Except for the families of the Twelve. They learned that the population of the city was 33,823 and that several women were expecting babies soon. They all chose to stay close together. Some built homes up in the meadow, by the crops, to tend them. Others in the city, and some, like Ian, chose to build homes in the forest just west of the city. They had a group of riders that built their houses in the trees near the dragons' lair.

The lair was on a cliff, near a lake and waterfall within the forest. They kept the hatchlings in an enclosure up in the meadow, and they stayed there until they were old enough to move to the lair.

"How are you still here?" Kenji asked. "It's been 500 years. You guys look like you're maybe in your seventies s."

"It was decided that twelve of us would go into cryofreeze to await your arrival," Ali said. "Life expectancy here is much longer than we had on Earth, but most of us pass on between 160 and 180 years. I was 92 and Kendra 90 when we went into cryo."

"We wake a couple of times a year, to share in some events. The birth of our grandchildren, and great grandchildren, or if there was a medical emergency or if they needed us on council for some reason. And every year, we have a festival to celebrate our arrival on Asteria. But we wanted to be here to greet you when you came."

"Charlie told us that Ian learned about us from classes with the AROE so, it's still working?" Kenji asked, referring to Christov Wagner's vision. He created eleven AI units, one for each ship. Artificial Recreation of Earth. He loaded holographic images of the masterpieces in art and literature, including history and documentaries and apparently movies and television.

"It is. We still have both of them. And have added more since then. We use them in school settings mostly," Kendra said. "But we've also set up libraries, and museums. I think Christov would be happy with how his vision has played a part in our development here."

"Tomorrow, we'll give you a tour of the city. I think you'll enjoy what we've built," Ali told them. "We made decisions to focus on community and the arts. We all work, and contribute to the whole, but we keep it all very simple. It was decided that we would not abuse the planet's resources and recreate the issues we had on Earth. We have no politicians, we have committees for city planning, finances, building, etcetera. We built our environment with what we considered essential necessities. Running water, indoor plumbing, electricity. But we chose not to crowd our new world with unnecessary technology. We have made significant advances in medicine and agriculture. And we collectively agreed to population control. Asteria is significantly smaller than Earth. We have only two continents, and with our extended life expectancy, we needed to take that into consideration.

"We didn't see any other communities, when we flew in," Kenji said. "Have you explored the rest of this continent? Or the one in the South?"

Sarah felt a change in Kendra and Ali. And there was a long hesitation before answering. "Yes," Kendra said. "We've had explorers, and there are smaller settlements, further away from here. But most of us decided to stay close."

"It's late," Lena said. "I'm sure you all must be tired. We have some empty housing we can put you in for now.

Why don't we get some rest and meet back here in the morning."

Kendra put her hand on Lena's cheek. "Our granddaughter is ever practical and worries for her feeble old grannies. But she's right. Let's turn in and meet for breakfast."

"Feeble my butt," Lena said as she hugged both of her grandmothers. "You're only ten years older than I am."

Kenji reached a hand down for Sarah and pulled her up then slipped his arm around her waist.

"This is nice to see," Ali said. "I was always hoping you two would finish dancing and find your way to each other."

Sarah smiled and leaned her head on Kenji's shoulder. "We're still dancing some," she said. "But it's looking good."

They were led to a row of little houses. It seemed like they had just kept building, knowing that more and more houses would be needed, as the community continued to grow. Kenji and Sarah were shown to a small two-bedroom cottage and although they were dancing, as Ali said, they weren't quite ready to share a room. The other team members were shown to other houses along the same row.

"These are some of the original cottages," Ian told them as he opened the door and led them in. "So, they're a little more rustic than our newer housing. But they're in good condition and everything works. And it's got a great view of the ocean out the back door. My mom had some of the kids come down and clean them up and make sure the bedding and linen were all freshened up for you. But if you need anything more, just let us know."

"This is great, Ian. Thank you," Sarah said.

After they said goodnight and closed the door to their little house. Kenji and Sarah looked around and explored. It was furnished with heavy wooden furniture and soft cotton cushions. The little kitchen had a round wooden table and chairs. There was a sink, refrigerator, and stove. Sarah turned on the water and found it did indeed have running water. And it appeared that everything was made of wood. Even the stove. But it had a hard shiny coat of something over it. Off each side of the living room was a bedroom. Again, a wooden bed and a chest at the foot of it, with soft mattresses and cotton sheets and covers. There was also a small bathroom with running water off a back enclosed porch. The sink and toilet seemed to be made from wood as well, but sanded and polished. There was also a little shower.

When Sarah stepped out of the bathroom and back into the kitchen, she just looked at Kenji who was standing looking out a window over the sink. They had a perfect view of the ocean.

Sarah just shook her head. "I have dozens of questions to ask them tomorrow," she said. "I understand there is an abundance of trees here. So, the fact that everything seems to be made from wood makes sense. But what is the gloss over all the appliances? It's got to be an insulation of some kind. Protecting it from heat and fire?"

"Looks like," Kenji agreed. "And there is no sand. The grass goes straight to the sea. So how did they make all the glass?" He tapped on the window.

"Yeah," Sarah said. "Dozens of questions. But for now, we should probably get some rest."

Kenji took another look out the window and gasped. "Sarah, come here. Look at this."

She walked over to him and saw a large pearl white dragon with golden tips on its wings flying in circles over the ocean. It dipped down and went into the water then flew straight back up letting out a roar with water spilling off its body and wings. It repeated the same dip and emergence several times, each time letting out its roar. Sarah thought it sounded triumphant and happy.

"I don't think I'm ever going to get used to seeing that," Kenji said.

Sarah shook her head. "Me neither. But I really want to ride one."

Kenji snorted out a laugh. "You would. And I bet you will." He pulled her close and gave her a kiss on the head. "I'm going to get some sleep."

After he went to one of the bedrooms, Sarah turned back to the window and watched the dragon for a while longer before finding her bed and sleep. And while she slept, she dreamed of riding that pearl colored dragon across the sky.

Ian sat on the cliff, watching Apollo dipping into the water and rising again. He knew the sound he was making was a call to his rider. He wondered which of the newcomers he was calling to. Apollo was part of the western herd. He had gone west after his rider, Jill, passed away. That was the dragon's way. He knew they mourned the loss of their riders and went west to live with the others who had lost theirs. He never saw one stay like this, after the others returned home.

He thought about the people who came on the *Destiny*. He was fascinated by their stories of the Center, and the other team members. He knew that there were some in the colony that were hoping they could travel there someday. But Ian couldn't imagine ever wanting to leave Asteria and the life he had there.

He felt Darcy coming. She landed softly next to him and laid down resting her head on her front feet. She spread a wing, and he leaned back against her and closed his eyes. He fell asleep listening to Apollo's call, tucked under his dragon's wing.

CHAPTER 2

O ver the next few days and weeks, all of the newcomers to Asteria started learning their ways.

The city was sprawling and spanned several miles along the coast with structures built into the side of the cliffs. There were community kitchens that always had food going. There were also large dining halls where people could gather and eat meals together, or they could take food back to their homes. Many chose to cook in their own houses, but the dining halls were always there if they felt like community.

Everyone worked in some capacity. There were carpenters and builders who were always creating new furniture or helping repair homes and buildings around the community. There was a hospital and small clinics throughout the city for anyone needing medical help, and an abundance of doctors and nurses. Others worked in the fields and greenhouses. Sarah was thrilled to find a small crop of coffee beans and bartered one of her bracelets for a bag; they provided a wooden coffee bean press as a gift. There were those that tended the dragons, and others that took care of the babies and children while their parents worked. Others tended the community itself, running shops and stores. The people earned credits, kept by a community record keeper, for the work they did, and could use those credits for purchasing things, or they could barter. But no one went without anything they needed.

Some of the trees produced an abundance of a cotton-like substances, and there were those that collected that, and brought it to those that could weave it into clothing, blankets and bedding. Other trees produced a sap that they used for sealing their homes and buildings. When it dried, it was as hard as cement. And still another tree had sap they used as a resin to finish the sinks, toilets, stoves and refrigerators. The resin created the smooth finish and made the wood water and heat resistant. Everything ran on electrical power created by solar panels and powered by the ships.

They had learned that there were several islands that had mountains of a crystal like substance that dragon riders would fly to and chip away to bring back and the smiths would melt it down to make the glass used for windows and doors.

There were artists who created the most incredible works. Paintings, sculptures, jewelry and tapestries. There were musicians and writers, teachers and chemists.

Gaia was right when she told them that they had built a beautiful life here. Sarah thought.

They learned that a group of explorers had gone to the southern continent and began building a colony. It was much colder there, and many chose not to stay, but some had and were building a life there. Then about twenty years ago, another ship had crash landed on the planet. The Asterians saw it go through the atmosphere and when some of the dragon riders followed it, they saw it crash into the southern continent.

They sent an expedition to the south, by sea and by air, to offer assistance but the species on the ship was hostile, and the language barrier was too much to overcome. They had weapons and attacked the settlers that were trying to help them. They lost many in battle that day, and the ships and riders returned home. Kendra and Ali's grandson and his children were all lost in the battle. Christopher, their grandson, had a gift for diplomacy and went to try to communicate with the strangers. Their great grandson, Kaleb was the captain on the lead ship and was the first to lose his life. Ali had given birth to Abby first, from the frozen embryos they brought with them on *Stonehenge*, and several years later Kendra gave birth to Jax, conceived the same way. Both their children went on to have families of their own and lived to ripe old ages. And Kendra fell in love with all of their grandchildren and found herself staying out of cryo for long periods of time, just to be with them.

There had been no further contact with the southern continent, and it was forbidden for anyone to go there. Every couple of months the dragon riders would travel the northern continent to check for any signs of invasion from the south, but so far, it had remained quiet.

As the days passed, all the members from *The Destiny* seemed to find their niche. Kenji was working with the engineers, finding and building new ways to stretch the power in the city and was adding to the grid with *The Destiny's* resources. As their numbers were growing with the newcomers, and the babies being born and those coming of age, more housing was needed, which required more energy. Mateo and some of the other crew from Zander's security team pitched in with building and creating furniture, glassware and toys for the toy store and helping build some of the houses needed. Holly and Paul, both nurses, and Beth the MD that traveled with them, all picked up shifts at the hospital and clinics. They spent time learning about the healing herbs and adding the equipment and medication they brought from the Center. Even Josh had found a place working in the fields. He discovered that he was loving being a farmer, getting his hands dirty and sowing the seeds they planted. He was even having a little house built up in the meadow by the orchards. Everyone was fitting in and finding their place. Everyone but Sarah. She offered to help with the solar energy project, but they had plenty of scientists and engineers on that. She helped out in the community kitchen, but she was a terrible cook, and found she grew bored of chopping vegetables and washing dishes. She was definitely not cut out for building or plowing fields. And she was a little awkward with the children in the day care.

She did enjoy stomping around on grapes, so others could turn the grapes into wine. And she loved swimming in the sea, but fishing was not something she was made for. But every night, she sat out on her back porch drinking coffee and watched the dragon, Apollo fly above the sea, diving and soaring and calling out his dragon song. She learned from Ali that Apollo had lost his rider over thirty years before. She had passed away at the age of 162, and Apollo had been in mourning ever since, and lived with the western herd.

Her heart broke for him, and she wondered why he didn't follow his herd mate's home. His roar that she once thought sounded happy and triumphant, now sounded sad and longing.

One afternoon, Holly and Beth had the day off from the clinic, and they, along with Sarah, were practicing their leap up the cliff. They had mastered the coming down part but getting up there was another story. Ian was topside, watching them, and just shook his head. He decided to take mercy on them and floated down to them.

"It's not really that hard," he told them.

They all just looked at him like they wanted his blood. They were out of breath and exhausted from nearly an hour of failed attempts.

He held up his hands in a I surrender move. "Ok, let me show you." He walked to Holly. He had noticed her a few days ago a cute little blonde with big brown eyes and curves in all the right places. He went to stand behind her and placed his hands on her stomach. "It comes from here," he said. "Fill your lungs with air. Squat down and jump. First, find a few places on the side of the cliff that you can use to propel yourself upward. Soon you won't need that, but for now, until you learn to control your jump it'll help. Watch me," he told them.

He took an exaggerated deep breath in, squatted down, then leapt into the air. There was a small rock protruding from the side of the cliff, about halfway up. He placed his foot on it and pushed off then landed on the top of the hill. He turned and saw all three women staring up at him. He jumped back down and floated to where they stood.

"Come on," he said. "Who wants to go first.?" They all just stared at him. "I'll even go with you, just to make sure you're safe."

"Ok, fine," Sarah said. "Let's do this, Ian."

"Do you want me to hold on to you this first time?" he asked her.

She shook her head. "Just don't let me fall."

He smiled. "You won't fall Sarah. You'll float. I think the fear of falling is what's stopping you."

She looked at him for a minute then gave him a nod and repeated. "Let's do it."

"See the rock?" he asked.

She spotted it and nodded. Together they took a deep breath, squatted down and leapt into the air. Sarah felt herself lifting up, found the rock and got her foot on it, then propelled herself the rest of the way. She overshot a little and landed on her butt at the top of the hill.

"Oh my God! I did it!" Sarah shouted. "I actually did it."

Ian flipped in the air and landed on his feet next to her, then held out a hand to help her up.

"Show off," she said but took his hand and let him lift her to her feet.

He winked at her then turned and went back down to help the other two up. Holly went next and asked Ian to hold her hand. He took her hand, together they took a breath, squatted down and jumped into the air. She overshot the rock a little but was able to touch her foot on the side of the cliff and propel upward. With Ian's help, she landed at the top, on her feet.

"What a rush!" she laughed and hugged him, then turned and hugged Sarah.

Together, they watched as Ian floated back down and helped Beth. She was a little more hesitant, and it took her two tries, but she made it up on her own.

They all wanted to try again, so they jumped down, and each took a turn jumping back up. Each of them made it back on their own. A small group had formed at the bottom of the hill, and a few more on top. They all cheered for each of them as they landed on the top of the hill.

They took a little bow then laughed and turned to Ian. "Thank you, Ian," Sarah said. "We could have been at that for days without your help. I hope we didn't keep you from your work."

"You're welcome," he said. "No, I was just heading over to the dragon pen, to check on the new hatchlings. You want to join me?" he asked them. He had a hunch and wanted to check it out.

All three women eagerly answered yes, and he led the way to an area where there was a short, solid wall in a circle. Inside the circle were three baby dragons, one red, one red with gold wings, and another all gold. There was a small pond in there with two more eggs lying in it.

"These are my girl Darcy's pups," he told them. "They hatched two days ago, so they're still finding their feet."

They all watched as the baby dragons moved around the enclosure. They looked a little wobbly, but they were adorable with big eyes, full of love. Sarah saw there were toys for them to play with, little swings, and bridges, balls and even some stuffed toys. There was a building on one side of the enclosure that looked like a barn and Ian told them there were stalls inside, with straw and blankets for them. They would go inside at night, but dragons loved the sunlight, and the warmth, so they would stay outside till the sun set.

The women were so enchanted with the babies, they didn't notice some of the herd moving toward them. But Ian did and went with his hunch.

"I'd like to try something, ladies," he told them. He moved Beth to the far side of the circle, then asked Sarah to move to the center, leaving Holly where she was.

They moved to the positions Ian put them in without question, still watching the little dragons. Sarah leaned over the wall to get a better look. She saw the little red one jump into the pond and start splashing around with its wings flapping and sending water everywhere. She laughed and reached her hand out. The little dragon saw her leaning in, and her hand reaching out. He wobbled over to her and sniffed at her hand. and Ian continued watching the herd move closer.

When they were about ten yards away, the herd stopped, and Apollo made his way from the center of the group to the front. He hesitated for a moment, then began moving forward again, until he was about 10 feet behind Sarah.

Ian watched as Sarah, who was still leaning over the enclosure, watching the little hatchlings, stand up and straighten her spine. He saw the moment the knowing entered her eyes, and she turned to face Apollo. She took several steps forward and stopped. Then Apollo bowed to her.

Sarah didn't even realize there were tears streaming down her face. She didn't realize that Ian had come to stand behind her, or that other dragon riders had gathered beside the field. She only saw Apollo bowing to her. She could feel his love and his longing. And felt the same in her heart. Then she heard Ian's voice.

"You are his, and he is yours, if you choose to accept his offer."

She never took her eyes off the magnificent dragon in front of her. She nodded. "Yes. I accept. Of course I accept. He is mine, and I am his, as it was always meant to be."

Ian smiled. "Then claim your dragon, rider."

She moved forward and reached her hand out to Apollo. She leaned her head against his, then looked into his perfectly blue eyes. She felt an overwhelming love form between them, and she laughed through her tears. "I am yours, and you are mine," she whispered to him. "From this moment, until our last moment. I will honor and cherish you every day of my life." And she felt his response in her heart That same love and commitment to her. She ran her hand over his beautiful pearl white scales and moved to his side. She leapt off the ground and landed on his back, just below his neck. She grabbed on to a horn on his lower neck and lowered herself into position. It seemed as natural as breathing. Then, when she was ready, she gave Apollo a little pat and they lifted off the ground and flew.

Sarah heard all the others on the ground cheer and saw the other riders run to their dragons. After a few minutes, they all mounted and joined her and Apollo in the sky.

They circled and dove in a beautiful dance to celebrate the joining of a new rider, and her dragon.

Kenji and the team of engineers were working in *The Destiny*, on the community power grid, when they heard the commotion outside. They all rushed out to see what was happening. Kenji saw groups of people looking up to the sky and cheering. When he looked up, what he saw took his breath away. Countless numbers of dragons, flying and dancing in the air. All with riders on their backs. They circled the community and fell into a formation with Ian and his Darcy in the lead. Then he saw the big dragon, they called Apollo, moving forward through the formation, to fall in just to the right of her and about a nose behind. Another large dragon, silver in color with black tips, came forward on Darcy's left side and took the same formation as Apollo.

Jason walked up to stand next to Kenji and put a hand on his shoulder.

"What's going on?" Kenji asked him.

"They're celebrating a new dragon rider."

The herd circled the city and came lower so all could see. Kenji's breath caught in his throat when he saw Sarah riding on the back of Apollo, her hair flying, arms lifted out to the side, and her head thrown back toward the sky.

Jason slapped him on the back "You've got yourself quite a woman, Kenji." And he walked toward the center of the town to join in with the others in celebration.

Kenji watched as the herd made several more circles around the city, then when it looked like they were coming in for a landing he ran to the cliff and launched himself up to the top.

He got there at the same time Sarah landed. She was quickly engulfed by people. Everyone was cheering and laughing. He moved through the crowd slowly, and when he spotted her, he thought she had never looked more beautiful. She was smiling and had a flush on her cheeks, her short hair was in a tangled mess on her head and her eyes were lit up with joy.

A lump rose in his throat, and the part of his heart that didn't already belong to her, fell. He watched her turn and spot him in the crowd. He watched as she moved toward him and an intensity and excitement shone in her eyes. Suddenly all the noise and movement around him blurred. There was only her. When they reached each other, Kenji grabbed her around the waist and pulled her to him. She reached up and cupped his face in her hands and they met in a kiss that held all the passion they had been holding back for years.

Another cheer went up from the crowd, but they didn't hear it. All they could hear was the pounding of their hearts.

Kenji broke the kiss, only long enough to scoop Sarah up in his arms and turned toward the edge of the cliff.

He jumped off the side and floated to the ground. He set her on the ground and hand in hand they ran and almost flew toward their little house by the sea.

Kendra slipped her arm through Ali's and smiled. "That was lovely," she sighed and leaned her head against Ali's arm. "I was a little worried that she would be too strong for him. That her personality would overpower his and he would lose his voice. But I think what I just saw proved me wrong."

"The entire community just saw that." Ali laughed.

CHAPTER 3

What felt like hours later, they lay tangled together in Kenji's bed. He was just looking at her, his eyes moving over every detail of her beautiful face.

"I'm in love with you Sarah."

Her sleepy eyes snapped open, and she looked into his eyes. "Oh," she breathed.

"You don't have to say anything right now," he told her and smiled. "I just want you to know where I'm at." He sat up. "Thirsty?" he asked her.

She nodded. Kenji stumbled into the kitchen to get them both a glass of water.

He grabbed a glass and turned on the sink faucet. As he held the glass under the running water, he glanced out the window and froze.

"Ummm, Sarah!" he called out.

"Yeah," her sleepy voice answered.

"Can you come out here for a minute?"

He heard her groan and start shuffling around the room.

He turned off the running water and took a long deep drink, never taking his eyes off the window.

He glanced over his shoulder, when he heard her come into the kitchen. "Can't handle filling a glass of water?" she asked.

31

She was only wearing the shirt that he'd been wearing earlier. He liked seeing her in his t-shirt hanging almost her knees. He was tempted to scoop her back up and go back to his bedroom and take it back off. But then he remembered what was going on out the back window.

He reached his hand out for her. "Come here."

She stepped forward and took his hand and he turned her toward the window. "Look," he said.

When she did, she saw Apollo standing in the grass directly behind their cottage. He was baring his teeth at Kenji and his tail was swishing back and forth. He looked fierce.

"Is that going to be a problem?" he asked her.

She giggled a little and gave him a quick kiss. "No," she said. "I'll go talk to him."

She headed toward the back door.

"Talk to him?" he asked.

"Yeah. I need to let him know that I'm ok. That you weren't hurting me."

"Um, Sarah. It's still daylight honey. You might want to put on some pants first."

She looked down at herself and started laughing.

She ran back to the bedroom and pulled on her pants, then ran out the back door to reassure her dragon.

When she approached Apollo, she immediately leaned her head against his and began stroking his neck. She could feel his love pouring out of him and knew he could feel hers. "It's ok, Apollo. I'm ok." He was smelling her hair. "That's Kenji. I think I might be in love with him. He's a good man. And he loves me." She pulled back and looked into his eyes. "But don't worry. My heart is big enough to hold both of you in it."

She heard the back door of the cottage open, and both she and Apollo turned to Kenji. She held her hand out to him. "Come and meet my Apollo, Kenji."

He moved to them, slowly, then took Sarah's hand. "Umm, hey there, Apollo," he said.

Sarah took their joined hands and put them up to Apollo's snout, so he could smell him. Apollo's eyes moved from Kenji to Sarah, and Kenji could see the love for her in those eyes.

"He's beautiful Sarah. Almost as beautiful as you. You two make quite a sight."

"We're a team," she said. "I need to go fly with him for a little while."

Kenji nodded. "Go," he said. "I'll run over to the community kitchen and bring back something to eat. We'll have dinner when you get back."

She leaned forward and kissed him. "Thank you for understanding."

"I'm a pilot. I totally get it."

Sarah jumped onto Apollo's back and Kenji's heart beat a little faster as he watched them lift off. He heard Sarah's laugh echo through the sky as they disappeared in the clouds.

He shook his head and went back into the cottage to take a shower then he'd go get them some food.

Suddenly life on Asteria took on a whole new meaning for Sarah. She found that the dragons were her niche. She shared Kenji's bed at night, and together they would walk to the community kitchen every morning and have breakfast together. Then, after a kiss goodbye, they went their separate ways, Kenji to the ships to work on the power grid, and Sarah to the clifftop to help take care of the hatchlings, and the younglings. She helped muck out the stalls of the two 5-month-old dragons, still staying in the barn at night. Ian told her they'd stay there until they were about 9 or 10 months old, then would join the older dragons at the lair.

She would spend hours with the little hatchlings, cleaning their pond, making sure their toys were in good condition and mostly just playing with them. She had to fight the urge to name them. Ian told her that would be for their riders to do.

She kept a close watch on the two eggs in the pond, Ian said they still had a few months to go, before they hatched.

In the afternoon, after all their work was done, most riders would meet in the field and fly.

The formation was always the same. Darcy and Ian in front. Sarah and Apollo at his right side, just slightly behind. And the silver dragon Titan, with his rider, Quinn, on his left. The rest following behind in their own places behind the alpha.

Sarah learned that Darcy was alpha because she was the largest female. A female was always the alpha of the herd. Titan and Quinn had been the beta, until Apollo chose another rider. Then Titan moved to the third spot. There was no animosity for the loss of position. Quinn just explained that it was the dragon way. Apollo was beta, because he was the largest and oldest of the male dragons with riders.

The riderless dragons had their own alpha and she always bowed to and followed the lead of the rider's alpha. In the evenings, Sarah and Kenji would meet back at the dining hall to have dinner before heading back to their little cottage. The first couple weeks, they had dinner with whoever happened to be there, but more often lately, Josh, Mateo, Shawn and Holly would join them along with some of the other riders. Ian, Quinn and Pax. And tonight, they were joined by some of security team as well. Bret, Kevin, Rick and Meg. They were becoming a large group of friends.

Sarah remembered a night when she and Kenji along with the other members of the Nine went to a little bar in Deadwood South Dakota. They danced and drank, laughed and ate and just enjoyed being young and alive. She thought she should talk to someone about building something like that here.

She needed to find out who was in charge of building, and community planning, and see if that could happen.

When the group broke up for the night, and started heading back to their homes, they heard a loud thundering in the sky. There had been a few rainstorms since the newcomers had been on Asteria, but this was definitely not thunder. Everyone looked up and through the clouds, they could make out the faint silhouette of a ship. Not one of the eleven ships from Earth, this one was very different, more oval in shape and black. And it was moving fast. As quickly as it appeared, it was gone, heading toward the southern continent.

"What the hell was that?" Shawn asked.

Ian was still staring at the sky. "It was a ship like the one the southern settlers landed in," he said.

"They didn't look like they were in distress," Kenji said.

"A rescue mission for the crash victims?" Quinn asked.

"Let's hope so," Ian said.

Ian saw all his riders coming toward the dining hall.

"Riders," he called out. "Let's do a little scouting mission. I'll meet you all up top."

The riders all turned toward the cliff and started jumping up to the top, to find their dragons.

Sarah stepped forward and Kenji grabbed her hand. "You have no experience with this Sarah, maybe you should stay grounded for this mission."

She stepped up to him and gave him a soft kiss. "Apollo will keep me safe. We'll be back before you know it."

She ran and caught up with Ian and Quinn and they jumped to the top of the cliff together.

Charlie stepped up to Kenji as he watched Sarah jump to go to her dragon. "Watching them go is so hard sometimes," she said. "They won't engage. And they won't get close enough to the southern continent to be detected."

"The *Destiny* is still able to fly," he said. "Should we follow them and see what's going on?"

Charlie shook her head. "It may come to that. But we don't want to provoke them. Let's let the riders do their thing and see what they find out. Then depending on what they find, we can talk about what if anything we need to do."

Kenji nodded. "So, what do you do with yourself while they're gone?" he asked her.

"I join other rider families in the pavilion and drink some wine. Why don't you join us."

At the top of the cliff, the riders were all standing by their dragons. Ian stepped forward to address them.

"This could just be a rescue mission for the ship that crashed twenty years ago. But we know that this species is hostile and violent. Our first priority is keeping our home safe. Pax, take Quinn and Sarah and a couple of others north and west. Make sure there are no signs of invasion or settlers. Micha, Alan and Jessie, take your scouts and head south west. I'll take Darcy and my scouts and head to the islands."

The riders all started mounting their dragons. "Remember, we are not trying to engage. Stay far enough away that you don't draw their attention. Pax, keep your group tight. I want everyone back here within two hours."

Ian went to Sarah and handed her what looked like a small telescope. "This is a tool used by all scouts. You can see anything moving on the ground. Stay close to Pax and Quinn."

She took the telescope and tried it out, pointing it up to the sky. It brought everything so close it looked like she could reach out and touch it.

"Awesome!" she said.

"One more thing," he held out a jacket, like one that all the other riders wore. They all matched the color of their dragon. Hers was white with golden trim. "It can get chilly up there after dark," he said.

36

She took the jacket from him and just stared at it. "It's beautiful, Ian. Thank you."

He nodded. "Be safe," he said as he turned to walk away.

She put her jacket on, and mounted Apollo. She saw Quinn and Pax circling above and before taking off to join them she leaned down and whispered. "Ok, my boy. Let's do this. I don't want to hold them back, or make you look bad," and she stroked the side of his neck. "Help me learn how to do this."

Sarah felt Apollo stand a little taller, then spread his wings and lifted up to meet the rest of the scouts.

Josh and Mateo were standing together by the field.

"I don't like this," Mateo said. "These people are peaceful. I think if they are invaded by a hostile species, with weapons, they'll be slaughtered."

Josh nodded. "Yeah. But you and I are not peaceful. And neither are some of the others we brought with us. We can teach them, Mateo. I think we're supposed to teach them."

CHAPTER 4

Sarah fell in next to Pax and his dragon Ruby, with Quinn and Titan on his other side. Six others fell in behind them and they headed west and north. She marveled at the change in scenery as they moved farther north. When they flew in on *The Destiny*, they went to the southeast. The northwest was breathtaking, but much less hospitable. There were rolling green hills that met huge, jagged mountains. They looked impossible to climb to Sarah. She saw no breaks in the mountains they were just straight up. The dragons started circling the mountain tops, while the riders looked through their telescopes.

The air was much thinner there, and Sarah started feeling a little lightheaded. Apollo must have felt it, because he let out a roar, and she saw Titan turn toward them and roar a response. Apollo went a little lower and a few of the other scouts followed them, while Quinn and Pax and the others stayed towards the top.

The ground at the foot of the mountains was covered with thick, dense shrubs and trees. As Apollo flew above it, she quickly realized that there was no way they could tell if there was any movement in there, without going on foot. In her mind, she started working on tracking devices, maybe something to distinguish heat sources so they could detect movement of life forms.

When the scouts above flew down to where Sarah and her group were, Pax waved for them to move on. A little while later they landed by a lake so they could get some fresh water and let the dragon's rest. The lake was fed by a waterfall flowing from the side of a mountain and next to the top of the waterfall were what looked like dozens of caves and ledges outside of them. She saw dragons lounging on the ledges and coming and going in and out of the caves. Sarah realized that she was looking at the Western herd's lair.

She was sitting with Apollo on the bank of the lake, and she could feel his restlessness. She reached out to soothe him and began stroking his neck. "This was your home for more than thirty years. Do you miss it?" He turned his head to her and gently, almost playfully, bumped her. She laughed. "Good," she said. "I want you happy, buddy. Because you've made me so very happy." She kissed his snout. "We're going to be here for a while, if you want to go see your friends. I'll be right here waiting for you." He nuzzled against her, then gently lifted up to one of the ledges in front of a cave and went inside.

"I love seeing his bond with you," Quinn said. She had come up behind and saw the exchange. "He loves you."

Sarah turned and smiled at her. "It's mutual," she said. "Never in my wildest dreams did I imagine this. It's pretty overwhelming."

Quinn nodded and sat down beside Sarah. She handed her a jug with water in it.

"Sorry about earlier. "Quinn told her. "We didn't even think about the thinning air being too much for you. We are all acclimated to it. You're so natural up there, it never occurred to us that you aren't used to it."

Sarah shook her head. "I don't want to be a handicap to you guys," she said.

Quinn looked confused.

"I don't want to hold you back or slow any of you down," Sarah explained.

"You don't. and you won't," Quinn told her. "Like I said, you're a natural. We'll probably need to head back in about twenty minutes. Ian wanted us all back in two hours, and we'll be pushing it. Next time, we'll take a different route and get to the western shore."

"What the heck does he have in his mouth?" Sarah said when she looked up and saw Apollo emerging out of the cave.

"Oh, wow," Quinn said.

Apollo flew down to Sarah, and she saw he had a small blanket hanging from his mouth. He dropped it at her feet and nuzzled at her hair.

Sarah picked it up and saw a plush white blanket about three feet long and wide. Sewn around the edges was the same gold braiding that was on her jacket. "It's beautiful!" Sarah said.

"It was Jill's riding blanket," Quinn told her. "Most of us don't use them, unless we're traveling far distances. His giving it to you is a great honor, Sarah. It's a gesture of his love and devotion to you. And he's showing you that you are his and he is yours."

Tears came to Sarah's eyes, and she put her arms around Apollo's neck. "It's the most precious gift I've ever gotten. I will cherish it, and you, Apollo, as long as I live. Thank you."

Sarah mounted Apollo and laid the blanket carefully on his back. She put her matching jacket on and took her position. Then she and Apollo lifted off to circle in the air and wait for the rest to join them.

As the Northwest scouts were flying home, they met the Southwest group, and they traveled back together. They landed in the meadow and saw that Ian's group hadn't returned yet.

They dismounted and waited. And waited. Some of the community had joined them in the meadow, including Kenji, Josh, Mateo and Charlie along with some of the other family members. They were all sitting on the ground with their dragons.

41

Sarah told them about the mountains and valleys she saw. She told them about the Western herd's lair and Apollo's gift. And about her idea for heat sensors.

It felt like it had been hours when Pax came up to Quinn and Sarah. "Micha and I are taking a few others to go look for them. It's not like Ian to be gone this long."

Quinn jumped up. "I'll get Titan and join you," she said. Pax gave her a nod. She ran toward Titan and mounted. Sarah got up too. "Apollo and I will go too."

Pax shook his head. "You're too new at this, Sarah. Sorry, but you're grounded for this one."

He turned and walked toward his dragon. Sarah watched him walk away with a protest on her lips. She turned to Kenji. "He's right," Kenji told her before she could say anything. "You've only been riding for a few days. They may run into trouble and need to maneuver. You're not experienced enough."

"Ugh," was her only response and she walked away.

"Dude," Josh told him and shook his head. "Do you know nothing about women? You should have taken her in your arms and told her you are outraged for her. Don't they know there's nothing she can't do? Now she's pissed at you instead of Pax."

Mateo snorted out a laugh when Kenji just stared at Josh.

Suddenly there were shouts, and they heard Pax holler, "Hold! They're coming."

When Ian and his group landed, he called for all of them to gather. Kenji, Josh and Mateo moved forward, they stayed back from the riders, but close enough to hear.

"Sorry we're late," he started. "I'll explain why in a minute. First, Pax and Micha, did your groups see anything unusual?"

Both answered no but said they didn't get all the way to the coast.

Ian nodded and asked them all to sit and then dropped to the ground and bowed his head, looking for the words to describe what they saw.

"We went to the islands off the coast of the southern continent, where we know their settlement is," he started. "We could see the ship that arrived today on the ridge above their settlement. It looked like they were having a celebration. There were bonfires, and a lot of laughing and cheering and what sounded like singing. They seemed drunk," he paused. "They had four young dragons, chained and penned. They aren't full grown. I'd say between six months and a year old."

"Why?" Quinn asked. "How did they get dragons?"

"I didn't recognize them, so I can only assume they are sea dragons His eyes met Quinns. "They didn't look good. They were obviously injured and malnourished. It looks like they have been there a while."

"What are they doing with them?" Quinn asked. "Are they trying to ride them? If they're under two, they can't be ridden, and if they're from the sea, they may never be able to. Not to mention, they would never bond with those that chained them and kept them hostage."

"They're not trying to ride them," Ian said. "They had slaughtered one and were roasting it over their fire. They're using them for food. For meat."

The response from the riders was rage and grief. They all started talking at once.

Quinn shook her head. "Oh Ian, no," she said, and tears sprang to her eyes. "We can't let this happen. We have to do something."

Ian nodded. The pain from Quinn reflected in his eyes. "Yeah, we do." He looked at the three men standing at the edge of the group. "Any suggestions?" he asked.

Josh stepped forward. "We have soldiers and security teams that were former special forces. We have navy seals and green berets. Black belts in Karate and jiu-jitsu," he told them. "Let us help you plan a rescue mission for the dragons. Then let us help you prepare for what will come next."

Ian nodded. "Please come join us."

They talked into the night. Some of the town members joined them and added their input. Then they asked the soldiers and security team members to join them as well.

By dawn, they had a plan.

"We should get some rest today," Ian said. "We'll leave at sunset tonight. But I need everyone up here two hours before that for your assignments."

When Mateo got back to the little cottage by the sea that he shared with Josh, he paced around but couldn't settle. Josh had gone straight to bed, and he could hear him snoring through the closed door. He decided to go down by the sea and do some Tai-Chi. It always relaxed him and put his mind at ease.

He sat cross legged on the lush green grass, just feet away from the rolling ocean. He closed his eyes and took some deep cleansing breaths. After a few minutes of breathing, he stood in one fluid motion and began the slow precise movements of Tai-Chi. He kept his breathing even and his body fluid, moving from one position to the other.

Quinn was restless as well and found herself on a little ledge overlooking the sea with Titan by her side. She saw Mateo emerge from his cottage, remove his shoes and shirt and sit on the grass by the shore. Then she saw him get up and start moving in a slow and graceful dance. She was fascinated with the movements of his body. She saw him spin slowly back toward the cottage and hold a position with his left leg stretched out to the side, and his arms stretching in the opposite direction. Each movement he made was slow and precise. Then she saw him stiffen and move back into a standing position. She saw an enormous red dragon come from the sea and stop behind him. She saw the moment of knowing come into him, and he turned toward the dragon.

Mateo moved from one position to the next and held between each movement. Suddenly, he felt a presence behind him. He straightened. And slowly turned to face a huge red dragon.

She was beautiful. She had flame red scales, with black tipped wings and black markings on her head. It looked like she was wearing a black crown.

She stepped a little closer and Mateo could see her green eyes, looking into his. Then she bowed. He felt an overwhelming love and longing enter his heart and when she raised her eyes to look into his, he bowed back to her. He moved closer and leaned his head against hers. The words came from his heart, and he knew they were right, and that she heard and understood.

"I am yours and you are mine," he told her. "From this moment, until my last breath. I will honor and cherish you."

He felt her response in his heart and could almost hear her words in his mind. "I am yours and you are mine, Mateo. I will love and cherish you until my last breath."

"You are Yemaya," he said with a smile. "The great mother who lives in the sea. You protect what is in the sea and bless those that live on the shore." He could feel her anguish over the younglings taken by the Southern Continent inhabitants. "Don't worry, Maya. We are going to get your children back." She nudged his head with hers. "Yes, my beauty, you will help."

Quinn watched with wonder, as Mateo mounted the red dragon, and lifted off to circle above the ocean. She had never known of a sea dragon being ridden and never heard of one bonding with a human. But as they circled, she saw dozens of sea dragons lift their heads out of the water and let out a roar.

Mateo felt a freedom and belonging he had never felt before. He saw the other dragons of the sea raise their heads and welcome him. And he saw Quinn and her Titan

on the ridge above the sea watching them. He smiled and
sent her a salute. Then Yemaya lowered to the sea and
floated on the water. An idea started to form, and he asked
her to start swimming. She dropped just slightly below the
top of the water and started moving. Mateo did a lot of surfing
when he was younger and lifted himself up to stand on her
back as she moved forward under the water. He put his
hands out to the sides of his body, found his balance and
began surfing across the water, standing on the back of a
dragon.

CHAPTER 5

When Mateo saw the village start to wake with people moving around, he left Maya with the promise to return soon with the tools to put their plan in motion. It was amazing to him how clearly they understood each other. He wondered if all riders had the same communication ability with their dragons and thought he would ask Sarah about that later.

He grabbed his shoes and shirt off the shore and started running to Jacob's cottage.

Jacob was a builder but also an artist and visionary. He created unusual and usable tools that had made life in the community much easier and more efficient. They had already agreed to talk to him about making weapons they might need for a possible battle with the southern continent.

When he reached Jacob's cottage, Mateo found that there was already a group there talking to him, including Ian, Josh, Kenji and some of the other soldiers. They were talking about designs for weapons.

"Hey Mateo," Josh said as he approached. "I thought you were still sleeping."

Mateo sat next to Josh and shook his head. "I've been up all night. I'll explain later."

He saw there were diagrams and maps showing the southern continent, the islands and where the ships were located.

"Our first priority is getting those dragons released, before they kill another one," Ian said. "Once that is done, we will start training every man, woman and child in the community, how to defend themselves in case of an invasion. How quickly can you and your team start working on weapons, Jacob?"

"We already have some," Jacob told him. Some were on the ships when they got here and we created more after the first ship crashed and our rescue mission was attacked. We can start with those and do any repairs needed to get them in your hands later today."

"The language barrier is a problem," Meg said. "I wish there was a way to know what they're saying."

"I may have something to help with that," Sarah said. She had come up behind the group with Quinn and had been listening to their plans. She moved forward and dropped a small bag into Ian's lap.

When Ian opened the bag, he saw a bunch of small round objects made out of some kind of metal. He pulled one out. "What is this?" he asked her.

"They're universal translators," Sarah said. "Gaia gave them to me before we left the Center. She said we might need them."

"The nine sisters of the Center created every planet within the universe," Sarah told them. "So, every language spoken on every planet is programed into this translator." She grabbed one out of the bag and placed it behind her ear, to demonstrate how to attach them. Then she took another and put it behind Ian's. and handed a third to Quinn. "Say something is Japanese, Kenji."

"Ohayo gozaimasu tomodachi," Kenji said.

"He said hello my friends!" Quinn gasped!

Ian looked up at Sarah and smiled.

"Anyone wearing one of these can understand any language spoken by any species," Sarah told them.

Quinn looked at Mateo. "Have you told them?" she asked.

He shook his head, but that got the attention of everyone in the circle.

"Told us what?" Josh asked.

"I bonded with a dragon last night," he said.

"What!" Sarah said. "Oh Mateo, that's wonderful!" She wrapped him in a big hug. "I'm so happy for you. So, you're a rider now too?"

"Which dragon?" Ian asked a little suspiciously. "I was with the herd all night and didn't notice any of them wandering off, and if they sensed a new rider, they would have rallied and let us know."

"Her name is Yemaya. And she is of the sea," Mateo said.

"You bonded with a sea dragon?"

"He did," Quinn said and stepped forward. "I saw it happen. And when he took his place on her back, all the sea dragons raised their heads from the water and welcomed him."

"That's never been done," Pax said with awe in his voice. "A great red sea dragon gave Kendra eggs, almost 500 years ago. But no one has ever bonded with or mounted one."

"Congratulations, Mateo," Ian said and clasped his hand with Mateo's. "What can you tell us of them? Are they willing to help with our mission?"

Mateo nodded. "They are in anguish over the loss of their younglings. They'll do anything to get them back. And I think I may have an idea for that. Can we move this down to the shore? I'll show you what I have in mind."

Jacob turned to a group of younger people who were standing off to the side. "Why don't you guys start working on those weapons. Make any repairs they need and make sure they're ready to go by nightfall." he told them.

They all headed to the ridge where Ian had sat with Darcy watching Apollo call to Sarah, and where last night, Quinn sat with Titan watching Yemaya and Mateo meet and bond.

They jumped and floated down to the shore, just as Yemaya emerged from the sea. Mateo walked to her and leaned his head against hers in greeting. "Let's show them what we can do, Maya." He removed his shoes, then leapt on to her back. She turned back to the ocean and submerged just below the surface. Mateo stood and they started moving down the shoreline. More of the sea dragon herd emerged above the water to watch.

After a few minutes, Mateo sat back down, and Maya rose to the surface. They returned to the group standing on the shoreline. Mateo jumped down and turned to Jacob. "I need straps," he told him. "Something that can go around her torso, behind her front legs. Something I can hold on to. If we could get enough of them, other sea dragons would like to take riders as well. We could circle the far end of the southern continent and come up from the opposite side of the settlement and release the pups. They wouldn't be expecting us to come from the sea, so we could probably do it without being seen."

Ian nodded. "It would be better than us coming in by air. Can you make the straps he needs, Jacob?"

"Yeah, we can make them," he said.

"How do we choose the riders?" Josh asked.

"We don't." Mateo nodded to where some of the dragons had come closer to the shore. "They do."

They spent the rest of the morning and early afternoon talking to people and explaining the new plan. Jacob brought in more craftsmen and women to work on the straps, and weapons.

Ian, Quinn and Pax flew out to the islands, to check on the dragon pups in confinement and see if they could tell where the best entry point might be.

Josh was working out training schedules with the other members of the miliary and security teams, finding out their strengths and who could teach what techniques and weapons training to the community members. He saw Amelia, one of the farmers he had worked the fields with, coming toward him, carrying a large sack. She was a sweet girl, with long golden curls and big brown eyes. She told him that her great grandmother had been an original ship member and was a chemist. He stood and met her when she reached his group.

"I was told that some of the dragon pups are injured," she told him. "There are ointments, and medicine in there, for them,"

He took the bag from her. "Thanks Amelia. I'll make sure they get this."

She nodded. "I and some of the others will be waiting on the shore. Ask the riders to try to get the pups to us as soon as they are able, and we can work on healing their wounds. What is in the bag should help ease their pain until you can get them back to us."

He nodded and she turned and walked away. He watched her for a few seconds and shook his head. She was kind, and gentle, and exactly the kind of person who would be slaughtered if they were invaded. He felt a protectiveness over her, and the community of people like her. They had been living in peace and harmony for so long they couldn't even imagine what could come for them.

He turned back to his group and continued making plans to defend and teach them to defend themselves.

Later that day, a large group went to stand on the shore. Several dragon riders were circling in the sky to watch, and other community spectators were standing in groups behind them and off to the side. Mateo was mounted on Maya, floating in the water near the shoreline with his new strap around her body and long reins attached for him to hold on to.

Yemaya let out a loud roar and a group of sea dragons emerged from the ocean and looked at the people standing on the shore.

A black female with silver tips rose from the sea and moved forward toward the group. She hesitated for a second then moved to where Shawn was standing. She looked into his eyes, and they all saw the moment of knowing enter him. He stepped forward and the dragon bowed. He moved toward her and laid his head against hers. They saw him whisper the words to her then he lifted his head and smile. "This is Ebony," he told them. "And I am hers and she is mine." He mounted her back and together they rose into the sky to fly with the riders circling there, then came back to the sea to float next to Mateo and Maya.

Mateo nodded to him. "A whole new way to fly, huh, brother?"

"Yeah." Shawn let out a breath and laughed. "I've been a pilot all my adult life but never experienced anything like this. What a rush!"

They saw a greenish blue female come to the shore next. She went to stand before Gill, a young fisherman from the far side of the city. She bowed and he moved to her without hesitation. The selection continued for nearly an hour. Mateo saw two more dragons near the shore. There were others further out in the sea, watching them. The next dragon was an opal white, almost iridescent female, with pink tips. She stepped up to Rob, one of the soldiers that worked with Josh at NORAD on Earth. She bowed to him, and he responded by putting his head against hers and saying the words. "This is Shiloh," he said and mounted her.

When Rob and Shiloh landed beside the other sea riders, there was a long pause. There were eight new riders selected and Mateo began wondering if that would be all. But suddenly the last dragon emerged from the sea. He was huge, and golden in color. He had no other markings or colors on him. Only gold, with golden eyes. He had a horn mane around his head. He turned to Meg and bowed. She stepped forward and looked at him with awe. He was the most beautiful thing she had ever seen. As she took another step toward him, he raised his eyes to hers. She could see amusement in them, and he exaggerated his bow. As if saying, 'Are you coming or not?' She laughed and came to stand directly in front of him. "Hello, Leo," she said, then put her head against his. "I am yours, and you are mine," she told him, then pulled back and looked into his eyes. "You and I are going to do great things, my king. And have a lot of fun doing them," she whispered to him. She jumped to his back and hollered. "This is Leo, I am his and he is mine."

Then they lifted off and began circling the sky before landing with the others in the sea.

They spent the next several hours with their dragons. Each was given a strap to put around their torso to hold on to. They practiced standing on their backs while they raced just below the surface of the sea. They also sat and held on the straps while the dragons went a little lower into the water and really moved with speed. They held on while they did turns and spins, and when they lifted up into the air to soar among the clouds.

It was decided that they would meet four hours after nightfall. The air riders would fly to the islands to watch and send any warnings needed. And the sea riders would start heading for the southern continent. Each of them was given a translator to wear. The plans were gone over again and again, until there was no question that each of them knew exactly what to do.

Mateo decided to get a couple hours sleep before they headed out. He'd been up for more than thirty hours and was starting to feel exhaustion fall over him.

He walked to Yemaya who was laying in the grass behind his cottage. She opened her wing for him, and he curled next to her and dropped immediately into a deep sleep.

Denise Coulson

54

CHAPTER 6

Mateo woke after a few hours and felt rested and ready. He gave Maya a scratch and rub. "I'm going to go grab something to eat and take a shower," he told her. "I'll see you soon, gorgeous." As he turned and walked to his cottage, she went into the ocean.

When he got out of the shower and went to the kitchen, wearing only a towel, he found Josh sitting at the table sharpening the blade of a dagger on a stone. "There's a big fish fry for all the riders, up at Jacob's cottage."

"Sounds good," Mateo said. "Everything ok with you, brother?"

"Yeah," Josh said without looking up from his blade. "They've got some good weapons. And are starting more. I just want to say, be careful out there tonight." He looked up and Mateo nodded. "If you can make it look like a natural escape, that would be best. If you can make it so they don't know the humans had anything to do with it, do that."

Mateo grabbed a glass of lemonade and joined Josh at the table. "Ok. What are you worried about, Josh?"

"These people aren't ready for a fight right now, Mateo. We need more time to work with them. We can't afford a retaliation from the southern continent right now. There just aren't enough of us to protect them."

"Understood," Mateo said. "And I agree. I'll do what I can to keep that from happening." He stood up. "I'm going to go up and see about some food at the fish fry."

"Mateo, one more thing." Josh stood. "I know the dragons are important. But nothing is worth losing a human life. I mean it when I say, be careful. We don't know what these creatures are, but we know they're capable of killing."

Mateo nodded again and went to get dressed.

When Josh and Mateo arrived at Jacob's cottage, he saw it was more than just for the riders, their families were all there too. Kids running around and tables set up everywhere some heavy with big containers of potato salad, and coleslaw, more with fish and French fries and there were groups of people gathered everywhere eating and laughing. They even had musicians set up and some were dancing.

They grabbed plates and went to sit with a group of riders. Ali, Kendra, Lena and Charlie were there with Ian. Jason and Brad sat with Shawn, Kenji and Sarah. Kristen was there with her husband Micha, who Mateo recognized as one of the sky riders. Josh had given Shawn the bag from Amelia along with her instructions, and it was sitting next to him.

"We'll all leave a little before midnight," Ian said. "We'll escort you from the air, as far as the islands, then we'll take position there. We'll watch your progress through our telescopes and come if you need us."

"You need to understand what you're up against," Ali said. "They have space travel technology, so they either stole it, or they have a high intelligence. I would assume the latter. You have to know that. But know also that they are brutal. They are very large, more than seven feet tall, and are all brawn. They have guns that shoot lasers and are deadly. They also have shields and blades. They are big, and strong and fast."

"It's our hope that they'll be asleep when you get there. But you need to stay alert and be prepared for any that might be on guard," Kendra added. "You must not be seen. And you must use extreme caution."

Ian gave each of the sea riders a telescope. "Use these to scope your area before going ashore. You each have a translator, listen carefully to everything you hear. Get in and get out, as quickly as you can. And abort if necessary."

The sea riders all looked at each other. Each had bonded with a sea dragon. None of them was going to leave those babies there to be killed and feed those monsters' bellies. But they each nodded at Ian.

Ian looked at each of them in turn. He was a rider too and understood the bond. "Really guys, be careful and no unnecessary heroics."

Jason handed Shawn a bag. "What's this?" Shawn asked.

"We had five of Zander's security team on *Stonehenge*. three of them came on board, after the battle, wearing their night vision goggles." He nodded to the bag as Shawn opened it and pulled out a pair. "I checked them earlier today. They still work."

Later, Jacob handed out weapons to all the riders going on this mission. Each was given a handheld laser blaster, an electric taser, a dagger and a breast shield. They were also given belts to hold the weapons.

In addition to the nine sea riders, ten sky riders were equipped with the same weapons. Ian saw Mateo and Meg showing their riders how to use each one. He saw Kristen who worked in a kitchen. And Gill, the fisherman watching closely as Meg showed them how to aim and shoot. His heart clenched a little knowing they may have to use those weapons.

A little before midnight, the nine sea dragons were lined up on the shore, their riders ready with their weapons at their sides, and a sack filled with tools that might be necessary to break chains or cut through the pen holding the pups. Shawn, Meg and Mateo all had the night vision goggles around their necks.

Above on the ledge were ten sky riders with their dragons waiting to fly with them to the islands: including Sarah who would not be grounded for this one.

All the other riders were on standby. Jessie's dragon Sky was mated with Kyle's Rose. If they need back up, Sky would send the word to Rose and the other riders would come.

Ali and Kendra stood on the shore hand in hand with tears in their eyes, remembering the day they watched their grandchildren sail to that place, and never come back.

Amelia and a group of healers were gathered on the shore. They were putting out medical supplies for when the pups arrived.

Every other member of the riders' families and friends were gathered on the shore or on the cliffs to watch the departure and pray for a safe return.

Mateo nodded to each of the sea dragon riders. "Ok. Let's go get those babies." Yemaya and he launched into the water with the other riders falling in behind him. At the same time, Ian lifted off the cliffside, with the sky dragons falling into formation behind him.

They turned south and west and were flying faster than Sarah ever had. Apollo was keeping his place next to Darcy, but Sarah felt like he was holding back for her. "Ian," she shouted. "Don't hold back for me. I can take a faster pace."

Ian nodded and stroked Darcy's neck and they really started moving. Sarah lowered herself over Apollo's neck and held on.

Below, she could see Mateo leading the sea riders and saw between thirty and forty riderless sea dragons following behind them. Up ahead she could see the faint outline of huge mountains lifting into the sky from a tiny group of islands. The moon was full and bright, and seemed to be reflected off the mountains, giving off more light. As they got closer to the islands, Sarah saw that the mountains rising out of the lush green grass of the islands looked like solid mountains of crystal. They were breathtaking, and powerful. She could almost feel a vibration coming from them.

They circled the islands and landed on the south side. She saw Ian and Quinn pull out their telescopes and extend them to full. She did the same, and when she looked through it, she could see the southern continent and the sea dragons moving toward it. They were moving to the far northwest so they could circle back and move in from the opposite side of the settlement.

Mateo and his group stopped about 100 yards from the shore of the southern continent. They all pulled out their telescopes to search the area before moving any closer. He could see the enclosure with the four dragon pups inside. It didn't look like opening it was going to be a problem. It looked like a corral, the sides were at least 12ft tall, made from thick wood. There was no roof, but he saw that each dragon had a steel collar with a chain attached and staked into the ground. There was no slack in the chains, so the dragons were forced to lie on the ground.

He checked the surrounding area and saw two figures lying down a few yards from the enclosure. From what he could tell, it looked like they were sleeping. There was one other leaning up against a tree on the opposite side of the enclosure, drinking out of a large mug and just looking out to the sea. He was big, with long thick hair around his face so it was hard to make out any features. Mateo couldn't make out his eyes, but it looked like that was the only part of him not covered by that thick hair. He was wearing pants and a shirt, that almost looked like it was made of some kind of thin metal.

When Mateo lowered his telescope and looked at his team, he saw they were all looking at various locations along the coast. Meg lowered her scope. "They're like chain mail wearing sasquatches," she said.

Mateo laughed a little. "Yeah. Ok, team, we need to deal with that one that's awake. He's too close to the pups to not notice us freeing them. Rob and Brett, I need you two to take care of that. See if you can come up behind him and knock him out."

They nodded. "No problem," Brett said.

"Shawn, I need you and Gill to keep a close eye on the two sleeping. Once Rob and Brett have incapacitated the one that's awake, I need you guys to keep watch." He took off his night vision goggles and tossed them to Brett. "Meg and I will get the enclosure open and start working on those chains. Kristen, be ready to lead the freed pups to the sea."

"Ok," Rob said. "Let's move, Brett."

They moved toward the shore, to come up behind the creature leaning against the tree. They had both been Navy Seals, in their life on Earth, so Mateo knew they could move quietly and quickly. As soon as they reached the shore, each of them started moving forward. Shawn and Gill moved toward the two sleepers while Mateo, Meg and Kristen moved toward the enclosure.

Mateo saw the creature by the tree slump down to the ground and Rob lifted his hand and circled it in the air signaling to the rest of them all clear.

Brett stayed with the one they had taken down, and Rob moved to where Shawn and Gill were watching the other two.

Mateo saw the opening to the enclosure and slid the bar aside to open it. He could feel the fear coming from the pups, and they started moving around and snorting.

"Shhh," Mateo put his finger up to his mouth. "We're here to help you, babies. We're going to get you out of here." He and Meg went into the enclosure with Kristen standing to the side. He walked slowly up to the first pup and saw a pretty serious wound on his side and blood coming from the collar around his neck where he had struggled to get free. He tried pulling the stake from the ground, but it wouldn't budge.

"Maya," he whispered. She and Leo moved forward. They went to the stakes and took them in their mouths and pulled. They came out of the ground easily for them, then they moved to the other two and did the same.

Mateo stroked the dragon, to let him know he was going to be ok, then pulled some large cutters out of his bag and went to work on the chain, below the collar. He saw Meg doing the same with a little blue dragon on his left. It took longer than he would have liked, but finally he got the chain off, and Kristen came to lead the dragon to the sea.

Mateo went to the third dragon, a small red male. He looked defeated, and Mateo's heart broke for him. "It's ok, little guy. We're going to get you back to your family and fix you up." He stroked his head and started cutting through the chain. He saw that Meg got the chain off her first one and was coming back from leading him to Kristen.

"Mateo," Meg whispered. "This little girl is really sick."

He looked over and saw Meg kneeling down in front of the pale gold female. He finished cutting the chain on his little male and led him to Kristen then went back to help Meg. He could see she had tears in her eyes, and she was trying to soothe the little female. He kneeled down and started cutting the chains. They heard a low shout and a scuffle behind them. Mateo turned and saw the large creature Rob and Brett had knocked out had regained consciousness and was overpowering Brett. He was reaching for the laser gun at his side when Leo reared up and picked him up in his mouth. The entire top half of the creature was engulfed in his mouth. The creature let out a muffled scream as Leo shook him like a rag doll, blood was splashing everywhere, then Leo threw him into the ocean. Mateo saw that the noise had woken the two sleeping creatures, but Rob and Vince had gotten their guns and were holding them down with a blade to their throats, and their own guns at their heads.

Thanks to the universal translators, their guttural noises were easy to understand.

"Disgusting creatures," one was saying. "You will die for this. We will invade your land, and kill each and every one of you, and take all of your dragons for food."

Leo came up behind the one doing all the talking just waiting for word to rip him in half.

Mateo and Meg got the chains off the last little dragon and helped her to stand. Kristen came in and began rubbing ointment on her wounds and brought her some water. Two sea dragons had come ashore to take her to the sea.

"We've got to get rid of these chains" Mateo told Meg. "We need to make it look like a dragon rescue. Leo helped with that, by killing one of them."

"Mateo, we can't leave those two alive. They'll tell them about us, and they'll come for us."

"Yeah. I know. I'm going to go talk to Shawn. Can you and Kristen manage to get the chains out of here?" She nodded and he went to stand with the four men holding the giant creatures at gun and knife point.

He looked down at them lying on the ground. "They really do look like sasquatch," Mateo said with a smile that didn't reach his eyes.

The larger of the two hostages was still cursing and hissing out disgusting words about their imminent death. The smaller one was lying very still just watching the men surrounding them.

"Gill, do me a favor, and give me your translator, then I need you to go with Meg and Kristen and help them get those chains disposed of and start leading the pups back, so our people can help them."

Gill looked down at the ground for a moment, then took his translator and handed it to Mateo. "You don't have to send me away," he told him. "I know what has to be done, I'm not afraid to do it."

Mateo put his hand on his shoulder. "I know you're not afraid. I just don't want you to have to live with what is about to happen. And I would feel better if you were with the girls, helping them get those babies back. A couple of them are really hurt."

Gill nodded and handed the gun he had been holding to Mateo, then walked over to Megan and Kristen. He saw Meg look over at them once, then signal for Leo to join her. She mounted Leo and led the rest out to sea. Mateo could see the other dragons surrounding the pups and helping them swim away.

Yemaya came and took Leo's place standing over the two creatures still lying on the ground.

"Let's get the big talker on his feet," Mateo said. When he was standing, Mateo walked up to him. Hair was indeed covering every inch of his face with it cut just enough around the eyes for him to see. His eyes were red and angry with just small black dots in the center. He turned away from him. "Take him, Maya," he whispered.

Yemaya pounced on him and muffled any sound he would have made. Like Leo had done, she started shaking him and tore him in half. When she was done, she spat out his upper body and went to the ocean to drink.

The last hostage began trembling and muttering in his guttural language.

Mateo knelt next to him and put the translator behind his ear.

"Quiet!" Mateo barked at him.

He could see the confusion in his eyes, as suddenly he could understand what Mateo told him.

"Be very quiet or I will let my dragon do to you what she just did to your friend. Understand?"

"Yes," the creature whispered back.

"Good. Now, stand up," Mateo said.

When he stood, he towered above all the men. He was definitely close to 7 feet tall, and every exposed part of him was covered with thick hair. Like the other two, he was wearing the same metal clothing.

"What are you thinking?" Shawn asked him.

"I think we need to take him back with us. Find out what we can about their plans. Hopefully, the others will think the dragons drug him out to sea and ate him."

"What is your name?" Mateo asked him.

"Altvi" He answered.

"And what is your species called?"

"We are Chartins. From the planet Chartin."

"Ok, Altvi from Chartin, move. If you call out, or make any sound at all, I'll let my dragon tear you apart. Understand?"

He nodded and they walked him down to the shore.

Mateo took his knife and cut a sleeve off his shirt, then cut it in half. He rolled one half into a ball and shoved it into Altvi's mouth, then used the other piece and tied it around his head to keep the ball in place. Then he cut a large piece of Maya's rein and used it to tie his hands behind his back and bound his legs at the knees.

Rob and Shawn did one last look around the area to make sure they hadn't left anything behind, then joined them on the shore. They all mounted their dragons, Mateo with Altvi draped in front of him over Maya's back. Without a backward glance, they headed home.

CHAPTER 7

W hen Mateo caught up with the other riders, he slowed his speed to watch the pups. They were each flanked by two riderless dragons and being helped through the water. His passenger, Altvi, was trying to keep his head from hanging in the water so was flailing around some and begging Mateo to let him sit up. Remembering the condition of those dragon babies, Mateo didn't care much about his comfort.

He could see the sky dragons above, circling to make sure they made it back safely. There were only four of them, so he assumed the others were holding on the island to make sure no one was following.

After about another hour on the water, Mateo could just make out the shore of the northern continent and breathed a sigh of relief. He started moving a little faster, so he could get to shore and get everyone organized for the treatment of the pups, and guarding Altvi.

Meg picked up her speed as well, and they arrived on shore together, just as the sun was starting to rise.

Kendra, Ali, Amelia, Josh and Kenji met them as soon as they came in. "What the fuck, Mateo?" Kenji said when he saw him pulling Altvi off Maya's back.

"Kenji, Altvi," he said as if making a casual introduction. "Altvi, Kenji." He started dragging Altvi toward a large tree off to the side of the prep area. "Meg, I'm going to need something to secure him to this tree. Then I need

Leo to help Maya hold him here until we can figure out what to do with him."

Meg unlatched her strap from Leo and brought it to him. Mateo kept Altvi's hands behind his back, still bound by the strip he had cut off Maya's strap. "Sit," he told him. Altvi sat with his back against the tree. Then Mateo started wrapping Megan's strap around his body and securing it behind the tree.

Maya and Leo didn't need to be told what to do, they both hovered over Altvi, showing him their teeth and roaring low in their throats.

"Make one wrong move, and these dragons will rip you apart. Understand?"

Altvi nodded.

"He understands what you're saying?" Kenji asked.

Mateo tapped his translator. "He's wearing one too."

Josh came over and met Mateo and Kenji as they started walking back. "What are you planning on doing with that?" Josh asked with a head nod toward Altvi.

"I don't know. Question him? Find out what the hell they're planning? The dragons killed the other two guards, that one was trembling in his boots, man. I didn't know what else to do. I couldn't leave him there to alert the others, but killing him seemed, I don't know, wrong."

"How bad was it?" Josh asked.

"It could have been worse. But pretty damn bad. All the pups are hurt. Two worse than the others, and one of them really bad," Mateo said. "Let's get those babies fixed up and I'll brief you all at once."

Josh nodded and they headed over to help the others with the pups that were just arriving on shore, leaving Yemaya and Leo guarding Altvi.

Mateo could see how frightened and exhausted the pups were. And he could see the concern in the eyes of all the adult dragons.

The healers were gathered around each of the babies, putting ointment on their wounds, and covering them with large leaves from a tree that Mateo didn't recognize.

Jacob and his apprentices arrived carrying tools that looked like huge scissors and started cutting off the collars.

Kendra and Amelia were working on the small gold dragon, with the worst injuries. Amelia had her head resting in her lap trying to soothe her, while Kendra tended to her wounds. Josh knelt down next to her. "What can we do to help?" he asked her.

Amelia looked at him and he saw tears streaming down her face. She shook her head. "I don't know," she whispered. "Josh, what kind of monster would do this to these beautiful, innocent creatures?" He shook his head but looked over to where Altvi was slumped against the tree, watching them with his red eyes.

Throughout the day, someone was kept on guard with Altvi, while other arrangements were being made for his confinement. Two dragons were with the guard at all times.

Jacob and his team started working on transforming a small storage building, isolated on the far west side of the meadow, to use as a cell.

The two larger dragon pups were patched up and given a good meal and some love and snuggles, then released to go back to the sea with their families. The green male pup had some pretty serious wounds on his neck and a couple of deep punctures to his legs, and side. They had given him some herbs, to help him rest, so they could clean and treat his wounds. The healers seemed pretty optimistic about his recovery.

The little gold female, however, was failing. Her wounds were deep, and some were infected and one of her wings was severely damaged. She wouldn't take any food and only small amounts of water. She was lying on her side, and Amelia could see her struggling to take every breath. "Fight, sweet girl," Amelia whispered to her. "I'll help you, and I'll keep you safe. But I need you to fight to stay here with me."

It seemed every dragon rider, both air and sea, stopped to check on her. Every healer, doctor and nurse in the community stopped to see how she was doing, and most of the community stopped by and offered to sit with her. Amelia refused every offer and refused to leave the little dragon's side. Kristen brought her a plate of food from the community kitchen. Amelia thanked her but couldn't find her appetite.

As the sun started to set, she watched as a group from the Destiny's team came to get the prisoner. They along with two dragons and escorted him away. 'Good,' she thought. The more she had to sit on that shore, looking at him the angrier she became. Every time she saw his red blood eyes look her way, the more she wanted to grab a rock and bash him with it. She heard some of the riders talking about the sea dragons killing two of the guards during the rescue and the thought did not make her fear or shudder as it normally would. She felt satisfaction that they were able to exact some revenge for these poor pups.

Amelia felt the little dragon stir under her stroking, and saw her eyes flutter open. "Hello, beautiful," Amelia said and leaned down to kiss her snout. The dragon's nostrils started sniffing, and she turned her head toward the plate that Amelia had set aside. "Are you hungry, baby?" She grabbed the plate and broke off a small piece of fish. She held it to the pup's mouth, and when she took it, Amelia smiled and breathed a small sigh of relief.

Josh got back to his cottage, after helping to escort Altvi to the hut that Jacob had constructed. He left the interrogation to others better equipped to get information out of him. He went to the kitchen to brew some coffee. He liked the cottage, and Mateo was proving to be a good roommate, but he was looking forward to moving into his little house in the meadow. He had chosen a spot near the orchard, but close to the crops. About 50 yards from his back door was a cliff, dropping to the shore, so he had a nice view of the ocean. Jacob told him that in another week or two, they would be finished installing the plumbing, and he could begin choosing his appliances and furniture. When he was back on Earth, he always imagined buying his own home. Something large and lavish. Taking on a mortgage that would put him in debt for thirty years or so. But now, he couldn't imagine being more excited about moving into the little cottage he had designed and helped build.

It made him think of Hank, his college roommate and friend. He was one of the nine once, along with Hank. Helping build and plan the journey to the Center. Hank was an architect and designed the ships. He would have liked to have his input on designing his little house. Hank was pretty pissed when Josh betrayed the team and went to his father with information about them and their mission. His dad was a 4-star general and had pulled every detail out of him. He had definitely made a misstep there, and had lost his place on the team, and his relationship with the best friends he ever had.

He shook his head, to try to get those thoughts out of his head. He was building a new life here on Asteria. And he was enjoying every minute of it. He poured a cup of coffee and went to the back door of the cottage to watch the sun set. He saw Amelia sitting on the shore next to the little golden dragon, feeding her pieces of food from her plate. The sun was setting behind her, and the sky was orange and red. He could see her smile and talk to the pup. And wished he had a camera, or any kind of artistic skill. He would have captured that moment and called it 'Innocence'. Amelia with her golden curls and golden brown eyes, and the little golden dragon looking up at her as she ate out of her hand.

Josh went with instinct, and poured a second cup of coffee, then grabbed a couple blankets and a pillow from his room and balancing them all, headed down to the shore.

Amelia felt the fear come into the pup and looked over to see Josh heading their direction. "It's ok, baby," she soothed the dragon. "He's our friend, he would never hurt you, I will never let anyone hurt you again." She kept stroking the dragon's head as she watched Josh, never taking her eyes off of him.

She smiled when she saw he was carrying two mugs, with two blankets thrown over each shoulder and a pillow tucked under his arm.

"Hi," she said.

"Hi. I see she's awake. That's great. How's she doing?"

"She's ok. She still has a long road to recovery, but she ate a little and is holding it down. That's a really good sign."

He handed her one of the mugs. "I hope you like coffee. If not, I think we have some lemonade."

"I love coffee," she said and took a sip. "Thank you."

"May I join you?"

She nodded and Josh handed her his other mug. "Can you hold this for a minute?" He took a blanket and wrapped it around her shoulders, then took the other one and draped it over the pup. Then set the pillow next to Amelia's knee. He took his mug back and sat across from her. "It can get chilly down here after dark," he told her. "I don't want you two to get cold."

"Thank you, Josh."

He nodded and looked at the pup. He could see the wariness in her eyes and felt a tug on his heart. He held out his hand like he would with a strange dog, so she could sniff it. She kept her eyes locked on his, and sniffed his hand, then lay her head back down on the grass. "What's her name?" he asked Amelia.

She blushed a little. "Only a rider is supposed to name a bonded dragon."

"Kind of a dumb rule," Josh said. "She loves you. So, what's her name?"

"Molly," Amelia said.

Josh smiled. "The Unsinkable Molly Brown."

They talked well into the night, and after Amelia gave Molly some more medicine, and changed the leaf bandages and checked her wounds, then covered her again with the blanket he had brought for her. Josh could see her eyes getting heavy and circles appearing under them. He took the pillow he brought down and laid it next to the little dragon. "Why don't you get some rest," he told her. "I'll sit with you both for a while, and make sure you're ok."

"You don't have to do that, Josh," she said. "You must be tired too."

He shook his head. "Not even a little." He patted the pillow.

She laid down with her head on the pillow and pulled the blanket a little tighter around her. "Thank you, Josh., For the coffee, the blankets and the company. And for not trying to talk me into leaving her."

He smiled at her and shook his head. "You're welcome, Amelia."

While Josh and Amelia were on the shore, a large group was gathered outside the little shed, where they had chained and locked up Altvi. They had taken his translator, so he couldn't understand what they were talking about. They gave him some food and water, and a blanket with a mattress on the floor. They shackled his ankles to chains and bolted them to the floor. He could move from the mattress to the little makeshift toilet they put in there for him. There were no windows, and the chains would not reach to the door.

Outside, Ali and Jason were sitting in a circle with ten others, trying to decide what to do with Altvi. Kendra had removed herself from the conversation. This was one of the creatures that had killed her family, and she couldn't be objective. Mateo bringing him here had opened the wounds left by the death of Christopher and Kaleb.

She moved to the cliff and looked down over the ocean. She could see Josh and Amelia sitting together next to the little golden dragon. She saw Holly and the healer, Mari, watching over the green pup. And she saw other sea dragons circling in the water, staying close to the shore. She sat down and dangled her feet off the side of the cliff. She heard someone approaching and turned to see Sarah walking to join her.

"Do you want some alone time?" Sarah asked. "Or may I join you?"

"Please join me." Kendra patted the ground next to her, Sarah sat and dangled her legs over the edge as well.

Sarah took a deep breath, and looked down over the shore, the city, the sea and the dragons. "What an amazing life you've built here Kendra. If I were to imagine a paradise, I think this is what I would see."

Kendra nodded. "Sometimes I miss driving," she said. "I used to love driving my little car around Pheonix. I had a Mustang convertible. God, I loved that car."

"I miss cable TV," Sarah said. "I used to get hooked on those stupid reality shows."

Kendra laughed at that. "Really?"

Sarah nodded. "That was my dirty little secret."

"You should reserve some time with Christov's AROE. He put a lot of Earth's culture in there. You might be able to find something you'd enjoy watching. There are some classic television shows, and a ton of movies."

"I haven't found time to do that. I'll have to make the time," Sarah said. "Hey! We should find a chick flick, and get a bunch of girls, and do a girls' night with wine and a movie."

Kendra put her head on Sarah's shoulder. "I'd like that."

"Kendra, I'm so sorry about your boys. And I'm sorry that this has brought all of that back."

"I hate that creature in that hut. I'm sure he wasn't involved in Christopher and Jax's death. I have no reason to believe he was even there. But I hate him. That goes against everything I thought I knew about myself."

"That just makes you human. We aren't a perfect race, but we're a good race. And you are one of the best I've ever known. I can't imagine what you went through, but I know that what you're feeling now is perfectly human."

Kendra patted Sarah's hand and sat up. "You've seemed to settle in here nicely," she told her. "A dragon rider! That's so exciting."

Sarah shook her head. "I still can't believe it. I have to pinch myself sometimes just to prove it's real. Apollo is such a gift!"

"And Kenji?" Kendra asked with a twinkle in her eye.

"Yeah, Kenji. I think I'm in love with him. He told me he was in love with me. That's another gift, I never saw coming."

"Really?" Kendra asked. "I saw it coming a mile away. So, are you planning on settling here? Or do you think you might return to the Center?"

"I can never leave Apollo. I think it would break both of us, beyond repair. I miss Jewel and my parents, but I know they're doing well at the Center. And it's been 250 years. It would take another 250 to get back there. I don't know if they would still be there. I know Kenji misses his family. Akemi and Kai, his father. I'm hoping he'll stay. But I have no desire to ever leave Asteria."

"Good. You belong here now."

Sarah nodded and looked at Kendra. "I do. Do you?"

"Sometimes I regret that I never got to see the Center. I miss some of the friends I made at Area 51. Ali and I made a life here. We raised a family. I get to spend time with our children's children, and they are all a joy to me. I'm proud of what we built here. So, yes. This is my place."

Sarah linked her arm through Kendra's. "Good."

Together they sat and watched the sun set over the ocean.

CHAPTER 8

Josh was sitting at the kitchen table drinking coffee and waiting. He heard the door open, and Mateo came in, grabbed a mug, and slumped into a chair at the table.

"How was your day, dear?" Josh asked.

Mateo laughed. "Brutal. Yours?" He shook his head and took a big gulp of coffee. "I have half the community thinking I'm a freaking hero, and the other half pissed at me for bringing Altvi back here."

"You did the right thing, Mateo," Josh told him. "Did you guys get any information out of him?"

Mateo nodded. "Quite a bit, actually. Jacob is a master interrogator, believe it or not. He brought in a bunch of menacing looking tools and laid them on the floor in front of him, and the dude started spilling his guts."

Mateo spent the next hour filling Josh in on what they learned.

"The planet Chartin is several systems away. It's a planet of ice and snow, and they built their homes in caves deep inside of mountains. They're fairly intelligent, but lazy. They're violent and highly misogynistic. The females are only for doing the cooking and having babies. A couple of ships landed on the planet a couple of hundred years ago. They stole them, killed the crew of each ship, took their weapons and started invading planets and stealing more technology. They're cowards and thieves, but strong, and self-important. They never tried to develop their own technology, just kept stealing others. The first ship crash landed on Asteria, after attempting to go through the asteroid field and taking a hit that crippled their ship. They sent out a distress signal that went unanswered until now." Mateo hesitated for a moment. "Josh, the reason they even answered the distress signal, after so many years, is because they saw us. They saw the *Destiny* approaching Asteria. We led them here."

"Well, shit," Josh said. "So, what are their plans?"

"He thinks they're getting ready to leave. They spent the day packing up the rescue ship. But they were leaving some here to await the arrival of more ships." Mateo looked into Josh's eyes. "They scanned us on their way in. They know how many of us there are and knew they couldn't overtake us with the numbers they have now. They want our ships, our technology, our dragons and our women. And will be coming back for them."

"How much time do we have?"

Mateo shook his head. "Altvi didn't know. It could be a week, or a day or a month."

"Well, shit," Josh repeated. "Do we have a plan?"

"Jacob is going to work his team around the clock, to make weapons. The scientists are going to start working on some kind of electrical weapons, powered by the ships. Kenji is going to move the *Destiny* off the runway and hide it somewhere. And we start training today."

Josh nodded. "Ok. Why don't you get some rest. I'm going to go up and see where I can help."

Mateo drank the last of his coffee and rubbed his hands over his face. "Yeah. Do me a favor, and come get me in a couple of hours, if you don't see me up there."

Josh nodded. "Will do."

Over the next few days, the people of Asteria were broken into groups. They learned how to use the weapons they were making, make traps and engage in hand-to-hand combat. The dragon riders practiced shooting from the air on dragon back. The sea dragon riders did the same from the backs of their dragons. Mateo led martial arts training. They used the AROE to teach other skills in combat, strategy and planning.

Dragon riders rotated time at the islands keeping watch over any activity at the southern continent. They also filled bags with crystals from the mountains, to help the scientists with more power for the weapons they were building.

The doctors, nurses and healers spent time making new bandages, medication and herbal remedies.

Kenji's group studied the laser guns that the rescue team brought back and were trying to duplicate the technology with electrical power. They had made crystal generated tasers that could zap an electrical current into the body, incapacitating that body, the downside was it had to be at close range, meaning they had to get past the weapons the Chartins had to use them.

The little green dragon had recovered enough to return to the sea, and Molly, the little golden dragon, was making progress but was still struggling. Amelia wanted to move her up to her cottage in the meadow but wasn't sure how. She could walk, with a little difficulty, but the healers said the damage to her wing was extensive and she may never fly, so getting her up the cliff could be a problem.

When Meg came to check on her, Amelia told her of her dilemma. Meg just smiled. "I may have an idea," she said.

She went to the edge of the sea, and Leo came out of the water. Amelia caught her breath, he was by far the largest dragon she had seen, far bigger than Ian's Darcy, or Apollo or Titan. She watched him lower his head to Meg, then look over at Amelia and Molly.

Both Leo and Meg came to stand before them. "He can carry her up," Meg told her.

Leo lowered his head and nuzzled little Molly. She had no fear of the huge dragon and seemed to know he was there to help. She stood and he gathered her, gently in his front talons, then lifted off and flew to the cliff.

"He's beautiful!" Amelia said.

"Yeah. He really is. He'll be very careful with her."

Together Meg and Amelia ran to the cliff and lifted up to the top. They saw that Leo had set down near the pup enclosure and was watching as Molly explored the field where other dragons were watching and grazing.

Amelia approached Leo and reached her hand out to him. "Thank you, Leo," she laid her hand on his head. "I promise I will take care of her and keep her safe." He gave Amelia a slight bow then turned to Meg. After some kind of silent acknowledgement, he lifted off and returned to the sea.

Sarah had been in the baby dragon enclosure, walked over to join them and watch Molly in her new surroundings. "Looks like she's doing well in her recovery," she said.

"She is," Amelia said. "She has a long road ahead, but she's eating now, and able to walk further without tiring."

"I can prepare a stall for her if you want me to," Sarah said.

Amelia shook her head. "I think I would like to keep her close to me for a while. I'm going to ask Josh to help me prepare a place for her at my cottage."

Sarah nodded. "I think that's a great idea."

"I'm going to go check on her," Amelia said and walked away toward where Molly was laying in the field.

"Female dragons usually only bond with males and vice versa," Meg said. "But those two are definitely bonded." Sarah nodded. "Yes, they are."

"Well, I think I'm going to go steal some time with an AROE" Meg said. "I want to work on my hand to hand for a while. You want to join me?"

Sarah laughed. "Hand to hand? Not even in my worst dream. I'll stick to shooting from Apollo's back," she said. "I'm actually getting pretty good at that."

Meg nodded. "Yeah, you are. I'll see you tonight at dinner?"

"Yeah. See you tonight."

Meg headed off toward the AROE building they had set up as a training facility and Sarah watched Amelia and Molly for a few more minutes, then went back to the enclosure to play with the new hatchlings.

When Meg entered the little domed building that housed the AROE her first reaction was annoyance at finding it already in use. Ian was there and had a martial arts program running. He was working on kicks and punches. He had really good form. He was barefoot and had taken off his shirt. Sweat had formed on his body and face. She was impressed with his muscle structure. He was ripped. Her annoyance turned to curiosity. She leaned back against the wall to watch.

He knew she was there, watching him. He felt her the minute she walked in.

He thought about stopping the program and cutting his training short but then decided against it. Let her watch, he thought. God knew he had watched her enough. She was petite, but he knew she was a warrior. On Earth, she had been a special forces officer in the military, then became a security member on Zander's special ops team. She was definitely not his type. He preferred women with long hair and lots of curves. She was small and built more like a young boy, with short choppy hair and big blue eyes.

But he still caught himself watching her. She had moves and knew weapons. He had seen her training some of the women. She seemed fearless. And when Leo, the largest and most elusive of the sea dragons chose her to be his rider, he started looking at her a little closer.

She always seemed to be moving. Pitching in helping, working on weapons training, helping build. She never seemed to rest. Even when she joined in for the evening meal, she ate quickly and was the first to leave to find something to do.

He ended his program and grabbed his water. He took a long drink then turned to her. "Sorry, did I run over on my time?" he asked.

"No. I didn't sign up for time. I just thought I'd take a chance and find it open."

"Well, I'll get out of here and let you get to it."

"No rush," Meg said and moved to program the AROE

"Can I ask you a question?" Ian asked her.

"Sure." She laid a mat on the floor and started doing warm up stretches.

"Are we ready for this battle?"

Meg stopped stretching, took a deep breath and looked into Ian's eyes. "No. But you will be. You guys are learning and preparing. Most of the population are young and strong and in great shape. And more important than all of that, you guys have something worth fighting for here."

"Why do you think they're not coming?" Ian asked. "Why haven't they attacked yet?"

"I don't know. Maybe they changed their minds We have no idea how long it's going to take them to organize an attack or call reinforcements. But the more time it takes, the better for us to prepare."

Ian nodded. "What are you working on tonight?"

"Kickboxing," she said. "Have you tried it? You're welcome to stay and work out with me."

Ian laughed. "Hell, no. I just did an hour with the Karate program. I'm spent. I'm going to grab something to eat and get some rest. I'm on the morning shift on the island."

"Yeah?" Meg said. "Me too. I'll see you at the islands then."

He grabbed his shirt and pulled it on as he walked out the door. "See ya."

Meg shrugged and hit play on the AROE to start her workout.

The next morning Meg and Mateo met at the shore at dawn. Their dragons were already there, waiting for them. They mounted up and headed for the islands to relieve the night watch. They looked up when they saw a shadow of sky dragons and saw Ian and Quinn flying above them. Mateo gave them a two finger salute, and he and Meg increased their speed to get to the islands.

When they arrived, they saw Ebony and Maxie swimming close to the island shore. Shawn and Vince were waiting to go home. They reported no activity that night.

Meg saw Ian and Quinn relieving Pax and Micha. Then the four dragon riders mounted and headed back to the city.

Ian and Mateo, who had become good friends, decided they would start filling bags with crystals while Quinn and Meg took watch on the south settlement. Meg watched them walk toward the crystal mountain and shook her head. "They just want to go play," Meg said.

Quinn shrugged. "Let them. My gran made fresh bread this morning and a delicious spread to go over it. And I have fresh potato salad from the kitchen. If they miss out on it, their loss."

Meg let out a little whoop and sat down on the blanket Quinn had spread on the ground. She dug into the bread and spread some of the whipped dressing over it. "Oh, my God!" she said through a mouthful of bread. "This is delicious!"

"My grandmother's bread is the best," Quinn said and pulled out her scope to check in on the Chartins. "It looks like they're still sleeping. I don't see any movement over there."

"Can I ask you a question, Meg?"

"Sure," she said. "What's up?"

"My gran was the granddaughter of one of the original travelers from Earth. She died long before I was born, so I never knew her, but she told gran's mother stories about Earth, and they were passed down. She was one of you. One of the warriors that was on Zander's team."

"Really? Meg asked. "Who was she?"

"Her name was Paula," Quinn said.

"Paula was your great grandmother? She was my friend, Quinn. A really good friend. We served together in the Navy, and she's the one that introduced me to Zander." Meg tilted her head and looked a little closer at Quinn. "I see her in you. Now that I know, I can really see her in you. Who did she hook up with?" She saw Quinn's puzzled look and rephrased the question. "Who did she get together with, start a family with?"

"My great grandfather's name was Colin. I believe you may have known him too,"

Quinn laughed. "Yeah. I knew Colin. He always had a thing for Paula. He was a good man. I'm glad she gave him a chance. So, what's your question?"

"On Earth, you and my great grandmother were fighters. You were warriors. Can you teach me to be one too?"

"I can. You're a dragon rider, so most of what we will need you to do is shoot at the bad guys, from the air. But yeah. I can teach you to fight, to defend yourself."

Quinn nodded. "Can you tell me about her?" she asked. "About Paula?"

Meg smiled. "She was fearless. She was the first one to volunteer for a mission. The more dangerous the better. She was fierce. But she was funny, and kind. She had a very definite line of what was right and what was wrong. And she insisted on always doing what was right. I think you share that trait."

"Thank you for saying that, Meg. I want to do what is right. I want to do everything I can to protect my people and our life here."

Meg nodded. "Then you will. Something else you share with her is your looks. She was freaking gorgeous! All that long wavy chestnut colored hair, big, long, green cat eyes. She turned heads everywhere we went."

Quinn's mouth dropped open. "Thank you for that. But I'm very average looking. You are the gorgeous one. With your pale and perfect skin, black hair and blue eyes.

Your hair is shorter than some of the men here, but it's very flattering on you. I've seen more than one of the village men looking your way."

Meg laughed. "I'm sure they're looking your way too, honey. You should look in the mirror more often."

"Well, Ian certainly looks your way often enough," Quinn said, dismissing that.

"Really? Well, I might have to look back sometime. He's a cutie."

She grabbed her scope and took another look at the south shore.

While Meg and Quinn were feasting and having some girl talk, Ian and Mateo found a tall tree next to a crystal mountain. They jumped from limb to limb, until they reached the top, and started chiseling crystal from the mountain.

"I'm starting to get itchy," Mateo told him. "I don't like how long they're waiting to leave. Don't get me wrong, the more time we have to train the better. I just wonder what they're waiting for."

"Maybe they're doing their own surveillance on us," Ian said. "With the arrival of the *Destiny*, which we know they saw, they may not know what kind of weapons we have."

"Yeah. Makes sense. Sometimes, I wonder if we should just attack them and get it over with."

Ian shook his head. "The elders will never approve that. The last time we went to the southern continent, they slaughtered us. Let them come to us. Let them head into our traps. And the ones slaughtered this time will be them."

"Yeah," Mateo said. "Like I said, I'm just itchy."

"Maybe what you need is a woman to scratch that itch."

Mateo cracked up laughing. "Yeah, maybe. It's been a while."

"Well," Ian said. "I'm sure you won't have any trouble finding one. So, you and Meg aren't?"

"Aren't what?" Mateo asked. "A couple?" He saw Ian nod and laughed. "No. Just friends. Why? Are you thinking about looking there?"

Ian shrugged. "Probably not. She's not really my type. I was just wondering."

Mateo raised an eyebrow. "Meg is every guy's type," he said. "Well, my bag is about full. How about we head back down and get some lunch."

Ian smiled. "I'm sure they have food down there."

"Perfect."

They jumped to the ground and took their bags full of crystals back to the shore to join the girls.

CHAPTER 9

Altvi was kept in his cell, with no windows and only one door. There were some cracks between the wooden slats in one of the walls that let in a little light, and he found if he squinted, he could see some of the activity outside but couldn't really make it out.

They had given him a soft platform to lie on. They called it a mattress. It was very nice, and better than sleeping on the ground or hard floor, which he had done his entire life. The Chartins had nothing like a mattress. They also gave him a toilet. He was unfamiliar with the toilet. The Chartins had nothing like that either. The one called Mateo explained what it was for and demonstrated how to use it. He liked the idea of the toilet, and found he enjoyed using it, as opposed to shitting outside like the animals.

He wondered why these humans had treated him with such generosity. They provided him with food three times a day, and fresh water. One time the one called Ian brought him a glass filled with something called lemonade. It was sweet and very tart and made his cheeks feel strange, but he enjoyed it.

When he was first captured and tied to a tree on the beach, he saw that women worked beside the men. Many of them wore the same clothes as the men as well. He also saw both men and women riding the dragons. He thought this strange, but when he asked any questions, they always went unanswered. There was one with long gold hair. She cared for the little dragon they had been going to slaughter in the morning for the next feast. He found himself looking at her more and more as he sat there at that tree. If he could find a way to escape, he would take her for his own. She was pretty, and dressed as a woman should. And she could care for him the way she cared for the little dragon.

Two or three men would come to question him every day. They would put the strange device behind his ear, and he could understand their questions, and they could understand his answers. This technology they had was much like magic to him. If he could take these back to his people, he would be a hero.

Altvi was only 19 when he took his first space voyage, and it was about two years into the voyage when they were hit by the space rock and crashed on this hot miserable planet. He lost track of how long they had been here but knew he must be nearly 40 years old now.

He wished they would just return home. Now that the rescue ship had gotten there, Altvi wished they could just return to their beloved Chartin. He disliked killing and stealing. He wasn't very good at it, so he was often given the jobs of women. Cooking, and guarding prisoners. And because he was smaller than most, he was often used as a female in other ways as well. He disliked that very much.

He would like to see his family. He would like to see if they had made changes on the home world. He didn't think he would volunteer for another voyage. He would like to find a female and have children and just live his life without taking orders. If he could escape this place, he would find a way back to the settlement and tell them that they could not win a battle here. He would tell them they should flee before they came for them. That they had thousands of their species who were warriors with weapons far superior to theirs and their dragons were fierce and would devour them.

Maybe if he told his captors that he would do that, they would let him go. Maybe they would be pleased with his idea and let him have the golden haired female to take with him.

Amelia knew that the new dragon eggs were due to hatch anytime, so after she finished her morning chores she and Molly walked to the pup enclosure to see if they had arrived yet.

As they got closer, they saw Ian sitting on the wall of the enclosure, and she could see Sara's head poking up from inside it. Amelia could feel Molly's distress. She started walking very slowly behind her. She loved going to see the dragon babies but was still terrified of humans.

Amelia stopped and let Molly catch up. She leaned in and put her head against the little dragon's. "It's ok, Molly. No one here will hurt you. Those two are my friends, they are dragon riders and love you too. I promise you're safe, Molly."

The little dragon looked into Amelia's eyes and with one more look at the enclosure started walking cautiously forward. She was still limping from the wounds to her leg, but they were healing, and Amelia suspected she would soon be able to walk without the limp.

Ian saw the exchange with Amelia and Molly and understood the little dragon's fear. She wasn't quite so timid with him; he figured it was because she saw him often when they visited the pup enclosure but he stayed very still, just watching as she approached a few steps behind Amelia.

He looked into Molly's eyes and smiled, then turned his attention to Amelia. "You're just in time!" he told her.

"They're here?" she asked?

"They're coming now. One of them has almost broken through his shell, and the other is starting to crack."

Amelia let out a little scream of joy and jumped up and down. Molly watched her closely, backing up a step. "Come on, Molly, the babies are coming!"

She moved to the wall and leaned over it. Molly went to the other side of Amelia, away from Ian, and peered over the side.

Sarah was sitting down on the ground next to the little pond. Amelia could see little legs pushing out of the shell, pieces broken and lying around in the water.

"Ian won't let me help him come out," Sarah said with a little sulk, never taking her eyes off the little dragon. "He said he has to do it on his own."

Amelia smiled. "I know, it's hard not to help them break through. But he's almost got it."

"But he's breech," Sarah said. "Water from the pond is starting to fill up in the egg. What if he drowns?"

"He, or I should say she, won't. Dragons are from the water. She'll be fine."

"She?" Sarah asked and saw that she had rolled onto her back and pushed most of the back legs and lower body out of the shell."

Amelia put her arm around Molly. "You're about to be a big sister, Molly." She could feel the dragon's excitement. It had overcome the fear of being around people. She watched very closely as the little dragon started pushing out of the egg. She was a deep purple with gold tipped wings. While they watched the little pup emerge from the egg, they heard a loud crack and looked over and saw a little black arm push out of the second egg.

A couple of hours later, Amelia, Ian and Sarah sat on the wall watching the little hatchlings get acclimated to their new environment. They put gruel out for them to eat, and watched as they gobbled it up, then watched as they curled together and slept, a little purple girl with gold tips on her wings, and the little black boy with just a touch of silver around his eyes.

"They're so beautiful!" Sarah said.

Ian smiled. "Yeah, I remember when Darcy hatched. It was the first time I had seen a hatchling. It's a magical moment. We'll probably have another couple eggs come this season from the sky dragons, then that will be it for this season."

"So, they self-regulate their population?" Sarah asked.

"I guess," Ian said. "I just know that we usually only have four females bring us two or three eggs each season. We've had two from the sea, and one from the sky, so we should be getting another sky dragon bring us hers."

"That's incredible," Sarah said. "What about the dragons in the West? Do they bring eggs?"

"They never have," Ian told her. "Once they lose their rider, they stay in mourning, unless they bond with another human. We've never had a mourning dragon bring eggs."

Sarah thought of Apollo and was even more in awe, and grateful that he had chosen her.

Amelia saw Josh heading toward them. He was walking out of the orchard in the southern field. She immediately smoothed her hair, and wished she was wearing something other than the old dress she used for doing chores.

Molly noticed him coming in their direction and moved closer to Amelia. She put her arm around her to comfort her, and together they watched Josh's approach.

"Hey," he said as he walked to the enclosure. "What's up?"

"We had babies!" Sarah told him and pointed at the little hatchlings.

"Yeah?" he asked and took a seat near Ian. "Well, look at that! They're about the size of my grandma's chihuahua!"

"You're grandma's what?" Amelia asked.

He smiled at her. "Her little dog. I've been working over at my place and was wondering if I could get your opinion on a few things," he asked Amelia.

"Of course!" she said and swung her legs over the wall. "Take care of our babies," she told Ian and Sarah. "Come on Molly, let's go for a walk."

"Hmmm," Sarah said as she watched them walk away.

"What?" Ian asked.

"Something's happening there," she said.

Ian looked over as Josh and Amelia walked toward the orchard with Molly following behind them. "Yeah. She kind of lit up when she saw him."

"So did he," Sarah said. "This could be interesting to watch."

As they walked through the orchard, toward his cottage, Josh suddenly felt awkward. He wasn't sure what to do with his hands, so he shoved them in his pockets and searched for something to say. He looked back at Molly, who was following at a safe distance, staying closer to Amelia and giving him the side eye.

"Molly seems to be adjusting well," he said.

Amelia looked back at the little dragon and smiled. "She is. Her wounds are mostly healed. She just needs to learn to trust. She's still so afraid of everything."

"She trusts you," he said. "She'll learn to trust the rest of us in time. She just needs to believe no one here will hurt her."

Amelia nodded. "She's grown some too. Now that she's eating. I think she may reach full size. But the healers say she may never be able to fly."

"She's of the sea, isn't she?"

Amelia shook her head. "No, she's a sky dragon. She's one of Apollo's."

"Then how did they get ahold of her?" Josh asked. "The others were of the sea and have returned to the sea. How did they get a sky dragon?"

Amelia shook her head. "I don't know."

Josh looked over at Molly. She shrank back from him. He reached up and pulled an apple from the tree behind him, then took his knife from his pocket and started cutting it into small pieces. He took a bite, then sat on the ground. He took another bite, and looked at Molly, who was suddenly very interested. He held out his hand. "You want a bite, Molly?"

Amelia smiled and sat next to Josh. He handed her a piece of the apple, and she bit it. Then he held out a larger piece to Molly.

Josh kept his hand held out, then turned to face Amelia. "So, I was thinking I could barter with you. I can really use your help in the garden I want behind my cottage," he told her. "And I could use some ideas for some of the space inside. I thought in return I could build a larger and more secure space for Molly, at your place."

"I would love to help with your cottage, Josh. You don't have to barter your time for my help. I would do it, just because I enjoy doing it. And I'd like to think we've become friends. But I'm not going to turn down your offer. Maybe you could come over sometime, and we could compare ideas for a new enclosure for Molly."

Neither of them missed the fact that Molly had been inching closer to Josh's outstretched hand, as they talked.

Josh turned and looked into Molly's eyes and the little dragon froze in mid step.

"I'll never hurt you, Molly," he told her softly. "And I will never let anyone else hurt you either."

She took another step toward him, never taking her eyes off his. One more step and she was close enough to snatch the apple from his hand, but she just looked at him. "It's for you, sweetheart," he told her as he leaned toward her and held his hand up toward her snout. She slowly and gently took the apple, then lay down in front of him. When he reached out and rubbed her back, she didn't flinch and looked at Amelia with no fear in her eyes.

"I think you just made another friend."

When they got to the end of the orchard, Amelia just stopped and stared. She had seen the house in the early stages of construction, but now it looked complete, and it was beautiful. It was two stories, and he had added a wooden porch that ran the entire front of the house. There was a picket fence running the length of the porch. And he had transplanted three young flowering bushes and planted them in front of the fence. Amelia knew that when those bushes started to mature, they would grow up and entwine with the fence. It would be lovely.

"Oh Josh. It's incredible!" Amelia told him.

He had been watching her face, as she looked at his home, and was delighted with what he saw there. Then he looked back at the cottage. He loved it. His first home. He still needed to get the shutters up on the windows. And he was deciding what color he wanted to paint them. And the entrance door was still brown. When he decided what color to paint the shutters, he would paint the door and the fence the same color.

"Have you moved in yet?" she asked him.

"Sort of. I haven't gotten furniture yet. But I have a bed, so I've been spending most of my nights here. Do you want to see inside?"

"Yes! Please!"

When they got closer to the cottage, Josh stopped. "What color do you think I should paint the door?" he asked her.

"Blue," she said without hesitation. "Like the sky and the sea."

He nodded, and he could see it. His little white house with blue shutters, door and fence. Then he grabbed her hand. "Come on." He led her to the house and opened the front door.

When Amelia stepped inside, she stopped and tried to see everything at once. She saw that the second floor did not run the entire length of the house, so the living area had a high vaulted ceiling with dark wooden beams. The second floor stopped at the back of the living area and there was a half wall, so you could stand upstairs and look down over the area. There was a staircase, the same dark wood as the beams, running up to the second floor, along the back wall, so it didn't take any room away from the living area.

There was a large window looking out over the front of the cottage. Then under the floor of the upper level, a full wall that enclosed the kitchen. It was large, and there was another half wall holding a countertop separating the kitchen from a larger area with another wide window, looking out at the orchards.

Josh was watching her as she ran her hands over the breakfast bar and was looking around the kitchen. There were upper and lower cabinets, all the same dark wood. "I thought I could put a big dining table here, by the window," he said. "Maybe the same wood as the staircase and beams. Kind of tie it all together."

There was a closed door off the side to the right of the kitchen; she opened it and found a bedroom. It was empty of any furniture, but it had a window overlooking the meadow and cliffs. She backed out and closed the door, then wandered to the back of the kitchen to the small, enclosed porch where she knew the bathroom was. She opened the door to the bathroom and found it was very large with a huge shower. Instead of wood, he had used pale stone for the walls, and it was beautiful. Outside the bathroom door was a bench where you could sit to take off your shoes, and hooks along the wall to hang your jacket.

When Amelia turned to go back into the kitchen, she saw Josh standing there looking nervous. She realized she hadn't said anything since she had entered the cottage, and he must think she didn't like it.

"Josh, this is the most beautiful home I've ever seen," she told him. "It's so grand! And it's deceiving from the outside. It looks like a sweet little cottage, then you walk in and it's just grand! Everyone is going to be jealous and want to copy it!"

Josh let out the breath, he didn't realize he had been holding and smiled. "Thank you. Do you want to see upstairs?"

She nodded. "Absolutely!"

As they walked back through the living area toward the staircase, Josh stopped in front of the window. "Amelia, look." He pointed to the window.

She saw Molly lying in the front yard, flat on her back, basking in the sun. Amelia laughed. "I've never seen her lie like that! She feels safe here. You may find her visiting your home often."

"She and her mother are welcome here anytime," he said with a smile.

When they reached the top of the stairs, Amelia looked down over the half wall and saw the living area. She could imagine what it would look like once he brought in furniture. She could see him lounging on a big sofa, in front of the window. She hoped he would get a large area rug to put in the center of the room and match colors with a sofa and chair. She could see little tables, holding wildflowers in little bottles. She smiled and turned back to the large room behind her. It was a huge room with just a mattress in the middle. She realized he would be using this as his bedroom. There was a closet with sliding doors. And when she opened the door, she saw it was large enough to walk into and ran almost the entire length of the room. At the back end of the closet there was another door, and she was thrilled to find another little bathroom with another, smaller, shower, again with stone walls.

When she came out of the enormous closet, she noticed large double doors at the back of the room. "What's through there?" she asked him.

He smiled and opened one of the doors. It opened to an outdoor porch. It had another half wall surrounding it. When Amelia walked to the wall, she could see a view of the cliffs and the sea. She gasped. "Oh! Josh, it's so beautiful!"

"I always dreamed of having a house, with a balcony overlooking the sea," he told her as he looked out at his view. "Who knew I would have to travel millions of miles from my home to make it come true." He leaned down on the wall and pointed to the ground. "I'd like to put a little garden there. Maybe put some chairs and a table. So, you can sit outside and enjoy the flowers."

"That would be lovely," Amelia said. "I can see it, in my mind."

"So, will you help me?" he asked her. "I have no eye for design. I need help decorating this place, and planting the flowers to make it appealing, but easy to care for."

"I would love to help you! When can I start?"

Before he could answer, they heard a loud rumbling overhead and looked up to see the Chartin ship flying low in the sky. Once they reached the edge of the continent the nose lifted up and the ship disappeared.

"They're leaving," Amelia said.

"They're going for reinforcements." Josh told her, still looking up at the now empty sky. "We need to be prepared for their return."

CHAPTER 10

Amelia's days suddenly became very full. She would spend her early mornings in her greenhouse, tending to her flowers. Then she would work in her vegetable garden. She would have a quick lunch then head to Josh's.

She was particularly excited today. Jacob was delivering the stones she had ordered for pathways, and she was ready to get her hands dirty, and give her back a workout, laying those stones.

As she approached Josh's house, she was surprised to find him home and painting his front door. She saw that he had already painted the fence a pretty sky blue. He had also hung the shutters, the same blue, on the lower windows. The color was perfect. Exactly what she had envisioned. She saw that Josh had removed his shirt, and she could see the sweat glistening on his back. And the muscles on his arms.

She put her hand on Molly's neck. "Well, that's a pretty sight, isn't it, Molly?"

They moved forward, and Josh spotted them as he turned to pour more paint into his tray. He set his brush down and opened his arms. "What do you think?" he asked.

"It's perfect, Josh!" she said. "It's beautiful and perfect."

He nodded. "I think so too. Jacob brought a wagon full of rock this morning. He put it around back."

"I didn't know you were going to be home this morning. I was hoping to have the stone laid before you got here. I wanted to surprise you."

"No way am I going to let you do that alone," he told her. "Consider me your work horse today. Just tell me what to do."

She started to protest and saw the look in his eye. "Ok. It'll go twice as fast with you doing the heavy lifting. Why don't you finish painting this door, and I'll go get us something cold to drink."

"Yes ma'am. I'm about done here. I'll meet you out back."

Amelia and Molly walked to the back of the cottage, and Amelia was thrilled with the wagonload of rock. It was exactly what she wanted, thin slabs of rock in different shapes and sizes. Paving stones, Jacob had called them. She would start them from the back door and run them in different directions through the garden.

She had ordered more uniform, brick shaped rock for the little patio she wanted to create by the back door under the cover of the balcony. Jacob said he would be able to deliver those next week. So, once they laid the pathway, she would start clearing the space for the patio. She had already handpicked the flowers she wanted for each area of the garden, and she could really see it taking shape in her mind.

As at home in his kitchen as she was in her own, Amelia went inside to get some lemonade from the fridge. And she watched, through the back window, as Molly wandered closer to the cliff, to graze in the grass then reached into the bag she brought with her to pull out two big glasses for the lemonade. Josh had no dishes yet. He said he didn't cook, so hadn't bothered to get anything but a big coffee mug for his morning coffee. He took all his meals at the community kitchen. So, Amelia had been slipping little things into his kitchen. She brought over the pitcher she made lemonade in the day before. She also brought over a couple of dishtowels she had hung over the sink. Today she added the two glasses, and another coffee mug. She also brought a big wooden bowl she set in the middle of the breakfast counter and filled it with fruit from her personal garden and fruit trees.

She was just placing the last apple in the bowl when Josh walked in from the back door. He saw her fussing with the fruit bowl and just stopped and stared. He loved seeing her in his kitchen. He thought he'd better be careful, or he'd start wanting her there all the time.

"Hey," he said. "That's nice."

She turned and saw him and started laughing. He had blue paint all over his chest, hands and splattered in his hair and on his face. "You're a mess," she said.

He looked down at his chest and pants. "Yeah. I'm a messy painter. I really like the bowl. It matches the wood in here."

She nodded. "I saw it at the free store and thought it would be a good fit."

"Thank you," he said. "Thank you for everything you're doing here. You're usually gone before I get home, but I wanted you to know that I've noticed all the little touches you've done. I appreciate you, Amelia."

She blushed, then walked to the fridge to pull out the glasses of lemonade. She handed one to him and took a sip of hers.

"Well, you're going to earn it today," she told him. "Drink up, work horse. Let's get those pavers down."

Amelia showed Josh the design she drew up and he really liked it. He started following the lines she had drawn and brought the pavers over and started laying them according to her instructions. While he did that, Amelia started clearing the ground for the patio.

As the sun started to set, they stood side by side on the balcony looking down at the work they had completed. "It's going to be beautiful," Amelia told him.

"It really is. Amelia, I don't know how to thank you for all the work you're putting in here."

"No thanks necessary. I'm loving every minute of it," she told him. "And I'm getting requests from some of the others in the city, asking for my help with their homes."

"Yeah? That's great! You're going to have your own little business as a landscaper."

"Maybe," she said. "I'd never thought about it. But that could be fun."

"Amelia's Design's," Josh said. "I can see it."

"Hmmm. I like that. You must be exhausted Josh. I worked you pretty hard today."

He shook his head. "I'm ok. But I'm hungry. Do you want to join me at the community kitchen? Grab some dinner?" he asked her. "Or I'm sure you're tired. You worked pretty hard yourself."

"I'm not tired at all. I actually made a casserole this morning. I just need to put it in the oven and warm it up. Why don't you clean up and come to my cottage? I can show you the flowers I picked out for your gardens. And you can have dinner there. Help me eat that casserole."

"I'd like that," he said.

"About an hour?"

"I'll be there," he said.

She smiled and nodded, then he watched as she walked away to head downstairs. He saw her go through the back door and call for Molly. She looked up and smiled and waved to him, before she and Molly headed back to her place.

"Oh, shit," Josh said and ran his hands over his face. You have no business falling for someone like her, he told himself. He should stay far away and keep their business professional. But even as he thought it, he headed to the shower. He should think of this as a business dinner, not a date.

When Amelia reached her cottage, she gave Molly a kiss on the snout and watched as she went to her little enclosure to lay on her bed of hay. Then she ran in and turned her oven on to warm. She put the casserole in and headed to her own little shower. As she stood under the warm running water, she realized she had nerves building in her stomach. "Calm down, Amelia," she told herself.

After her shower, she chose a yellow dress from her little closet. It was casual, but pretty. It had a scoop neck and showed off her shoulders. She pulled her hair back in a loose ponytail, leaving some of the curls to hang around her face and shoulders. She wished that she had makeup, like Sarah wore around her eyes. But she had never seen the need for it. Until now.

When she had herself put together, she went back to her little kitchen to check her casserole, and make sure she had fresh bread ready to cut. She set her little round table with plates and her good cloth napkins. Then started putting a salad together with lettuce, tomatoes, cucumbers and carrots she had picked from her vegetable garden.

She jumped when she heard the knock on her door, then laughed at herself. Her nerves really were jumping. She wiped her hands on one of the dishtowels hanging over her sink, then went to open the door.

Josh was standing at the door, feeling stupid. He was holding some wildflowers he picked on the way over. He looked over and saw Molly peeking out at him from her enclosure. "Hi, Molly. Don't worry, I was invited," he told her with a smile.

When Amelia opened the door, all words just left his brain. "Wow," was all he could come up with. Amelia raised her brows and smiled at him. "You look great," he told her.

"Thank you," she said and moved aside so he could come in. "Those are lovely." She gestured to the flowers he was holding. "I was just wishing I had taken time to pick some for the table."

He looked down at the flowers he forgot he was holding, then handed them to her and looked around at her little cottage. It was just one great room with the kitchen flowing into the living area. The only other door opened to the back porch where her closet and bathroom were. It was like a studio apartment, he thought, and figured she must sleep on the couch. It was tidy and pretty, with beautiful pieces of art hanging on the walls, and lace curtains over the windows.

Amelia took a vase from under her sink and started filling it with water for the flowers. She watched him as he looked around her home.

"It's small," she said. "Nowhere near as grand as yours. But it serves me well."

"No, it's lovely, Amelia. It's you."

She smiled and put the flowers in the center of her little table. "Dinner is going to be a little while yet. Would you like to see the flowers and plants I've selected for your gardens?"

"Sure."

She turned up the heat on her oven, then led him out the back door. They walked to the greenhouse, and Josh realized it was twice the size of her cottage. There were flowers, and plants and young trees in rows. There were tables set off to the side with soil and pots stacked neatly. He saw gardening tools hanging on the wall above the tables. She had gloves folded neatly on shelves.

"This is amazing, Amelia. I had no idea you had all this. What do you do with them all?"

"I use them to barter with. And once a year, we have a large festival where everyone brings their crafts, and art. I take what I have here and set up at the festival. We trade our wares, then at night the dragon riders put on an air show. Musicians play, and we dance and drink wine or ale. It's a big party and a lot of fun."

She walked over to an area where she had a mixture of flowers and plants. "These are some that I thought would go nicely in your garden," she told him.

He walked over and looked. "I trust your expertise on this," he told her.

She smiled at him. "These will bloom in different colors and shapes. It will be really pretty."

He nodded. "I had no idea you had such an enterprise going here."

"I don't know about an enterprise. But it's my passion."

After dinner, Amelia gave Josh a glass of blackberry wine that she had made from her own bushes.

He took a taste and looked at her for a moment. "This is delicious! So, you cook, you bake amazing bread, you make wine, tend your gardens and your greenhouse, you make healing balms, and help heal the wounded and sick. Is there anything you can't do Amelia?"

"I can't fight," she told him. "I think I need to learn to fight."

He shook his head. "I hope to God not," he told her.

"I need to be prepared to defend what's mine, Josh. Will you help me?"

He stared at her for a long time. This beautiful and gentle woman. Finally, he nodded his head. "Yes. I'll teach you how to fight, Amelia. I'll teach you how to use the weapons we have. And pray every day that you'll never need to use those skills."

"I pray the same thing. But thank you."

"Will you do something else for me?" he asked her.

"Of course."

"Will you go shopping with me tomorrow? I'd like your input on furniture for the cottage. And maybe some art. And I should probably have more than just a coffee cup to my name."

She laughed. "I would love to go shopping with you! I was hoping you would ask. Tomorrow morning? Then we can work in your garden in the afternoon."

"Perfect." He stood up and started clearing the table.

"Josh, you don't have to do that. Guests don't clean."

"No, but friends do. I really feel like we're friends, Amelia."

She smiled and nodded.

They cleaned the kitchen, stored the leftovers, then Josh washed the dishes, while Amelia dried and put them away. When they were done, Josh took the leftover casserole Amelia insisted he take home and headed for the door.

"Thank you for dinner. It was the best I've had since I've been here. I'll swing by about nine in the morning and pick you up for our shopping excursion. If that works for you."

She nodded. "Nine works for me."

He leaned in and gave her a kiss on the cheek. "Sleep well."

He opened the door and headed toward his cottage. "Night Molly," he called out to the little dragon, peeking out at him.

Amelia took a deep breath and sat on her front step to watch him walk away. Molly came to her and put her head on her knees.

"He thinks of me as a friend, Molly," she said while stroking the little dragon's head. "I may have to change his mind about that."

CHAPTER 11

Josh wandered around his cottage. It had been two weeks since he and Amelia had finished furnishing it. There was a big fluffy couch in front of the front window. It had deep maroon cushions and dark wood frame. It was long enough that he could fully stretch out on it for a nap. There were a couple of chairs with ottomans, with the same dark wood and maroon cushions. Amelia found a big oval area rug with the same maroon, and other accent colors in it, and she made throw pillows in those colors, and had placed them artfully around the room. There was art hanging on the walls and on the end tables and the oval coffee table held more little sculptures he had picked up from the community artists. Amelia would not give him any input on the art. She said it had to reflect his taste. But he watched her face carefully as he chose the pieces and could tell she approved. He had a spot picked out in the corner of the room for a personal sized AROE unit he was working on.

In the kitchen, he saw all the added touches. The wooden bowl on the breakfast bar which now had two tall stools. Amelia had made yellow cushions and attached them to the seats. There were dish towels, and a ceramic spoon holder on the stove. She had made lace valances in bright yellow that she hung over the windows. There were little pots with pretty plants on the windowsill. Inside the cabinets there were now dishes, glasses and cookware.

They still hadn't found the perfect table for the dining area yet. But Amelia was working with Jacob on that.

His guest room now had a bed and chest with pretty blue curtains over the window and matching spread over the bed. There were little bedside tables with matching lamps and a chest placed at the end of the bed. He noticed that she had added more throw pillows here too.

His bedroom now held a huge four poster bed with matching tables on each side and a long chest across the foot of the bed holding sheets and extra blankets. He had chosen a deep blue spread, and more dramatic art for the walls. Amelia had changed out the doors to the balcony, and they were now more like French doors with windows running the length of each one. She had made sheer curtains in the same blue as his bed spread to hang over them.

Josh opened the doors and stood on his balcony to look down at his garden. It was glorious with flowers blooming, and green ground covering. The stone paths he laid according to her design flowed throughout the area. And under the protection of the balcony roof was a seating area with a little table and two chairs.

His home was complete, furnished, and exactly as he had imagined it. And now that Amelia 's work here was done, it felt empty.

He was still unsure how he had paid for all this. He didn't really understand the way currency worked here. But Amelia did. She told him that he was earning credits with his work in the fields, and all the training he was doing with the Asterians.

He wandered down to the kitchen and opened the fridge to get a glass of lemonade. He found a casserole dish on the top shelf with a note on top of it. 'Heat in the oven on medium heat for an hour. Then turn up to high for 30 minutes. There is fresh bread in the bread box.'

Bread box? He didn't even know he had a bread box.

Josh knocked on Amelia's door but got no answer. He stood on her porch for a few minutes and was torn between disappointment and relief. It was probably for the best.

He started to head back home, when he heard a little scream from the back of Amelia's cottage. He raced to the back and found her sitting on the ground in her little garden laughing. She had something in her hands and seemed to be examining it.

"Amelia?"

She looked over at him with pure joy on her face. "Josh! Look!"

He walked over and kneeled down next to her. She was holding a small worm in her hands.

"Are you ok? I heard you scream."

"Josh, it's an earthworm!"

"Ok," Josh said.

She carefully put the worm back on the ground. "We've never had them before. We didn't transplant them here." She started laughing again and threw her arms around him. "We're evolving!"

Josh breathed a sigh of relief then leaned down to look at the little worm. "That's amazing," he said.

"You heard me scream all the way over at your cottage?" she asked him.

"No, I was on your front porch." He sat back up and looked at her. "I found the casserole in the fridge. Thank you for that."

"You're welcome," she said and was studying his face. He looked suddenly awkward and unsure.

"It's a big casserole," he said. She just kept watching him. "I, uh, was wondering if you would like to come over and help me eat it?"

"I'd love to," she said without hesitation. "Just give me a little bit to clean up." She stood up and started brushing the dirt off her hands.

"Don't clean up," he told her. She was wearing dirt-stained pants with an oversized white shirt. Her hair was pulled up into a messy bun on top of her head with a dirt smudge on her cheek. He didn't think he'd ever seen her look more beautiful.

"Josh, I'm a mess."

"You're not," he said and stepped toward her. He brushed his thumb over the dirt smudge on her cheek. "You're beautiful. I miss having you in my house. It's different when you're not there."

She tilted her head and looked up into his eyes. "Ok."

He took her hand, and she called for Molly. The little dragon came running from behind the greenhouse. Together they walked to Josh's cottage.

This became their normal. A few days a week Josh would work with the farmers in the fields. The other days he worked with the security teams, training or making traps. He would often sit in with Altvi, asking questions or learning about his species. He and a couple of Jacob's apprentices built an enclosure for Molly at his cottage. And in the evenings, Amelia and Josh would have dinner together. They'd talk about their day and just enjoy being together. And every night he would walk her back to her cottage and leave her with a kiss on her cheek.

Amelia grew frustrated that Josh never made a move. He never tried to kiss her, or touch her, or try to convince her to stay. She could see the look in his eyes when he looked at her. It was more than friendship he felt for her. But he never made a move. She mentioned it to Sarah one afternoon, while they watched the hatchlings playing in their enclosure.

"I think it's because he respects you," Sarah told her. "Josh always had a way with the ladies. He was always looking for the next good time, if you know what I mean. But he never got serious with anyone. Maybe he doesn't know how to move on someone he actually respects."

"So, what should I do, Sarah?"

"Maybe you need to make the first move."

"I have no idea how to do that," Amelia said.

Sarah just smiled at her. "Of course you do, Amelia; you are a beautiful, confident, independent woman. You know who you are, and what you want. Let him see that." Sarah saw the look of uncertainty in Amelia's eyes. "Or you can try something else."

"Something else?"

Sarah nodded and had a gleam in her eye. "Yeah. Make him miss you."

That evening, when Josh got home, he was surprised to find his cottage empty. There was a note on the counter. It said there were leftovers in the fridge, or the guys were having dinner at the community kitchen. They were having a ladies' night, and she wouldn't be around tonight.

Josh opened the fridge and looked at the leftovers, in storage containers. They held no appeal. He didn't want to have dinner alone. He closed the fridge and headed out to the community kitchen to meet the guys.

There were now three AROE enclosures with the addition of the *Destiny's* unit, built on the north end of the field. One was used for training. It had mats and open space for workouts. The second was used for education and the third for entertainment. Those were the original units. Others had been added since, but had limited information loaded. The entertainment building had big comfy couches and chairs with large pillows and plush rugs on the floor. Amelia approached the hut with two big jugs of her blackberry wine, and a sack full of glasses and cookies she baked that morning. She smiled at the sign hung on the door. 'Reserved for a PRIVATE PARTY' it read.

When she entered, she found Sarah, Quinn, Meg and Kendra already there. "Am I late?" Amelia asked.

"Nope, right on time. We're still waiting for several more to get here," Sarah said. There was music playing in the background, and Sarah and Quinn were setting up a table with drinks. Kendra was fussing with another table full of snacks. Amelia set her cookies on the snack table and Kendra snatched one off the plate and bit in. "Mmmm. You still make the best!" she told her and gave her a peck on the cheek. She took the jugs of wine to the beverage table and set them out.

"Who else is coming?" she asked.

"Holly, Jessie, Kristin, Lena and Charlie," Kendra told her.

"Ali isn't coming?"

"No, she's on shift tonight. But sends her love."

When Kristin walked in, she brought a tray of brownies from the kitchen. "There are a lot of grim faces at the dining hall tonight," she laughed. "The boys are pouting."

"Good," Sarah said. "They need to miss us, so they can appreciate us. Right Amelia?"

While ladies' night turned into a party with dancing, drinking, laughing and a chick flick on the AROE, Altvi worked out a plan. The hut where the party was going on was close enough to his so that he could hear the music and the laughter.

He had been pulling against the restraints on his feet and could feel the chain loosening from the floorboards. He found a loose piece of wood behind the toilet, and had pulled a small piece of it off, and had been rubbing it on the stone floor, sharpening it. Soon he would have a weapon and be free to sneak out and escape.

Josh, Kenji, Ian, and Mateo moved their little pity party to Kenji's cottage. Ian had brought a jug of ale, and they sat at the little kitchen table and played cards. "Poker just isn't the same without cash," Mateo said. He threw his cards on the table and folded.

"My grandmother taught us how to play with little rocks," Ian said. He looked around the table and saw the guys all scowling at him. "Just sayin'," he shrugged.

Kenji stood up and went into his room. When he came back a few minutes later, he was carrying a small wooden box. "Before I set this down, I want to say that I want every penny in here back."

He put the box on the table and opened it. Josh let out a whoop and reached over to touch and feel the familiar coins and bills. Kenji had pennies, nickels, dimes and quarters. There were a couple of 50 cent pieces and a couple of silver dollars. He even had a Susan B. Anthony dollar. There were rolls of ones, fives, tens and twenties, He also had euros, pesos and yen rolled into small bundles with a rubber band holding them together. In the bottom was a credit card.

Mateo started laughing. "Dude, why? What did you think you were going to do with this?"

"I don't know," Kenji said. "I got the box from my dad when I was a kid and started putting money in it. It's sentimental, you ass."

They noticed Ian was just staring at the pile of money. "This is what you used as currency on Earth?" he asked and reached out to touch the bills.

Kenji nodded. "The root of all evil."

Ian pulled his hand back. "What do you mean?"

"This led to greed and power. The want and need for it. People stopped caring about each other and only cared how much of this was in their bank accounts."

Josh grabbed the cards and started shuffling. "True story, but it's going to make poker a whole lot more fun!"

Back up on the cliff, ladies' night was winding down. Lena and Charlie helped Kristin stand, then each of them put their arms around her to help her walk out. "I think this is her first good drunk," Lena said on the way out the door.

"It'll be her first good hangover in the morning too," Charlie said. "I have a feeling I'll be taking her shift in the kitchen in the morning."

Holly was curled up on one of the couches, snoring quietly, and Kendra was asleep on the floor with her head on a cushion and her feet up on a chair.

"She's in her 90s," Jessie said looking over at Kendra. "Do you think we should wake her and move her to a couch?"

Sarah tipped her head and looked over at Kendra. "She looks pretty comfortable to me. I'll wake her up and help her home when I leave. But I think we need to finish off this jug of outstanding blackberry wine first."

Sarah filled up Amelia, Quinn, Jessie and Meg's glasses and just flopped down on the empty couch.

"This was so much fun, girls," Amelia said and sat next to Sarah on the couch. "We should do this once a month!"

"Agreed!" Meg said.

"Now, I think we should talk about Amelia's Josh dilemma," Sarah said.

"Amelia's Josh dilemma?" Quinn asked. "What dilemma? He's nuts about you! Don't you like him?" She sat on a cushion on the floor in front of the couch.

"Of course I like him," Amelia said.

"That's the dilemma," Sarah told them. "He hasn't made a move yet."

"Sarah!" Amelia gasped out.

"What? We're all girls here. We've each been in a similar place. So, ladies, what should our little Amelia do about Josh?"

Meg came and joined the group. "I can't believe he hasn't made a move. That's not like Josh. Maybe he did and you didn't notice."

They all cracked up at that. "I think I would have noticed," Amelia said.

"Maybe you should try to make him jealous," Jessie said. "That worked with Ryan. I started flirting with someone else and he just about lost his mind!"

"I don't know if that's a good idea with Josh," Sarah said. "He's liable to beat the crap out of someone. I think you should make yourself unavailable for a while. Make him appreciate you. Let him know you have a life and aren't at his beck and call."

"Honey," Kendra said, still lying in the same spot and position. "You need to make the first move with him."

They all looked over at Kendra. Her eyes were still closed, and she hadn't moved at all.

"How? I don't know how to do that."

"I think if you show up in his bed, naked, he'll take it from there." She opened her eyes and looked over at the girls. "Now, if someone would hold the ground still for a few minutes, I think I should go home and throw up."

Sarah and Jessie helped Holly and Kendra back to their cottages down below, leaving Meg, Quinn and Amelia to tidy up the hut. Then they closed up and headed to their homes. Quinn to the trees, Meg to the shore and Amelia across the field. As she and Molly reached the edge of the south field she stopped. Should she go right to her cottage? Or left through the orchard to Josh's?

"What should I do Molly?" She looked at the dragon who was no help at all. She was just looking at her wondering why they stopped.

Amelia took a deep breath. "Granny used to call wine and ale liquid courage," Amelia giggled. "Let's be brave, Molly," she turned left toward the orchard.

Josh left Kenji's cottage when Sarah staggered in. Her eyes were glazed, and she was holding on to the wall like it was a lifeline. She smiled, waved, and went straight to her room. "She's plowed," he told Kenji with a laugh.

Kenji nodded. "Guess ladies' night was a success." They looked over at Ian who was still sitting at the table but had his head lying on it, snoring. Mateo had already passed out on the sofa so Josh figured he would need to help Ian home.

After he got Ian settled in his tree house, Josh headed across the field to his cottage. When he got to the end of the orchard he stopped and noticed a dim light glowing from his bedroom. He didn't remember leaving a light on up there. He started moving quicker to the cottage, a little prickle at the base of his neck rising up. He moved around to the side of the cottage and let out a breath, when he saw Molly sleeping in her enclosure. His relief in realizing he didn't have an intruder in his house changed to curiosity then concern. What was she doing there? Was she sick? Was she hurt? He rushed back to the front door and went in quickly and quietly then ran up the stairs. When he reached the top, he stopped and just stared.

She was standing on his balcony. The doors open wide. She was framed there, with her back to him wrapped only in a sheet she must have pulled out of the chest. The moon was full and bright in the sky, and she had her head thrown back looking at it. There was a slight breeze blowing through her hair and the sheet blowing against her legs. He could tell that she had the sheet pulled up over her chest, but the back had slipped down and was draped just above her butt showing off her slim but muscled back.

She turned to move back into the room and froze. Then let out a little laugh. "I didn't hear you come in. You startled me," she said.

"I startled *you*?" he asked. His voice came out a little harsher than he meant it to. "What are you doing here, Amelia?"

She took a couple steps into the room, leaving the doors open. Then looked down at the sheet she was holding, covering her naked body. "You're a smart man Josh. I'd think you could figure that out yourself."

He shook his head. "You're drunk, Amelia."

"I'm not. I had three glasses of wine over a very long evening. I think I'm the only one that left that hut semi sober." She took a few more steps toward him. "I feel wonderful. I know what I'm doing here, Josh." She took two more steps toward him and dropped the sheet.

God she was beautiful! Tiny waist, perfect breasts, long firm legs. It was all he could do to keep himself from lunging on her to take what she was offering. He shook his head again. "You don't know me, Amelia. I'm not a good man. I've done so many things I'm not proud of. You deserve so much more."

She smiled and took the final steps to reach where he stood. "Josh, I know all I need to know. You are strong and kind. I've seen how gentle you are with Molly. You help in the community. The men turn to you for advice and guidance. The women look at you like you're a juicy piece of forbidden fruit they want to take a bite of. But you don't see that, or don't respond to it. But I've seen you look at me, Josh. And I know there's more than friendship in that look. If I'm wrong, tell me. I'll get dressed and return to my cottage and we'll go on as we have. Your past, the life you lived before you came to Asteria is gone. It's what you're building now, how you're living now, that matters. I see who you are now, and I want you, Josh. I want to feel your hands on me." She reached up and touched his lips with her fingertip. "I want to feel your mouth on mine." She leaned forward and pressed her body against his. She kissed his neck and whispered, "I'm not an innocent child, Josh. I'm a woman grown, and I know what I want. I want you. I want to taste you. I want to feel you inside of me."

He let out a low moan and grabbed her hair, yanking it back so she was forced to look into his eyes. His breath was coming faster, and she could see the look she needed to see in his eyes. She was close enough to feel him going hard through his pants.

"Be sure, Amelia. Be very sure."

"I'm sure, Josh. Don't make me leave." He still had his hand in her hair, and he pulled her against him. His mouth came down on hers more roughly than he intended. She wrapped her arms around his neck, and he reached down with his other arm, and lifted her to him. She wrapped her legs around his waist, and he walked her to his bed.

CHAPTER 12

Josh woke the next morning with the sun shining brightly through the still open doors. He looked over at Amelia. She was curled on her side facing him, her breathing deep and even, and she had a slight smile on her lips. He wanted to reach out and run his fingers through her hair and replay last night, in the light of the day. It took everything he had to get up out of his bed instead. He crept into his closet to grab clothes, and instead of showering in the upstairs bathroom, went downstairs so he wouldn't wake her.

He saw Molly out the back porch window, grazing in the meadow behind his house. She was as at home here as she was at Amelia's place. He just shook his head and headed to the shower.

He stood under the warm spray of water longer than usual. He remembered every second of the night before. Never in his life had he experienced anything like it. She was sweet and passionate. Giving and powerful. The moans and the gasps that came out of her as he made love to her drove him even further. He couldn't get enough of her and only let her sleep when the sky started to lighten up with the morning sun.

"Fuck!" he said under his breath and turned the shower from warm to cold. He had no business taking any of that, no matter how generously offered. She was obviously experienced. She was no virgin. And he allowed himself to become angry instead of grateful. Any hot blooded man would have done the same when a naked, willing, beautiful female threw herself at him.

He turned off the shower, got dressed and went to the kitchen to brew some coffee. He was already behind schedule because of her. He needed to get to the fields and help with harvesting the corn ready to be pulled. Then he had weapons training with some of the community members.

He stiffened when he felt her arms come around him from behind. "Good morning," she said in a soft sleepy whisper.

His first impulse was to turn and wrap her up in his arms and carry her back to bed. But he fought that and said instead, "Good morning. I overslept and need to get going. I promised Thomas I would help him this morning in the corn field."

"Ok," she squeezed a little tighter. "Would you like some breakfast before you go?"

"No. Thank you."

She released him and backed up. When he turned, he saw that she was wrapped in that blasted sheet again. Her hair was a messy tangle around her face. Her lips were full and swollen from his kisses and she had a mark on her neck where he sucked her into his mouth while he plunged into her.

He shook his head "I've got to go." He filled his mug and headed for the front door.

"Josh?" Amelia said. "What's wrong?"

He stopped and let out a long breath. "Last night was a mistake, Amelia. It shouldn't have happened. Don't get me wrong, it was fun, and much needed so thanks for that. But it was a mistake."

He saw the shocked look on her face. "Thanks for that? For what, scratching an itch? Is that what it was for you?"

"Yeah," he said with a little smile. "Sorry if it was more for you. Feel free to stay as long as you like. But I've got to go."

"Fuck that, Josh!" Amelia said. He saw pain and anger in her eyes. "And fuck you! It was much more than that, and you know it. I'm falling in love with you, you bastard."

"No Amelia, you're not. You don't even know me." He saw her head jerk back like she had been struck.

"Don't you dare tell me what I feel, Josh." Her voice was quiet and calm. "You have the right to not feel the same. But you have no right to tell me what I feel. What I know." A single tear slipped from her eye, and it just about undid him.

"Amelia," he started and took a step toward her.

She shook her head and took a step back, away from him. "You're late. You should go now." She turned and walked away from him.

He stood for a moment and watched as she walked up the stairs. Then turned and walked out the front door.

Josh worked in the corn field the rest of the day. He loved the fields. It was quiet and no one bothered him while he worked. It gave him time to think. He realized he had taken the wrong approach with Amelia. He should have been kinder. He should have told her how much he valued her and depended on her, but he could only be her friend. He felt a little sick to his stomach. He was afraid he had blown any chance of staying friends now. No, that was unacceptable. He needed her in his life. He needed to see her and be around her. She was a loving, forgiving woman. He would give her a few days to cool down. Give her a few days to come to her senses and realize she wasn't in love with him. God, he heard those words come out of her mouth and it almost put him on his knees. He almost caved. He could almost see himself building a life and a family with her. Oh, God. What had he done?

Sarah sat cross legged on the little couch in Amelia's living room, an amused look on her face as she watched Amelia scrub every inch of the place like the devil was chasing her. She listened to her rage, getting angrier every time she replayed the conversation with Josh.

"Why are you smiling?" Amelia demanded.

"Was I?" Sarah asked. "Sorry."

Amelia started scrubbing the table she had already cleaned twice. "He acted like it was just a little fling. He acted like it meant nothing. But let me tell you, while it was happening, it sure felt like something!" She turned in a circle, looking for something else to clean. "I could have been the best thing that ever happened to him, the ass!" She realized there was nothing left to clean and flopped down on the couch next to Sarah. "He kept telling me he wasn't a good man. He said he had done things he wasn't proud of. Do you know what he's talking about, Sarah?"

"Yeah. I think I do," she said. "But it's not my story to tell. I think he will tell you, though. When he stops being afraid. The thing is, what he did was a lifetime ago, and when it mattered, he did the right thing."

"What should I do?"

"Stay mad for now. Make him come to you, and I believe he will. Because you're right. This was no fling. I've seen him with his flings. He's never looked at anyone the way he looks at you, Amelia. He'll come around. But you make him work for it."

Amelia nodded. "It's getting late. You should get home to Kenji."

"I can stay. We can eat cookies and drink some more wine and bash men."

Amelia smiled. "I appreciate the offer, I really do. But I think I'd rather be alone tonight. I'll probably end up cleaning every inch of this place and getting my mad back. I'm not going to keep you from your man two nights in a row."

"He'll survive," Sarah said. "If you're still pissed after you clean your place, you can always come do mine."

Amelia laughed and stood. She reached out and helped Sarah to her feet then wrapped her in a big hug. "Thanks for being here and for listening to me rant. I feel better."

Sarah nodded. "If you change your mind, and want some company just holler."

"I will. Thank you. I think I'll take a walk, maybe pick some apples for a pie."

Molly raised her head as Sarah passed by the spot where she was sleeping, her enclosure. "Night, Molly." The little dragon watched Sarah jump from the cliff and laid her head back down to wait for Amelia.

Inside the cottage, Amelia lost interest in cleaning anything. She waited until she knew Sarah would be gone and headed out to the apple orchard.

Her mad had worn off, and the sad was setting in. It was time to have a good cry, then figure out how to move forward. What she told Josh was true. She was no innocent child. She'd had boyfriends, and male friends with benefits. She was extremely selective about who she took to her bed and hadn't had many partners. But the 18 year old boy she was sure she was in love with and has allowed to take her virginity had dumped her a month later and had broken her 17 year old heart. She had been very cautious since then and had never put her heart into a relationship. If she felt someone getting too close, or too attached, she would back away. She always tried to be kind, and she was still friends with some of them, and their wives now. Until Josh. The night he brought a blanket for her and Molly on the beach she had felt the crack in the shield around her heart. And every day after that, the crack widened. The pain she felt as a 17-year-old was nothing compared to the pain she was feeling now.

But she would go home, have her cry, then pull herself together, bake a pie and live her life. She would rebuild the shield around her heart. And go on. She wished she could talk to her grandmother. She had died three years ago, and she still missed her every day. Her mother had died in the Chartin slaughter over twenty years before. She could hardly remember the sound of her voice, or what she looked like. She had been 7 when the slaughter happened. Amelia was one of the last cryo babies. So, she had no father. Her grandmother took her in and raised her and loved her until the day she died.

Amelia shook the tears away. No, those would need to wait until she got home. She would pull her curtains and lock her doors and take the time she needed to grieve. She took a deep breath and leaned down to pick up the basket she had been filling with apples. When she stood up, she felt a fierce pain in the back of her head, and the world went black.

Josh got home later than usual. He went to the community kitchen for dinner and found Ian and Mateo. They had dinner together, then went to the shore to have a nightcap. The sun had set, but he had no desire to go into his cottage. She was everywhere in there. So, instead, he walked to the back to sit on his patio and look at his garden. Unfortunately, she was there too. He had pictures of her in his mind, kneeling in the dirt, clearing the pathways, planting flowers, helping him lay the brick for his patio. Always laughing, smiling at him like no one ever had. He saw her in his kitchen, making dinner and singing. He saw her in her garden holding a little worm like it was a miracle. He saw her taking care of a baby dragon who was wounded and scared, and with her tears, and her care, brought her back from the brink of death and taught her to trust again. And he saw her standing in the moonlight, naked and perfect. Offering him everything. Her body, her heart, a future. He saw her head thrown back in passion crying out as she came. And he saw the look in her eyes when he broke her heart the next morning.

"Fuck!" he shouted and ran his hands over his face.

"I hope that is you realizing what an ass you are," Sarah said from the back doorway of his cottage.

He spun around and saw her leaning against the door, watching him.

"What are you doing here, Sarah?"

"I stopped by to see how you're doing. I knocked on the front door, but you didn't answer, so I let myself in. Great place, by the way."

"Thanks," he grumbled at her. "Look, I appreciate the wellness check, but I'm really not in the mood for company."

She nodded and sat next to him on the patio. "Ok."

"That wasn't an invitation to sit down, Sarah."

She nodded. "I know. I won't stay long, but you need to hear what I have to say. Then I'll go."

"Fine. Just make it quick."

She just smiled at him. "Josh, you have a real chance here. You're building something in this special, amazing world. You're doing really good things here. Don't fuck it up because you're afraid."

He started to object, just on principle, but stopped himself. "I am afraid. I saw my mother and father in their marriage of convenience. They never spoke to each other. He gave orders and she followed them. They never spoke to me. They told me what to do, when to do it. How to do it. It was not to be questioned, just obeyed. When I finally disobeyed him and went to college instead of the military, it felt like I was finally free. Then I met Hank, you and the team, and felt, for the first time in my life, like I was following my destiny, making my own mark. And then I fucked it up. And started following orders again. I don't trust myself to not fuck this up too."

"Yeah," Sarah said. "You fucked up. And then you did the right thing. You laid down your weapons, you tried to convince your father to lay down his. You stepped away. You can write the rest of your story any way you want to, Josh.

Don't throw away a life that could make you really happy, because of a miserable past."

Suddenly they heard a strange screeching noise coming from the front of the cottage. They both jumped up.

"What the hell is that?"

"It's a dragon," Sarah said and started running to the front yard, with Josh right on her heels. Molly was running full speed in their direction, screeching and calling out. She spotted Josh and ran straight to him. He put his hands on her to steady her. "She's shaking," he told Sarah. "What's wrong, Molly? You're ok, girl. You're safe. Where's Amelia?"

She took a hold of Josh's sleeve and started pulling him forward. His face went pale, and he looked at Sarah. "Amelia!"

Josh took off at full speed, following Molly across the field toward the orchard.

Molly led him to the end of the orchard, where he found Amelia's basket lying on its side with apples spilt on the ground. Sarah was just a few steps behind him. He knelt down and ran his hand over a spot on the grass. When he pulled it back, his hand was covered in the blood that had pooled there.

"Oh, God," Sarah said. "Tell me that's not blood."

Josh shook his head. "Yeah. It's blood." He stood and saw Molly, still screeching and turning in circles toward the opening of the orchard.

"Maybe we should go down to the clinic. She's probably there, if she hurt herself."

"Maybe," Josh said. He was still watching Molly. She had stopped turning and was staring in the direction of the Chartin's cell. The shed was further back in the field, and closer to the trees, but Josh noticed that there was no guard at the door.

He started moving quickly toward the shed, with Molly following behind him. When he opened the door, he saw Pax on the floor unconscious, with a bleeding wound in his gut. Josh knelt down and felt for a pulse. Then breathed a sigh of relief when he felt it. He ripped off his shirt and wadded it up and held it over the wound and applied pressure. He was losing too much blood. He heard Sarah enter behind him and heard her gasp. "He's alive. But he needs help fast." He looked at Sarah. "Go get the medics. Call Apollo and have him fly you down. As quickly as you can. Tell everyone to be on high alert and not to go anywhere alone. I don't think he's around here, but everyone needs to be on alert. Tell Mateo to take a few men and go check Amelia's cottage. She's not going to be there but have them check anyway."

"What are you going to do?"

"I'm going to find him. He's got Amelia."

"Josh, you don't have a weapon. Come down with me. We can organize a scouting party."

Josh tore the sheet off Altvi's bed and ripped a long piece from it to wrap around the wound and add pressure under Pax's shirt.

"Sarah, get Apollo and get help for Pax. He doesn't have time for us to stand here and argue. Let everyone know what's going on and send them out to find me. But I'm not waiting another minute." He rushed out of the cabin and headed into the trees with Molly following behind him.

Altvi realized he had made a mistake. He should have waited. He should have planned better. He had no food, and he was beginning to think he had hit the female too hard. She should have woken up by now. He also had no way to get across the sea to his people. But he had pulled the chains free that morning, and his weapon was sharp and ready. He still had the translator that the man called Pax placed behind his ear, so he could understand them. When Pax bent over to put the device behind his ear, Altvi didn't think, he just plunged the weapon into his stomach and smashed his fist into his face and ran. He saw the blonde female in the trees. She was bending over picking up a basket from the ground. He came up behind her and hit her on the back of the head.

He had been carrying her over his shoulder for miles, and she hadn't stirred. He was staying in the trees. He knew that once they discovered the dead man and missing woman, they would start searching for him. He knew that they rode dragons and would be able to see him in the open, so he would stay in the trees. He would look for a cave and water, and hide, until they stopped searching. He figured he had time. They would not find the dead man until morning, when they came to relieve him. And he hoped the woman didn't have a family that would miss her tonight. So, he had time to put more distance between himself and the settlement. He would rest during the day, and travel at night. Once he found a cave, far away from the human city, he would wait there until his people came back and destroyed them.

When Sarah burst through the doors at the clinic, she saw Ali, Holly and one of the male nurses, she couldn't remember his name, standing at the reception counter. They turned when they heard the door open, and went on alert when they saw the tears, and terror on Sarah's face. Ali moved quickly to her. "Sarah, honey, are you ok? What happened?"

Sarah shook her head. "It's Pax. He needs help. He's hurt really bad."

"Ok, what are his injuries, and where is he, Sarah?"

"He's at the cabin, where they are holding the Chartin. He has some kind of stab wound in his stomach and was bleeding a lot. Josh put his shirt in the wound and tied a sheet around it to try to stop the bleeding. But he's unconscious, and it looks like he's lost a lot of blood. His face is bruised and bleeding too."

"Ok. Holly, grab our bags," Ali said calmly. "Is Josh still with him?"

"No," Sarah said. "I've got to go and get him help. The Chartin escaped. He took Amelia, and Josh is going after him."

126

"Oh, shit," Holly said.

"Go, Sarah; we'll take care of Pax. Get Ian and Mateo and the riders," Ali told her.

Sarah nodded and raced back out the door.

"Kelly!" Ali called out for the nurse's aide, who was taking her lunch in the break room. Kelly poked her head out the door. "I need you to ring the bell."

"What?" Kelly said. "Why? What's happening!"

"I don't have time to explain. Just do it!." Then get Kendra and come back here to wait for us to get back." She turned and ran out the door with Holly and Michael to get to the cabin and Pax.

Sarah went to her cottage first to get her weapons. She wished the heat sensor she had been working on was finished, but with everything going on, it had been put on the back burner. When she opened the door of her cottage, she was relieved to find Mateo there. He and Kenji were at the kitchen table drawing some kind of diagram of the city. As soon as she entered the cottage, the bell rang.

Mateo jumped to his feet. "Are they coming? Are we under attack?"

"No," Sarah said. "The Chartin escaped. He stabbed Pax and took Amelia."

Kenji grabbed Sarah and looked into her eyes. "Are you ok?"

She nodded. "I need to get to Apollo and the others. Josh went after them by himself. Ali is on her way to the cabin, to help Pax, but we need to go after Josh. Mateo, he wants you to check Amelia's cabin. He said he didn't think they'd be there, but we should check."

"I'll check," Kenji said. "Mateo, you should get Yemaya and the other sea dragon riders and meet the rest up top."

"Don't go alone, Kenji," Sarah told him. "Take a few others with you."

Mateo ran to the shore and found his fellow riders, already assembling. "I ran into Holly, she filled me in," Meg told him. "She is sending others to the rest of the community to let them know what's happening and to stay in their homes."

When they got to the top of the cliff, they found the other riders, and all the dragons, including the riderless, waiting in the fields. Ian was giving orders and assignments. He put some of the sea dragon riders with others of his group, then told Meg and Mateo to come with him, Sarah and Quinn. Everyone mounted and flew up to go to their designated areas and start searching.

Josh followed Altvi's trail into the trees. He was grateful that the Chartin was stupid and didn't even try to cover his tracks. He didn't know exactly how much of a lead he had on him but figured it couldn't be more than an hour. Pax's injuries were still fresh, as was the blood in the orchard. He shook his head. He couldn't think about that blood. He couldn't think about the possibility that Amelia was hurt, and scared. He couldn't think about what an ass he had been the last time he'd been with her. He refused to think that might have been his last interaction with her. He needed to stay focused and find them.

He would stop occasionally, to check the tracks that Altvi left. A couple times, he thought he had lost them, but quickly picked them back up, moving deeper into the trees. He saw that Molly was keeping up with him pretty well. She was surprisingly quiet and light on her feet.

And each time they stopped, she would look at him with fear in her eyes. "We're going to find her Molly. Don't worry.

CHAPTER 13

Altvi was cursing himself, again. He had been walking all night, carrying the female. He was tired, hungry and hot. He hated this hot miserable planet. He almost fell to his knees when he saw the river. He took it as a sign that he had done the right thing.

He approached the edge of the river and pulled the female off his shoulder. He just let her drop to the ground and watched as she flopped down. He was disappointed that the fall didn't wake her. He stepped into the river and sighed in delight to find the water was cool. He cupped his hands together and drank, then just put his face in the water and gulped the cool refreshing water. Where he was standing, the water came to his knees. He decided he would walk in the river for the rest of the night, following it deeper into the trees. At least he would stay cool, and he would still be protected from the sky dragons as the trees were still thick and dense ahead. He looked at the female lying on the shore and thought about leaving her there. She was probably dead or would be soon. Or he could put her in the water and let her float away to the sea. That idea appealed to him, then when her people found her, they would think he went into the sea, to return to the Chartin settlement.

He approached the shore, to get the female and let her go into the water, but he saw the rise and fall of her chest. He put his hand over her mouth and felt the shallow breath. Huh. So, she wasn't dead yet. Maybe she would live long enough for him to find shelter. Then he could do with her as he pleased, and if she died after that, he would toss her in the river. He noticed that there was a great deal of blood on her face, coming from a deep gash on her forehead. Must have happened when he hit her, and she fell forward. He grabbed a handful of leaves from a bush growing from the side of the river and put them over the wound. Then took her arm and dragged her to the side so he could pick her up. He threw her back over his shoulder and started walking in the water, north, away from the sea and deeper into the trees.

The longer he walked in the water, the deeper and wider it became. He had to take the female off his shoulder, or her head would be under the water. So, he carried her in his arms like a baby.

He walked in the water for more than an hour, when he saw a waterfall up ahead. It was flowing from the mountain. So, this is where the river started, and he would need to leave the water, and continue on the other side. He started to cross to the other side of the river, when the bottom dropped out and the water became very deep. Deeper than he could stand touching the bottom. It threw him off balance and he lost the female. She was quickly submerged in the water and again he thought about just letting the water take her. But then he saw her eyes open, and she gasped. So, he reached out and grabbed her and swam to the other side of the river.

As he approached the western shore, the water became shallow again, so he stood and threw the female to the shore. He pulled himself out and sat for a moment and looked around trying to figure out where to go. That's when he saw it. Behind the waterfall, a series of holes in the mountain. Caves!

Ian and his group of riders followed the tree line. He had sent other riders out in all directions, but he had a hunch. Altvi would want the cover of the trees. He knew that Josh had headed into the trees as well, so they kept a close eye out to see if they could see any movement. They reached the Asterian river and set down.

"There's no way they could have gotten this far this soon," he said. "We are going to need to go in on foot."

Amelia woke with a blinding flash of pain in her head. She was lying on a hard surface, but it was too dark to tell where she was. Cold panic ran through her when she realized she couldn't move her arms or legs. They were bound tight. There was something in her mouth keeping her from screaming and she could taste blood. Her vision was blurred and when she looked down, she saw that she was naked. She was cold and started shivering, then fear set in, and she started shaking uncontrollably. She tried to look through the pain and double vision. She needed to focus and then she saw the Chartin and his red eyes looking at her. Her eyes rolled back in her head, and she lost consciousness and slipped back into the blissful black.

Josh had been following Altvi's trail through the increasingly dense forest. He had cuts across his arms, chest and back from the tree limbs. He wished he had his machete so he could cut through them. He heard the rush of water and came to a wide river. He and Molly ran to the water and started drinking. Then he sat and dropped his head into his hands. He looked across the river and couldn't see any sign that they had exited on the other side. Molly was examining a bush a few yards away. Then she let out a low growl. Josh jumped up and went to her. The first thing he saw was a pool of blood on the ground. Then he saw several shredded stems on the bush that Molly had been sniffing.

Molly backed away from the bush and sniffed at the blood pooled on the ground. Josh recognized the bush. Amelia had cleared several of them off his land. She told him they were poisonous and could cause hallucinations, lethargy, then a deep sleep, coma and eventually death, if not treated. They had burned the bushes together, and she pulled him back away from the smoke, because ingesting the smoke could cause the same effect. She told him that they learned about the effects of the plant because when the first settlers found it, they were drawn in by the aroma. It had an appealing scent, and they thought it might be an herb, but found out quickly the deadly consequences of eating or smelling it.

"Fuck!" Josh said under his breath. "Altvi, what have you done?"

He sat for a few more minutes, looking to see if he could pick up Altvi's tracks, then stood up and started following the river north with Molly following closely behind him.

Ian sent Sarah and Quinn back into the air with instructions to fly as low as possible and see if they could see any movement below. He, Mateo and Meg started the trek north, following the river. When the tree line became too thick for the dragons to walk, they leapt into the water and started swimming. The three of them just looked at each other, then called the dragons to the shore, and each jumped onto their dragon's back and picked up their pace in the water.

Josh reached the end of the river and saw the waterfall, just as dawn was starting to lighten the sky. He dropped down to the ground in despair. He started thinking he had lost them. He had no idea where to go now. What if they had entered the river and gone to shallower waters. The river here was wide and deep, and the waterfall caused huge currents. It ran from high on the mountain, crashing into the river below. Molly watched him for a moment, then spread her good wing, and jumped into the river. She swam to the other side and sniffed the ground. Then looked back at him and threw her head back and her front legs started doing a little dance. Josh couldn't hear her but had gotten to know her body language. She had found something. He looked at the river, warily. He was a strong swimmer, but the current here could easily take him downstream and he would lose valuable time. He moved back to the tree line and started running toward the river at full speed. He launched himself into the air and flew. And he almost made it. He dropped just a few feet from the bank of the western side of the river. He landed in the water with a splash, but landed on his ass and found it shallow enough here so he could stand and climb out. His shoes, socks and pants were soaked. When he stood on the bank, she saw Molly staring at him with an amused expression in her eyes. He stood up and rubbed her neck. "Laugh it up, miss smarty pants," he said. "Show me what you found, Molly Brown."

Josh looked over at the ground and could see the imprints from Altvi's feet, and a depression in the grass, where it looked like someone had been lying. The footprints were heading toward the mountain. He followed the tracks more cautiously now, and when he reached the side of the mountain, he saw a series of caves, nestled behind the waterfall.

He leaned his head against Molly's. "Yeah, I think she's up there. You stay here, baby girl. I'll go get her."

Josh followed the narrow clearing behind the waterfall and started pulling himself up the rock wall to the largest opening.

Altvi was tired of waiting. He decided that he would throw the female into the river, and let the water take her to the sea. But he wanted his reward first. He wanted his reward for carrying her through the trees, and the water, and dragging her up the side of the mountain, and through the cave. He had stripped off her clothes because they were wet, and she was shivering from the cold. Then he ripped them into strips, to tie her hands and feet and he had gagged her because he grew tired of listening to her cry out. He would take his reward, then toss her out of the entrance to the cave. He walked to where she was laying, naked and bound. She had blood in her hair covering her face, she was still shivering but no longer thrashing around. Her breathing was shallow and there were long pauses between each breath. She had large breasts that appealed to him, and the hair covering her woman parts was nice. He untied her legs, so he could spread them and examine her there. He was pleased to find her parts were very much like Chartin women. He knelt down between her legs and reached up and grabbed her breasts. He pinched and pulled quite hard, hoping that would wake her, but she didn't move. He sighed but decided he didn't need her awake to claim what he wanted.

He moved his hair away from his privates and released his male member. It was hard and ready. But before he could plunge it into her, he was grabbed from behind and thrown back against the wall of the cave.

When Josh entered the cave, he found it was huge and empty. It was dark, but he could make out the walls, and back of the cave. He started to think he had chosen the wrong entrance, but before he turned to leave, he heard a noise echo from the back. He moved slowly and found an opening in the rear wall. It was wide, but only about 5½ feet tall. He stooped down and entered. He could make out Altvi's footprints, and it looked like he had been dragging something heavy behind him. A few feet in, Josh lost the light from the entrance of the cave and the world went black. He had to stop and let his eyes adjust to the darkness and proceeded by feeling his way along the wall. When he reached the opening of the tunnel, he entered into another large cavern. It was still dark, but not as bad as the small tunnel. He could make out Altvi, with his back to him, positioned between Amelia's spread legs. All he saw then was red. A red haze clouded his vision, and he sprung, grabbing Altvi from behind and swinging him away from Amelia. Josh saw him hit the wall of the cave and didn't waste time for him to get his bearings. He started using his fists, beating them into Altvi's face again and again. Then he used one of the martial arts kicks Mateo had shown him and kicked him in the balls. Altvi doubled over with a grunt, but what should have taken him down didn't. He bent over then rammed Josh mid body with his head rushing him and pushing him back into the other wall of the cave. Josh saw his fist flying toward his face, and barely dodged a blow that would have taken him out. He moved his head slightly and Altvi's fist just grazed the side of his head and rammed into the wall. While Altvi recovered from the pain of hitting the rock wall, Josh swiped out with his legs and took Altvi down to the ground. He punched out again and leaned in with his forearm against his throat. But Altvi's size and weight worked in his favor, he bucked up and flipped Josh to the ground. He rolled on top of him and started punching his body and his face. He could feel blood running down his face, and into his mouth. He knew his back was shredded from the wall of the cave. And with the next body punch, he felt something deep inside of him snap and tear. That's when he knew. He was going to die here. Amelia was going to die here. He was going to fail. Altvi grinned down at him and placed a hand around his throat and started to squeeze.

Just before Josh lost consciousness, he heard Altvi scream. He released his hold on Josh's throat, and the weight on top of him was gone. He rolled over gasping for breath, and saw Molly dragging him away from Josh. She had her teeth sunk into Altvi's leg and was ripping and shredding it. Blood was splashing from the wounds. Josh got slowly to his feet, just as Molly pulled his leg off, and threw it to the ground. Before she could pounce on him again Josh walked up behind the screaming Altvi. He put his left arm around his neck and took his right hand and placed it on the right side of his head and with one smooth movement, snapped his neck. The screaming stopped and Altvi slumped to the ground dead.

Ian held up his hand and looked at Mateo and Meg. "Do you hear that?"

They both listened and could hear screaming. It was faint, under the rushing water from the river and waterfall. But it was unmistakable screaming. The dragons heard it too and swam to the west side of the river. Ian saw the cave openings, behind the waterfall, and motioned for Mateo to follow. As they approached, Ian turned to Meg. "Maybe you should stay here," he told her. "We don't know what we're walking into up there."

She squinted her eyes at him. "All the more reason for me to go. I'm a soldier, cowboy. You may need me up there."

Before he could say anything else, she pushed ahead of them and went behind the waterfall.

Mateo shrugged and followed her with Ian now bringing up the rear. Mateo stooped down and put his hands together. Meg put her foot in his hands, and he lifted her up. She grabbed the ledge to the largest opening and pulled herself up and into the cave. She looked around and found it empty, but heard one final blood chilling scream, then silence.

She lay down on the floor of the cave and stuck her head out the entrance. Mateo cupped his hands again and lifted Ian. She grabbed his arm and helped him pull himself up into the cave. Then he lay down and both he and Meg held out their arms to Mateo.

"Where did that come from?" Ian asked looking around the empty cavern.

"Back there," Meg said. They moved to the back and found the tunnel, then they all pulled their weapons and entered.

When they reached the end of the tunnel, they saw another large cavern. Mateo pulled out a lantern that he had in his pack and pulled it open. In the light, they could see Josh holding a naked Amelia in his arms. He was sitting, propped up against the wall of the cave with his head tipped back. He was covered in blood, and his eyes were closed. They also saw Molly lying in front of them. She was letting out a long deep growl. Meg moved to stand in front of the two men and went down to her knees.

"Hey, Molly. It's ok, sweetie. We're here to help. Let us help them, girl."

Ian was pulling off his shirt and moved around Molly to Josh and Amelia. She recognized him and let him pass but kept her eye on him.

Mateo was looking around the cave and saw the blood splatter on the walls. He saw Altvi's leg lying by the tunnel entrance, and his body slumped on the ground a few feet away.

Ian was covering Amelia with his shirt, and talking to Josh. He had opened his eyes and was responding to questions.

When Meg and Mateo approached, Ian stood. "They're both in really bad shape," he whispered. "We've got to get them out of here."

Mateo nodded and knelt down. "Hey, Josh." His eyes fluttered open and he tried to focus on Mateo. "I'm going to take Amelia, ok? I'm going to carry her out of here and get her help. Meg and Ian are going to help you get to your feet. We're going to get you both out of here and back to the clinic."

Josh nodded. "Is she alive?"

"Yeah. She's got a pulse. But we need to move. Ok?"

He nodded again and let Mateo lift Amelia out of his arms. He was careful with her limp body and tried to keep Ian's shirt in place over her body. "Help him up. I've got to get her out of here fast."

Mateo moved to the tunnel, with Molly following quickly behind him.

Ian and Meg went to Josh. "Can you stand?" Ian asked him.

"I don't know. Something is torn inside of me. God, he really beat the crap out of me."

Ian smiled. "Yeah. He did. But looks like you dealt with him."

"Molly did," Josh said with a smile.

"What's this?" Meg asked when she spotted the leaves in Josh's hand.

"Don't touch that, Meg," Ian called out. "Josh, you need to drop those leaves."

He did and looked at Ian. "He had these over the wound on Amelia's head. Guess he was trying to stop the bleeding with them. I know what they are. I ripped them off of her as soon as I got to her."

"What is it?" Meg asked again.

"They are leaves from the sopor bush. They're deadly," Ian told her.

"Let's get you out of here, Josh," Meg said. She and Ian each reached down and put their arms around Josh's waist to help him to his feet, then followed Mateo through the tunnel.

When they reached the mouth of the cave, Meg could see Josh was in a great deal of pain. He was sweating even though the air was cool in the cave. He had gone very pale, and his breathing sounded ragged. With each step he took he grimaced, and she could see it took everything he had not to cry out.

"Ok, Let's take a break here, buddy."

Josh shook his head. "I need to go with her."

"You will, Josh. Mateo has her, and we'll be right behind them. I promise. I'm going to try to get Leo up here." She looked at Ian. "I don't think he can take jumping down to the ground."

Ian nodded at her. Before she could jump to the ground, Ian put his hand on her arm. "Just call him, Meg. You're bonded. Just close your eyes and feel him. Call him to you and he'll come."

She looked at him for a moment, then closed her eyes. I need you, Leo. She reached out with her mind and felt him. I need your help. Please hurry. She opened her eyes and felt him coming. Suddenly he appeared through the waterfall. He turned his body and lined himself up against the entrance. Meg jumped on his back and reached her arms out for Josh. Ian helped him to the edge, and carefully, Josh stepped onto Leo's back, in front of Meg. Once he was on the dragon, he slumped over Leo's neck gasping for breath.

"Go," Ian shouted. "Darcy and I will be right behind you. I'll get Sarah and Quinn and meet you back home."

Meg nodded and Leo turned and headed back through the waterfall to the river. They splashed down into the river, and Leo started swimming. Meg and Josh were soaked, and cold and Josh started shivering. She put one arm around him, to keep him from falling then leaned down over his body and held on to Leo. She could see Mateo and Yemaya up ahead of them and breathed a sigh of relief when the tree coverage above started getting thinner and more light was coming through.

She saw Yemaya spread her wings and lift out of the water, then shoot up into the sky and turn east.

Sarah and Quinn had been circling the river and mountains, praying to see some kind of movement. Sarah heard Quinn shout out and turned to see her pointing. She saw Yemaya rising out of the river, and flying, fast, toward the settlement. They turned Apollo and Titan and headed toward him. Then they saw Leo following a few minutes later. Finally, Ian and Darcy joined them.

Ian saw Quinn and Sarah flying toward him and was grateful he didn't need to try to find them and fill them in. He just lowered himself over Darcy's neck and urged her to pick up speed.

Mateo was still holding Amelia in his arms. He didn't want to risk letting her go. She was deathly pale, and her mouth had gone slack. Her body was cold, and he could only pray that she was still alive. Maya set down outside the clinic and laid down on the ground. Still holding Amelia, Mateo flipped his leg over and slid down Maya's body to land on the ground. He ran to the clinic doors and met Ali and Kendra who were running toward him with a gurney.

"How long has she been unconscious?" Ali asked.

Mateo shook his head. "She was like this when we found her. She never woke up." He laid her down and stepped back. "Meg is right behind me with Josh. He's hurt pretty bad."

Ali called for Beth and Michael and told them to get another gurney and get outside to get Josh.

Suddenly there was movement and people everywhere. Mateo backed up against the wall to stay out of the way and just watched. He saw them wheel Josh in followed by Meg and Ian with Sarah and Quinn behind them.

Ian ran up to Kendra and told her about the leaves they found from the sopor bush and asked about Pax.

Kenji had seen the dragons and burst through the clinic doors in search of Sarah. He spotted and ran to her, grabbing her in a hug then just looked into her eyes. "Are you ok?"

She nodded and clung to him. "But Josh and Amelia aren't."

He ran his hands through her tangled hair, then led her to a sitting area off to the side of the room. He sat with her on a little couch and pulled her tight against him.

The rest followed them and found seats. All they could do now was wait.

CHAPTER 14

Word spread quickly through the community. The Chartin was dead, Josh and Amelia badly injured. It seemed like every person in the community stopped by to see if they could do anything.

Kristen brought some sandwiches, coffee and water and set it on the little table in the waiting room. They smiled and thanked her, but none of them had the stomach to eat or drink.

Hours passed and the longer it took, the more their fear grew. Finally, Kendra came out and walked toward them. They all stood up and tried to read her expression. She smiled at them and told them to sit, and she would tell them what she knew.

"First, Pax is ok. The stab wound didn't hit anything major. They were able to stop the bleeding and sew him up. He has a concussion, but he was released and is staying with his sister for a few days," she started. "Josh just came out of surgery. He had a ruptured spleen, which they removed. He has severe bruising to his liver, kidneys and larynx. His sternum was broken, and they were able to use screws to stabilize it. He had multiple broken ribs that punctured his right lung. They drained the blood from the lung and reinflated it. He's lucky he has such a hard head, and he only has a fracture to his left cheek bone. He was very, very lucky that you found him when you did. He's still sedated and in recovery, but you should be able to go back and see him in a couple hours."

"Amelia?" Quinn asked her.

Kendra shook her head. "I don't know. Her right shoulder was dislocated. And she suffered a significant blow to the back of her head. She is in a coma, and we have her on a ventilator to help her breathe. The concern is the amount of time she was exposed to the sopor poison. When he put the leaves over the wound on her forehead, the poison entered her bloodstream. We injected the antidote, but we don't know how long she was exposed to it. We have her on an antibiotic drip and are hoping that with the antibiotics and the antidote she may have a chance. All we can do for her now is wait and pray."

"What about a transfusion?" Mateo asked.

"This isn't Boston General, Mateo. We don't have blood types on file. Or stocks of blood in a freezer back there."

"I'm O negative," Mateo said. "I'm universal. Take my blood and give it to her."

Kendra's eyes went sharp, and she stood up. "Let me go talk to Ali," she said and hurried back to the hospital section of the clinic.

A few minutes later, Holly poked her head out the clinic door and called Mateo back. He followed her to a room and sat on the bed. There was a curtain separating the room, and he could hear Ali and Kendra talking on the other side of it. Holly handed him a large glass of apple juice and told him to drink up. He did, then lay back on the bed. Kelly came in with a bag and Holly put a tourniquet around his arm and started looking for a vein.

"You're going to need another bag," he told her. "You need to take two pints at least. Maybe three."

"Absolutely not, Mateo," he heard Ali's voice say, she opened the curtain and looked at him. He could see Amelia lying on a bed on the other side of the room.

"Look, I can lose up to four or five pints and be ok. I'll recover. She needs it, Ali."

Ali just stared at him for a long time before nodding. "Kelly, get two more bags. We'll take two, Mateo. No more," she told him. "You're going to be weak and feel like shit. But you're young and healthy and should replenish it in a week or so."

When Josh opened his eyes, he saw Sarah looking down at him. "Welcome back, ass," she told him.

He laughed a little and groaned. "Don't make me laugh. It hurts. Did anyone get the license plate of the truck that hit me?" His voice was raspy, and his throat hurt.

Sarah smiled. "Yeah. Looks like you dealt with it."

She saw his eyes clear, and panic enter them. He started looking around the room. He saw Kenji standing behind Sarah. "Amelia?" he asked and tried to sit up.

Kenji moved forward and put his hand on his shoulder to hold him down. "Don't try to move, Josh," he told him. "She's alive. They're working on her now."

"She's alive?" He looked back at Sarah.

She nodded. "Yeah." She didn't add 'for now'. "You need to rest. Don't try to talk. You need to heal."

He nodded and settled back down. "What happened? How bad am I?"

"You took a pretty good beating. But you'll live." Sarah sat on his bedside and proceeded to tell him about his injuries and what they did to fix him up. Then told him they were using Mateo's universal blood type to transfuse Amelia. He calmed down, closed his eyes and fell back to sleep.

Kenji convinced Sarah to go home for a while. Shower, change her clothes and eat something. They checked in on Mateo before they left and found him sleeping. Quinn was sitting with him watching him sleep.

"How's he doing?" Sarah whispered.

"He's ok. Just tired. They took two pints of blood, so he just needs to sleep for a while."

"Any word on Amelia?"

Quinn shook her head. "Not yet."

"Ok. I'm going to go home and change, but we'll be back in a while. You should do the same," Sarah told her.

Quinn nodded but made no move to leave. Sarah and Kenji left the clinic and found Molly lying outside the front door. Sarah went to her and knelt down. She gave her a kiss on her snout and rubbed her head. "Hey there, you sweet, brave girl. I bet no one told you what's going on, did they?" Molly just looked deeply into Sarah's eyes. "Josh is going to be ok. He'll be here for a little while. He needs to recover. But he's going to be ok. They're still working on Amelia. But I believe she's going to be ok too. You need to eat and drink and stay healthy. And I think your mama will be home soon."

Kenji came up behind her and knelt down next to her. He put an arm around Sarah and his other hand on Molly. "You think she knows what you're saying?" he asked her.

"I know she does."

Kenji nodded. "Why don't you come with us, Molly? You can stay with us until Amelia is back on her feet."

He stood up and pulled Sarah up. They both looked at Molly. She glanced at the clinic door, then stood up and followed Sarah and Kenji home.

"I need to go deal with Altvi's body," Ian told Meg. They were still sitting in the little waiting area in the clinic.

Meg stood up and stretched. "I'll go with you." She saw the protest before Ian could say anything. "Don't," she cut him off. "Don't even say it. I need to do something other than sit here and wait," she told him. "I'm not some helpless female, Ian. I'm a soldier. I've been to war zones. I've seen and dealt with dead bodies."

Ian nodded and they left the clinic together.

Meg headed to the sea to get Leo and told Ian to gather some others, and she'd meet them up top in a few minutes.

He gathered three dragon riders he passed on the way to the cliff, and all headed up to wait for Meg. He saw her flying toward them on Leo and gave the signal. They all mounted and flew up to meet her and head toward the Asterian River and the bloody cave.

Two days later, Michael had Josh up and walking in the hall. He was weak, and in quite a bit of pain, but he walked. He asked Michael to take him to Amelia. She was in a room by the nurse's station. She was still so pale, and on the vent to keep her breathing. They had cleaned the blood off her face and stitched up and bandaged the gash on her forehead. He could see that her arm was in a sling and strapped against her body. "Can I have a few minutes with her?" Josh asked, never taking his eyes off her.

Michael pulled a chair to the side of her bed and helped Josh sit. "I'll give you some time. Don't try to stand up without me," he told him and left the room.

Josh reached through the rail on Amelia's bed and took her hand. He leaned down to place a kiss on her palm. He didn't even realize there were tears pouring from his eyes. "I'm so sorry, Amelia," he whispered to her. "I'm so sorry I wasn't there. I'm so sorry for everything I said to you. I'm sorry for hurting you. I didn't mean one word of it." He looked up at her face and reached out to brush her hair back. "Come on, baby. Wake up. Come back to me, please. I need you, Amelia. And I love you so much!"

He didn't hear Sarah enter the room. He didn't see her come up beside him. But when she sat on the arm of his chair and wrapped her arms around him, he turned to her and didn't try to stop the tears. He began sobbing into her shoulder and let her hold him while he wept.

The following week, they took another pint of blood from Mateo and tried another transfusion. Ali saw a little color come back into Amelia's cheeks and was hopeful. They discharged Josh the next day. Ali gave him strict instructions. Rest, stay ahead of the pain. Take meds when he needed them. No physical labor until she said so. No lifting. Take the antibiotics she gave him twice a day until they were gone and come back to see her in three days but sooner if he had any problems. In return, she promised she would send word immediately if there were any changes in Amelia's condition.

Sarah walked him out and took him home on Apollo's back. She didn't want him to risk jumping up and ripping his stitches or something. She told him that Kenji and Molly were waiting for him at his cottage with food and a cup of ale if he was a very good boy and cleaned his plate.

When Apollo set down in front of Josh's cottage, they slid off his back and Josh saw Molly coming from her enclosure next to the house. He walked to her and wrapped his arms around her. "Thank you," he whispered. "God, you've grown even more." Her head was now above his and he had to look up to see her eyes. He saw the question in them. "I don't know, girl. But we need to believe she's going to be ok." She lowered her head and rested it on his shoulder. He stroked her neck for a minute. "Let me go get rid of our company, and I'll come out and see you in a while," he told her.

He turned and saw Sarah watching them. "Dragons only bond with one person. But I swear, she is as much yours as she is Amelia's."

Josh shook his head. "No. We just both love her."

Sarah linked her arm through his and they walked into the cottage together.

After dinner, Sarah sent the boys out back with their cups of ale, while she cleaned up the dinner dishes. Kenji and Josh sat on his little patio, looking out at the garden.

Josh started talking. He told him about searching for Amelia, following Altvi's trail. He told him about finding the cave and what he walked in on. "I told Ali. She said she checked her and didn't see any sign of ..." Josh shrugged and looked at Kenji "You know."

Kenji nodded. "Yeah."

"She was unconscious, barely breathing, and he was going to..."

"But he didn't," Kenji said. "Ali wouldn't bullshit you, Josh."

He nodded. "If I had gotten there two minutes later, Kenji."

"But you didn't," he said again. "You can't do that to yourself Josh. You did get there. He didn't get a chance to do anything to her. And you and Molly took care of business."

"She wouldn't have been there if I hadn't been an ass to her earlier that day."

"Stop. You can't change what happened. I get it, Josh, I really do. Christ, if anything happened to Sarah I'd lose my fucking mind. But you can't change the past, man. All you can do is go forward, and make sure you do everything you can to make it right."

"Yeah. She has to wake up first."

Sarah offered to stay with him that night. She told him that they could bunk in his guest room. They'd be there if he needed anything.

"I appreciate it, Sarah. I really do," he told her. "But I'm good. I think I'd like to be alone tonight."

She nodded and wrapped him in a big hug. "Ok, but please holler if you need anything at all. And I want to see you down there in the morning for breakfast."

"I'll be there. I want to spend some time with Amelia."

He walked them out and watched them walk hand in hand toward the cliff. As soon as he saw them jump down, he went to Molly's enclosure. He sat down next to her on the fresh hay someone had laid for her. He leaned his head back against the wall and she put her head in his lap.

The next morning, Josh awoke in Molly's enclosure. At some point during the night, he must have laid down and when he opened his eyes, he was face to face with a dragon, her big blue eyes staring at him. He smiled. "Good morning, sweetheart," he said. "You know, in my entire life, this is something I can honestly say I never imagined. Waking up next to a beautiful female was something I did from time to time," he told her. "But waking up next to a beautiful dragon? Nope. Never in my wildest dreams."

When he tried to sit up, he found that he was stiff and sore. Molly gave him a nudge and he slowly stood up. "We need to get you something softer than hay to sleep on, Molly my girl."

He went to his cottage to get cleaned up, change his clothes and get down to the clinic to see Amelia.

Josh followed the same routine each day. He spent the days with Amelia. He would sit with her, talk to her. Told her stories and wished he had books that he could read to her. He would watch as one of the doctors came in and did an exam. But there was never anything new to report. No change. She had a steady stream of visitors, each staying for a while then they would leave with a look of pity for both Amelia and Josh. He would meet Kenji and Sarah for dinner at the community kitchen. Go back and spend a few more hours with Amelia. Then go home and spend the night with Molly. He had a few of Jacob's kids haul up a mattress for her enclosure. So, he would stretch out on it, and she used it as a pillow.

He lost track of how many days or weeks it had been. His life became sitting with Amelia. Waiting for some sign from her that she was still in there. Kenji and Mateo tried to talk him into a poker night. But he just wasn't interested. Sarah tried bullying him into getting out and doing something, anything. But he wouldn't engage, and she stormed out.

The only one that didn't harass him was Quinn. She would come in, pull up a chair on the opposite side of Amelia's bed and hold her hand. She would talk about their childhood. They had been next door neighbors, and best friends their entire life. She told stories that made him laugh, about their adventures. He learned that, even at a young age, Amelia had a gift for healing and children that got cuts or breaks would seek her out to fix their injuries. Josh learned so much about Amelia from Quinn. And with each story and memory, he fell more in love with her.

During one of Quinn's visits, Ali and Kendra came into Amelia's room. They looked very serious, and Josh felt a dread fall over him.

Kendra pulled a chair over next to Josh and sat and Ali stood at the foot of Amelia's bed. "We need to talk," Ali told him.

Josh shook his head. "No, we don't," he said.

Kendra took his hand. "Just listen, Josh."

He looked at Quinn and saw tears forming in her eyes. She gave him a little nod.

"Ok. Talk."

"We think it's time to remove the vent and cut back on the sedation. We need to see if she can breathe on her own," Ali told him.

"And if she can't?" he asked.

Kendra squeezed his hand. "Then we think it's time to let her go."

He looked at Kendra. She could see the disbelief, the denial, the pain and rage all reflected in his eyes. "Josh, we've done all we can do. We can't leave her like this, honey."

"We don't know the extent of the traumatic brain injury," Ali picked up. "We don't know if she'll ever wake up. But we know that she won't if we keep her in this state."

"No! We're not going to just let her die!" Josh shouted. "I'm not going to let you kill her!" He jumped to his feet and clenched his fists, ready to fight anyone that tried to get near her.

"Josh," Quinn said quietly. "Amelia is my best friend. My sister in all but blood. Our mothers were friends when they carried us inside of them and spent every day together. I've known and loved her since I was born. Look at her, Josh. Do you think this is how she wants to live? Is it how you would want to live?"

She reached down and put her hand on Amelia's cheek. "I want to remember her laughing, and dancing. I want to see her in my mind working in her gardens and helping people. I don't want to remember her like this. Coming to this room and looking at her wasting away, with tubes in her body. And I know with every fiber of my being that she wouldn't want that for me either. And she wouldn't want it for you. You know that. Josh, look at her."

When he did, they saw his body go limp. He slumped back into his chair and rested his head on the railing on her bed.

"So, what happens now?" he asked after a long silence.

"I'll remove the breathing tube, while Kendra stops the IV with the sedation. We should know in the first few minutes if she can breathe on her own," Ali told him.

"And if she can't?" Josh asked. He had a lump in his throat and felt panic rising. He had a pain in his chest. It felt like his heart was breaking.

"Then we sit with her," Quinn said softly. "We hold her hand and tell her we love her. And we respect her decision to stay or to go."

Josh looked into Quinn's eyes and finally gave one quick nod.

Ali and Kendra went to Amelia. Kendra clamped off the IV tube and began removing the needle from her arm. At the same time, Ali began pulling the tube from her throat.

Josh wasn't sure what he was expecting. But it wasn't nothing. Nothing at all happened.

Ali moved from Amelia's head, to remove the feeding tube in her stomach, then stepped back with Kendra and they stood hand in hand to watch.

It felt like a lifetime, but seconds later Amelia gasped. Her body went rigid, and she gasped again. Josh and Quinn each reached out and took one of her hands.

"Come on, baby," Josh whispered. "Fight, Amelia. Please stay."

Her body relaxed, and she started breathing on her own.

Amelia was breathing but not waking up. Quinn left to go do some work she had been neglecting but told Josh she would be back tonight. Ali and Kendra stepped out and told him they would be close and if anything changed he should come get them. And Josh just sat holding her hand. He lowered the railing on her bed and pulled his chair as close as he could and just held her hand, trying to will her to wake up.

People came and went, once word spread that she was off life support and breathing on her own. Sarah came in and told him that Molly was pacing outside, waiting for him to take her home but he refused to leave Amelia's side. Kristen brought him food from the kitchen, but it went untouched. Ali came in and checked her vitals. Her temperature was normal, breathing was good, and heartbeat was strong. All good signs, but still, she didn't wake up. Kendra came in later and told him that she and Ali were going to go home for the night, but Michael and Holly would be there overnight, and they'd be back in the morning. She tried to convince him to go home and get some rest. He refused. He would not let her wake up alone.

At one point, Josh put his head down on the bed and tried to pray. He wasn't sure who to pray to. God? The universe? Gaia? Before he could begin, he fell asleep.

When Amelia opened her eyes, she was disoriented and confused. Her arm hurt, and she saw that she was in the clinic. She couldn't remember why. She saw Josh asleep in a chair next to her, with his head resting on her bed. He was holding her hand. That made no sense either. The last thing she remembered was him telling her that the night they spent together was a mistake. She remembered him leaving his cottage. Then nothing. Trying to remember was making her head hurt. Her throat felt raw and sore, and she was thirsty, hungry, and weak.

She squeezed Josh's hand and tried to speak his name, but it came out a raspy croak. She cleared her throat and tried again. "Josh?" she squeezed his hand again and she saw his eyes open and snap to hers.

He sat up slowly, and she saw bruises fading on his face. "What happened?" she asked him.

He smiled, and tears formed in his eyes. "Oh, God, Amelia!" he gasped out. He sat on the side of her bed and carefully leaned down to place a kiss on her cheek then buried his face in her hair. "Welcome back, baby."

CHAPTER 15

O ver the next few days, it seemed that every person in the community stopped by to see Amelia. They brought her flowers and plants and little paintings and knickknacks. But no one would tell her what happened. They told her to focus on getting stronger, and not to worry about anything.

She grew more and more frustrated. The only thing she did remember was that she was pissed at Josh. So, when he came to visit on the fourth day, she spoke very little, thanked him for bringing whatever trinket he would bring and told him she was tired and would pretend to sleep until he left the room.

A couple of times a day someone would come in and help her up to walk or pee. They brought her food and told her she needed to get her strength back.

She discovered that she was a terrible patient, made even worse because everyone was treating her like she was a fragile piece of glass that would break with one wrong move.

"Josh," Amelia told him on one of his many visits. "I don't think you should come here anymore."

"What?"

"You made it perfectly clear what you thought of me and our time together."

"Amelia, I didn't mean anything I said to you. So much has happened since then."

"Really?" she snapped at him. "What? What has happened since then, Josh? Please tell me, because no one else will."

Sarah, who had been listening at the door, slipped into the room. She walked up to Josh and put her hand on his arm. "Kenji and Mateo could use some help over at our cottage. Why don't you go over and give them a hand," she told him. "I'd like a few minutes to talk to Amelia."

After a brief hesitation and one final look at Amelia, he nodded and left the room.

Sarah walked up to Amelia's bedside and took a seat in the chair. "You need to give him a little break, Amelia," she told her. "He hasn't left your side in weeks. I know you don't remember what happened, but you need to know he almost died trying to save you."

"Save me?" Amelia said. "From what? Sarah, no one will tell me anything. I have no idea what happened to me. It's driving me crazy!"

Sarah nodded. "I bet. I'd be pissed too. Ok. I'll tell you what happened." She reached out and took Amelia's hand and told her everything.

She told her about going to Josh's cottage and calling him out for being an ass. She told her about Molly coming and alerting them and them running and finding the blood and her basket of apples in the orchard where Altvi had hit her over the head and dragged her off. She told her about finding Pax wounded and bleeding out and how Josh had taken the shirt off his back to try to stop the bleeding. She told her about him running shirtless with no weapon and chasing after Altvi through the trees to find her. She told her what she knew of Josh and Molly finding her in the cave, with the sopor leaves covering the gash in her head. Of the fight with Altvi, of Josh almost dying until Molly pulled Altvi off him and ripping off his leg and Josh snapping his neck. She told him about Mateo and Meg and Ian finding them, with Amelia naked, and Josh holding her in his arms. She told her how they got them out on dragons' backs. She told her in detail each of Josh's injuries, and the surgery to remove his spleen and repair his broken sternum. And told her that the first words out of Josh's mouth when he woke was to ask about Amelia. How as soon as they got him up and walking, he walked to her. She told her about finding Josh at her bedside, weeping and apologizing for everything he had done. She told her that every day, all day he was there, and only left her side when they made him go. She told her that she had been in a coma and unresponsive for over three weeks.

"So," Sarah finished. "You might want to give him just a little break. Ok? He never gave up on you, Amelia. Even when others had. He never stopped believing that you would wake up."

"Oh, God," Amelia said. She put her hand over her mouth to try to stop the sob that wanted to escape. "I need to see Molly. I need to talk to Josh. Will you tell him to come back?"

Sarah nodded. "I will. But I happen to know that Molly is right outside. Why don't we go see her first."

Sarah helped Amelia to her feet and walked with her to the front doors of the clinic. Amelia was still weak, and suffering from some vertigo, but with Sarah's help, she made it to the door of the clinic. As promised, Molly was lying right outside the door. As soon as they saw each other, it felt like all was right in the world. Amelia wrapped her arms around Molly's neck and lowered her head to Amelia's shoulder. "Oh, Molly, my brave beautiful girl," Amelia sobbed into her neck. "I'm so sorry for what you went through. But thank you! Thank you for saving Josh." She leaned back and looked into her eyes. "And me. I love you, Molly. I am yours and you are mine. Now and forever, my precious girl."

Kendra was watching from the doorway of the clinic. She saw Molly lay back down, and Amelia sit and lean against her. She smiled and walked back inside the clinic.

Sarah turned to leave them alone and went to find Josh.

Later that day, Josh walked to Amelia's hospital door. He took a deep breath and knocked. Sarah told him that she wanted to talk to him. She didn't tell him why, or what they had talked about, only that he should go talk to her.

He heard her call for him to come in, and when he opened the door, he saw her sitting on the side of her bed, and Kendra picking up some supplies. "I'll let you two talk and be back with the meds for you to take home with you."

Josh moved into the room as Kendra went past him with a smile and stepped out closing the door behind her.

"They're letting you out?" he asked her.

"Yes, with a few conditions. Please come in, Josh. I have a few things I need to say to you."

He took a few more steps into the room, and suddenly felt awkward, and out of place. He shoved his hands in his pockets and looked at her."

She stood and turned to face him. "Sarah told me what happened. She told me what you did."

"Ok," he said.

She took an unsteady step toward him. "She told me you almost died, saving me. Why Josh?"

"Why what, Amelia?"

"Why did you do it?"

"Are you kidding me?" he asked. "He had you, Amelia. I didn't know if you were dead or alive. There was so much blood on the ground." He took a step toward her. "It was my fault, Amelia. It was my fault you were there. My fault you weren't safe."

Amelia moved to him and put her arms around him. "No, Josh. None of what happened was your fault. It was no one's fault but the Chartin's."

He buried his face in her hair. "I thought I lost you. I thought he was going to kill me, and then you. When we were in that cave. Then when we got back here, there were so many times I thought I was going to lose you."

"I'm right here, Josh," she pulled back and looked into his eyes. "I need you to say it, Josh."

"I love you, Amelia. I love you so much it makes me stupid. It terrifies me how much I love you! I can't imagine a world without you in it. Forgive me, please. I didn't mean a word I said to you that morning."

"There's nothing to forgive. I think you've paid for that mistake. I love you too, Josh. I love you so much it makes me stupid and terrified too." She took his face in her hands and brought him in for a long deep kiss.

That's how Kendra found them when she came back into the room. She cleared her throat, and they broke the kiss, but didn't back away from each other.

"I brought your meds," she said cheerfully. "I know you have herbs to make tea for nausea, so I didn't include any of that. But this is for the vertigo," she held up a small bottle with pills inside. "If that persists more than a few days, you need to come back, Amelia. It's perfectly understandable for you to be dizzy, but it should start subsiding. If it doesn't, come back."

"I will. I promise."

Kendra nodded and held up another bottle. "This is for the headaches. If you feel one coming on, take one. It's going to make you drowsy. So, take one and sleep it off. If the headaches get worse, or you have one that won't go away. I want to see you. And this is serious, honey. You experienced a pretty severe head injury. It's nothing to play around with. If you feel off in any way, you get yourself to the clinic. Got it?"

Amelia smiled. "Got it."

Then Kendra looked at Josh. "She needs someone to stay with her. I'm assuming that will be you?" Josh nodded. Kendra continued, "Good. Keep an eye on her. If you notice anything not quite right, I want to know about it. She's going to be a little off balance, that's normal, for a while. But, if you notice mood swings, memory loss, changes in eyesight, headaches that last too long, or seem incapacitating ..."

"You want to see her. Got it," Josh said and smiled. "Don't worry. I'll watch her like a hawk."

Amelia put her hands on her hips and frowned. "I'm starting to feel a mood swing coming on," she said. "I don't need a babysitter."

"No, but you need someone to keep an eye on you for a while. Or, if you'd rather, we can keep you here for another week or two."

Amelia squinted her eyes at Kendra. "Fine."

Kendra laughed and gave her a kiss on the cheek. "Let us worry and take care of you, honey. You gave us quite a scare. I'll stop by your cottage tomorrow, just to check in and see if you need anything."

"She'll be at my place," Josh said.

"Oh, Will I?"

"Yeah," Josh said and grabbed her around the waist and pulled her to him. "It makes more sense. My place is bigger and has actual beds. Unless you want me to sleep on the floor, because I don't think your couch is big enough for both of us. I mean I'm willing to sleep on the floor. But you know, I still get a little stiff from my injuries."

Kendra cracked up laughing. And Amelia shook her head. "Fine," she said again. "You're only going to be able to use that this one time ass."

He smiled. "Once is all I need."

Kendra left them to gather her things, and go file the discharge paperwork in her file, and Josh pulled her close again.

"I guess what I should have said is, I want you home with me. I haven't been able to stay there because you weren't there. It's not home without you in it, Amelia."

"Yes," she said and leaned into him. "That would have done it."

Suddenly the door swung open, and Kenji, Mateo, Quinn, Meg and Sarah all came in carrying boxes. "Ok, crew," Sarah said. "Let's pack up all this stuff and get this girl home!"

Later, after all the boxes were stacked on Josh's porch, everyone said they'd check in on her to see if she needed anything, and each headed home. Quinn was the last to leave. She wrapped her arms around Amelia. "I'll come by tomorrow. I'll bring breakfast. Make a list of what you want from your cottage, and I'll go get it for you. Then I'll help you get settled in here."

"Thank you, Quinn. I love you."

"I love you too. I'm so glad you're back. You scared me. Get some rest."

Amelia nodded and watched her walk to Titan and fly away.

Josh walked up behind her and put his arms over her shoulders and pulled her back against him. They stayed that way for a long time, watching the dragons flying overhead as the first stars started to appear in the sky.

"I don't know that I ever appreciated just how beautiful that is," Amelia said. "This really is an extraordinary place, isn't it?"

He kissed her on top of her head. "Yeah. It is. We should go in and get you comfortable."

"In a minute," Amelia said. "I want to check in on Molly. She ran into her enclosure when everyone was here."

They walked hand in hand to the side of the house and Amelia noticed that Josh had added a thick deep red curtain over the entrance. "Well, that's lovely, and luxurious," she told him.

"Yeah, well. She deserves her privacy. And she likes red," he shrugged.

Amelia looked at him and raised her eyebrows. "She likes red? Did she tell you that?"

"In a way. When I decided to add it, she went with me and picked it out."

"You took Molly shopping?" she asked.

He shrugged again. "I wanted her to like it."

"You're amazing, Josh."

159

"Wait till you see what we did with the inside," he said.

When Amelia opened the curtain, she just stopped and stared. Molly was lying on a huge mattress on the ground, covered with the same red material as the curtain. She noticed that he had expanded the walls out another 10 feet or more and raised the roof up. It was level with the top floor of his cottage now and had skylights in the roof. The mattress spread the entire length of the back wall. The walls were painted a pale blue, and along the outside wall was a long trough, filled with fresh water. She saw that there was a little spigot. "Check this out," Josh said and walked over to turn the spigot. Water started pouring out of it into the trough. Amelia laughed and clapped her hands.

"Kenji, Jacob and I connected a hose. We buried it underground and it connects in the back to my water system. And look, there's a drain in the back connected to another hose system. It dumps into the front garden. So, we can drain it and clean it out for her when we need to."

There was a long narrow window built in above the trough, with a red valance. Again, the same red as the curtain and spread. And hanging on the wall behind the bed was a painting. It was of her and Molly on the beach. The day they rescued her. She was wearing her yellow dress, and Molly was just a little thing, with her head in Amelia's lap. "Oh, Josh," Amelia gasped when she saw it. "That's beautiful."

"Yeah. I had one of the artists do it for me. I was going to hang it in my room, but Molly missed you. I thought she'd like seeing it every night before she fell asleep." She saw a pillow on the bed. And a large brown teddy bear.

"A teddy bear?"

"We went to the free store. She liked it," he shrugged again.

She walked to Molly who was lying on her bed. She looked happy and quite comfortable. "You lucky girl, Molly. Josh made you a bedroom fit for a queen!"

"Fit for a hero," he corrected. "Neither of us would be here without her."

"It's wonderful, Josh."

When they said good night to Molly and headed back into the cottage, Josh led her to the guest room. "I thought it would be easier to have you in here," he told her. "I'm not sure you should chance the stairs until you're steadier."

She shook her head. "No. I want to be in our room. I'll lean on you, and you can lean on me. We'll make it up the stairs together."

He nodded, took her hand and led her to the staircase, then swept her up in his arms and carried her up to their bedroom.

She giggled and told him to put her down. "Josh, you're still recovering," she said.

"Nope," he told her. "Ali gave me the all clear yesterday."

He set her down gently next to the bed, and went to his closet to find her something to sleep in. She noticed that there was only one pillow on the bed. "Where's your pillow, Josh?" she asked him. "You said you haven't been staying here. Where were you sleeping?"

He came back and handed her a shirt. "Here, you can sleep in this," he told her. And looked a little sheepish. "I can go grab another pillow from the guest room. I'll be right back."

She let him go and changed into the shirt. It smelled like him, and she decided he was probably never getting it back. She went to the far side of the bed and pulled the covers back. He came back a few minutes later carrying another pillow. He tossed it on the bed and stripped down to his boxers and climbed in next to her.

They lay down and he pulled her to him. She rested her head on his shoulder.

"Was the pillow on Molly's bed yours?" she asked him.

"Yeah," he said after a long pause.

"You slept with Molly?"

"Yeah," he said again. "We missed you together."

She smiled and curled in closer to him. "I love you," she whispered.

He wrapped her tighter in his arms. "I love you too, baby." He kissed her on the forehead, and they drifted off to sleep together.

CHAPTER 16

Quinn spent each morning with Amelia. They had it worked out that she would arrive just before Josh left. She would stay until after lunch, Josh would come home for an hour or so then Sarah or Meg would stay with her in the afternoon until Josh got home in the evening.

On the fourth day, Josh met Quinn on his porch. "Good luck," he told her. "She's in a mood today," he gave her a wink and headed off to the fields.

Quinn took a deep breath and opened the door. She could hear Amelia in the kitchen slamming cabinet doors and muttering angrily to herself. She walked into the kitchen and went to the coffee pot. Amelia gave her a side eye look and turned back to the sink. She was scrubbing potatoes and throwing them into a bowl. After Quinn poured her coffee, she took it to the little breakfast counter and sat.

After several minutes, Amelia swung around and glared at her. "What?" she shouted.

"I didn't say a word," Quinn told her.

"No, but you're thinking very loudly. So just say it!"

Quinn took a sip of her coffee. "I was wondering if I should call Ali or Kendra," she said.

"What? Why?"

"Mood swings, talking to yourself, I'm pretty sure those are signs they told us to watch out for."

"Oh, for God's sake!" Amelia said. She wiped her hands on a dishtowel and poured herself a cup of coffee. She

163

joined Quinn and sat. "I'm not suffering from effects of my injury. I'm just sick of being watched every minute of every bloody day! "

Quinn nodded. "I bet you are."

"I need my space, Quinn. I need to work in my gardens, go for walks with Molly in the orchards. I miss my greenhouse. I know Kristen has been tending it, along with your gram. But I need to do it! It's mine!" She took a drink of her coffee and took a long deep breath. "I appreciate you. I really do, but I wish you'd go away."

Quinn laughed. "Not going to happen, Amelia. I understand, honey, but you need to look at it from where I'm standing. From where Josh is standing. We almost lost you. And you are still suffering from your injuries. I can see the headache coming on right now. You're going pale, you're getting shadows under your eyes, and a little crease is forming on your forehead. Just yesterday you had a dizzy spell and had to grab on to the counter to steady yourself."

Amelia lowered her head in a pout. "It's not like I passed out cold on the floor, Quinn. I just turned too fast and lost my balance."

Quinn nodded. "Yeah, but what if you had passed out cold on the floor and you were alone? Do you have any idea what that would do to us?"

"Ok," Amelia said. "And you're right about the headache. The pills Kendra gave me just make me so sleepy I hate taking them. When I do, I don't know if I'm dizzy because I'm dizzy or because of the pills."

"I know, but I think you should take one anyway. Then lie down on the couch for a while and rest. Tell me what you want done with those poor potatoes and I'll do that while you sleep. When you wake up, we'll take a walk. We can go over to your greenhouse or pick apples in the orchard. I'll ask Meg to take my classes this afternoon and we can spend the whole day doing whatever you want. But I can't stand seeing you pale and in pain, Ami. So, please take the medicine and sleep it off."

"I'm a really terrible patient, aren't I"

"Yeah, you really are." Quinn smiled at her. "But I love you anyway."'

Amelia stood and walked to the counter where the little pill bottle sat. She opened it and took one. "There," she said.

"Thank you," Quinn told her. She stood and walked over to the sink. "Go lie down and tell me what to do with these potatoes."

"I'm making fish and chips for dinner. So, if you could peel them and slice them thin, then let them soak, I'd appreciate it."

"Done," Quinn said. "Now, go lie down!"

Amelia smiled. "Don't cancel your class, Quinn. I'm not sure I'm up to doing everything I want to do today. Maybe tomorrow."

Quinn eyed her. "Should I call Kendra or Ali to come check on you?"

"No, please don't. I'll feel better once this headache passes."

Amelia started toward the living room and called back over her shoulder. "Wash your hands before you do those potatoes!"

"Yes, Mother."

When Josh came home for lunch, Quinn was sitting on the front porch waiting for him. She watched him walk towards her and decided that her friend could definitely do worse.

"Hey there, handsome," Quinn said when he reached her.

"How's it going, gorgeous?" he returned, then sat down on the step next to her. "How'd it go this morning?"

"She was cranky, and she's bored out of her mind. She misses her greenhouse and her solitude. But under all of that, she had a headache."

Josh nodded. "Did you get one of her pain pills down her?"

"I did. And she's on the couch, sleeping. I think it was a bad one. I asked her if I should get Kendra or Ali, but she said no, and I didn't push it."

Josh nodded. "I'm taking the rest of the day off. I'll keep an eye on her."

"I have no doubt about that," she smiled and used his knee to help her stand up. "There's some pasta salad in the fridge, if you want lunch. And I've got potatoes soaking. She said she wanted to make fish and chips for dinner."

Quinn started to walk away, and stopped turning back to look at Josh. "She really loves you. You know that, right?"

He stood up. "I do. And I really love her. I hope you know that."

"I think I do. Have you told her your secrets?"

She saw Josh stiffen up. "What are you talking about, Quinn?"

"Josh, you came from a planet that we can only imagine. A planet that had wonders we can only learn about through the AROE You were a soldier, a scientist, a PhD. You're a man who looks like he knows how to take care of business. If you didn't have secrets, I'd be surprised and disappointed," she laughed a little. "I don't care Josh but be honest with her. It'll make you two closer, and it'll take her mind off of her condition. She'll never fully trust you if she knows you're hiding something. And you'll never be able to fully trust her if you don't share who you are."

"What if what I tell her makes her not love me anymore?"

Quinn let out a little laugh. "Were you a serial killer? A rapist or child abuser? Did you kick those little animals? What were they called? Puppies?"

Josh laughed too. "No. None of that."

"Then I think you're good."

Josh looked at her for a long time. "How can you be so sure, Quinn? How can you know that she'll still love me?"

"Because I told her mine. And she still loves me."
She turned and started to walk away. "Tell her to be ready in
the morning and we'll go check out her greenhouse."

Quinn thought about telling Meg not to worry about taking
her class that afternoon, but realized it was probably already
going on. She changed her direction and headed to the
AROE training facility. She still needed to work on her hand
to hand. She made a silent wish that it was empty. But when
she walked in, she found Mateo. She almost backed out, but
then saw he was working with a sword. So instead, slipped in
and stood just inside the door to watch. The program running
had two or three opponents, He would swing out, killing one
and it would vanish. He would attack another, and roll on the
ground, plunging his sword into his opponent's stomach, or
just swiping at their legs causing them to fall, then he would
jump up and take the killing blow. Once each opponent was
killed, three more would appear.

It was brutal, violent, and yet somehow beautiful.
Almost like a dance. He had his shoulder length wavy hair
pulled back in a leather tie and the tight shirt he was wearing
was drenched in sweat.

After his next three opponents were destroyed, he
set his sword against the wall and turned. He visibly jumped
when he saw Quinn standing inside the door.

"Holy shit!" he said with a little laugh. "Sorry, I didn't
expect anyone to be here."

"No, I'm sorry," she said. "I didn't mean to startle
you."

"Did I run over on my time?" he asked. "I thought I
had it booked for a few more hours, but I never know if I fill
out that damn sheet right."

"No, I'm not signed up. I just took a chance that it
might be empty."

"I can clear out if you want to use it," he told her.

She just shook her head. "I'm not going to impose
on your time, Mateo. There are other things I can be doing."

But she made no move to leave, just wandered over to where he had set his sword. She ran a finger over the hilt. "Where did you learn to do that?" she asked.

He shrugged. "I always had a thing for knives and swords. I used to collect them back home. In college I was on the fencing team and then joined a group of more hard core guys. They really taught me how to use it."

"You should teach a class," she told him. "I think if we're attacked, this would be a skill we should know."

"I've been working with a few of the community members. Some of them are getting pretty good."

"What were you going to do now?" she asked. "More of this?"

"No, I thought I'd cool down with some stretches and end with karate."

She nodded. "Well, I'll clear out and let you get to it."

"What were you coming in here to do?" he asked her.

"I need some work on my hand to hand. I'm good on dragon back with a bow and arrow. And I'm getting better with the gun, and tasers But, if something happens and I need to fight – well, I need some work on that. I've been practicing some with Meg. But I think I need a lot more practice. She puts me on my ass every time."

He laughed. "Yeah, she's a pro. Have you tried any martial arts? You might be more suited to that."

She shook her head.

"You're welcome to stay," he told her. "I could show you some of the basics."

"I'd like that. Thanks."

He sat on the floor and grabbed a big jug of water. "I just need a few minutes to catch my breath and rehydrate." He took a long drink. "Why don't you come over and sit with me. Tell me your strengths and weaknesses."

She sat on the floor across from him. "What do you mean?"

"Well, we've established that you're good on dragon back. You're good at archery. What else? "

"I run really fast," she said. "My legs are strong."

"Yeah?" He looked at her legs. They were hidden under tight brown legging type pants, but looked like she had some muscle tone there. "I used to love my morning runs but I haven't had a lot of time for that since I've been here. Maybe we can do that together some time."

"Ok."

"What else?"

She cocked her head to one side and looked at him. "Well, my grandmother taught me to make fantastic zucchini bread." She ignored his snort of laughter and continued. "That's why I'm here, Mateo. I have great aim and can run fast. Meg's been working with me on my upper body strength, and I've done some kick boxing with her. But I'm sadly lacking in that."

"Then that's what we'll work on."

"What are yours?" she asked him.

"Strengths and weaknesses?" he asked. She nodded and saw a wicked little gleam come to his eye. But he didn't follow up with the first answer that came to his mind. "I'm strong. I know how to use weapons, all different kinds of weapons. I know how to fight, and when I have to, I fight dirty, and I usually win. I'm pretty fast too. Weaknesses? I don't like it very much."

"Fighting?"

"Yeah."

He stood up and reached a hand down to her. When she took it, he pulled her to her feet. "You should probably take off the boots. The pants you're wearing are good, but the shirt needs to go. What are you wearing under it?"

She squinted her eyes at him. And made him laugh.

"No, seriously," he said and held up his hands. "It's too loose. It's going to get in your way."

She nodded, stepped back and took off her shirt. She was wearing a tight sleeveless undershirt in a shade lighter than her pants. He nodded. "That'll do." He looked her up and down. "Ok. Let's see what you've got."

Mateo had her move through a series of stretches. She was limber and her movements were fluid and graceful. He decided to start with some Tai Chi. He showed her movements and holds, explained that her strength would come from her core. She watched carefully and mimicked his movements.

After about an hour, Quinn asked. "This is great, but how is going to help me fight?"

"You're going to build your core strength, then we'll start working on defense and offense moves with karate and ninjutsu. Trust me."

"I do. But I need to get going. Thanks for this. Can we do it again?"

"Definitely," he said. "Do you want to meet tomorrow and go for a run?"

"Sure. I'll be on the western shore at dawn. Theres a curve just past the end of town," she told him. "That's where I usually start."

"Dawn?" His smiled faded. "Really?"

She laughed. "That's when I run. I have very full days, so, yeah. Dawn."

He sighed. "I'll be there."

He watched her walk away. She had a nice tight body and good moves. Put that together with long chestnut hair, big brown eyes and full lips; she was a nice package. He shook his head and shut down the program on the AROE. He had a full day too and should get to it. He headed to the shore. He had a date with Yemaya.

Mateo met Meg and the other sea dragon riders on the shore. They called their dragons and began their workout.

The sea dragons and their riders had become an entertainment outing for many of the community. Families would pack up a picnic dinner, and lay blankets on the shore. Children would gather and mimic their moves. So, the riders always did what they could to put on a show. But it was good bonding for the riders and their dragons, and it was good exercise. The dragons ate up the cheers and claps from the spectators, and Mateo suspected they enjoyed it as much as the watchers. He knew Maya did.

Mateo and Meg had been working on something, and decided tonight would be a good night to try it out.

They mounted their dragons, and the seven riders started out sitting, then as one, the dragons began leaping in and out of the sea, they grabbed their reins and jumped to their feet. Each time the dragon submerged then jumped up out of the water, the riders would jump and switch feet. Left front first, then right.

After a few minutes of that, the dragons submerged again, and the riders looked like they were standing on the water, moving through it as if by magic.

Kenji and he had made floating buoys, and they anchored them at 10ft intervals. The riders assembled in a single line, while still submerged with Maya in the lead, followed by Meg and Leo, Then the rest behind him. They started zigging and zagging through the buoys. It reminded Mateo of an agility course for dogs, back on Earth.

When they completed a couple rounds through the buoys, Meg and Mateo took Leo and Yemaya up into the sky, still standing and holding on the reins. They began circling, and the other dragons started circling in the water directly below them. Kristen took Romeo to the center of the circle and began throwing discs into the air. The other four riders pulled their weapons and started shooting the discs. After a few minutes of this, Kristen started throwing them higher, and those, Mateo and Meg began shooting, while still standing on their dragons' backs.

When Kristen signaled the discs were gone, Meg and Mateo gave each other a nod. They squatted down and Maya and Leo nosedived down toward the water.

They stood and turned, facing away from each other. Together they counted. One, Two, Three! And they dove into the water seconds before the dragons went in nose first at full speed. The dragons turned under the water together and headed toward their riders. Then went under them and both Mateo and Meg rose from the water on their dragons' backs and shot back into the air. Meg threw her head back laughing, and Mateo turned toward the shore and saw the spectators cheering.

Up on the cliffside, Josh and Amelia watched the show. They sat with their feet hanging off the cliff, eating the fruit salad Amelia had made. "They're spectacular," Amelia said.

"They are. Never in my wildest dreams could I have imagined this world. And now I can't imagine ever being anywhere else," Josh told her.

Amelia smiled and leaned her head over and rested it on his shoulder. "So, no regrets about leaving the Center?"

"None." Josh took a deep breath and a leap of faith. He pulled his legs up from the ledge and turned to face her. She did the same. "Amelia, I'm in love with you." He saw her eyes go soft and fill with light. But before she could say anything, he held up a finger to her lips to stop her. "Before you say anything, I need to talk to you about my life, before I came here."

He pulled his finger back and Amelia nodded. "Ok."

Josh took a deep breath and started. "My father was career military. He joined the army the day he graduated from high school. He and my mother were high school sweethearts, and she followed him to every base he served at, making his house and home exactly the way he wanted it. He climbed the ladder quickly. He was a soldier's soldier. He followed orders without question or hesitation and when he became an officer gave orders and they were followed, again, without question or hesitation. He ran his household the same way. Giving orders and expecting his wife and son to follow those orders."

Josh stopped for a minute and took a long drink of water before he continued. "In high school, I excelled at everything. It turned out that I was really smart with an extremely high IQ and I aced every subject, and they put me in college prep courses in math and science. I had a science teacher that was really cool. He kind of opened my mind to ideas. He told me that with my brain power, I could do really big things. I could help advance technology or medicine. It was always understood that I would join the military after high school. But suddenly, there were all these other possibilities. I was also really good at sports. I played baseball, basketball, football, you name it. I did it. I had girls throwing themselves at me and took a lot of them up on their offers."

Amelia smiled at that. She could see the looks he got from the community girls and women and had no doubt that he wasn't just bragging.

"When I was a senior in high school, that science teacher helped me apply for scholarships and send out applications to colleges. And when I started getting responses with offers for full ride academic and athletic scholarships, I bucked my dad's authority for the first time in my life. I went to Stanford University. God he was pissed."

Amelia interrupted for the first time. "He was angry because you wanted to go to college?"

"Yeah. So, I moved from Texas to Northern California, and my roommate in the dorm was Hank Ranson."

Amelia's eyes widened. That was a name she recognized as one of the original nine. The team that built the ships to escape Earth and move humanity to the Center.

Josh smiled at the memory. "Hank and I hit it off right away and after a few months, he introduced me to his brother. Ben Logan. I won't bore you with the details, but they asked me to join their team, and help them come up with the technology to build an engine for long term space exploration. I worked with the team and completed my education. I got my PhD, then moved to Philadelphia. I worked with Ben and Hank, Hank's wife Jewel, Sarah, Ishaan, Christov, Pete and Akemi. They became my family and my best friends. I lived and worked with them for years."

"I didn't know this, Josh. I didn't know that you were part of the original nine."

"Yeah. I got written out of that story," he told her.

"I don't understand." Amelia said.

"I got kicked out, Amelia. I betrayed the them and I got kicked off the team."

He could see the question in her eyes. But she didn't ask. She just waited for him to finish his story.

"I was pretty freaked out about what was happening to Earth. Ben had visitations from Gaia, and she would tell him what was coming. In turn, he told us. I saw increasing devastation. Global catastrophes and millions dying each time something else happened. I talked about bringing in the government, asking them to help, and the team shut that down. We made a promise not to tell anyone about what was coming. Ben knew the big picture. He saw what would happen to the government, the corruption and wars to come. So, it was decided we would move forward without saying anything."

"You went to your father?" Amelia asked him.

He nodded. "The CIA, Central intelligence agency," he clarified for her, "had already been nosing around. Trying to see what nine young scientists were doing in a big warehouse in Philadelphia. Buying products that sent up some red flags. But yeah. I told my dad. And I was off the team." He looked at her and saw no judgement in her expression, only curiosity, so he continued.

"After I left the team, I joined the military. With my dad's influence, my PhD, and my physical abilities, I moved up pretty quickly. I was stationed at NORAD, a military base inside of a mountain in Colorado. And I started using what I knew to try to duplicate the technology and build more ships, for more people. Then I was reassigned. I got sent to spy on my former friends."

"And you did?" Amelia asked.

"Yeah. At first. Then we found out that the New World Order had breached security and was watching the team. So, again, not to bore you with details, the team and my dad and some of his troops worked together to try to get ahead of them. We worked together to set traps and send out false information about the team's progress and departure date."

"I know about this from the AROE," she told him. "They attacked and you lost people in the battle, but you made it off the planet. Minutes before all the volcanoes erupted ending life on Earth."

Josh nodded. "When *Stonehenge* was hit by the asteroid, and it was determined that it wouldn't make it to the Center, they veered off and came here. *The Rapture* went with them, and rest of us continued to the Center. When we got there, my dad and some of his politician friends drew weapons on the sisters, the creators, and I think they were ready to try to take control. Gaia spoke to the troops, and asked them to come and feast with them, she asked them to lay down their weapons, and embrace a new way of life. Many of them did. My father called them deserters and ordered the remaining troops to open fire on them. Then he fired point blank at Gaia."

He heard Amelia gasp. "Oh, Josh!"

"She wasn't hurt. Neither were any of the troops. They had deactivated all of the weapons somehow." He reached out and took her hand. "But you need to know this about me, Amelia. You need to know that I come from that."

She squeezed his hand and held it tighter. "Did you open fire, Josh?"

"No, I laid down my weapon. I wanted what was offered. A new life. A new chance to live without war and hostility. I asked my dad to give it a chance." He shook his head. "He just couldn't imagine a new way of life."

"What happened to your father? The politicians and the troops that opened fire?"

"They were removed and sent to a moon called Kajax. They are sentenced to live there in isolation, with no contact with any outside worlds."

"You changed your life, Josh. You made a choice to embrace change. I know you may not feel this right now, but to me, you're a hero. You're an amazing man who sacrificed everything to save your friends, to save me. You're rebuilding yourself into the person who has always lived inside of you. Nothing about what you just told me makes me feel any differently about you. I'm in love with you. I don't think there is anything that will ever make me not love you, Josh."

He reached out and pulled her into his lap. He wrapped himself around her. "You make me want to be the man you see. I don't ever want to let you down, Amelia."

"The only way you could let me down is if you continue to believe you're not entitled to live the life you want."

"I want to share my life with you. I want you to move in with me, I want my home to be ours. It is already, because when you're not there, it's just empty. I want to build a life and family with you. I understand if you need to think about it."

"Josh!" Amelia interrupted. "Yes! I don't have to think about anything. I want you now and forever."

CHAPTER 17

The following morning, Quinn went to the shore to meet Mateo for their run. The sky was just starting to lighten, the stars starting to blink out. She sat on the shore and began her stretches and watched the sun start to peek over the ocean. This was her favorite time of day. Everything was still and quiet, the sea calm, the community, still sleeping, would wake soon to a new day. Gram had always told her that each new day was a new start. A new chance to make choices that would make your life a better place.

She was about to give up on Mateo. She could tell by his reaction yesterday that he was not a morning person. Just as she stood to begin her run, she turned and saw him coming toward her. He was wearing grey jogging pants, with a black T-shirt and white running shoes. His dark wavy hair was loose and hanging to his shoulders. He moved like an athlete with long strides, and fluid movement.

"Good morning!" she told him when he reached her.

"Morning." He started stretching and she saw he had a sleep line across his face. His green eyes were still heavy. It looked like he rolled out of bed and walked out the door. He always looked like he had a two-day growth of hair on his face. She wondered how he accomplished that? It made him look just a little dangerous.

She began jogging in place, so she wouldn't lose the warmup she started.

"So, how far do you usually go?" he asked her and began jogging in place next to her.

"There's an inlet about 2 miles west of here. That's my turn around point.'

He nodded. "Ok, let's do this."

He noticed that she had long strides, and after an initial warm up period, she turned on the speed. She didn't exaggerate, she was fast.

He felt Yemaya before he saw her. She was keeping pace with them in the water, then he noticed Quinn's Titan flying overhead. He hoped he never lost the amazement he felt each day of seeing dragons, living with them, riding them. He had to give it to Gaia, she had created quite a place here. He turned his thoughts quickly. Even thinking her name made him miss what he left behind at the Center. His brother, sister, mother. His nephew and friends he had made. He didn't regret the choice he made to come here. But he left them over 250 years ago, and he mourned them. He wondered if Zander and Akemi had more kids. He wondered what his nephew Kai had become. He thought it might be cool, someday, to go back to the Center and meet his descendants.

He saw the inlet ahead and kicked his speed up a couple of notches. Quinn matched his speed, and they reached their destination at a dead tie. Quinn went directly into the water to cool down, and Mateo just looked around. The half circle was surrounded by a jagged rock formation. The ground just stopped then continued on the other side of the water. The inlet was about 12 feet wide and had orange flowers growing along the edge of the water.

Quinn was treading water watching Mateo. This spot had always been special to her. It was her own personal sanctuary. She wasn't sure why she chose to bring him here. They could have run east instead of west. The eastern shore was beautiful too. It rounded the cliffs and opened to a meadow that led to the sea. But she wanted her spot today.

Titan landed on the other side of the inlet and lay down to watch them. Quinn moved onto her back to float and watch the sky. Mateo took off his shoes, sweatpants and shirt and jumped into the water next to where Quinn was floating. "Cannonball!" he hollered out and hit the water causing a huge splash.

Quinn moved quickly when she saw him coming but couldn't avoid it. She started laughing at the sheepish look on his face. "You're an ass," she told him.

"Yeah, but you've got to bring a little fun into each day, or what's the point?"

She cocked her head and looked at him. "I like that," she said and decided to add that to her gram's saying of making choices each day. She would choose to add some fun.

"This is a great place, Quinn," he told her. "I've probably flown past here a hundred times, and never really noticed it."

"I used to think about building a cottage here, just on the other side. I thought it would be my own little paradise," she told him. "But I didn't want to be so far from Gram if she needed me."

"It's just you and your grandmother?" Mateo asked.

"Yeah."

"What happened to your parents?"

"We lost my father in the Chartin slaughter when I was a kid. I remember him as a big, kind man. He was a hard worker and loved us very much," she smiled. "I still miss him."

"And your mother?"

Mateo saw the change in her face. The smile faded and her eyes went hard. "She died when I was 15." She swam to the shore and pulled herself out. "We better head back," she said. "I need to get up to Amelia. I promised her we could go check on her greenhouse today."

"Ok." Mateo said and followed her out of the water. He had obviously hit a nerve, mentioning her mother. That was a hard stop in their conversation. She started jogging back while he pulled on his clothes, then he ran to catch up to her, but stayed a few feet behind and gave her some space.

When they reached their starting point, Quinn turned to Mateo and gave him a smile. "I'll see you around," she said and headed for the cliff. She wanted to shower and change her clothes before going to Amelia's.

Mateo watched her retreat and muttered to her back. "You definitely will."

When Quinn reached Josh's cottage, she was surprised to see not only Josh and Amelia on the front porch, but Jacob and his crew as well. When she got closer she saw Ian and a couple of the other dragon riders too. "Having a party and forget to tell me?" she asked.

Amelia saw her and gave her a big smile. "Sort of," she came to stand with Quinn and grabbed her hand. "Let's go pick some apples," she said and grabbed a basket from the side of the cottage and called to Molly.

Molly came slinking out of her enclosure, then ran to follow Amelia and Quinn as they headed toward the orchard.

"What's going on?" Quinn asked her.

"I think Josh talked me into moving in with him last night."

Quinn stopped and raised her eyebrows. "Really? You think?"

Amelia nodded. "They are going to go move my greenhouse."

"Wow. That's big." They started walking again. "I'm going to need details, Ami."

"He loves me, Quinn. He wants to spend his life with me. He wants to make his home our home. We were up all night just talking. He told me about his past. Mistakes he made. He told me about his father, and his time in the military. He told me that I make him want to be a better man. He looks at me like no one ever has." She took a deep breath and put her hand on her stomach. "So, I said yes. Then first thing this morning he started recruiting everyone to come and start moving my greenhouse. He said he wasn't going to give me a chance to change my mind."

Quinn wrapped her in a big hug. "I'm so happy for you, Amelia. He is a good man, and he's getting the very best woman on Asteria! Once we get you settled in, we need to have a party."

They picked apples, slipping one to Molly every now and then. Once the basket was full, they headed back to the cottage. Amelia already had soup simmering on the stove and fresh bread made and cooling on the rack. She said she was going to make a couple of apple pies and send some home with everyone that came to help.

By noon, the crew that Josh recruited had moved the walls, floor and tables to the new location, carefully selected by Amelia. Jacob and some of his team were loading wagons now with her plants, flowers and herbs.

Quinn realized she had more than enough help and she would just get in the way, so she slipped out and headed to the AROE facility. She wanted to try out some of the programs Mateo showed her yesterday. Unfortunately, all the units were in use, so she turned and headed to the field and called to Titan.

She heard his call and looked up to see him circle above her before landing next to her. She walked to him and put her head against his. "I'm in a mood today, my handsome. Let's fly." She jumped to his back, and he lifted off.

Titan knew that Quinn had no destination in mind, so he just flew. He went out over the ocean, then back toward the mountains. They flew past the Asterian river and moved toward the Western shore. He circled the mountain range, and she sighed. She knew where he was going, and a part of her wanted him to turn back. But she knew he needed to see it. Just as he knew she needed to see it as well.

He set down in the field next to a ruin of a cottage. It was a beautiful spot. High on the mountain, a large plateau, a meadow with wildflowers everywhere. A tree line nestled against the mountain behind it and the small cottage in front of the trees. There was a waterfall flowing from the mountain that fed a small lake.

Quinn jumped from Titan's back and began picking wildflowers as she headed toward the lake, Titan following behind her. She bypassed the cottage. There was no need to go there, she knew exactly what it held. As she reached the shore of the lake she turned toward the mountain where there were three stone markers. She laid some of the flowers at the base of the first marker. It had just a name carved into it; 'Glory'. Quinn ran her hand over the stone. "You will forever have my gratitude, Glory. For your sacrifice and for your son." She moved to the next marker and saw Titan lie on the grass and put his head on the ground in front of the marker of his mother. The next stone had another name carved into it, in the same handwriting. It read, 'Jackie'. Quinn knelt down and placed a handful of flowers in front of the stone.

"I'm so sorry I couldn't protect you, Jackie. I hope you know how loved you were and still are. I miss you every day sweet baby brother."

She allowed the memory of the sweet and shy little boy to come. Running through the meadow, chasing after the dragon that loved him so much, flying into Quinn's arms with a laugh and a kiss.

The next marker had no name and no words. Her mother didn't deserve it. She only placed the stone, so that she would never forget. She laid a single flower on her mother's site then turned away to move to the lake. There was one more who died that day, who didn't even deserve a marker. She wanted no memory of him to ever exist in this or any world.

She stripped out of her clothes and jumped into the cool water of the lake.

When Quinn and Titan flew home, the sun had already set, so she had him go directly to the lair. He landed on the ledge in front of his cave, and she kissed his snout before hopping down and heading to her cottage in the trees.

As she approached she let out a soft curse when she saw Ian sitting on the stairs waiting for her. He watched her walk toward him and gave her a smile. "I was about to send out a search party. You were missed this evening," he told her.

"Titan was restless," she said. "And I suppose I was too. We needed to fly." She sat down next to him. "How did the move go?"

"Good. We got most of her stuff moved over. Just a few odds and ends to go. Amelia sent over some soup and apple pie. I put it up in your kitchen." He stood and looked down at her. "You know, Quinn, we've been friends our whole lives. If you ever need me, I hope you know that I'm here."

"I do know that, Ian. And I thank God for you and your friendship every day. Sometimes I just need to get away. It's been a hell of a month."

He nodded and looked into her eyes. "It has indeed. Guess I'll head home. I've got island duty in the morning. Good night, Quinn."

He turned and walked toward his tree house. "Night, Ian." She watched him walk away and climb the stairs to his cottage built into the tree across from hers. She sat for a few more minutes and headed up the stairs.

She loved her little cottage in the trees. It was built into the branches and stood firm against the large trunk. She had picked out every piece of furniture, every painting, and knick-knack. Every dish and glass and pot and pan. It was all hers. Only Ian, Amelia and her grandmother had ever stepped inside it and that was fine with her. She valued her solitude and her space too much to let anyone invade it. She and Ian had built a little outdoor porch off the kitchen overlooking the meadow and she had a porch swing built for two sitting on it. Jacob had built it for her, but when he offered to deliver it and set it up, she told him she had it covered. She and Titan had done it themselves.

She stood at the kitchen sink and ate one of the two pieces of apple pie Amelia had sent her. She decided she'd save the other for morning. She guzzled a large glass of blackberry wine, then headed to her bedroom and fell into bed without taking off her clothes. She prayed that the wine would give her a long dreamless sleep.

The next morning, she arrived at Josh and Amelia's cottage just as Josh was leaving. "I'll be home in a couple hours," he told her. "I'm just doing a class, then I'm free for the day."

"I'll keep her busy till you come back." Quinn told him.

He gave her a wink and a nod and hopped down off his porch to head to the new training grounds. When Quinn walked in she had almost turned and run back out. There were boxes everywhere. But she heard Amelia singing happily in the kitchen so walked back to find her up on a small ladder, placing plants on the shelf above the cabinets. When she turned to climb back down, she spotted Quinn watching her.

"Good morning!" Amelia said with a song in her voice.

"I'm not sure you being up on a ladder is what the doctor ordered, Ami."

Amelia rolled her eyes. "I'm fine. I feel great today!"

"I see that." Quinn told her, then looked around at all the boxes. "So, where do you want me to start?"

"Do you want breakfast first? There's still some left over from this morning."

Quinn shook her head. "I just ate the second piece of pie you sent over. Thanks for that."

"Where did you disappear to yesterday? I turned around and you were gone."

Quinn lowered her eyes and started looking through one of the boxes on the breakfast counter. "You had plenty of help, and I was just in the way. So, Titan and I went for a little scouting trip."

Amelia walked toward her. "A scouting trip?" she asked. "Where?"

"What the hell is this?" Quinn asked pulling out a strangely shaped bowl from the box.

"Where did you go Quinn?"

"We went to the western shore."

"Dammit, Quinn. Why? And why didn't you tell me?"

"I didn't know we were going to go there until we were there. I was restless and needed to fly. I told Titan the direction was up to him. And that's where he went."

"And?" Amelia asked her.

"And it was fine. I laid some flowers on the markers, took a dip in the lake, and flew home. Really, I was fine. And so was Titan. Every time we go there it's a little less. You know what I mean?"

"A little less?" Amelia asked.

"Yeah. A little less painful."

Amelia cocked her head to one side and looked at her like she didn't believe a word she was saying.

"I can't leave him there alone, Ami. I have to go and let him know I love him, and I'm sorry. He's only 3"

"Quinn, he's not there," Amelia said softly. "He's not in pain, or lonely. He lives here now." She reached out and put her hand over Quinn's heart. "And you have nothing to be sorry for. You didn't do anything wrong."

"I didn't protect him."

"You were 15. Protecting him wasn't your job."

Quinn nodded. "Yeah. Now, can you please tell me what this poor hideous little misshapen bowl is for?"

Amelia knew she had to let it go, for now. "It holds my sponges. I put it on the back of the sink and put my sponges in it. Ian made it for me when I first moved into my cottage. He was trying his hand at being an artist. Thank God that phase didn't last long."

Quinn held it up again and they looked at it with pity, then they cracked up laughing and Amelia took it from her and placed it by the sink and put two sponges in it.

"He improved some by the time I got my cottage," Quinn said. "The one he gave me is on my bathroom sink, holding my hand soap."

It didn't take long for them to get the kitchen boxes unpacked and they had moved into the guest room when they heard a knock on the door.

"You expecting someone?" Quinn asked her.

Amelia shook her head. "No."

They walked to the front door together and Quinn opened it. They saw Jacob and one of his apprentices unloading a huge table from his wagon. Amelia let out a little scream and ran to them. "Oh, Jacob! It's beautiful! It's perfect!" she threw her arms around his neck and gave him a noisy kiss on the cheek.

Quinn walked over to take a look, and saw it was more than just a dining room table. It was a work of art. It was the same dark wood that ran throughout the cottage. It had a large turning carousel built into the center, and the corners were decorated with carvings of flowers that flowed down the curving legs of the table.

"Wow." Quinn told him. "This really is beautiful Jacob. You outdid yourself on this."

He just smiled and ran his hands over his work. "It's a housewarming gift," he told Amelia.

"Oh Jacob! It's too much! I know we talked about what I'd like to have, and this is definitely it! But I'll pay for it. You don't have to give me a gift like this."

He shook his head stubbornly at her. "It's a gift," he repeated. "And I hope you will pass it down from generation to generation."

Tears filled Amelia's eyes, and she nodded then just wrapped him in another long hug. "I promise," she said. "And thank you."

Once they had the table and matching chairs in the dining area, and Amelia had chosen the perfect vase and flowers for the centerpiece they stood back looking at it.

"It's perfect," Amelia said.

"Yeah, it really is."

Josh walked in a few minutes later and began fawning over the table and all that Amelia had accomplished in the cottage. Quinn figured that was her escape.

"Don't you want to stay for lunch?" Amelia asked her.

"Thanks, but I'm going to go spend the afternoon with Gram. I've been neglecting her the past few weeks."

Amelia nodded. "Give her my love," she said and watched Quinn walk out the door.

Quinn smiled when she heard Amelia let out a little squeal, and she turned to see through the large window, Josh scoop her up and head up the stairs with her in his arms.

Quinn found her grandmother sitting on her front porch with a glass of lemonade. She was wearing her gardening clothes, loose tan pants, stained with dirt, an oversized man's white shirt that Quinn knew had belonged to her grandfather and ugly brown boots that were ancient when Quinn was born. She had a silly straw hat that she had made in a class years ago with a bright pink scarf tied around it.

She stood when she saw Quinn approaching and smiled then opened her arms, took her granddaughter in a tight hug then pulled back and gave her nose a little kiss. "There's my beautiful girl," she said and looked into her eyes. They stood exactly the same height and had the same

187

brown eyes; Quinn imagined she was looking into her own face in fifty years.

"Go grab another glass and the pitcher out of the fridge and sit with me for a while."

Quinn nodded and went into the house. Donna sighed as she watched her go. She knew her Quinn had been dealing with quite a bit lately, and saw the pain hidden in her eyes. She sat back down in her little patio chair to wait.

When Quinn came back out, she had the pitcher of lemonade and another glass. She refilled her grandmother's glass, then filled up her own. She set it on the little table and took the chair on the other side.

"The gardens look great, Gram. Sorry I haven't been around to help with them," Quinn told her.

"You've been pretty busy lately, honey, don't worry about me. I can still take care of myself. How is our Amelia doing?"

"She's great. We got her all moved into Josh's cottage. They are going to be really happy there. She's been adding all her special touches and turning it into a real home."

Donna nodded. "She deserves to be happy. I thought I'd visit tomorrow and take her a loaf of my zucchini bread."

"She'd love that," Quinn said. "You know, her cottage is empty now. You should think about taking it over."

Donna raised her eyebrows. "Why would I do that?"

Quinn shrugged. "It's smaller. This place is way bigger than you need. Amelia is already worried about her gardens there and is going to try to juggle between her work, her new gardens and taking care of those at her old place. It's a beautiful spot, overlooking the meadow and the cliffs behind it. It would be easier upkeep for you."

"Your grandfather and I built this house and raised our family here. I can take care of it just fine."

"I know. It just takes a lot of your time to keep it up. You know, Kylie and Lucas are expecting their second baby and are talking about building a second bedroom onto their place. If you moved to Amelia's cottage, they could take this one, and they'd have a room for everyone."

"Hmmm."

"Just think about it."

"So, tell me what you've been doing, Quinn. You look tired and sad."

"I'm ok. We've been putting in a lot of training with the dragons. Everyone is still on alert since we learned the Chartins are planning on coming back to attack. No one knows what they're waiting for. We hope that they just change their minds and leave us alone, but they left a handful of their people on the Southern continent, so I'm sure they're coming back for them. And leaving alone is not their way. We learned from Altvi that they attack and take what they want before they move on. So, we train, lay traps and wait. It's wearing on everyone's nerves. Then almost losing Amelia." Quinn stopped and put a hand on her stomach. "It was terrifying. Josh told me that he got to the cave just in time to stop Altvi from raping her." Tears came to Quinn's eyes. "I can't get that picture out of my mind, Grandma."

Donna stood and went to her granddaughter and wrapped her in a hug. "I know, baby." She held her while she wept, then pulled her chair over to sit in front of her and look into her eyes. "But Josh stopped it from happening. What did happen to her was horrible enough. But that didn't happen, baby."

Quinn nodded and wiped her eyes with the back of her hands. "I went west yesterday," she said quietly. "I guess Titan and I both needed to see it. I laid flowers for Glory and Jackie. And put one on your daughter's stone for you."

Here it is, Donna thought. Here was the sad she saw in Quinn's eyes. "Josh saved Amelia and thank God he was there. But there was no one there to save you. So, you saved you, my darling girl. You survived."

"But not Jackie, or Glory. I couldn't save them. And then I killed my mother. Your daughter. How can that be forgiven Gram?"

"Quinn, look at me."

Quinn raised her tear, soaked eyes and looked at her grandmother.

"There is nothing to forgive. You did what you had to do, honey, and the only one who hasn't forgiven you is you. And, baby, you will never find peace until you do."

Quinn just shook her head and threw herself into her grandmother's arms and wept.

CHAPTER 18

The next morning, Quinn went to the shore to take her run. She was surprised to find Mateo there waiting for her. She walked up to him and started warming up with stretches. "I didn't know you would be here today," she told him.

"I was restless and got up early. I wasn't sure you would be coming today. It's a little late for you, isn't it?"

"Yeah. Look Mateo, I'm not very good company today. If you want to take a run, I recommend the eastern shore, it wraps around the cliffs and has a beautiful view."

He cocked his head and looked into her eyes. "Are you asking me not to run with you this morning, Quinn?"

His tone put her back up. "Of course not! I'm just saying you might enjoy seeing the eastern side of the shore."

He shook his head. "I've seen it. I'll just run with you. Don't worry, I won't expect any conversation." He smiled at the look on her face when she realized she had just backed herself into a corner.

"Fine," she snapped out. "Don't try to keep up."

She turned and ran west at full speed. He shook his head. "Damn, she really is fast," he said to himself and took off behind her.

Mateo grew up with a mother and sister. He had two aunts and four female cousins. So, he was smart enough and experienced enough to know when a woman was in a mood and a dangerous mood at that. If he had any sense at all, he

191

would just head back now and let her run off her mad. But he was enjoying the view watching her from behind, so he just kept following.

When they reached the little inlet, he expected her to jump in like she did before, but to his surprise, she jumped over the inlet and kept going. He loved this planet. He loved the thin gravity, and the ability humans had to jump higher, and farther, run longer and faster and live longer and healthier. He leapt to the other side of the inlet and slowed down. He decided to let her run. He figured that she would come back this way when she got tired enough, so he stripped down to his underwear, and jumped into the water. He floated around the inlet for a while, then heard Yemaya's call, so he swam out toward the sea to meet her.

Quinn ran further than she had before. She heard Titan calling to her from the sky and slowed to a walk to cool her system down. When she finally stopped, she dropped down to the ground holding her side, her breath coming in fast pants. Titan let out another call then circled and landed beside her.

"You always have my back, Titan." She leaned against him, and he turned his long neck back toward her and nuzzled against her hair. "I love you too, big guy. Sorry I'm such a mess. I'll pull it together and we'll get back to normal. I promise." She stood and went to the water's edge to take a long drink. "We should head back. I guess Mateo gave up on us." She felt a little guilty for the way she treated him but shook that off. She told him she would be lousy company today.

Instead of running back she walked. Just wandered along the edge of the sea, enjoying the new scenery. She saw fish jumping in the distance and dragons scooping down trying to catch their breakfast.

When she was younger, before she bonded with Titan, she wondered why people didn't just fix the ships and fly away. Take whoever wanted to go, and head to the Center. Now, she could never leave Titan. She had no desire to leave

Asteria. But, maybe once the Chartin threat was gone, she and Titan would go to the southern continent and explore and colonize it. She had always wanted to see what it held there. She knew it had a cold season, and in the far south the mountains became snowcapped. She thought she'd enjoy seeing snow.

When she rounded the curve to the inlet she was surprised to see Mateo. He was lying back on a blanket with his arm propping up his head. He had a fire going and a blanket spread with a little basket next to it. Yemaya was diving and swimming in the water near the shore and he looked relaxed and happy watching her.

Yemaya saw her first and stopped swimming and watched her approach. Quinn could see wariness and some condemnation in her stare. Quinn smiled and continued to Mateo's little picnic. She sat down next to him, and he was watching her with the same wariness, but she saw no condemnation. "Your Yemaya loves you," she told him.

"Well, she has outstanding taste," he said. "And the feeling is mutual."

"I can see that. I thought you'd give up and go home."

He shook his head. "I really like this spot. You were running like demons were chasing you, and I didn't want to get rolled over by them, so Maya and I went to the community kitchen and got some breakfast. Thought you might be hungry when you got back." He opened the basket and took out bowls of fruit and a pan with oatmeal. He put the oatmeal over the fire and started stirring it.

"Thank you," Quinn told him. "I am hungry."

"Did you outrun the demons?"

She shook her head. "Do you ever really? But I lost them for a while."

He looked into her eyes, and saw the mad was gone, but there was plenty of sad still in there.

His gaze caught her off guard. His dark wavy hair was loose and hung almost to his shoulders. He had his two-day growth of hair on his jaw and cheek, and green eyes were staring into hers. She felt her heart beat a little too fast, and thought he looked like one of the pirates she read about in books from Earth in the AROE library.

She looked away quickly and he pulled the pot of oatmeal from the fire then poured sweet syrup into it before ladling it into bowls. He handed one to her along with a bowl of fruit and a spoon. Then took his and poured the fruit on top of the oatmeal and dug in.

She took a few bites of each and found herself charmed and touched that he had gone to the trouble for her. Unfortunately, those traits caused alarm bells to start ringing in her head. She knew better than anyone that charming and thoughtful could turn to demanding and abusive in a moment.

They ate in silence for a few minutes, then she started searching for conversation. "You said you went to college on Earth. What did you study?"

"Criminal Sociology," he said.

"Really? That is not what I expected you to say."

"What did you think I'd say?" he asked.

"I don't know. Not that. Why?" she asked him.

He scraped the bottom of his bowl and set it aside. Then looked at her again. "My father was killed when I was 14," he told her. "He was a cop. A good one. He was off duty and walking home from the subway. We lived in New York. He was a block and a half away from home and noticed that the corner store we went to frequently was being robbed. The couple that owned the store were an older Asian couple. Really nice, good people. And one of the robbers had Mr. Lee on his knees and was holding a gun to his head. Mrs. Lee was behind the checkout counter, with another of the robbers holding a gun on her. She was shoving money into a bag, begging them not to hurt him. My dad went in to help. I guess he tried to talk them down. Told them to take the money and go. He was in plain clothes, so they didn't know he was a cop.

He stayed calm and tried to reason with them. It didn't work. The gunmen killed them all."

"Oh, God, Mateo. I'm so sorry." Quinn said quietly.

"They caught them a few hours later. Two white 17 year olds. They came from money and lived in penthouses on the upper east side. They didn't need the money. They just wanted to do it. And I needed to try to figure out why."

"Did you?" she asked him. "Did you figure out why?"

"Not really. Some people just enjoy hurting people. But I learned about others and was able to help the police in some cases. But those two kids, they were just assholes." He was watching her face and saw her look down and her hands. "Quinn, if you ever want to talk to someone about those demons chasing you, I hope you know, you can talk to me. I'm a really good listener. I might even be able to help you chase them away."

She smiled at him. "I'll keep that in mind. But I have a class to get to now. Thanks for breakfast." She stood up. "I'll see you around."

He watched as she walked away then saw Titan swoop down out of the sky and land in front of her. She jumped to his back, and they flew up and toward the cliff.

Mateo watched until they were out of sight, then put out the fire, loaded the blanket, bowls and pot back into the basket and went to Maya. "Guess we should start our day too girl." He climbed on her back and flew back to the shore by his cottage. When he jumped down, he went to Maya and put his head against hers. "I think we're going to start annoying the hell out of her, my girl. That woman is a puzzle, and there's nothing I love more than solving a puzzle." He picked up the basket and headed toward his cottage. Maya watched him until he went inside and closed the door, then lifted off and returned to the sea.

The next few days were filled with activity. The annual festival was coming, the day they celebrated coming to Asteria, and it seemed the entire city was working to create fares to trade and show off and sell. The entire meadow on the cliff was transformed into a fair ground, with booths set up and a huge stage erected in the center. Quinn spent hours with Amelia, Charlie and her gram, making balm, soap, and lotion. When she wasn't doing that, she was helping Gram make zucchini bread. It seemed like she made hundreds of loaves in all sizes. And in between those activities, she was taking her island patrol, teaching archery classes and taking Meg's defense training. And she was trying to squeeze in time to learn her role in the dance and performance for the festival. She fell into bed each night exhausted and baffled. Baffled because it seemed Mateo showed up wherever she was. He told her he decided to take a refresher course when she asked him why he was in Meg's class. He told her that he needed to get more practice and experience when he showed up in her archery class. He told her that Kendra asked him to help her out when he showed up on Amelia's doorstep carrying bags of assorted herbs. He joined her little circle of friends in the community kitchen most nights and always found the seat next to her. He just seemed to be wherever she was. He never tried anything, sometimes he didn't even try to make conversation with her. But she watched as he engaged with everyone else around them. He seemed so easy and sure of himself. He always spoke with the people around him and was so comfortable in his own skin. She found herself watching him more than she was comfortable with, so he baffled her.

But the day he showed up in Ian's place on her morning island patrol, she blew up. When she went to the meadow and found Titan waiting for her, but no Ian or Darcy, she figured they had gone on without her. She had overslept after a late night at Amelia's and was running behind schedule.

When she reached the island, she expected to find Ian and Darcy. Instead, she saw Yemaya floating in the water off the island shore, and Mateo sitting on a blanket with his telescope out looking toward the southern continent.

She jumped down from Titan's back and stormed up to him. "What are you doing here?" she demanded.

He didn't lower the telescope. "Watching the Chartins. You?" He could hear the tone in her voice and kept his calm.

"You know what I mean, Mateo," she told him. "I'm supposed to be on watch with Ian this morning."

He kept looking through the scope. "Oh yeah. He had a little family emergency and asked me to take his watch."

"What family emergency?" she asked suspiciously.

"Charlie took a little fall and twisted her ankle, so he needed to help her get her booth ready for the festival."

Quinn dropped down to her knees, on the blanket in front of him and took his scope. "What do you mean a little fall? Is she ok?" Her voice turned from anger to concern.

"She's fine. Ian said she missed a step off her porch and twisted her ankle. He took her kicking and screaming to the clinic and they wrapped it up. Said nothing was broken. Gave her some balm for the inflammation and sent her on her way."

He saw her take a deep breath and exhale. She nodded and said, "Ok." She moved to sit next to him and pulled her scope from her bag. "Anything happening over there?" she asked.

He shook his head but kept watching her as she lifted to scope to look. "Nothing new in Chartin land," he said. "Quinn, can I ask you a question?"

"Sure," she said, not looking at him. She started adjusting the scope to focus. He waited until she was done and looked at him.

"Is it something personal with me that pisses you off or are you just naturally unfriendly?"

Her mouth dropped open. "I'm not unfriendly!"

"Not with Amelia and Ian," he said.

"Amelia and Ian are family. We've been friends since we were babies."

"Not with Sarah and Kenji, or Josh," he continued. "You've known them as long as you have me. So, it's just me you don't like."

"I don't NOT like you Mateo."

He raised his eyebrows at her and smiled. Quinn realized how that sounded and laughed. "Sorry. That sounded terrible."

"Not at all," he said. "I can work with you not, not liking me. So, what is it about me that puts you on edge, Quinn?"

Her first impulse was to deny but that wasn't fair. So, she decided to be honest. "Look Mateo, you're great. You really are. You've fit into the community like you've always been here. You pitch in and do your part. Yemaya, the queen of the dragons, chose you to be her rider. You became the first Sea Dragon rider ever. That alone, tells me you're a good man. Everyone loves you and the women swoon and bat their eyelashes anytime you're near them."

"Swoon?" Mateo asked.

"You know what I mean." Quinn snapped back. "You're just too good looking for your own good, buddy."

He flashed a big smile at that. "Thanks. So, what's the problem? You'd like me better if I was ugly?"

She gave him a look and didn't dignify that question with an answer. "Look Mateo, I like you, ok? But you are EVERYWHERE! Every time I turn around, there you are. You're always in my space and I don't understand why!"

Mateo nodded. "That's fair," he turned and faced her and looked directly into her eyes. "I like you, Quinn. I like looking at you. I like being around you and, yeah, I've been trying to be around you more, because I'd like to get to know you better."

She shook her head. "I appreciate that, I really do. But friendship is all I have to offer. I'm not interested in anything more with you, Mateo. You should really start noticing those other women watching you. I could introduce you to some of them."

"I'm good with friendship. Are you a lesbian?" he asked.

"What? No. I'm not a lesbian."

"Is there a man you're seeing, or interested in?"

"No."

"Is there some long lost love who has stolen your heart so you can never love again?"

She snorted out a laugh. "Definitely not."

He nodded. "Ok. In that case, I'm not interested in getting to know anyone else. And I'm not going to stop trying to be around you. But I'll take friendship. To start anyway."

"That's all you're going to get from me. It's all I've got to offer," she told him, and there was a look in her eyes that told him she was truly sorry about that.

"I'll take it." Mateo picked up his scope and focused his attention back on the Chartin community. "But now that I know you like the way I look, and you think I'm a good guy, I'm pretty confident I can change your mind."

"You won't. I'm not built for more." She said it quietly and with regret in her voice.

"We'll see," he said.

CHAPTER 19

The following morning, Mateo walked with Kenji from their cottages to the festival on the cliff. Sarah had left before daybreak to start helping set up and practice with the other dragon riders for the opening of the evening festivities.

There were dozens of booths set up and it looked like the entire community had arrived before them. The booths were actually colorful tents decorated with ribbons and curtains. They circled the north meadow. Each tent displayed food, baked goods, sculptures and paintings. Jacob had a huge tent with clever furniture. There was another tent with musical instruments. Guitars, banjos, violins, flutes, even small pianos. There was jewelry, clothing, hats and shoes. Blankets, pillows, and bedding. There was literally anything you might possibly need on display.

"How do we buy stuff?" Mateo asked Kenji.

"I have no idea. I think we are supposed to have things to barter," he told him.

"Like what?"

Kenji just shrugged.

"You have that box of money," Mateo said.

"I'm not using my money to trade for stuff."

"What else are you going to use it for?"

"It's sentimental, Mateo," Kenji told him. "I'm not spending it. These people have no use for it anyway."

"Neither do you," Mateo mumbled.

They spotted Josh and Amelia at a booth with ceramics and stoneware. Amelia was in deep conversation with the shopkeeper, while Josh looked at her with a dumb grin.

"Hey, Josh, what's up?" Kenji asked, as they joined him at the booth.

"Apparently we need a new set of dishes," Josh said.

They watched as Amelia wrote something down on a piece of paper, then both she and the shopkeeper signed it. They shook hands, and Amelia made her way back to where Josh was standing with Mateo and Kenji.

She wrapped her arms around Josh and smiled. "Are you sure you like those?" she asked him.

"Honey, if you like them, I like them," he told her.

She narrowed her eyes at him and put her hands on her hips. He quickly corrected himself. "They're great, Amelia. Really, they're going to look fantastic."

She smiled. "They really are!" She turned to Kenji and Mateo. "Hi, guys. Are you enjoying the festival?"

Mateo shrugged. "I guess. It's like a big market."

"It is. Just wait till the sun goes down! Then the entertainment starts," Amelia said. "We'll have music and dancing. The dragon riders put on a show. It's amazing!"

"How do you buy stuff?"

Amelia looked at him with a blank look on her face. "What do you mean?"

"I mean, we don't really have anything to barter or trade. So how do we buy stuff?"

"Mateo, you're a dragon rider. You saved the baby dragons and take shifts on the islands. Not to mention the classes you teach. You must have a ton of credit."

"I do?"

"Yes! You could go to any of these stands and buy just about anything you want. Haven't you been collecting crystal shavings from the island mountains?"

"Well, yeah," Mateo said. "But I give most of that to Jacob or the glass makers."

"Then you have credit for those too. Honey, you're loaded if you haven't spent any of that," she told him with a laugh.

"What about me?" Kenji asked.

"Umm, I'm sure Sarah has banked quite a bit. And you're working on the electrical grid, so you should have credit for that."

"Amelia," Mateo said and put his hands over his heart. "Would you be so kind as to show these stupid Earthlings how to shop on Asteria?"

Amelia laughed. "There is nothing I would love more!"

Mateo grabbed her hand and spun her twice under his arm then dipped her in a dramatic finale dance move, before kissing her quickly on her cheek.

Quinn watched the scene with Mateo and Amelia as she and Sarah walked toward them. After the dip, Mateo stood up quickly and grabbed Amelia's hand and together they ran off toward one of the tents.

"What was that all about?" Sarah asked as she slipped her arm through Kenji's.

"Mateo just found out he has a wad of credits to blow. Amelia is going to show him how to spend it," Kenji told her. "Do I have any credit to spend?"

"I don't know, but I do! Let's go play! You want to join us, Quinn?"

"I'll catch up with you later. I'm going to see if Gram needs some help at her tent."

"You should probably come with us, Josh. We'll see if we can catch up to them before Mateo runs off with your woman," Kenji said as they moved off in the direction Mateo and Amelia went.

Quinn helped her grandmother sell her baked goods and healing balms, then went with several other riders to give the children dragon rides. When the sun moved further to the west, and she set down with her last ride, she helped 7-year-old Kayden down from Titan's back. He looked up at her with his big brown eyes, his blond hair messy from the ride. He threw his arms around her waist.

"Thank you, Quinn," he said. "I'm going to be a dragon rider, just like you. My dragon will be as big as Titan and we're going to fly across the sky every day!"

She leaned down and kissed his head. "I bet you will, Kayden. I bet your dragon is out there waiting for you."

"I know she is. I dream about her all the time!" He looked up at her and memories of Jackie filled her. "Can I thank Titan?" he asked her.

There was a lump in her throat, so she just nodded.

When he approached Titan, he lowered his head so the little boy could stroke his snout. "Thank you, Titan." He leaned his head against his and whispered something she couldn't hear. All she saw was Jackie leaning against Glory with pure joy on his face. Titan looked over at Quinn and she smiled through her tears.

When the bell rang to signal the feast was beginning, Kayden pulled away with a smile. "Time to eat!" he hollered and flew past Quinn to join his mother, waiting for him across the field.

Quinn gave Titan a rub, then turned to cross the field and help her grandmother close up shop. When she got there, she found her tent was already shut down and she was nowhere to be found. Quinn spotted Meg and Josh sitting on a blanket with Mateo, Ian and Kenji, so she grabbed a plate and made her way over to them. As she got closer to the group, she saw Mateo leaning back against a large rock. He was holding a guitar, and strumming the strings in a quiet, but hauntingly familiar tune.

She sat across from him on the blanket and saw Ian leaning in, getting the tune, then he pulled his little wooden flute out and joined in.

"Where are your women?" she asked Josh and Kenji.

"Sarah's finishing a last dragon ride," Kenji told her. "She'll be along soon."

"Amelia and your grandmother went over to Amelia's old cottage. She said they'd be right back," Josh said.

Quinn picked at her food and listened as Mateo and Ian made music.

When Sarah joined them a few minutes later, she sat between Quinn and Kenji and picked a fried potato round off of Quinn's plate. Absently, Quinn handed her the plate. "You sure?" Sarah asked.

"Yeah. I'm not really hungry."

"I'm starving," Sarah said, grabbing the plate and digging in.

Amelia showed up a few minutes later and put her arms around Josh's neck from behind. "Mateo!" she exclaimed. "You play beautifully!"

He winked at her. "Thanks. One of my greatest loves was my guitar. I couldn't bring it with me when we left Earth, and I've been missing it."

"We should move this party down to the beach," Sarah said. "We have time before the evening festivities, don't we?"

"We do," Amelia said. "They just started setting up the chairs around the stage, so we have about an hour."

They all stood and started cleaning up the area. Once the blanket was folded and the plates taken back to the food tables and all trash disposed of, they ran to the cliff and jumped.

Quinn saw others had the same idea. There were families picnicking on blankets, lovers cuddling on the shore. There were other groups sitting around fire pits drinking and laughing and some walking in the sea holding hands.

They picked their spot on the shore and Mateo went to the sea to call to Yemaya. He felt her response and waited. She showed up seconds later and rose from the sea to join him on the shore. Leo showed up a few seconds after that and called to Meg. The group moved closer to the shoreline, and the dragons. Ian pulled out his flute and started to play and Sarah and Kenji began to dance to the music. Not to be outdone, Josh grabbed Amelia and joined in with their own dance. Quinn watched as Amelia and Josh swayed together, looking into each other's eyes. Amelia looked beautiful and in love. Quinn felt something tighten in her chest as she watched her best friend and the love of her life smiling at each other as if there was no one else in the world but them. She was happy for Amelia, no one deserved love and happiness more, but there was a little place inside her that mourned the loss of having her all to herself, and she found herself a little jealous because she knew that she would never have that for herself.

She saw Meg take Mateo's guitar and go sit with Ian. She began to play and started to sing. She had a husky alto voice and sang a song that Quinn didn't recognize about memories. It was slow and lovely. She watched as Mateo turned from Yemaya and began walking toward her. He held his hand out to her. "Dance with me, Quinn." Instinct told her to say no, but she put her hand in his and let him pull her close and lead her in a dance, slow and lovely like the song.

When Meg ended the song, they all watched in silence as the sun dipped below the sea line.

Amelia gave Josh a kiss, then turned to Quinn. "We'd better get going. We need to change before the opening ceremony."

Mateo gave Quinn a kiss on the cheek. "Thanks for the dance."

She smiled. "Thanks for asking."

Ian put his flute in his pocket and joined Quinn and Amelia. "You guys should get up top soon," he said. "You are going to want a front row seat for the show."

Then the three of them ran to the cliff together, leaving the rest to follow behind.

Donna and Kendra saved front row seats for Mateo, Josh, Meg, Kenji and Sarah at Ian's request. Mateo found himself sitting next to Quinn's grandmother, Donna. He gave her a smile and started looking around. He saw the community gathering around the enormous platform that had been placed in the center of the field. There were torches placed around it and in areas throughout the seating area, putting out enough light for everyone to see where they were going. There was a small orchestra seated behind the platform, with a bass, cello and violins. And he saw Ian join them and take out his flute. One of the AROE machines sat on a pedestal in front of the stairs leading up to the platform. There were eight large mounds of flowers placed around the stage, and one in the middle. He found himself excited to see the show. "You guys do this every year?" Mateo asked Donna.

"We do," she told him. "But today is special. It's our 500-year anniversary on Asteria. We have a history here now."

The crowd became quiet as Ali climbed the stairs. She was wearing a long mustard colored robe type dress with brown slashes through it, and a matching headpiece. She looked tall, regal and commanding. She found a spot in one corner of the platform and nodded to the crowd. The torches went out and the AROE came on with a holographic picture of Asteria showing just above the platform.

"Welcome my fellow citizens of Asteria," Ali started. Her voice carried through an unseen speaker, so all could hear her. "Welcome to the 500th anniversary of our arrival." The image of the planet started rotating slowly above. "Each of us knows the story of our arrival. Some of us here remember it. But it's important for us all to understand. Each and every one of us comes from a planet called Earth. A planet in a solar system far. far away." Suddenly the image of Asteria was gone, and a small white light was traveling through space showing planets, stars, black holes and all the colors of the universe, as it traveled through system after system until it stopped in the Milky Way.

"We all know that the universe was created by the great Mother and Father, who reside at the Center of it all.

They had nine daughters, and each daughter was given a portion of the universe to create and build life." The orchestra began playing softly a beautiful classical rendition of one of the masters. Mateo thought it might be Beethoven. Then, one by one, the mounds of flowers rose from the floor, and Mateo saw that they were young women from the community dressed in the flowers. As each one rose, they began throwing dust into the sky and in that part of the sky planets, suns and moons appeared. Mateo saw Amelia representing one of the sisters and smiled as she threw her dust into the air. Then each sister began dancing around the stage, in beautiful and enchanting moves, showing their grace and excitement at what they had created.

"Our home world was created by the daughter known as Gaia," Ali said and the mound in the center of the stage started to rise, and Mateo saw Quinn was beneath it, her hair flowing long and loose, and her dress of blue flowers clinging to her. She turned her head up to the image of Earth and she threw her dust in the air. Suddenly the planet started rotating. Quinn started rotating as well, then leapt from her spot in the center and began dancing around and through her sisters showing pure joy in her creation.

"Gaia loved her creation, and carefully planted the seeds to grow life on her beloved Earth," Ali continued. The image closed in on the planet, showing the continents and the oceans. It kept moving closer, showing rivers and mountain ranges. Quinn kept dancing around the stage in joy. Then she stopped and sat cross legged in the center, watching her planet as it grew life. The AROE image began fast forwarding through the evolution of Earth while Ali narrated the story, going through the dinosaurs, crawling from the ocean and dominating the planet. Then the meteor hitting Earth and destroying all that was there. It continued on to the evolution of humans from the apes to the first men. Ali told the story as the images went through the Dark Ages and the Renaissance. Between each era, Quinn would rise and spread more dust into the sky, dancing with complete abandonment and joy.

Ali kept talking about the home world as the AROE showed the pictures of an evolving Earth. It began showing war, from the crusades up to the many revolutions across the globe among the countries trying to get more than they had. She talked about the rise of automobiles, airplanes, from the beginning of their conception to what they became. She talked about modern technology, the rise of political corruption, and the effects of greenhouse gases on the planet. It showed children starving and animals dying. There were pictures flashing of wildfires, floods, drought and tornados, hurricanes, volcanoes and the devastation of nuclear weapons. While Ali explained what was happening, Quinn's dance became sad and desperate until she collapsed on the stage in complete despair. The music also became slow and sad. Then images started appearing on the stage of scientists, educators, politicians and Quinn rose. She began dancing around each image, whispering in their ear. Each one turned away without acknowledging her.

"Gaia tried for a hundred years, to get the attention of society. She tried telling them of the damage being done to the planet. She tried to get them to turn from the path they were on. But none listened and the damage continued."

Quinn turned dramatically from the Earth and bowed her head. The images on the stage all disappeared. Only the image of Earth above the platform remained. As the image rotated it showed pollution covering the atmosphere, disasters happening across the globe and a dark cloud above it, lowering to cover the picture of Earth.

Suddenly the music became more joyful, and a mist began covering the stage. A small boy that Mateo recognized from the community began climbing the stairs. He had shaggy, dirty brown hair and a small frame. He walked to the center and looked up. Quinn turned and saw him and reluctantly joined him. She kneeled down and whispered in his ear. He smiled and nodded and together they began dancing around the stage.

"In 2025 Gaia found Ben Logan, a 5-year-old boy with all the potential she needed. He listened and believed all she told him." Ali paused and a picture of Ben rose into the air. "Gaia told Ben what was coming. She told him he needed to build a team and together they would build ships to leave their dying planet and repopulate the human race." More pictures appeared next to Ben. His brother Hank, then their friend Ishaan, followed by Josh. Then came Kenji's sister, Akemi, followed by Sarah and Christov then Pete and Jewell. Finally, Kenji appeared. Other pictures rose above and below the ten photos of the original team. Ben and Hank's parents, Kim and Henry Ranson. Then Kenji and Akemi's father Mr. Hurato Tanaka. Head of Tanaka security, and Mateo's brother, Zander Delgado and last was a picture of Jenna Blair, Mr. Tanaka's assistant and Akemi's best friend. Mateo glanced at Josh and saw his mouth drop open and tears fill his eyes, when he saw his picture appear in the air. Mateo felt the same overwhelming joy and grief at seeing the image of his older brother Zander.

Ali continued, "Ben built his team and continued to communicate with Gaia. These amazing young scientists, with the support of their friends and family, grew and built what was needed to survive while Earth continued to fall apart."

Ali spoke about the team's single focus; to build these ships and save humanity. She talked about the US government's involvement and their request to have two ships for their people to join the expedition to the Center. She talked about relocating to Area 51 in Nevada and finally building the eleven ships. She paused as images of the ships appeared. The *Destiny, Gem, Quantum, Okinawa, Stonehenge, Rapture, Enterprise, Cor-Cordium* and *Victory.* Then the two government ships, *Justice* and *Freedom.*

"As the team continued their work, the planet fell further into chaos. A New World Order became the political superpower. It joined Russia, China, North Korea and the United States and was led by Iran's leader Khaled Saud-Khan. These world leaders cared only about power. They were corrupt and careless, trampling over the globe killing any that stood in their way."

Mateo watched as a holographic image of Ben appeared in the center of the stage, and Quinn approached him from behind. She leaned forward and whispered in his ear.

"When the team and Gaia became aware of the New World Order's plan to attack the base, and take control of their ships, they devised a plan to escape ahead of schedule. Gaia plotted a new route for them to follow to avoid hostile species that would be patrolling in the area of the original route. They input that into the AI program that would be running the ships. They loaded all the passengers into their cryotubes with the exception of the original team, the pilots and the military and security teams. They taxied the ships to the runway. But somehow the NWO knew and attacked."

Suddenly the AROE began showing what they had experienced as they prepared to launch.

Mateo watched as the NWO burst through the Area 51 gate, killing the guards. As they passed a bus it exploded and the first NWO truck burst into flames, throwing bodies into the air. He heard his brother's voice shouting orders, moving his team into position, and he saw the military protecting the ships. He glanced over at Kenji, Sarah, Josh and Meg. They were sitting forward, holding hands, their eyes glued to the images in front of them. Each of them had lived through this battle. Mateo had been frozen in his cryotube and had no knowledge of what was going on. He turned back to watch the battle. He watched as an image of Meg ran to the back of a bus to hold off incoming soldiers. He watched as Zander and his best friend Chad climbed on top of a bus and began shooting rockets at trucks, then incoming helicopters dropping more soldiers to the ground. He heard Christov's voice telling everyone to get to their ships. They were going to launch. Then he watched as Chad was hit and fell. He watched his brother kneel by his friend and take a shot in his shoulder, then two more in his leg and his gut. He saw Josh run to join the line in front of Zander then he and Meg, and several others began firing on the soldiers that had come up behind them, while some others on Zander's team lifted him and carried him to the *Destiny*.

Mateo didn't realize that tears were running from his eyes until he felt Donna reach over and take his hand. He turned to look at her and she reached up and wiped a tear away.

He turned back and saw an image of all the ships lifting up into the air, then the image of Area 51 exploding below them.

When they entered space, an image of the Earth appeared. It showed all the volcanoes erupting at once and covering the planet with ash. The orchestra music, which had gone low and sad, began rising in volume and turned to a more peaceful and uplifting melody. The picture of Earth faded. It became smaller and smaller until it was only a dot in the distance.

The women dressed in flowers, representing the nine sisters, filled the stage again, each dancing in their own space, each dancing very different dance moves but each beautiful and somehow all seemed connected.

Ali continued her narration and as she did Quinn moved back to center stage. She lifted her head to the stars and watched as the small fleet of eleven ships followed their course to the Center.

"The passengers of Gaia's fleet slept in their cryosleep state for over 3,400 years," Ali started. "Every fifty years, a member of the team would be woken by the AI program to track their progress. They were awake for 24 hours before returning to cryo and waiting another fifty years for the next team member to take their 24-hour shift. And as they slept, as they progressed in their voyage, Gaia kept watch."

Suddenly the image of the eleven ships lowered and began circling Quinn in the center of the stage. She spun amongst the ships and imitated wrapping her arms around them. There was joy and pride in her face. Her body moving in graceful fluid movements. Then with a swipe of her hands, she sent the ships back up to the sky.

Quinn watched them rise, then quickly threw dust into the air. A handful to her right and a handful to her left. And in each of those places, a planet emerged.

In the sky, the image changed to show an asteroid field. It filled the sky. Everywhere you looked there were giant rocks. At the far side of the field was a bright white spiral, surrounded by pink and purple. The wormhole. The two planets Gaia created were situated at the midpoint of the asteroid field, one to the left and one to the right. Quinn raised her arms and pulled the planets down to her on the stage. She began sprinkling dust on each one. Then with a kiss threw them back to their places in the sky, and with another swish of her hands, they started spinning. Quinn raised a hand to her lips, then threw her kiss into the sky and a small sun appeared above the planet to the left along with a bright moon. She repeated the movement and sent another sun and moon to the planet on the right.

With one final sweep of her arms, Quinn parted the asteroid field, just enough for a small pathway leading to the wormhole. She then spun and went down on her knees with her head raised to watch for the ships to arrive.

"Gaia knew that the ships would need to travel through the asteroid field to reach the wormhole. The final leg of their journey to the Center," Ali said. "She knew the danger, and the possibility that the ships could be hit by one of the asteroids. So, she created two planets just outside of the field, each capable of sustaining life, each with the possibility of being the home for her beloved Earthlings. Now, all she could do was wait for their arrival. It took over 3000years. But arrive they did."

The first ship, *The Destiny,* entered from the far left side of the asteroid field. And Mateo heard Kenji's voice. He glanced over to where Kenji was sitting. He was leaning forward, clutching Sarah's hand. "Ok, guys, single file. Let's reduce speed and keep alert. These rocks are huge, and they're moving."

Each captain from each ship responded. "Copy that."

"The team had programed the AI to wake each pilot when they approached the field, just in case manual maneuvers around the asteroids was needed," Ali said.

They all watched as a huge asteroid came up from below and impacted the bottom of *The Destiny.* "Shit!" Kenji shouted, "We've been hit from below, it just grazed us, and we have no damage to the *Destiny* but it's going to kick back on you guys." Kenji turned the ship and moved it into a slow upward direction.

"Jason, Report!" Kenji said as *Stonehenge* took a direct hit from the asteroid.

"We're hit," the pilot, Jason, said. "Kenji, we've got some serious damage here. Looks like direct impact to the bottom, one of our thrusters is out. I'm going to have to drop down, or we're going to get rear ended by the ships behind us. We've got minimal power. I'm going to steer toward that planet to the right. I think that's one of them that Ben told us about. Looks blue and green to me. If I divert power from the cryotubes, and put it toward the engine, we should be able to make it."

"We'll follow you down," Brad, the pilot of *The Rapture* said.

"Negative!" Jason said. "We'll make it. The rest of you get to that worm hole."

They watched as Jason turned his ship and fell out of formation.

"Kenji," Brad said. "I've got to go with him. I'm taking *The Rapture* down. There's only 125 people on that ship. They'll stand a better chance with 125 more."

Kenji took a deep breath. "Go," he told him. "I'll bring a recovery mission to get you guys as soon as we get to the Center. Stay safe and I'll be back for you. I promise."

"God speed, brother," Brad said.

They watched as *The Rapture* dropped out of formation and followed *Stonehenge* to the little blue and green planet on the right.

The remaining nine ships reached the wormhole and disappeared through it while The *Stonehenge* and *Rapture* entered the atmosphere of Asteria.

"The 250 souls survived and thrived on their new world. We created, built and planted. We grew our families as well. And true to his word, Kenji did return. They reached the Center safely, then he brought his *Destiny* along with his friends and colleagues and they found their place here with us. We have been here 500 years today. And each year we will continue to gather and come together to remember where we came from and promise to never repeat the mistakes of our ancestors. We will give our thanks to Gaia, for her service, and her compassion, for saving this flawed but overall good group of people and giving us the chance to continue." As Ali spoke, Quinn stood and began her dance of celebration. She was joined by the other eight, all dancing in a circle around her. Then she leapt from the platform and lifted high into the air, just as Titan swooped down to catch her on his back. They flew low over the crowd, spreading flower petals over their heads and the AROE trailed them with a brilliant rainbow.

Mateo couldn't take his eyes off of her. Donna noticed and smiled. "She was brilliant, wasn't she."

"She's everything," he responded, never looking away from her as she sailed across the sky.

CHAPTER 20

After the performance, chairs were moved, and a band took the stage. A beverage station was set up on each side of the platform, with ale and wine, and punch for those too young or not inclined to have alcohol.

Mateo helped move chairs, then got himself a jug of ale. He stood back as people started filling the space in front of the stage and dancing. He was relieved to hear familiar music playing. Songs he knew from Earth. He figured they learned from Christov's AROE. He watched, impressed, as Sarah and Kenji began dancing. They looked like professionals. He smiled as he watched Donna and Jacob twirling by him. And he kept an eye out for Quinn to appear.

While he waited, he danced with a couple of the community girls who asked him, only to be polite, and never more than once. He danced with Kendra, and with Charlie, then spotted Amelia, Ian and Quinn at the beverage station at the far edge of the stage. They had changed out of their flower gowns, and Amelia was wearing a bright yellow dress and Quinn had on a cream-colored blouse that hung loose, showing off her shoulders, and a flowing gypsy style skirt. He was pleased to see she left her hair unbound. It hung in long waves to her waist. He didn't think he'd ever seen her hair untied before. And knew he'd never seen her in a dress. She was stunning. And he felt a tightening in his chest, as he made his way across the field. Before he could reach them, Ian pulled Quinn to the center of the field for a dance. Josh and

Meg connected with Amelia, and they were pulling chairs up to a small table off to the side of the field. When he reached them, he set his jug on the table and scooped Amelia up in a big hug.

"You were amazing!" he told her. "That was a great show."

She smiled and kissed his cheek. "Thank you! It was so much fun!"

Mateo turned to Josh. "I didn't realize the part you played in saving my brother." He put his hand out. "Thank you." Josh looked a little shocked but took his hand.

"It was pretty intense," Josh said. "Your brother is a good man. A good leader. I admired him a lot."

"Me too," Mateo said.

One by one their little group came together. Kenji and Sarah came to the table, breathless from dancing, then Ian joined them. Mateo looked for Quinn and spotted her dancing with another partner.

Meg walked up to Mateo and followed his gaze to Quinn. "If you want to dance with her, you are going to have to cut in, buddy," she told him. "She's the belle of the ball tonight."

"Yeah," Mateo agreed. "Let's dance," he grabbed her hand and drug her out to the field.

Quinn felt like she was never going to be able to sit down again. As soon as one song ended, she was scooped up by someone else for the next one.

"Ian, you should go rescue our Quinn," Amelia said. She had seen Quinn's strained smile, as she spun by with a new dance partner. "She needs to sit and get something to drink."

Ian started to rise, but Mateo put his hand on his shoulder to keep him in his seat. "I got her."

Mateo made his way to her in the center of the field. He tapped the shoulder of her current dance partner. "This dance was promised to me. Mind if I cut in?"

He could see on his face that he did mind, but he nevertheless nodded and stepped away.

"I'm here to rescue you," Mateo said as he put his hands on her waist and pulled her close. "You want a break?"

"God, yes!" she breathed out.

He smiled at her. "Put your arms around my neck, Quinn, and I'll dance you over to our table."

She did, and he swayed and stepped to the music as he led her to the side of the field.

"You were spectacular tonight," he told her.

"Thanks. It was fun. Kenji recorded the entire show on the AROE so I can watch it later."

They reached the table, and Amelia slid a glass of wine over to her. Ian raised his glass and everyone else followed. "To Quinn, and Amelia, our little shooting stars. Well done tonight, my girls!"

"To Quinn, and Amelia!" they all said together and clinked their glasses.

"It really was incredible," Sarah said. "Where did that footage from Area 51 come from?"

"Christov recorded everything onto *The Destiny's* AROE," Kenji said. "It was still on the ship, when we left. I just dug it out."

Mateo shook his head. "I'm sorry I wasn't awake to help. I knew you guys had a battle to get off planet, and I knew Zander took some bullets, but by the time they woke me from cryo, he was already recovering. I guess I didn't realize how bad it was."

"It was terrifying at the time," Sarah said. "Somehow watching it tonight wasn't as scary. It looked like we had it under control. Our side knew it was coming and were prepared."

"We were," Josh agreed. "Instead of being caught in a trap, we laid one." He made eye contact with Kenji. "That's what we need to do here."

"The Chartins?" Ian asked.

"Yeah. The Chartins," Josh said.

"Tonight is for celebrating," Amelia said. "Let's not think about them tonight."

"You're right," Josh said and kissed her on her head and pulled her close. "Let's celebrate."

They spent the rest of the night dancing, drinking and enjoying each other's company. The band called Mateo up for a set and handed him a guitar. He played a few songs and even sang in one of them. His voice was lovely, strong and clear as he sang an old classic called *Faithfully*. Quinn found she couldn't take her eyes off him as he performed. And she noticed that throughout much of the song, he looked at her. The song was slow and talked of lovers rediscovering each other.

Donna stood to the side of the field, enjoying the show. She was watching Mateo look at her granddaughter, and she looking back at him. A little glimmer of hope for Quinn rose in her heart. She spotted Ali and Kendra sitting at a table near her, so she walked over and joined them.

"What do you know about that boy? Mateo?" she asked them.

"Umm, not much really," Ali told her. "I knew his brother better. Why?"

Kendra laughed a little and put her hand on Ali's arm. "Honey, you're so blind sometimes. I did Mateo's intake on Earth," she told Donna. "He comes from a loving family, with strong ties. He has a college education in Criminal Sociology, he knows right from wrong, and will do everything he can to always do the right thing. He has a keen sense of justice, and is not afraid to fight for what he believes in. He's charming and friendly. Always willing to jump in and help out. And from what I've seen tonight, he's incredibly talented. It looks like he's turned his eyes to your Quinn, and I don't think she could do any better. Not to mention, he's about the sexiest thing I've ever seen in real life." She sighed and took Donna's hand. "Quinn is gorgeous, if she lets him in, I think they would be a lovely couple."

"Mateo and Quinn?" Ali asked.

Kendra shrugged. "Maybe."

The three of them turned to the stage and watched Mateo take a little bow after his performance, then he handed the guitar back to one of the band members and jumped down from the platform. He went straight to Quinn and spun her around into a dance move and led her to the center of the field.

"They do look pretty together," Ali said.

"Hmm." Donna tipped her head and watched them dance.

When Mateo and Quinn made their way back to the table, they found Sarah talking excitedly about some plans she was making.

"Jacob said he could start on it late next week!" she was saying.

"What did we miss?" Mateo asked.

"Oh, my God, Mateo! Why didn't I know you could sing and play like that! You have to play at my new place!"

"What new place?" he asked.

"I'm going to open a bar!"

"A what?" Quinn asked.

"A bar. Like a pub. I talked to Kendra and Jacob, and I'm going to build a bar. A place where people can come, and drink and dance and I'll have live entertainment," she said with a pointed look at Mateo. "It'll be a place to just hang out and have some fun."

"I love that idea!" Amelia said. "Can I help?"

"Absolutely! I'll need your decorating skills for sure!" Sarah told her with a wink. "We're going to put it at the far east end of the community, on the shore right around the bend, so the noise won't bother anyone. It'll be far enough from the cottages. I'm calling it The Dive," she looked at Kenji. "The bar where Kenji and I had our first dance. It was in South Dakota."

221

"That was the night I found out Sarah had a temper. But she was dressed in these tight little jeans, so I forgot to notice her tantrum."

"You must not have known her long," Josh said. "I was introduced to her temper the second time I met her. She bit my head off for talking about building a warp drive."

Sarah threw her head back and laughed. "Oh Josh! You were obsessed with the warp drive!"

"It would have made everything a lot faster," he grumbled.

"And taken a hundred years to figure out how to build it. We didn't have a hundred years."

Amelia and Quinn looked at each other and shrugged.

"I was more of a Lucas Sagas fan," Mateo said.

"What's that?" Quinn asked.

Everyone at the table stopped talking and stared at her. "What? Is that something I should know?"

"You've never seen the Lucas Sagas?" Ian asked. "How is that possible?"

"What is it?" she asked again.

"Only the best set of science fiction stories ever made," Mateo said.

"Which set?" Josh asked him.

"Well, the original of course. But the third one is probably better. But the first is a classic."

"You mean episodes four, five and six, right?" Sarah asked.

Mateo nodded. "One, two and three were just sad. Seven, eight and nine were a great ending for it, though. But then the side stories, all of them were great!

"Yeah," Ian said. "There were what, ten or twelve others that were all good!"

"You all watched it on the AROE?" Quinn asked.

"Amelia and I did," Ian told her.

"It was a favorite on Earth. I think they were remakes from old twentieth-century films. I didn't see any of those, but the remakes came out in the late 2020s and were phenomenal," Meg said.

"Huh," Quinn said. "Well, I'll try to watch it sometime, so I can keep up with you all."

"Oh my gosh!" Amelia jumped in. "I completely forgot to tell you, Quinn. Your gram and I went over to check out my cottage, and she said she wants to take it over!"

"What?" Quinn asked. "I feel like I'm suddenly the last person to know everything!"

"She talked to Jacob, and they're going to remove Molly's enclosure and add a bedroom on for her, and as soon as he's done with that, she said she'll be ready to move in. That's probably why he can't start on your place till next week, Sarah."

"That's great!" Quinn said. "She and I talked about it a while back, and she was dead set against it."

"You're not upset, are you?" Amelia asked. "I know you lived there too, most all of your life."

"No, I'm the one who planted the idea. That house is way too big for her. And I know she loves your gardens at the cottage. I think it's wonderful!"

"I guess she's going to talk to Kylie and Lucas about taking her place. Now that they are expecting their second baby, she said it would be good for them to have the extra room," Amelia continued.

Quinn just shook her head, as she heard Amelia echo the exact words that she had said to her grandmother.

"Let us know when she's ready and we'll all be there to get her moved in," Ian said.

Meg leaned forward. "So, Sarah, tell us more about The Dive. You can't have a bar without a pool table and dart board."

The eight of them sat talking, laughing and drinking until the sky started to lighten, and the stars twinkled out. They hadn't noticed that the band stopped, or that most everyone had gone home. Tables and chairs were folded up and moved to the edge of the cliff. Food was put away and moved back to the community kitchen.

When Amelia let out a big yawn, she tilted her head back and looked at the sky. "Wow, it's almost daybreak," she said. "Molly is probably going crazy wondering where we are."

"Yeah, we should get home," Josh said and stood, then reached down for Amelia's hand then pulled her up behind him. "You all want to meet up tonight? We can go check out the spot for Sarah's Dive?"

"Sounds good to me," Meg said as she stood up. "Why don't we meet up for dinner at the community kitchen, and we can head over there, after."

They all agreed and folded their chairs, then headed off in their separate directions. Ian and Quinn walked together to their tree houses, Josh and Amelia to the orchards, Kenji, Sarah, Meg and Mateo to the cliff and their cottages by the sea.

CHAPTER 21

Quinn slept for a few hours but couldn't rest. She felt itchy and uncomfortable, so she gave up and decided to go see her gram. They had a lot to talk about. She showered, made coffee then guzzled down a mug, and headed out. When she reached the edge of the trees, she saw Titan laying in the shade waiting for her. He rose as she approached him and bowed. She put her head against his. "Good morning, my love," she told him. "I need to see Gram, but I promise we'll fly later today." She kissed his snout. "You want to give me a ride?" He nuzzled her neck and made her laugh. "Ok, big guy, let's go." She jumped on his back, and he lifted off.

Titan began circling the field, and Quinn let him go, she saw that all evidence of the party had been removed from the field. They circled wider, and Quinn saw her grandmother walking toward Amelia's cottage with Jacob. She patted Titan's neck, and he lowered when he saw them too. Before he could land, Quinn threw her leg over the side and leapt from his back, floating down and landing just in front of where Donna and Jacob were walking.

Donna jumped back, putting her hands over her chest, and Jacob started laughing. "You have just taken five years off my life, girl!" Donna scolded, then smiled and embraced Quinn. "You used to do that when you were younger. Always scared the life out of me."

225

"Sorry, Gram. So, where are two headed off to?" Quinn asked.

Donna looked a little sheepish and turned to Jacob. "Can I have a minute with Quinn? We'll meet up with you in a few minutes."

He gave a quick nod, and a wink for Quinn, then started walking across the field.

Donna linked her arm through Quinns and started walking, slowly, behind Jacob. "I'm sure Amelia already told you."

Quinn batted her eyes and looked at her grandmother with mock innocence. "Told me what, Gram?"

"Alright, missy. I thought about what you said, and you were right. Kylie, Lucas and little Brax need a bigger place. Especially once the new baby gets here. And there's no point in me having a three-bedroom house. So, I asked Amelia about it, and we went over last night. It really is a sweet little cottage. The view of the sea is breathtaking, and Amelia's gardens are just lovely."

"Oh, Gram, I'm really glad! I think you'll be so happy there."

"I do too, baby. But I'm too damn old to sleep on a couch. I want my bed, so I need a bedroom. Jacob thinks he can easily put a door on the side of the living room and build a bedroom for me in no time at all." Quinn could hear the excitement in her voice and just smiled as she went on. "And once that's done, he's going to have a few of his kids come and build me a greenhouse in the back field. Nothing as extravagant as Amelia had, but my own little greenhouse! Can you imagine, Quinn?"

"I can Gram. I can see you puttering around in the gardens, and in your own little greenhouse. It's going to be perfect."

As they approached the cottage they saw Jacob, Josh and a couple of Jacob's guys disassembling Molly's enclosure. Molly was lying in the grass watching them with disapproval, huffing and snorting out her objections. Amelia was painting the front door a pretty pale pink, Donna's favorite color.

"Oh, my darling girl!" Donna gasped. "I couldn't imagine it being any more perfect, but you found a way. It's just beautiful! I love that color."

Amelia smiled. "I know you do. I wanted to make it all yours, and soon it will be." She stood and put her arms around Donna. "I love thinking of you living here." She backed up and took Donna's hand. "Come around to the back, I have a surprise for you, but I want to let the paint dry before we start going in and out through this door."

She led Donna and Quinn around to the back of the cottage. They both just stopped and stared.

In the center of the garden was an octagon shaped gazebo. It was painted the same white as the cottage. It had a round table that Quinn recognized as the one that used to be in Amelia's kitchen, and four chairs around it.

Donna put her hands over her mouth to stifle a sob. "Oh, Amelia, it's just beautiful!"

"I thought you and your friends could sit out here and visit or do your crafts. And I laid some stones, over there." She pointed to the far edge of the field. "That's where my greenhouse was. It gets the perfect amount of morning light." They saw the stones laid out in a long rectangle shape.

Amelia saw tears in Donna's eyes. "Oh, Donna, if it's not what you want, or what you imagined, we can change it," she told her.

Donna shook her head and grabbed Amelia in a fierce hug. "It's absolutely perfect. It's so much more than I could have hoped for, my darling girl."

Amelia let out a breath. "Oh, I'm so glad! I have a pitcher of lemonade in the fridge. Why don't we sit in the gazebo and chat. I'll run in and get it."

Donna shook her head. "This is going to be my home. I'll go get it. You two go sit, and I'll be right back."

She ran her hand over Amelia's cheek and headed to the back door.

Quinn shook her head as she watched her grandmother walk into the cottage. "You've outdone yourself, Ami. When did you have time to do all this?"

Amelia linked her arm through Quinn's, and they walked to the gazebo. "I already had the idea in my mind for the gazebo," she said. "So, I had the wood and had already painted it. When Jacob's guys got here this morning, I just told them what I wanted, and they put it together. While they were doing that, Josh and I laid the rocks for the greenhouse."

"We were up till dawn, when did you sleep?" Quinn asked.

"We didn't." Amelia wiggled her eyebrows. "It's amazing how energizing shower sex can be."

Quinn let out a laugh at that.

"Really, you should try it sometime," Amelia said with a giggle. "I think Mateo would be more than happy to show you."

Quinn rolled her eyes but shushed Amelia when she saw her grandmother coming back juggling the pitcher and three empty glasses.

Donna set the glasses on the table and poured each of them a glass before sitting. "Amelia, it's just lovely in there. It looks so much bigger with all the furniture gone. Now, what were you two talking about."

"Shower sex," Amelia said, and Quinn spit out the mouthful of lemonade, she had just taken in.

Donna handed Quinn a napkin and smiled at Amelia. "Nothing better," she said.

A couple of hours later, Josh and Amelia went home to get some sleep before they all met for dinner. Donna went home to start packing and Quinn and Titan took their fly around. Titan could sense Quinn's exhaustion, so took her to the little bend on the shore. He lay down and she slid from his back. He lifted his wing, and she curled under it and fell asleep.

Mateo had been out working with Maya in the sea. He saw Titan heading toward Quinn's spot, so led Maya in the same direction. When they got there, they saw Titan covering Quinn with his wing, and she was fast asleep. He jumped down from Maya's back and started walking toward them. Titan let out a low rumble in warning and watched Mateo with cautious eyes. Mateo stopped and held up his hands. "I'm not going to hurt her, Titan," he whispered. "I promise I will never hurt her." He started walking forward again and leaned his head against Titan's. "She is yours and you are hers. And I think she's very lucky to have you." When he pulled back and looked into Titan's eyes, he saw acceptance. He put his head down on his enormous feet and sighed.

Mateo motioned for Maya to come closer. She lay down and he leaned back against her and watched Quinn sleep. He realized it was the first time he had seen her rest. She looked completely relaxed and at peace. She was beautiful.

"Oh, shit," Mateo muttered. "I think I'm in trouble."

He put his head back against Maya and closed his eyes. He dozed off and on until he saw the sun move further to the west. He stood and stretched then gave Maya a rub, to get her up as well. "You should wake your girl pretty soon, Titan. She has dinner plans with her friends tonight."

"I'm awake," he heard Quinn say from under Titan's wing. He looked down and saw she was lying on her stomach, with her head resting on her arms. Both eyes were still closed. "Why are you here, Mateo?"

"Just enjoying the scenery," he told her.

She opened one eye and looked at him.

He smiled. "No, really. This is a great spot," he told her. "I went to Mexico one time, for Spring Break. They had these big bed type swings. Covered with thatch roofs. They lined the beach. People would just crash there watching the ocean, and napping. You should do that here. Just one. Just for you."

Quinn tapped Titan's wing, and he lifted it, so she could sit up. "Why would I want to build a big bed here?"

"It's not really a bed. I mean it's a mattress, but it's on a swing. And it has a roof covering it." Mateo shrugged. "I'll draw a picture of it for you. It would be a hell of a lot more comfortable than the ground, for taking a nap." He reached his hand down to her. She only hesitated a moment, then took it and he pulled her to her feet. Then he dropped her hand and walked to Maya. Before he jumped up, he turned and looked at her. "I was thinking, while I was watching you sleep. I have patrol the next couple of evenings, but then I've got a few nights free. How about I grab a couple of bottles of that wine you like, you bring the glasses, and we can meet up at the AROE hut to watch some of the Lucas Sagas. I'll introduce you to the wonders of a galaxy far, far away."

Quinn caught the no, before it left her mouth. It was an automatic response. "Why not," she said instead. "I can probably make that happen."

He flashed a smile and jumped to Yemaya's back. "Cool. We'll firm up the details later. See you at the community kitchen?"

"I'll be there," she told him.

Quinn was the last to arrive but found her group of friends huddled together at a long table. She grabbed a plate of fish tacos, salad and rice, then headed over to join them. Mateo saw her and moved over to give her a seat on the bench between him and Amelia. Josh and Kenji were deep in conversation about building a mini AROE for people to have in their homes. Sarah, Meg and Mateo were talking about all the aspects needed for a successful bar. Ian was stuffing his face with tacos, keeping track of both conversations and injecting comments between bites.

Amelia turned to Quinn with concern in her eyes. "You look tired, honey. Are you ok?"

Quinn leaned her head against Amelia's and nodded. "I am tired. But I'm good. Just need a full night's sleep."

"Why don't you stop by the house when we're done tonight? I'll give you some tea to help you with that."

Quinn picked at her food, then pushed her plate away. Ian reached over and grabbed a taco off her plate and bit in.

"That's your sixth taco," Meg told him. Her tone both impressed and disgusted. "How do you eat like that and not get fat?"

"Good metabolism," he said with a smile and a mouth full of food.

A little while later, the eight friends stood on the east shore listening to Sarah's plans for her little bar. Quinn could see it in her mind as Sarah explained. Built to look rustic. With raw logs. An open front, facing the sea with both indoor and outdoor seating, booths along one wall, and a long sleek bar across the back. Tall and short round tables, and a large platform for a band with a dance floor in front of it. The outdoor seating area would have a log fence surrounding it with an opening to the shore. There would be a flat surface on top, so people could sit on stools and look out at the sea while they enjoyed the music and their drinks.

"And there will be a huge sign arched over the top, lit up in bright lights," Sarah said as she waved her hands in the air. "The Dive."

"Oh, Sarah! I can see it. It's going to be wonderful!" Amelia said.

"I know! Right?" Sarah said. "I already have people volunteering to work here when it's ready and we open."

"Well, sign me up!" Amelia said. "I'd love to help out!"

Josh put his arm around her waist. "I'm not sure my wife should be working in a bar," he told her.

Everyone froze and looked at them.

"I'm sorry, what? Wife?" Sarah asked.

Amelia elbowed Josh in the gut. "I didn't want to say anything tonight. I wanted it to be all about you and your place, Sarah." She pulled a little chain holding a ring from under her blouse. "But apparently Josh can't keep a secret. He asked and I said yes!"

Congratulations and hugs were exchanged and Josh helped Amelia take the ring off the chain and he slipped it on her finger. Sarah wrapped her in a hug. "You're not stealing my thunder," she told her. "You've just added to the joy. I'm so happy for you two!"

"I wish the bar was open," Mateo said. "I'd buy a round to celebrate."

"I'll remind you of that when she opens," Josh told him.

They sat in a circle in the grass and talked, laughed and made plans for the future. Each of them forgetting for a while about the threat across the sea.

CHAPTER 22

For the next few days, Quinn spent every waking moment with her grandmother, helping her decide what to take to her new cottage and packing it up. Kylie and Lucas stopped by to look at the furniture. Most they would keep, with the exception of what Donna was taking with her. Kylie was so heavy now that she waddled when she walked. Quinn did everything in her power not to show how freaked out she was when Kylie grabbed her hand and put it over her belly so she could feel the baby kicking.

"There's a real live person in there, Kylie," Quinn told her.

"There is! And I think she's about ready to come out. I know I'm ready!"

"She?" Quinn asked.

Kylie just shrugged. "I don't know for sure. But she feels like a girl. It feels different than it did when I carried Brax."

They tagged what was going to the new cottage with green and what needed to go to the free store with red. Everything Kylie and Lucas would keep were left without tags. Kendra, Charlie and Amelia all showed up to help. They said they were there for the packing party. They got the kitchen packed up in crates. And by the end of the second day, everything was organized, packed and ready.

Jacob finished the bedroom ahead of schedule. He was laying the floor and putting in windows. He said that the

233

floor would need to set for 24 hours and then she could start moving in.

The night before the big move, Quinn and Donna sat together, going through the last few boxes pulled from one of the guest closets. They held little mementos Donna had kept through the years. They had their last dinner at the old dining room table. They laughed and cried over the memories they had in the old house. And talked and dreamed about the new cottage.

They held each other tight on the front porch before Quinn left to go home and promised she would be there bright and early for moving day. She decided to walk home rather than fly with Titan, when she left her grandmother. She was sad, and worried and just needed to clear her head before she dragged herself up to her cottage and tried to sleep.

She watched Titan fly overhead trying to keep pace with her. He made circles in the sky over her head. When she stopped in front of the forest of trees that led to the tree houses, she lifted her hand to her lips and threw him a kiss. He sent her that special purr of his, that he reserved just for her, and flew on to his lair.

When Quinn approached her tree, she saw Mateo sitting on her steps. She closed her eyes and took a deep breath. "Mateo, why are you here?"

He could hear the wariness and exhaustion in her voice. "You stood me up."

He saw her face go blank. "What?"

He pointed to the bottle of wine sitting on the step next to him. "I brought the wine. You were supposed to bring the glasses, and I was going to introduce you to the greatest movie trilogy ever made."

"Oh, shit." She flopped down on the step below his and leaned her head back against the railing. She looked exhausted and Mateo was immediately concerned.

"I'm sorry. I completely forgot. Can I take a raincheck?"

Mateo was watching her closely and saw the sad under the exhaustion. "I don't know, Quinn. A second date is a monumental thing."

Her eyes snapped to him. "Second date? When was our first date?"

He gasped and put his hand over his heart like he was wounded, but she could see the sparkle in his eye. "I can't believe you don't remember. Four nights ago, we had dinner, then took a walk on the shore and watched the sun set, then went dancing."

"That wasn't a date Mateo. We had dinner at the festival with our mutual friends, then went for a walk with those friends to wait for the entertainment to start. I danced with everyone. So did you if I remember correctly."

"We seem to remember it differently," he said.

He got the smile, and little laugh he was hoping for.

"How about you make it up to me now," he said. "Invite me up for a nightcap. We'll open this bottle of exceptional blackberry wine, and you can tell me why you stood me up for our second date. I mean, I did wait for you for over an hour."

He could see the protest in her eyes and on her lips and was genuinely surprised when she stood up and said, "Fine. Come on up. I could use a glass of wine." She started up the stairs, and he sat for a moment to make sure he heard her correctly. When he figured he had, he grabbed the wine and hurried up behind her.

She walked into her cottage and left the door open for him to follow. He stopped inside the front door and looked around. "Quinn, this place is great!" he said. The living area held a large fluffy couch in a deep burgundy. There were two oversized chairs across from the couch in a plush tan material and a low coffee table with a gorgeous sculpture of a dragon in the center. Toward the back of the room were three steps going up to an open door. He could see a four-poster bed with a blue spread and fluffy pillows all over it. To the left of the living area there was a half wall that opened to her little kitchen. It had a small round table with two chairs and a vase with a bouquet of wildflowers in the center. There was a long counter that looked like white granite, and above it held open cabinets with white square plates and matching bowls.

Quinn pulled two long stemmed wine glasses down from another cupboard. The stem and rim were white and held a large deep cup. While he poured the wine, she opened a back door off the kitchen and went out to a small deck overlooking the west field. There was a glider with a small table on each side, and another closed door at the end, that he knew held her bathroom.

She sat on one end of the glider and kicked off her boots, then took off her socks and put her feet up on the railing of the deck. He handed her the glass and sat next to her.

"I've been to Ian's place a couple of times, and it's just a big bachelor pad. But this," he said gesturing with his glass, "is a home. It's a great place, Quinn."

"Thanks. I love it here." She took a sip of her wine and leaned her head back with a sigh. "I really am sorry about tonight. I should have let you know I got tied up. I just got involved helping my grandmother and completely forgot."

Mateo nodded. "Ah, tomorrow's her moving day."

"Yeah. I was helping her pack up the last of her things. It was rough. She's lived in that house for sixty years. I know it's the right move for her. But it was rough."

"I'm sure it was. You lived there most of your life too, didn't you?"

"I did. That place holds a lot of memories. We were going through boxes that have been sealed up longer than I've been alive. It was hard to see her sad. She cried and I felt so helpless and guilty. I almost told her to forget it. To start unpacking She could tell Kylie and Lucas to make other arrangements. But they're so excited about moving in." Quinn took another deep drink of her wine and shook her head. "But then she would wipe her tears and start talking about how great it was going to be in her new place. It would take less upkeep so she would have more time for her gardens and her herbs. She wants to have Jacob, and his kids build her a greenhouse like Amelia's so she can experiment with more propagation. It was like being on a swing. Swinging from one emotion to the next before I could catch my breath."

"I'm sure that's what it felt like for her too," Mateo said. "Excited and sad. Energized and melancholy. Memories of the past and dreams for the future. That was a lot for both of you to go through in the span of one evening."

She turned her head and looked at him for the first time since they sat down. His green clear eyes focused on her with complete understanding in them. "It's nice to talk to someone who gets it," she told him. "Thanks."

"Anytime, Quinn. Really." He reached over and brushed a stray hair away from her face and he felt her freeze up at his touch. "I should let you get some rest. It's late." He stood up and reached out his hand to pull her up behind him.

"Yeah." She took his hand. "I have to be over there at first light to get everyone organized."

"Can I help?" he asked as he pulled her to her feet.

"I would be stupid to say no to an extra pair of hands and some more muscle. And I am definitely not stupid."

"Then I'll be there. First light you said?" He put a little pained expression on his face and a whine in his voice.

She laughed. "Or when you wake up. We'll be dealing with it all day, and I know how you feel about early mornings."

They reached the front door, and before Quinn could open it, he stopped her.

"I want to try something," he told her and moved toward her. He kept his hands at his sides, but leaned in and gave her a slow, gentle kiss. He moved back a few inches and waited for her to open her eyes. When she did, he saw what he needed to see and moved in again, this time pulling her close. He put one arm around her waist and deepened the kiss backing her up against the door. He felt her arms come around him and her lips relaxed against his, and he plunged his tongue between them. She returned his kiss with her tongue and pressed her body closer to his. For a few minutes, she was with him completely, sweet and giving. And he felt the second she started to fight it. He released her and looked into her eyes and saw terror. She pushed against his chest and started shaking her head. Then her breath started coming in desperate pants, not out of passion but out of fear.

"I can't" she said with a sob and started to go down to the floor.

"Ok," he told her and held her up. "It's ok, Quinn. Just breathe, slow even breaths." He started breathing with her. "Long breath in and let it out slowly," he kept repeating it until she was doing it. When it seemed like her panic attack had subsided, he just leaned his forehead against hers. "Oh, baby, who hurt you?"

She shook her head again. "I'm sorry, Mateo. I just can't give what you're asking for."

He pulled back a little and looked into her eyes. "I'm not asking you for anything, Quinn. But I'm telling you that I think you're incredible. You're strong and loyal, sweet and fierce. And you're fucking beautiful. And I'm not going anywhere. And most importantly, I will never hurt you. I'm not built that way, Quinn. And one day you're going to know that." He gave her a kiss on top of her head. "I'll see you in the morning." He moved her aside and opened the door. "Have another glass of wine and get some rest."

She nodded at him and watched as he stepped outside and closed the door behind him.

As Mateo went down the stairs, he became angrier and angrier with each step. When he reached the ground, he didn't hesitate. He went directly to Ian's tree and climbed his stairs. When he reached the landing, he pounded on the door. He could hear Ian shuffling around inside, and his anger and impatience grew. He knocked again harder and longer.

"Hold on, I'm coming!" Ian shouted. Then Mateo heard a crash and a curse from behind the door.

Ian opened the door in his underwear, rubbing his knee. It was obvious he had woken him up. His already crazy hair was standing up all over his head and his eyes were still glazed from sleep. "Mateo, what the fuck? Did I sleep through the bell? Are we under attack?"

"No," Mateo said and pushed passed him. "I need a beer." He walked into Ian's kitchen and went to his fridge. Ian closed the door, and followed him, flipping on a light as he went.

"Dude. I have to be up in a couple of hours for an early patrol, then go help Donna move to Amelia's cottage. Don't you have ale at your place?"

Mateo stood in front of the fridge with the door still open and took a long drink directly out of the jug. Finally, he closed the fridge and leaned back against the counter. "You've known Quinn all your life, right?"

"Yeah. I'm a year older, but my mom, hers and Amelia's were all friends. We grew up together. Why?"

"What happened to her?" Mateo asked.

Ian sat down on one of the chairs at his kitchen table. "What do you mean?" He kicked the vacant chair away from the table and motioned for Mateo to sit.

Ian could see the simmering anger in Mateo's eyes as he took another swig of ale and sat.

Ian took a deep breath. "I don't know, Mateo. I really don't. I think the three of us kind of bonded after our parents were killed in the Chartin slaughter. My dad, Quinn's dad and Amelia's mom. It was a rough time. My mom was a rock, man. And she along with Amelia's granny and Quinn's gran were great. But her mom really fell apart. We didn't see her much. And they moved in with Donna. Quinn had a hard time. Her dad was a really good man. He and Quinn were really close, and I guess it was like she lost both her parents, cause her mom just checked out, you know?"

Mateo nodded.

"About a year later, her mom started working in the community kitchen a few days a week, and she hooked up with a man. I think his name was Victor. A big burly guy. A loner. My mom said he had a weakness for ale. A few months later they got married and moved to the cottage at the north end of the field. Where Pax and his lady live now," Ian said. "I don't know much more, I was only 9 or 10. But I do remember hearing my mom and Donna talking one time and saying he was a bully and there was a lot of arguing and crying in that cottage. Quinn didn't come around as much. I think Victor made her stay home. When she did come round, she was different."

"Different how?" Mateo asked.

Ian shrugged. "Quiet, her clothes looked too big, like she had lost weight, or wasn't eating well. She didn't really want to hang out like we used to." He let out a breath and leaned back in his chair. "Then one day she was just gone. The cottage was empty, and they were gone. I asked my mom, and she said Victor wanted to explore more of the continent and they headed west."

"Had anyone in the community done that before?" Mateo asked. "Just leave to go explore?"

Ian shook his head. "Not in my lifetime. I know back in the early days, they explored. But they settled here and used the ships' resources to create an electrical grid. If anyone ventured too far out, they wouldn't have access to those resources."

"How long were they gone?"

"Years," Ian said. "Then, one day, Quinn was back. Victor and Katie were still gone, but Quinn came back with a dragon and moved in with Donna."

"Did she say what happened to Victor and her mom?"

"Not really. She just said they died and didn't want to talk about it. But I know whatever happened out there was bad."

"Why do you say that?" Mateo asked.

"She was really different after she came back. I mean, she was 15, a dragon rider and hot as hell. But she wouldn't let anyone near her. I tried to give her a hug when I first saw her, and she pushed me away. There were guys that tried to get close to her and she wouldn't have anything to do with them. I had to kick some of their asses for calling her a cold fish or other stupid shit, because she shut them down."

Mateo smiled for the first time since entering Ian's cottage. "You're a good friend Ian."

Ian shrugged and squinted his eyes at Mateo. "I'm not going to have to kick your ass, am I? Is she ok over there?"

Now Mateo let out a short laugh. "Like you could, brother. But no, she's ok. I just needed some back story." He stood up and returned the jug of ale to the fridge, then squeezed Ian's shoulder as he walked to the door. "Sorry I woke you. See you over at Donna's later."

After Mateo was gone, Ian went to his window and looked over at Quinn's cottage. It was dark, all but the fairy lights she had around her bedroom window. So, he knew she was sleeping. He decided to try to catch a couple more hours himself, before he had to take his patrol and went back to his couch.

CHAPTER 23

Quinn woke the next morning, and the sun was already shining brightly through her window. "Oh, crap!" she exclaimed. She jumped out of bed and threw on some clothes, then braided her hair. She was late. She told her grandmother she would be there at daybreak. She scrubbed her face clean, brushed her teeth, then put on her shoes and flew out of her cottage. She found Titan waiting for her at the edge of the trees. She ran to him and jumped on his back. "We're late buddy! Take me to Gram's house."

When they landed a few minutes later, Quinn saw organized chaos. Dragons were everywhere. Two of them were hitched to a huge wagon, heading away from the cottage moving toward the free store. The wagon was loaded with furniture and boxes. She saw Kendra standing on the porch, directing some of the community members carrying boxes to another wagon waiting on the side of the house. As she approached the porch, she could hear Charlie hollering. "Ian, get some help moving that hutch! I'm going to whop your ass if you break that glass."

"I'm not going to break it, Ma," Ian answered. "Mateo, you want to give me a hand? Before my mom has a nervous breakdown."

Quinn cringed. Even Mateo had beaten her there. "I'm late," she told Kendra.

"Yes, you are. But we have everything under control."

243

Quinn stepped out of the way quickly, as Ian and Mateo carried out her grandmother's beloved hutch.

"Wrap that in a blanket before you lay it in the wagon," Kendra told them as they walked by.

"Where's my grandmother?" Quinn asked.

"She's at the new place," Kendra said, still eyeing Mateo and Ian as they wrapped the hutch. "We've already taken several loads up, so she's directing traffic there.

"How can I help?"

"You can go make sure those boys have that wagon packed correctly. Then make sure they get Apollo and Darcy hooked up correctly. We have a smaller wagon, with boxes almost ready to go. Once Sarah and Ian get off the ground, we can hook it up to your Titan and Yemaya."

Quinn nodded and went to check the wagon. She passed Ian and Mateo heading back to the house as she went. "Morning," Mateo said with a smile as he passed her. She found Sarah checking the hooks and reins on Apollo. "You know, I never gave a thought to how we were going to get everything down here, up there," Sarah said when she spotted Quinn. "It's freaking genius!"

"Well, we've had hundreds of years to perfect it. Just give thanks that the dragons love us and are so willing to help."

Quinn checked the hooks and cinches on Apollo to make sure they were secure. One over his neck, attached to the front of the wagon, one over his rump attached to the back. Satisfied that they were good, she moved to Darcy and did the same.

"Looks like this is ready to go," Quinn said, giving everything in the wagon a tug to make sure it was secure. "Let's get a tarp over the wagon."

Together, Quinn and Sarah pulled a long black tarp tight over the top of the wagon, securing it by tying it to hooks underneath.

Ian and Mateo joined them. Each carrying a glass of lemonade. "Ready?" Ian asked Sarah.

"As I ever will be," she said. Ian guzzled down the lemonade and handed the empty glass to Quinn.

They each mounted their dragons, and Ian looked over at Sarah. "On three," he told her. They counted down together, then Darcy and Apollo lifted up together. They flew steadily to the cliff and headed east toward Donna and her new little cottage.

"That's so cool," Mateo said watching them fly away.

"Yeah. I guess we're up next. Is Yemaya willing to do that?" she asked him.

"She is. I think she's excited about it."

Quinn nodded and looked down at her feet. "Mateo, I need to apologize to you."

He moved toward her and put his finger under her chin to lift her face to his. When her eyes met his he just shook his head. "Quinn, please don't. You have nothing to apologize for."

She held his gaze and nodded. "Ok."

"Ok," he said, then stepped back and clapped his hands together. "Let's get this wagon loaded!"

Titan and Yemaya landed just as Ian and Pax were unloading the last of the wagon Ian and Sarah had taken up. Donna spotted Quinn and ran to her. "I'm so glad you're here!" she told her as soon as Quinn jumped to the ground.

"I'm so sorry I was late, Gram," Quinn said. "The addition is perfect! It looks like it's always been there."

"Jacob does good work," Donna said with a nod. "Come in and see it from the inside." She started dragging Quinn to the cottage. "I think I've brought too much. Amelia keeps telling me that everything will fit, but I just don't see how."

"If Amelia says it will, then it will."

Quinn saw a little arched doorway off the living room. She walked through it and saw Amelia and Sarah hanging pretty pink lace curtains over the windows. They already had her bed placed against the back wall with little tables on each side. She had her matching quilt thrown over the top of it.

They heard Ian shout from the other room. "Where do you want this hutch?"

Amelia rolled her eyes. "I'll show them. You show Quinn your little bonus."

She moved out of the room and Donna grabbed Quinn's hand. "Come see this!" Next to the bed was another arched doorway leading to a large closet. It had rods to hang her clothes and lots of extra room for storage. There was another doorway, that opened into the bathroom at the back of the cottage.

"So, if I have to pee in the middle of the night, I don't have to walk all the way through the house," Donna laughed. "Wasn't that thoughtful?"

Quinn nodded. "It's great, Gram!"

Quinn spent the rest of the day with her grandmother, helping her unpack and organize. Donna had arranged for Kristen to bring up food from the community kitchen for everyone that helped with the move, and Amelia had baked her famous apple pies.

As everything started winding down, and the sun was starting to set, Quinn stood at the kitchen sink washing dishes and saw Mateo enter the room. He walked up to her grandmother. "Miss Donna, I'm going to head home now. I just wanted to say thanks for feeding us. And if you need any help getting things moved around, just give me a holler."

"You're a sweet boy, Mateo." Donna gave him a kiss on the cheek. "Thank you for all your help today. Here, take some pie." She handed him one of the containers already packed up with the pie.

"I will not say no to that," he told her and took the container. "I was wondering if I could steal Quinn away for a minute. I need to show her something."

"Mateo, I'm up to my elbows here," Quinn said

Donna grabbed a towel and handed it to her. "Go, I can wash my own dishes."

Quinn took the towel and started drying her hands.

"It'll be quick. I promise," Mateo said and dragged her outside with him.

They started walking to where Yemaya was waiting for him. "Your grandmother thinks I'm sweet," he said and gave Quinn a little shoulder bump.

"My grandmother is a feeble old lady. She probably has dementia."

Mateo laughed out loud. "Your grandmother is as sharp as a whip and there is nothing feeble about her."

He reached in his pocket and pulled out a folded piece of paper. "Here," he said.

She opened it and saw he had drawn a picture of her little cove with the swinging bed on the far side of the inlet. "Wow. This is a really good drawing," Quinn said. He had captured it perfectly. He even drew in the flowers surrounding the inlet. And she had to admit, now that she saw the swinging bed, she wanted it.

"I told you I'd draw it up for you," he told her. "What do you think?"

"I think I want it!" Quinn told him.

He smiled at her, and she cocked her head to look up at him. "So, you're an artist, a musician, a dragon rider, and a fighter. What other talents do you have Mateo?"

He wiggled his eyebrows at her. And gave her a mischievous smile. "Stick around and you might find out. I am quite a catch, Quinn."

"I guess I forgot to add humble to the list."

He took her hand again and led her around to the other side of Maya to avoid the curious eyes he knew were staring out the windows at them.

"I'm going to keep trying this, until you get used to it, Quinn."

He leaned in slowly and kissed her lips. He was gentle and quick.

247

"Mateo," Quinn started and before she could say more he put a finger over her lips and shook his head.

"Quinn, I'm interested in you. It's only getting stronger, not going away. And I think you are too."

She took his hand away from her mouth and looked at him. He saw some sadness in her eyes but no fear this time. "If there was anyone that I could be interested in, it would be you," she shook her head. "But I can't."

"You can," he said. "And you just said all I need to hear."

He leaned in and gave her another quick kiss. "I'll see you around."

She watched as he and Yemaya lifted off and headed for the cliff. After a few minutes, she turned back to the cottage and saw her grandmother sitting on the porch in one of her rocking chairs. As Quinn approached, Donna pointed to the other chair.

Quinn sat and just waited for her to start talking. "That is one good looking man," Donna said finally.

"He is," Quinn said.

"But he doesn't seem to be vain or arrogant about it. Like some are. He's just comfortable in his skin." When Quinn stayed quiet Donna kept going. "He seems to have taken a shine to you."

"A shine? Really?"

"Honey, I watched him watching you when you weren't aware he was. He looks at you the way any hot-blooded woman would want a gorgeous, sexy, good man to look at them."

Quinn shook her head. "But I don't want that, Gram."

"Stop." Donna cut her off before she could say any more. "Honey, you've spent so much time deciding you don't want what your mama had that you haven't let yourself try to have something different. Quinn, look at me."

Quinn raised her eyes to her grandmother's and saw tears streaming down her face. "My Katie was weak and spoiled. Your daddy was a good man and loved her beyond reason. He enjoyed taking care of her, and you. He never saw anything but sweet in my Katie. I raised her, but I must not have done a very good job because she had no spine. And when Kurt died, she couldn't survive without him. That's why Victor was able to do what he did. You went through something no child should ever have to go through. But you survived. And now you are a strong, independent woman. You have good friends who love you. You are a dragon rider. And I hate thinking that you are going to grow old and never know what it's like to be loved by a good man. You'll dote on and spoil the children of your friends, but you'll go home alone and never know what it's like to hold your own. I can't bear the thought of you closing yourself off to something wonderful because you're afraid. Be brave, Quinn." She stood up and wiped her eyes on her sleeve. "Now I'm going to go see to the rest of my guests." She leaned over and gave Quinn a quick kiss on the cheek. "If you have a brain cell left in that head of yours, you'll follow that boy and let him show you what he has to offer." She turned and went back into her cottage.

Quinn ran from the porch and jumped on Titan's back. They lifted off, but she didn't follow Mateo. She had Titan land at the entrance to the trees and went home alone.

CHAPTER 24

The next morning, Donna and Amelia were overseeing the construction of Donna's new greenhouse. They were actually sitting in the gazebo, drinking coffee and watching the construction.

"Where is your Josh this morning?" Donna asked.

"He's helping Thomas get some crops planted. He said our rainy season is coming early this year and wants to get the corn and wheat in."

"If anyone knows, it's Thomas."

"Jacob asked me to start working with him, learning the community books," Amelia said.

Donna turned to face her. "Oh honey, I think that's brilliant."

"Really?" Amelia asked. "I'm kind of excited about it. But nervous too."

"There's no one that could do any better than you. You've always had a head for numbers. You're honest, trustworthy and reliable. You would be who I want to take over the community accounts."

"Only help." Amelia corrected.

Donna nodded. "For now," she said. "But Jacob is in his 80s. He's not going to be able to keep doing all he's doing forever. Someone needs to know how to take it over and not one of his kids has a head for that. They can design and build like no one else, but trusting them with the community finances?" she shook her head.

"Why do we call them Jacob's kids?" Amelia asked. Looking back at the builders. "I mean, none of them are really his kids. He's never married or had children. And most of them are definitely not kids. Tad is in his 50s."

Donna laughed. Jacob just collected kids. He took four of them in when they lost their parents in the Chartin war. The older ones started working with him when they were teenagers. Then they had kids, and they started working with them. They all just became 'Jacob's kids'."

"I thought Quinn would be here today," Amelia said.

"No, we had a little talk last night and I figure she's still licking her wounds."

"A little talk?"

"Well, I talked. What do you think of Mateo?"

Amelia smiled. "He's dreamy, isn't he."

Donna laughed. "He sure is. But that's not exactly what I meant."

"I like him a lot. So does Josh. He's funny, quick witted, smart. He's always there to help anyone. He was the first person to bond with a sea dragon, so that has to say something about his character. He risked his life to rescue the baby dragons. Molly loves him, so I know he's gentle. And I think he's absolutely perfect for Quinn. I see the way he looks at her. I think he'd be good for her."

Donna nodded. "Me too. I just wish she'd figure that out."

Mateo was up at dawn. He got ready and left his cottage and shook his head. This being a morning person was the pits. He walked past the community kitchen but just grabbed a pancake and rolled it up and ate it as he walked to the free store. He had already gathered the wood he wanted, now he just needed the rest.

He and Yemaya made trip after trip, to get everything to the inlet. He thought about getting Ian or one of the other guys to give him a hand. But it didn't seem right.

This was Quinn's private place. She needed to keep it that way.

Mateo worked most of the day, and when he was done and satisfied that it was just right, he stood with Yemaya and admired his work. "I think she's going to like it, my girl," he said to Maya. "It's better than the picture I drew. Now we just need to get her down here to see it."

Yemaya sniffed at Mateo's neck and made a huffing noise. "You're right," he laughed. "I should probably shower first."

A little while later, Mateo figured he timed it so Quinn would be just about done with her archery class. He'd drag her down to see her spot, then maybe talk her into having dinner with him. When he got to the archery range, he found Meg teaching Quinn's class. He waved her over. "Where's Quinn?" he asked.

"Well hello to you too, Mateo," she said and put her hands on her hips.

He smiled. "Sorry. Hey, Meg, how's it going? Why are you teaching Quinn's class?"

"I have no idea. Quinn told Ian that something came up and she asked him to take her classes today. But he had patrol and then promised his mom he'd help her out at her place this afternoon. So, he asked me. And being the super nice person I am, I said ok."

"What came up?" he asked.

"Mateo, you know what I know," she told him.

"Ok, I'll keep looking. If you see her, tell her I need her to come find me." He turned and started walking away.

"Bye, Mateo," Meg called after him.

He just raised his hand and kept walking. Meg chuckled a little. "Atta girl, Quinn. Keep him guessing." Meg didn't imagine any other woman ever had. Damn, he looked as good walking away, as he did walking toward you. She shook her head and got back to her class.

When Mateo approached Charlie's cottage, he saw Ian up on the roof hammering down some shingles.

"Hey!" Ian hollered down at him.

"Hey. You need some help up there?" Mateo asked.

"Nah, I'm just about done. Be down in a few."

"Do you know where Quinn is?"

"No, why?"

"Meg told me she asked you to take her classes. I thought maybe she told you what she was doing."

"Correction," Ian said. "She slid a note under my door. She just said something came up."

"She's probably at her grandmother's, helping her settle in," Charlie said as she came out of the house. She was carrying a basket of clothes to hang on her line. "Have you been up there yet?"

"No, ma'am. I'm going there next. Thank you," Mateo told her. "Catch you later, Ian."

Charlie watched him walk away and had about the same reaction as Meg. Their little Quinn was a lucky girl.

"What' cha looking at Ma?" Ian asked as he came up to stand by her.

"Nothing, baby." She gave him a kiss on the cheek. "Thanks for taking care of the roof. Why don't you go in and make a sandwich?" She turned and started hanging out her laundry.

When Mateo reached Donna's cottage, he heard banging and laughing coming from the back, so he bypassed the front door and went around to where the noise was coming from.

He saw Donna standing next to a little greenhouse clapping and jumping up and down like a young girl.

"Oh, Mateo, look at that!" she said when she saw him. "Come give me a hug, there's no one here to hug me."

"Well, I'm here, Miss Donna. I'd hug you," Tad said.

"You're all sweaty. And you need to finish hanging that door."

Mateo grabbed her in a big hug and smiled at Tad.

"My very own greenhouse," Donna said. "I'm going to have so much fun in there." She pulled back and looked at Mateo. "So, what brings you to my door today?" she asked him.

"I was actually looking for Quinn. I thought she might be up here with you."

Donna's eyes sharpened just a bit. "No, I haven't seen her at all today."

"Hmm. Maybe I'll run by Amelia's and see if she's seen her."

Donna shook her head. "Amelia was here with me most of the day. She was headed over to Jacob's when she left. I don't imagine that she's made it home yet."

She saw concern cloud Mateo's face. "Do you know where she might have gone?" he asked her. "Meg took her classes today and no one has seen her."

Donna took a deep breath. "She has a little hideaway on the shore, just west of the town."

Mateo nodded. "Yeah. She's not there."

"You know about her hideaway?"

"Yes, ma'am, I do."

"Don't call me ma'am, it makes me sound like someone's grandmother." She sounded offended but smiled as she said it.

He smiled back. "Yes, ma'am," he said with a laugh.

"You were raised right, weren't you, boy."

"I like to think so Miss. Donna."

She nodded. "Better. Why don't you come inside for a minute. I might know where she is, but I need a cold drink."

He nodded and went to the back door of the cottage. He held it open for her and followed her in.

"Have a seat, Mateo." She went to her little fridge and pulled out a pitcher of lemonade, then two chilled glasses. She filled them and sat but took a long deep drink before she started.

"I don't know how much you know about my Quinn. She keeps to herself and doesn't share much."

He took a drink and smiled. "That's an understatement," he said. "I know more than she thinks I do. I've asked around."

Donna nodded. "I'm not going to tell you her story. It's hers to tell or not. But I'll tell you some of mine. My daughter Katie was not a great mother, but we all loved her and when she married Quinn's dad, then had Quinn, we all thought she would get her happily ever after. But then he died. The next year, she married a son of a bitch. His name was Victor. And he sure didn't like me. I noticed how unhappy Quinn was and I started making noises about bringing her to live with me. Katie was a woman grown and free to do as she pleased, but Quinn was only a baby, really. Just turned 9." She shook her head and took another drink. "Well, no sooner than I made those noises, I got a note on my door. It was from Quinn. I could tell he made her write it, and was probably watching as she did, and telling her what to write. It said that Victor and Mama and her were going on an adventure. They were going to explore their world and find a special place just for them. I ran to their cottage, but they were gone. I figured it would just be a matter of time before Katie got tired of roughing it and would come home. She wouldn't like living off-grid, with no lights or running water. But after a few weeks, they didn't come home and I got scared. We sent out search parties but never found them."

Donna looked up at Mateo. He was looking back at her with kind eyes. "That must have been so hard for you, Donna. I can't imagine what you went through. But then Quinn did come back, alone, right?"

"She did. And next to the day of her birth, it was the happiest day of my life. The rest of this story is not mine to tell. But what I will tell you is that sometimes, when Quinn gets in a mood, or something is bothering her, she flies Titan out to that place, where they lived. I think each time she goes, it's to try to get her head around what happened to her there."

"Do you know where it is?" Mateo asked. His eyes went sharp.

She nodded, never looking away from him. "I've been there once. She flew me out there so I could put flowers on my daughter's grave for her birthday. But only once. And I don't know that I could find it on my own, if I were to try."

Mateo leaned forward and took Donna's hands in his. "Can you try to tell me the way?" he asked.

"Just follow the mountain range west for several hours. You'll see the riderless dragons' lair, and you keep going for another 20 minutes or so. You'll see the mountain range start to go off in a couple different directions. Follow the original range to the right and go up. You'll come to a plateau on the far side. Theres a little lake being fed by a waterfall and nestled in the trees is a cottage. Or more of a shack really. That's where he took them. And that's where she goes when she disappears."

Mateo stood up. "Thank you, Miss Donna." He squeezed her hands and leaned down to kiss her cheek.

"Mateo," she said before he could reach the back door. "She may not be happy that you found her."

He smiled and winked at her. "I know," he said and walked out the door and called to Maya.

CHAPTER 25

Quinn floated in the little lake and just let everything she was feeling float with her. When she arrived that morning she was so mad! Just mad at everyone. Mostly her grandmother for her little pep talk. She made her feel weak, and worthless because she didn't have a man in her life! But she was mad at Amelia, too, for finding Josh, and being so damn happy and in love. It felt like suddenly her best friend was shoving what she could never have in her face, and she resented her for it. She was mad at Ian, for no reason at all, just because he was easy to be mad at. And she was mad at Mateo for making her want what she swore she would never have. She stood on that stupid mountain top and just screamed until her voice was hoarse. When she couldn't scream any more, she picked up every rock and stick she could find and started throwing it at the cottage. When she couldn't find anything else to throw, she walked over to the three gravesites. Victor didn't have a stone on his, but she knew exactly where she buried him. She began stomping on his grave, screaming at him and stomping on the ground. She was aware that she probably looked like a mad woman having a major tantrum, but she didn't care. There was nobody out here to see her. Today was the day she would get it all out. Today was the day she would decide what happened next in her life.

When she finally wore herself out screaming and stomping around, she just let herself flop down on the ground.

"You were a monster, Victor," she said quietly. "You took my childhood, my innocence and my safety away for no other reason than you could. You had to prove how powerful you were. You raped me and used me and hurt me, just because you could. You tried to take away any chance of me having a normal, happy life." She wiped a tear away. "Well fuck you, Victor. You have had this power over me for too long, and I'm taking it back. You're dead, you son of a bitch! And I'm not. You are nothing. And you don't get to rule over me anymore." She turned to her mother's stone. "And fuck you too, Mama. You knew what he was. You knew what he was doing. And you never tried to stop him. You could have saved us, but you never even tried. I will never be like you. I will never roll over and let someone I love be hurt. You didn't deserve me. And you sure as hell didn't deserve Jackie." As soon as she said his name, the pain in her chest came. She lay down over his grave and let herself cry it out. "I'm so sorry, baby brother. I'm so sorry you didn't get to see what could be. You and Glory would have been magnificent. You were such a bright light, even being brought into such horrible darkness. But I'm going to make you a promise right here, right now, baby brother. I'm going to live for both of us now. I'm going to let your light shine through me. I hope you're riding your Glory, wherever you two are now. Flying through the sky, free and strong."

She sat up and saw Titan inching slowly toward her, looking at her with caution. She smiled at him and stood up. She walked to him and put her arms around his neck. "Sorry, buddy. I had myself a little freak out, didn't I?" He nuzzled her and gave her his special purr. "I think I'm done now," she said. "But I'm going to take a dip in the lake for a bit and cool down." She took off her clothes and dove in.

She watched as the sun started to set and pulled herself out of the lake. She walked to her clothes and her bag where they lay on the shore. But instead of getting dressed, she reached into the bag and found the little torch and matches she kept there. She walked to the front of the cottage, lit the match, used it to light the torch, and threw it through the broken window. It only took a few seconds for it to ignite everything inside, and a few more minutes for the entire structure to erupt into flames.

That's how Mateo found her. Naked, standing in front of a huge structure fire, her hair loose and flying in the wind. She was staring into the flames as if in a trance. For a minute he feared she was going to walk into it. He jumped from Maya's back and ran to her, stepping in front of her, grabbing her arms and forcing her to look at him instead of the fire.

"Quinn, what are you doing? Are you ok?"

She looked into his green eyes and his beautiful face and smiled. "I am. You found me." She sounded a little dazed.

"Yeah, I found you." He started running his hands up and down her arms. "You're wet, are you cold?" He started to pull off his jacket to put around her.

Now, she laughed a little. "I'm wet because I went for a swim. I'm not cold because, big fire," she gestured over his shoulder to the flames.

"Yeah, big fire," he said, looking over his shoulder to make sure it wasn't coming near them. "Are you ok?" he asked again.

"I'm ok," she said.

"You're naked."

"Yes. I am."

Mataeo nodded. And just kept watching her. "So, is this some kind of ritual or something? Should I be naked too?"

He saw what he thought was amusement come into her eyes, and she cocked her head to the side. And started to nod.

"Yes. You should definitely be naked too."

She saw his head jerk back, and his eyes narrow suspiciously. She stepped closer to him and put her arms around his neck. "Get naked, Mateo," she whispered against his mouth. Then she jumped up and wrapped her legs around his waist because she knew he would catch her. As soon as he did, she devoured his mouth with a kiss. Passionate and urgent.

He might curse himself later, but right now, he had a beautiful, wet, naked woman wrapped around him and all he could do was respond. He lowered them both to the ground without breaking that kiss. As soon as she was lying down, she reached up and started pulling at his shirt. He pulled his arms out of the sleeves and left the shirt tangled around his neck, but when she started opening the button on his pants, he pulled back to look into her eyes. When hers opened and she looked at him, he whispered, "Be sure, Quinn."

She reached up and pulled the shirt from his neck and threw it. "I'm sure, Mateo." She pulled him back down and began kissing him again and went back to work on his pants. He broke the kiss one last time and rolled off her to kick off his shoes and finish removing his pants. He rolled back on top of her and looked into her eyes and smiled. "Well then, we're going to slow this down a little."

Before she could object, he burrowed into her neck, kissing and sucking, then going lower, taking his time with his mouth on her breasts while running his hands up and down her body, she arched her back and thought she was about to lose her mind. Then he went lower still. "God, you're sweet," he murmured. Quinn threw her head back and let out a little moan. She dug her nails into his shoulders and pushed herself harder against his mouth. She felt something building inside of her and she was afraid she was about to explode, Suddenly, he stopped and raised himself above her. He took her mouth with his as he entered her slowly, gently. Then pulling out again, each thrust grew a little harder, a little faster, a little deeper. Mateo felt it growing in her and held himself back. She was tight and wet, and only when she felt her body tighten around him and heard her let out a gasp, then a little scream, did he let himself go.

A little while later, she was curled up with her back against him and his arms tight around her. They were watching the dying fire.

"Quinn?" Mateo said softly.

"Humm?"

"You want to talk about what happened here?"

She smiled and rolled toward him. "Sure. Is it always like that?" she asked him.

He smiled and kissed her nose. "When it's done right," he said. "But not what I meant."

She sighed. "Yeah. I think I do. I think maybe you should know. Can we get dressed first?"

"Sure," he stood up and pulled her up behind him. She started to turn to get her clothes, but he pulled her back and kissed her. "I want you to know that I think you're amazing. I think I'm already halfway gone over you. And no matter what, I swear I will never hurt you or let you down."

She ran her hands through his hair and looked into his eyes. "I think I do know that, Mateo."

He nodded. "One day you won't have to think about it. You'll just know it."

A few minutes later they were both dressed and sitting cross legged next to lake, facing each other, with their knees touching.

As soon as Quinn started talking, he knew what kind of man Victor was. He didn't need the sociology or psychology classes to tell him he was a predator. He chose a vulnerable woman mainly because she had a young pretty little girl, and he began training her almost from the beginning. Isolating her, denying her anything she loved, rewarding her with little trinkets for what he considered good behavior and dealing out harsh punishment for anything he considered an infraction. The more Quinn talked the angrier he became. He had to keep reminding himself to stay calm. What she did not need right now was anger.

"When he brought us here, it just got worse. On my 11th birthday his gift to me was an upgrade to womanhood. That's what he called it," she told him. "Touching only. But it was ugly." She looked into his eyes.

He nodded. "Yeah."

"My mother got pregnant when I was 12. Up to that point he had never used his fists on me. Only on Mama. But he didn't touch her when she was pregnant with his child. But he touched me. He would punch me and throw me around. When I cried, he would pull my pants down and spank me. Then he'd rape me."

Mateo closed his eyes. "Jesus, Quinn."

She kept going. "Mama gave birth to Jack, and things got better for a while. But not for long. But he was just such a sweet happy baby. I really fell in love with him. Ya know?"

Mateo nodded.

"About a week after Jackie was born, a huge black dragon started coming around. She was beautiful and had little pink tips on her wings. I thought at first, she was there for me. To take me away. But it was Jackie, not me she was there for. Victor thought it was cool that she was there, but I could tell he was a little afraid of her. He kept his distance. But God, I wanted her to be mine." Quinn smiled as the memory formed in her mind. "Not long after she showed up, I was sitting on the ledge, holding Jackie, and she approached us, and rolled an egg to me. I realized she wasn't for me, but she was giving me her baby. I was so excited, and suddenly terrified. I rolled it back to her. I told her that if Victor found out, he would take it from me. He would kill anything that I loved. It was like she understood. She took the egg in her mouth and looked at me. I knew I was supposed to follow her." Quinn stood up and looked down at Mateo. "Will you come with me?"

He nodded and stood. She took his hand and led him around a bend in the mountain. When they reached the other side, she pointed to a small cave. "That's where Titan was hatched," she told him, with a smile on her face. She sat down next to the cave and Mateo sat next to her, keeping her hand in his. "I was sleeping one night, and I heard her calling out. I slipped out of bed and sneaked out the open window. The door creaked, so I knew he'd hear if I left that way. She saw me and led me to the cave. Titan's little black head was just poking out of his egg. I reached in, and pulled the egg out, and watched him hatch in my lap."

"What was her name?" Mateo asked.

"Glory," Quinn answered. "Not much changed over the next few years. Victor focused more on my mother, probably because I stopped fighting back. I think he liked the fight. But he never said anything about Titan. He mostly ignored him. But as Jackie grew, and Glory and he bonded. I think he was proud of that. That his son would be a dragon rider. Titan grew too, and I knew once he was two, I could ride him. I only had to wait a little longer, then I would take Jackie and Titan and Glory would follow, and we would run to Gram. I knew if we were there, she would keep us safe."

"What happened to them, Quinn?" he asked after a long pause.

She seemed to snap back from her memory and started talking again. "The day came. I had snuck out and practiced riding Titan. It was as natural as breathing." She smiled. "I woke Jackie and put my finger over my lips to quiet any questions. I grabbed his jacket, and my bow and arrows, the only thing he had let me keep. It had been a gift from my father, but I didn't tell him that. I was a good shot, so he thought it might be useful. Anyway. I grabbed it and we snuck out. Titan and Glory were waiting for us in the field. I told Jackie we were going on an adventure. And he was so excited! We started running. Before we reached them, I heard the door of the cottage slam and he was hollering at us. I picked up Jackie and practically threw him on Titan's back. But before I could get up there, he was on me. He yanked me back by my hair then punched me in the face. 'Where ya going, girl?' he asked me. 'You trying to run away with my son?' He punched me again, and I heard Titan let out a growl. I was dazed from him hitting me, but I saw Jackie jump from Titan on to Victor's back and I froze. "No, Dad!" Jackie yelled. "We're just going on a venture. Don't hurt my Quinn."

Quinn let her tears fall and pulled her knees up to her chest. She looked at Mateo and smiled through her tears. "That's what he called me. It was always, my Quinn. Victor just reached up and grabbed him and threw him to the side. He never even looked at him. He just threw him so hard. And you know the gravity here is light. So, Jackie flew through the air for what felt like forever. Victor didn't watch him, but I did. I saw him hit his head on a rock and fall limp. And as soon as I heard Glory's moaning cry, I knew he was dead. I don't know if you've ever heard the cry of a dragon when they lose their rider. But I think it must be the saddest sound in the entire universe. I was watching Jackie's little limp body and before I knew it, Victor was coming toward me with a dagger. It was a long nasty blade, and I knew he was going to kill me. The weird thing is, I was ok with that, Mateo. I was dizzy, and grieving, and I just lay there, waiting to feel the blade. But instead, I heard something else. Glory had come up behind him and bit down. She tore him apart, shaking him like a rag doll, and spat him out. I didn't even realize my mother had grabbed the blade. All I could see was Victor and all that blood."

Mateo saw what Maya and Leo had done to the Chartins, so he understood. But he couldn't understand how a traumatized young girl could ever recover from that. From all of it. A lump had risen in his throat, and he couldn't speak, so he just reached over and pulled her to him. She came into his arms and laid her head on his chest and kept talking.

"Kendra, told me, years later, that I was probably in shock. I was shaking, lying on the ground watching the blood flow. My mother was screaming at me, telling me to look at what I had done. Telling me it was my fault. Glory was screaming. And suddenly Glory just stopped, and then Titan screamed. That's what snapped me out of it. I looked over and saw my mother stabbing Glory. Over and over in her head. Then she turned toward Titan. I screamed at him to fly away, but he wouldn't leave me. I jumped up, grabbed my bow, and shot my mother through the heart. She was dead before she hit the ground."

"Oh, baby," Mateo choked out. He pulled her into his lap, and she curled into him. He started rocking her while she finished her story.

"I think I passed out after that. But when I woke up, Titan was lying next to me in the field. He was watching over me. I got up and together, we dug four holes. And together we buried the four bodies. When we were done, I climbed on Titan's back and we went home, to my Gram."

She took a deep breath and went on. "I don't remember a lot of those first few days, back at the community. Gram told me that I didn't speak. I showed up on her doorstep covered in blood. I had two black eyes and blood dried under my nose. And in my hair. She brought me in and ran to Charlie's. She told her to get a doctor and ran back to me. She said that Titan never left her front yard. Not once. He wouldn't eat or drink until he saw me almost a week later."

They sat in silence for a few minutes. Mateo figured she'd had enough for one day. They had all the time in the world to talk about how she recovered.

"So, today was the day you decided to burn it all down?" he asked.

She smiled and moved in closer to him. "Yeah," she said. "Today was the day."

He tightened his hold on her, and he felt her body relax as she fell asleep in his arms. "Good," he whispered and kissed her head.

At some point during the night, Mateo had laid them both down. He woke and had his back pressed against the mountain, and had Quinn pulled close against him in the front with her head cushioned on his arm. He could feel her breathing soft and even. He didn't want to move her and wake her up, but he had a screaming pain in his shoulder, and his left arm was numb. He opened his eyes and saw the dragons had moved closer. They were lying side by side, about three feet away, watching them. He tried to move his arm out from under Quinn's head, so he could get some blood flowing, but as soon as he started moving, she turned towards him and looked into his eyes.

"Hi," she said and smiled up at him.

"Hi." He forgot all about the pain in his shoulder as he looked down into her beautiful face. She looked relaxed with a little smile on her lips, her dark brown eyes, clear and full of fun.

"You ok?" he asked her

She nodded. "But I think we should see if we can still do it right."

Mateo smiled and leaned in for a kiss. Soon, clothes were flying and the dragons got up with a huff and turned their backs on them.

CHAPTER 26

Donna was drinking coffee in her little kitchen, worrying about Quinn. She didn't regret what she told her, but she probably should have been a little gentler. Her girl was so strong and fierce, sometimes she forgot that inside she was still fragile. She heard a knock at her front door and opened it to see a crowd. Amelia and Josh, Sarah and Kenji, Meg and Ian were all standing on her porch. Even Molly was there sitting in her yard with concern in her eyes.

"Sorry to just drop by like this Miss Donna," Ian told her.

Donna nodded. "It's ok, Ian, I'm worried about her too. And no, I haven't seen her since the move in."

"What about Mateo?" Meg asked. "He's missing too."

"He came looking for her yesterday. He was going after her," Donna said.

"After her where?" Josh asked.

Donna looked at Amelia with a knowing look.

Amelia nodded. "They've been gone an awful long time, Donna."

"The Chartin threat is still out there," Josh said. "We're going to organize a search. Can you give us an idea of where to look?"

Donna felt a little clutch in her chest at the mention of the Chartins. She looked up to the sky, and her eyes narrowed, then she smiled. "Look to the sky," she said.

They all turned and followed Donna's gaze. They saw Titan lowering through the clouds, with two riders on his back.

Titan circled the field, and Mateo leaned forward and whispered in Quinn's ear. "Looks like we have a welcoming party."

When Titan set down, they slipped from his back. Mateo put his arm around her shoulders, and took her hand with his free hand, pulling her close. They started to walk toward the little cottage. "I was hoping for a little time with my grandmother," Quinn said quietly.

"You'll get it," Mateo said and kissed her head.

Tears filled Donna's eyes as she watched them walk as a unit toward her. Then she let out a laugh when she heard Sarah say, "See, told you guys they were off somewhere hooking up."

When they reached the porch step, Ian said. "You guys had us worried."

"Not me," Sarah said.

"Where's Yemaya?" Meg asked.

"I sent her home by sea. She'd been on land too long and was missing it," Mateo told her.

"Sorry, everyone," Quinn said. Then looked at her grandmother. "It won't happen again."

Donna nodded and smiled at her baby. "Why don't you all come in, I'll make some breakfast."

"Thanks, Donna, but I think we're going to give you two a little time," Mateo told her. "We all have work to do."

"I don't," Ian said.

"Yes, you do," Mateo said without looking at him. He gave Quinn a kiss and leaned his head against hers. "I'll see you later."

She nodded. "Yeah, you will."

He gave Donna a little nod and a smile, then turned and grabbed Ian around the neck in a head lock and started leading him away.

Meg called after them. "Ian, we have island patrol after lunch."

"I'll be there, partner," he hollered back. Then she ran toward the cliff and jumped down with a hoot and a holler.

They all started moving out, Kenji and Sarah walking away hand in hand, she to the baby dragons and he to work on the power grid.

Josh gave Amelia a quick embrace and headed off to work with Jacob on some traps they were setting for the Chartins when they arrived. She stepped in front of Quinn and looked her in the eye. "Are you ok?"

Quinn grabbed her dearest friend in a fierce hug. "I'm ok, Ami. We'll talk later, all right?"

Amelia nodded. "You bet your ass we will," she said and Quinn let out a little laugh. "I'll be home all afternoon. Come see me."

Quinn nodded again. "I will."

Amelia turned and gave Donna a kiss on the cheek. "I'll see you tomorrow and we can have one of our little gossip sessions?" she asked.

"You bet your ass we will." Donna repeated her words and made Amelia laugh.

When Amelia walked away, Quinn turned and walked into her gram's open arms. They just held each other for a long time, then Donna pulled back and looked into Quinn's eyes.

"You're really ok?" she asked.

Quinn nodded. "I'm really ok. I burned it all down Gram. And I never have to go there again."

"Good," Donna said. "Let's go in and talk."

Arm in arm they walked into the cottage and closed the door behind them.

When Mateo and Ian reached the opening to the trees, Ian asked, "You want to come up and talk?"

Mateo nodded and they continued to Ian's tree house. Ian started up the stairs but stopped when he saw Mateo standing on the ground, staring up at Quinn's place. Ian sat on the steps and waited. He saw Mateo's fists clench, and his breathing started coming fast and hard.

Every emotion Mateo felt, and held back while Quinn was talking last night, suddenly came bubbling to the surface. He couldn't keep it in any longer, and he wished with every fiber of his being that the bastard was still alive, just so he could kill him again.

Ian watched as Mateo started pacing back and forth muttering to himself. He couldn't make out everything he was saying, but he caught some words. "Sick, twisted motherfucker" was coming out a lot. Suddenly he stopped and swung around to look at Ian, rage coming out of every pore in his body and his eyes flashing. "Did you know?" he asked. His voice low and dangerous. "Did you know what that sick bastard did to her?"

Ian kept his body relaxed, but ready. He shook his head. "I suspected. But no. She never talked about it with me."

Mateo started pacing again. "I need to hit something. I just need to beat the shit out of something!"

Ian lowered his head and looked at the ground for a minute. Then he let out a long sigh. He looked back at Mateo and shrugged his shoulders. "All right," he said and stood up. He started back down the stairs. "Come on," he told Mateo when he reached the ground.

"I'm not going to hit you, Ian."

"Damn right you're not! Come on."

He led Mateo around to the back side of the giant tree, and Mateo saw he had a full blown gym back there. He just stopped and stared at everything. He had a punching bag hanging from a branch on a long rope. There was a wooden bench, with a bar holding stones ground into round discs with holes through the center. And another bar hammered into the tree. It looked like he used it for pull ups. "Good metabolism, my ass," Mateo muttered.

Ian went to a chest and opened it and pulled out some boxing gloves. He tossed them to Mateo. "Here, put these on."

Mateo caught them and started checking them out. "How did you get these?" he asked. "How did you make all this? How did you know how?"

"I watched an old movie on the AROE when I was a kid. It was about a boxer," Ian told him. "I was a scrawny little thing when I was a kid. And I watched that movie over and over. I dragged my mom and dad with me to watch it and told them I wanted to do that. Dad and I figured out how to make the bags and mom learned to make the gloves. I told Jacob what I wanted, and he carved the stones for the weight bench. I pulled some bars out of the ships, and voila," Ian said. "Every couple years, my mom will make me a new pair of gloves for my birthday. So, I have a few sizes in here if those don't fit."

Mateo pulled them on, and Ian started lacing them up for him. "These are great. You were lucky in your childhood, Ian. I mean, I know how hard it is to lose a good dad. I lost mine too, when I was young. But you and me, we were lucky."

Ian went to stand behind the punching bag and grabbed it from behind and gave a little tug to make sure it was secure. "Yeah. We were."

Mateo went to stand on the other side of the bag. "Quinn wasn't."

Ian looked into Mateo's eyes. "No," he said. "She wasn't."

Mateo nodded. "I guess there are monsters in every corner of the fucking universe."

Ian braced himself, and Mateo let loose. Punching, kicking, tackling the bag. He let the rage and the need to kill out. Ian didn't think he had ever seen anyone unleash so much. He felt every impact as he held the bag. He figured he was going to have a whole chest full of bruises before Mateo got it all out.

Both men lost track of time. It could have been minutes or hours. But Mateo started slowing down. His arms were limp, and his legs ached. After he threw his last half-hearted punch, he just put his head against the bag and tried to catch his breath. Ian peeked around the bag and saw tears streaming down Mateo's face.

"He beat her," Mateo said in a whisper. "He punched her. He whipped her and he raped her." Ian dropped his head to the bag opposite Mateo's. He knew. She never told him anything, but he always knew. And hearing Mateo say it, confirm it, broke his heart. He reached around and gripped Mateo's arms and Mateo gripped his in return. No more words were needed. They stood together, both leaning against the bag between them, arms gripped around it and wept for the woman they both loved.

Mateo pulled himself home, thanking God that he didn't run into anyone that wanted to talk. He didn't think he had it in him to make conversation. He went straight to the kitchen and guzzled about a gallon of water. He looked out his back window and saw Maya resting in the sea right off his shore. He stripped and left his clothes where they landed on the kitchen floor and walked to his shower. He stood under the running water until it started to cool, then washed quickly. When he was done, he slipped some clean clothes on and went out to Maya. He climbed on her back and had her swim to Quinn's little hideaway. He climbed down and went to lay on the big thick mattress. He was asleep before his head hit the pillow.

A while later he felt Quinn lay beside him and he pulled her close. "Thank you, Mateo," she said and gave him a soft kiss. She curled closer to him, and they slept.

Ian showered, changed his clothes and was only a few minutes late meeting Meg in the field.

"I didn't see you at the Kitchen for lunch," she said, so I brought food. She held up her bag.

"Thanks," he said. And held up his own bag. "I brought dessert."

"Nice! Well, let's ride, cowboy!"

They jumped to their dragons and flew to the island. Pax and Delainy, their group's newest dragon rider bonded with Bandit, saw them coming, so they mounted their dragons and headed up. As they passed in the air, Pax gave them a thumbs up, to indicate nothing to report and flew home. Ian felt a little pang of guilt. He had let Pax take control of Delainy's training and hadn't even checked in to see how she was doing. He made a mental note to spend some time working with her. There were actually several new riders he needed to spend time with. He wondered if it was just evolution or something else that had so many dragons choosing new riders.

When they landed, Meg pulled a blanket out of her bag and spread it on the ground, then grabbed her scope and started surveying the Chartin community. Ian pulled out two containers of apple pie he had left over from Donna's moving party and sat down on the blanket.

"Doesn't look like anything's going on over there," Meg said and collapsed her scope. She turned and saw Ian digging into his pie. She came and sat by him just watching him eat. "I thought you said that was dessert," she said.

"It is," Ian answered between bites.

"Dessert is for after a meal."

He looked at her. "Why?"

"I don't know, it's like a rule or something."

He picked up her container and handed it to her. "I'm not much of a rule follower," he said.

"What the hell," Meg said and sat next to him to dig in to the pie.

275

When Ian was done, he set his container aside and pulled out his scope. He started watching the Chartins. He didn't understand what they were doing. Why had they left these twenty or thirty behind and why weren't they coming back for them. What were they waiting for?

In the more than twenty years they'd been there, they never built a settlement. They lived and slept in their ships. He only occasionally saw them fish or cook. There were no little Chartin monsters running around. So, they weren't reproducing or building anything. It had been weeks since the ship left. He couldn't imagine that they weren't coming back for them. Meg ate half her pie then put it aside, and looked at Ian, as he watched the Chartins. He really was a cutie with his dark caramel colored skin and lanky, muscled body. He had full lips, and light brown, almost amber colored eyes. His hair was just crazy. Long and sticking up everywhere, like he never gave it a thought.

"You should let me cut your hair," she told him.

"Nope," he said without hesitation, and without looking at her.

"Come on! I'm actually really good at it. I've trimmed Mateo's hair, and Josh's."

"Nope," he repeated.

"I could just give it some shape. I could even put it in rolls for you, or braids. Or if not, just shape it and give it some style."

He lowered the scope and looked at her. "My hair has style. It's my style."

She just smiled and shook her head.

"Why do you want to chop at my hair?"

She shrugged. "Because I'm good at it. That's how I made my living before I joined the military. I was a hairdresser and got my barber's certificate too."

He studied her for a long minute. "Nope."

"Fine," she huffed out and picked up her scope. "Keep going around looking like a scruffy, unkempt ruffian."

Ian let out a short laugh. "Ruffian? What the fuck is a ruffian?"

"I don't know. Scraggly."

"Hmm. I'll think about it," he told her.

She smiled. "I'll wear you down. And when I'm done, you'll thank me."

"We'll see."

The rest of their shift was uneventful, and when their relief came, they mounted their dragons and flew back to the community. Meg to the shore, and Ian to the upper field.

When Meg slid from Leo's back, she lowered her head to his. "I'll be back after dinner. Gather the rest, and we'll work tonight. I feel like something is coming." She kissed his snout and went to her cottage to change before heading out to the community kitchen to meet her friends for dinner.

When Meg arrived, she grabbed a dinner plate and located her friends at their regular table. She slid in between Ian and Sarah. She wanted to talk about the traps they needed to set and the training taking place to ready the community for what she knew was an imminent battle. But when she looked around the table, she saw Kenji and Sarah deep in conversation about The Dive. Josh and Amelia were only half listening to them, probably thinking about their upcoming wedding. And Mateo and Quinn were sitting close enough to each other that no air could pass between them and giving each other such smoldering looks that Meg was surprised they both didn't erupt into flames. Ian just had his head down, shoving food in his face. She let out a frustrated sigh and did the same.

After dinner, Meg met with the other sea riders and their dragons at the shore. They had added four more dragons and riders so with Mateo and Maya, they were up to eleven now. Of course they were nowhere to be seen tonight.

"Ok, let's get to work everyone," Meg said and mounted Leo.

While they rode and practiced maneuvers in the sea, Meg was relieved to see Ian doing the same with his riders in the sky.

CHAPTER 27

Meg went to bed that night frustrated and angry. Mateo had never shown up for their work out with the dragons. She understood he was in love and wrapped up with Quinn, but he had obligations to the team. The other riders. He rode the alpha female of the sea dragons, and he needed to be there to help organize.

She was pissed at Quinn, Josh, Kenji and Sarah too, but Mateo had the misfortune of living next door to her. So, the next morning, she was pounding on his door. When there was no answer, she rolled her eyes and walked in.

She only grew angrier when she found he wasn't home. So, she left and decided to wake him up at Quinn's.

When she reached the tree houses, she bumped into Quinn as she was coming down her stairs.

"Good morning!" Quinn told her.

"Morning," Meg mumbled back. "Is Mateo up there?"

"No. Why? Is something wrong?"

"What's wrong is I can't find him."

"Did you check down at the ships?"

"Why would I check there?" Meg snapped back.

Quinn saw the fire in Meg's eyes now and was concerned. "You left dinner early last night. I forgot," Quinn said. "Why don't you come up and have some coffee and I'll fill you in."

Quinn turned without waiting for a response and went back up her stairs. After a brief hesitation, Meg followed her.

She followed Quinn to her little kitchen and watched as she went to heat the percolator on her stove.

"You left before the conversation switched to community safety last night," Quinn told her.

"Community safety?" Meg asked.

"Yeah, Ian said he was feeling itchy. He thinks we need to start making plans for the Chartins' return. Mateo said he was feeling the same way. I think we all are, actually." Quinn brought two cups over to the table and motioned for Meg to sit. "So, Kenji started talking about a grid he was working on. An electrical grid around the ships. We know those ships are going to be their primary focus, so our number two priority is to protect them."

"Number two?" Meg asked. "Why is that number two?"

"Because human life has to be number one, Meg."

"Right," Meg mumbled. "Why didn't they come get me? I know a little about military strategy."

"Mateo said he was going to fill you in today. But he knew you'd take the sea riders through drills last night and felt that was important. So, Ian, Sarah and I went up with our dragons while Mateo, Josh and Kenji went to the ships. We saw you working with the sea riders. I figure we were all doing what we needed to do."

Meg nodded and took a drink of her coffee.

"You came over here on a rampage," Quinn said. "Why?"

Meg shrugged, feeling a little like an ass.

"Are you angry about me and Mateo, Meg?" Quinn asked. "I mean, I know you two are close. But you said there was nothing romantic between you."

Meg almost choked on her coffee. "No, God! I am definitely not interested in Mateo, or jealous of you and him, if that's what you mean."

"Good," Quinn breathed out. "That would make things a little awkward."

"Yeah, but no," Meg said. "I'm happy for you two. I just thought..."

"You thought he was up here playing house with me, instead of attending to his duties."

"Playing house?" Meg laughed. "Yeah. I guess I did."

"There is nothing more important than protecting what we have here, Meg," Quinn said. "And we all know that."

"You're right. And I'm sorry I jumped to conclusions. Where were you heading out to?"

"I was going to go over to Amelia's. She and my grandmother are meeting a few of the others to work on healing balms."

Meg stood up. "I'll let you get to it."

"I'd rather not," Quinn said. "Do you have time to knock me on my ass a few times? I haven't trained in hand to hand for a while."

Meg looked at her and smiled. "Quinn, there is nothing I would enjoy more."

A few hours later, Meg limped to the field to meet Ian for their island watch. Quinn had developed some good moves and had definitely improved. She got a couple good hits and kicks in and Meg was feeling those. But she felt a keen sense of pride too. And she felt more relaxed. Nothing like a good fight to get out some frustration.

When she and Ian got to the island, Meg spread her blanket and pulled out her scope. Ian told her he was going to go gather some crystal. He wanted some larger cuts that could be forged into weapons. When he returned a little less than an hour later, he had two bags full. He sat next to her on the blanket and started sorting through them.

"Aren't you worried that you are going to deplete these mountains?" Meg asked him.

Ian just looked at her for a minute. "What do you mean?"

"I mean, back on Earth, people would mine for silver and gold, and they would deplete their mines. Pretty soon there was no more. Or oil fields, would run dry, because they would deplete the fields."

"That's because money ruled there," Ian said. "At least that's what I learned in my AROE classes. People were greedy, and the more they took, the more they wanted. We don't work that way here. We only take what we need. Besides, it would take thousands of years to even put a dent in these mountains." He went back to searching through his bags. "And once the Chartins are gone, we can go back to exploring the southern continent. There are islands even bigger than this one. Hundreds of them."

"Really?" Meg asked. "Hundreds?"

"Yeah. The early settlers did a lot of exploring. There are maps, with locations of crystal mountains. Lakes, different types of plants and trees. They had areas where new settlements could be built. I can show them to you sometime if you want."

"Yeah, I'd like to see those."

He nodded and smiled. "Found it!" he said and pulled a huge chunk of crystal out of his bag and handed it to her. "Here. I got this for you."

She took it and couldn't take her eyes off it. "Oh, God, Ian. This is gorgeous! It looks like a castle." She ran her hands over it. It was probably 10 pounds, 10 inches long, about 6 inches wide and over a foot tall. It had peaks on top that looked like towers. "Thank you!"

"You're welcome," he said. "I thought you could put it in your back window. When the sun hits it, it will send a rainbow of color into the room."

"I love it," she said. She looked over and saw he was putting all his other crystals back into his bags. "You know, all of our friends have hooked up."

"Yeah, I noticed that," he told her.

"They're probably wondering when we will."

He looked at her. "When we will what?"

"Hook up, dummy."

"Oh." He had no answer to that. "Ok."

"We should probably have sex, and just get it over with," she told him.

He raised his eyebrows. "Just get it over with. Well, that's the most romantic thing I've ever heard, Meg."

"Oh, give me a break. You're a guy."

"I am," Ian agreed.

"We are both healthy, attractive and unattached adults. I just thought we could have some fun. Since all of our friends are getting regular nookie."

"Nookie?"

She gave him an exasperated look. "If you're not interested that's fine. I've never seen you with a woman, so I figured you are single and free. If I'm mistaken, that's ok. Or if you're just not interested, then no harm, no foul."

"Meg, I'm interested. You just caught me off guard."

"Good," she said. "Think about it and let me know what you decide." She picked up her scope and focused it back on the Chartins.

He just stared at her for a few minutes and stood up. He leaned down and took her scope and pulled her to her feet. "I don't have to think about it. But let's try this first." He grabbed her waist and pulled her close. He saw the surprise in her eyes and attacked her mouth with his. It was fast and hard and demanding. She melted right into it and put her arms around his neck.

When he pulled back, he rested his head on hers. "Yeah, this could be fun," he said.

"How long till our shift is over?" she breathed out.

They both heard a strange noise coming from the Southern shore and turned to see a small ship, all black, with two sets of propellers on top of it. It was lowering down to the Chartin community. "What the hell is that?" Meg said and pulled away from Ian to grab her scope. "It's like a helicopter. It almost looks like a Black Hawk. And not much bigger than one," she told him.

Ian grabbed his scope and watched the ship. It was midnight black, oval in shape and much smaller than the other Chartin ships. It had no markings on it and only one window in the front of the vessel. It didn't look like any helicopter he had seen in pictures or movies. Except for the propellers on top.

"We need to warn the others. Get some more riders out here," Ian said.

"Yeah. Why don't you take Darcy and go get Mateo and Pax."

"You should go," he told her. "You and Leo would be less conspicuous in the water."

"No way, cowboy. I'm staying. I might see something you could miss."

Ian narrowed his eyes, offended that she thought she was better at surveillance, but before he could argue a hatch opened in the ship and stairs dropped down. Five Chartins exited the ship. They were obviously Chartin, but they had shaved most of the hair from their bodies. They had beards, and some facial hair but they were definitely better groomed than any of the others. They had thick hair on their heads and were as tall and muscular as the group that began gathering around them. But they were dressed in some kind of uniform. Almost military-looking. It put Meg on alert.

"Look, Ian, we don't have time to argue. I'm trained in this. You know the community. And no one is faster than Darcy. Please, fly over there. Alert them. Then get Mateo. Have Pax or someone get Josh. We need his eyes out here. Then come right back."

"I don't want to leave you here alone, Meg. What if they see you?"

"They won't. I promise."

He only hesitated a minute. "Ok. But if they do, haul ass out of here," he told her. "You better be here when I get back."

She lowered her scope and looked into his eyes. "I'll be here."

He nodded and called Darcy.

Meg didn't take her eyes off the activity on the shore of the southern continent. They were having a deep conversation with a few of the long-term Chartins and the five newcomers. She could tell from the body language that those guys were in charge. She'd trade a year of her life to hear what they were saying over there. She saw two of the new guys walk back to their ship. They emerged a few minutes later, each carrying two large black canvas bags. Meg recognized those bags immediately. She knew exactly what they were. She focused in on them and saw the writing she knew would be there, on the sides of each bag. "Oh shit!" she said.

Ian didn't think he had ever flown so fast. He hated leaving Meg there alone. But he knew a stubborn woman when he saw one and she wasn't going to leave. He had Darcy set down near the ships. He knew that Mateo, Kenji and Josh were going to be working there today. He just prayed they were still there.

He saw the hatch open and the stairs down on Rap*ture*, so ran there and jumped in. They were all there, including Brent, Shawn and Sarah. They all turned when they heard him enter. Sarah jumped up when she saw his face.

"Ian! What's wrong?" she asked.

"The Chartins, another ship just landed. Smaller and different than any of their others. Five in military uniforms got off and they're planning something."

"Where's Meg?" Mateo asked.

"She wouldn't leave. She's still on the island watching them. She told me to get you and Josh."

Mateo jumped up. "Let's go."

"Should I get Apollo and follow you?" Sarah asked.

Ian shook his head. "No, I need you to alert everyone. Just in case they invade today. Get over to the clinic and let them know, then gather the sky riders. Tell them to be at the ready. Shawn, I need you to get the sea riders together at the shore. Wait there and we'll send word if we need you to come."

Kenji and Sarah watched the riders mount, with Josh behind Ian on Darcy, and they lifted off. Kenji gave Sarah a kiss and told her now might be a really good time for a drill. They could see how the community reacted and how quickly everyone could get to their posts.

"Yeah," Sarah agreed.

"I'm going to get Apollo, can you get to the clinic and let them know what's going on? They should probably ring the bell."

Kenji gave her one last kiss. Then they each headed off in different directions to run the drill.

When Ian, Mateo and Josh reached the island, they found Meg exactly where Ian had left her, standing alert with her scope, watching the Chartins.

"Any activity over there?" Ian asked her.

She shook her head. "Not yet," she lowered her scope and looked at Josh. "But something's coming. You need to see this." She handed him her scope. "Look over at the shore in front of the ship," she told him. He raised the scope as did Mateo and Ian.

"What are those?" Ian asked.

"Property of USA?" Mateo said and lowered his scope. "How?" he asked her.

"Those are military. US military. Special Forces or Navy Seals," Josh said.

"Yeah," Meg said. "MIB's. Military inflatable boats."

"From Earth?" Ian asked. "How is that possible?"

Josh shook his head and took another look through the scope. "I have no idea. But we need to find out. Because the ship came from Earth too."

"What?" Meg asked.

"Before I came to Grooms Lake, I was working at NORAD, trying to come up with ships to evacuate Earth," he said. "That is one of our designs. It was a transport ship. Housed on a larger one."

"A larger what? Ship?" Mateo asked.

"Yeah. They wanted a couple of those on each ship in case they needed it to get down to a planet or use as an escape for any important passengers."

"So, there could be a larger ship up there?" Ian asked.

"I don't know Ian. Yeah, I suppose there could be."

"Well, that's just great," Mateo said.

CHAPTER 28

W hile the group on the island were watching the Chartins, Kenji and Sarah were meeting with some of the community leaders. The drill was extremely disappointing. The riders knew exactly what to do when they heard the bell, however, the community did not. There was some panic, people were unsure where to go or what to do. They realized that most of the community had been trained in weapons, hand to hand and defense. But no one had any specific instructions on where to go or what to do when the attack came. The only silver lining was that most everyone did come out and meet in the upper field. Kenji realized they still had a lot of work to do to get these people ready for an actual battle.

"How could they have military gear from Earth?" Ian asked again.

"I don't know Ian. My concern is, if they have those boats, what else might they have?" Josh said.

"Like what?"

"Weapons, night vision, radar, scanners. Who knows what else," Meg said.

"Could they have stumbled on Earth at some point?" Mateo asked. "Maybe raided it, after the volcanoes erupted? All life on the planet was destroyed but under all the ash, buildings, equipment and weapons could still be there."

"There's no way to know," Josh said.

"We could take one of them hostage. Like we did with Altvi," Mateo said. "Question him and find out."

"I think we should just observe for now," Josh said. "We don't need to take any unnecessary risks."

"Agreed," Meg said quickly. "It's too risky, Mateo. We have no idea what technology these guys have. And if there is a ship in orbit, they could have the ability to survey us. If they have communication ability and warn them we're coming, it could be devastating."

"So, we just sit here and do nothing?" Ian asked.

"No," Josh said. "We watch and learn. Any information we get can only help us prepare for what is coming."

Ian and Meg returned to the community to organize new island rotations and brief the community leaders on what they had learned. Josh and Mateo would stay until their relief arrived and would instruct them on new island protocol. It was decided that two dragon riders, one from the sky and one from the sea would take a rotation together, and each would bring a military or security person with them.

Pax and Shawn took the next rotation with two of the soldiers from *Destiny*, Ty and Daniel, behind them on their dragons. Once they were briefed, Mateo and Josh mounted Maya and headed back to see what needed to be done there.

For the next few days, Meg spent every waking moment working. She held classes, did island patrols and ran drills with the community. She assisted the medical teams, moving equipment, medication and bedding up to the dragons' lairs. It was decided that they would take the wounded there for treatment. There were four caves, one large one that would be used for the children. It went deep into the side of the mountain, and had a back cavern, where they set up bedding rolls, toys, water and snacks. They figured that they would be far enough away from the entrance that the kids wouldn't be heard if there was any crying or noise making. They put lanterns in for lighting and knew that it would not be seen from the entrance. The three smaller caves would be for medical teams to set up for the wounded.

When she had time to sleep, she stumbled, exhausted, into her cottage and fell into bed. She managed to think about Ian, a little more than she should. That kiss on the island was better than she expected. And she dreamt about it every time she closed her eyes.

She knew he was working as hard as she was, with his classes and working with his riders and planning community security. Every now and then they would pass each other, and they shared a look promising more and she hoped he fell asleep dreaming about her and that kiss as well. It gave her some satisfaction thinking that his nights might be as restless as hers were.

On the fourth day, Meg was heading to her cottage after a particularly long and brutal day with back to back defense and kickboxing classes. She was hot, sweaty, cranky and hungry. She wanted to shower and sleep for a week. Just before she opened her front door, Sarah called out to her. "Hey!" she called out and came running up to her. "I'm glad I caught you. I was just heading back to The Dive. I know you're beat, but can you come with me? I promise I won't keep you long, but I really need to show you something."

Meg was about to say no, but she saw the look on Sarah's face and found herself saying "Sure" Instead.

Sarah linked her arm through Meg's and began leading her toward the eastern shore.

"This place is so special," Sarah said, "its people so kind and generous. I just can't imagine that Gaia would have created such a place, just to have it wiped out by a brutal, ugly race like the Chartins."

Meg stopped walking and looked Sarah in the eye. "They're not going to get wiped out," she told her. "If they are truly planning an attack, and we don't know that for sure, but if they are, we will fight. We will protect this place and its people. Worst case scenario, we lose. The Chartins take the ships, which we believe is all they want. But not all will be lost. They will rebuild. Find new sources of energy and go on."

Sarah saw the fierceness and determination in Meg's eyes and nodded.

They continued walking in silence until Sarah said. "So, what's up with you and Ian?"

Meg let out a short laugh. "Nothing, yet. But, we're getting there.

"He's a good man. A gentle heart. And probably a future leader of this place. I see the way he looks at you. You could do worse."

"Yeah." Meg nodded. "I know. He's special and has the weight of this world on his shoulders. I thought at first, we could just fool around, you know? Just relieve some tension. But the more I'm around him, the more I think it may be more. I'm not sure I'm ready for that."

Sarah laughed. "That's always when it happens."

When they rounded the bend to the eastern shore, Meg just stopped and stared. The Dive was built in to the side of the cliff, as if it had always been there. A large structure made with logs and an open front with a huge veranda overlooking the sea.

"Oh, my God, Sarah, it's incredible! How did it go up so fast?"

Sarah shook her head. "I have no idea. I swear Jacob has magic hands and a whole tribe of elves. One day I'm talking to Jacob about what I want and the next, he's creating it.

"It's beautiful!"

When they reached the steps leading up to the veranda, Meg saw Amelia and Quinn setting pots with flowering plants on each end of the enormous bar. There was no other furniture inside just the long bar running across the back of the building. It was dark wood and polished to a gleam. But she could imagine it with tables and chairs, a band playing on the stage off to the right of the room. She heard pounding coming from behind the bar and saw Kenji and Josh pop up with smiles. "We got it," Josh said.

"You've got running taps," Kenji told her.

Sarah clapped her hands and ran behind the bar. "Perfect! I can't believe this is really happening!" She gave Kenji a big kiss then turned and gave one to Josh too. "Thanks, you guys! Jacob is going to put in a long mirror on the wall back here," Sarah told them. "And I have shelves coming for glasses and cabinets for the wine. One of Jacob's kids is working on bar stools to line the bar, and the veranda."

"It's going to be the most popular place in the city!" Amelia said. "And here comes our celebration!"

Mateo and Ian entered carrying bags with wine, ale and glasses. Once the ale and wine were poured, they sat on the steps of the veranda and raised their glasses in a toast. "To the Dive," Kenji said.

"And to Sarah for imagining it!" Mateo added.

They clinked glasses and sat watching the sun set.

Once the sun had set and the glasses were empty, talk turned to the Chartins and the community. Drills were being held daily. It seemed that everyone now knew where they were supposed to go, they had their locations, either with units to fight, or hide. There had been no more activity on the Southern continent. The new ship and its five passengers were still there, but no others had arrived. They talked about the traps they were laying and the weapons that had been made and were still in production. Finally, they all headed home with the promise that in three days, when they all had the evening off, they would meet at Josh and Amelia's cottage. They wanted to host their first dinner party.

Meg understood that life went on, and everyone wanted to live as normal a life as possible, but business openings and dinner parties seemed a little premature until the Chartin threat was dealt with.

She stood under scalding hot water for a long time after she had shampooed her hair and washed. She was hoping that the hot water would wash away all the tension in her body and she might actually get a good night's sleep. She got out of the shower when the water started running cooler and wrapped herself in an oversized towel. She wandered into the kitchen to pour a glass of water, and her body went on alert when she saw a shadow sitting on her living room sofa.

"Hey," The shadow said, and she relaxed when she realized it was Ian.

"Hey back," she said. "What are you doing here, Ian?" she pulled the towel closer over her chest.

He stood slowly and walked into the kitchen. He kept walking until he was right in front of her. Then he reached out and grabbed her and lowered his mouth to hers quickly, demanding more. She let go of the towel and put her arms around his neck and the towel dropped to the floor. He never broke the kiss but walked her backwards until she felt the counter against her back. Then he put his hands on her waist and lifted her to the counter. As soon as she was sitting, he dropped his head and trailed kisses down her neck and across her chest, then took her breast in his mouth. She wrapped her legs around him and leaned her head back against the wall and plunged her hands into his hair to urge him on.

Suddenly there was urgent pounding on the cottage back door. Ian broke away and dropped his head to her chest. "You have got to be kidding me," he breathed out. "Give me a minute to go kill whoever that is."

The pounding continued and they heard Gill's voice calling out. "Meg! Meg, are you in there?" Ian pulled away and picked up her towel. He threw it to her and went to the door. Meg jumped down from the counter and as soon as she had the towel secured around her again, Ian opened the door.

"Ian?" Gill sounded surprised to see him. Then he saw Meg coming up behind him wrapped in a towel. "Oh. Sorry to, uh, interrupt, guys, but there's a boat in the water. Pax told me to come get you and Mateo and get you to head to the island asap!"

"The Chartins launched a boat?" Meg asked.

"Yeah. One of those inflatable ones. There are eight of them in the boat, heading west."

Meg nodded. "Give me a minute to get dressed and I'll call Leo," she said as she headed to her bedroom to throw on some clothes.

"Did you alert Mateo?" Ian asked.

"Yeah. I went there first," Gill told him.

"Ok. Get back to the island. We're right behind you."

Gill nodded and looked over his shoulder to catch a glimpse of Meg. Ian closed the door in his face and turned to see Meg coming out of the bedroom in khaki green pants and a tight grey t-shirt carrying a pair of black boots. "I'm going to call Leo and get to the island," she told him.

He nodded. "I'll get Darcy and meet you there" He started to walk to the back door but stopped and went back to her. He grabbed her and planted one last kiss on her mouth. And whispered. "We're not done here."

She grabbed him and brought him in for another kiss. "No, we're not even close to done here," she said.

He nodded once, then went out the back door, leaving it open behind him.

When Meg left her cottage, she found Leo already waiting for her on the shore. She mounted and headed to the island. She could make out the outline of Darcy and Titan in the sky ahead of her, and Yemaya in the sea. She lowered herself over Leo's neck and whispered, "Faster," and he picked up speed. When the island came into sight, Meg saw Quinn and Ian split up. Quinn turned toward the island and Ian turned out to sea, moving higher. Up ahead, she saw Mateo and Yemaya turn to follow Ian. There were several riderless sea dragons surrounding Maya and joined Mateo as he veered away from the island. She was torn between following Quinn to the island or following the guys out to sea, but when she heard a roar from the sky and saw Apollo coming in low with Sarah and Josh on his back, she opted to go to the island and see what was going on, and what needed to be done.

Leo and Apollo reached the island at the same time, and all their riders dismounted and went to Pax and Ty who were waiting on shore.

"Report," Josh told Ty.

"One MIB entered the water with eight Chartins on board," Ty told them. "They headed away from the island and toward the northern continent. Looks like they were heading to the far west. They're loaded with weapons, though. Guns, machetes. Looks like they have night vision."

Meg grabbed her scope and turned it toward the south. "It doesn't look like there's any other activity over there," she said.

"No," Pax said. "They blew up the one boat, and the eight launched. The rest of them went back into the ships."

"It might just be a scouting group," Josh said.

"Maybe," Meg said. "But I don't like it. Ian and Mateo went after them. I should follow them. Make sure they don't need back up."

Josh shook his head. "I had Gill wake the other sky dragon riders. They are going to patrol the shore to the west. They'll find them."

"Ian told me that we should stay here and wait for them," Quinn said. "They'll send word if they need us."

Meg blew out a frustrated breath and lifted her scope. She turned it to the northwest but couldn't see anything in the air or the sea. When she lowered it again she saw Leo in the water, looking at her. She could feel his impatience and concern. She gave him a quick nod. "Go," she said. He turned and raced through the water following Yemaya's path.

Ian stayed high in the air following the Chartins. He was relieved to see Mateo and the sea dragons staying far behind the boat. If they saw the dragons following them, they would think it was just a pod of sea dragons swimming.

He didn't like the fact that he was unarmed. But he wasn't really thinking when he ran out of Meg's cottage and called Darcy.

When the Chartins came within about 100 yards from the shore, they began circling back toward the east, following the shoreline toward the community. They passed by Quinn's little nook and kept going until they saw the ships, *Stonehenge*, *The Rapture* and *Destiny,* all lined up. The boat hesitated, getting a good look at them, then turned and moved back to the west.

They went on shore about 3 miles to the west of the community. Ian saw the other sky riders coming toward them and held up a hand to hold them off. He saw Mateo move further to the west with the sea dragons.

Ian landed on the cliffs behind where the Chartins were starting to make camp. The other sky dragons joined him there, and all pulled out their scopes to keep watch.

Mateo saw Leo coming in fast and wasn't sure if he was relieved or disappointed that Meg wasn't on his back.

They watched as equipment was moved from the boat to the shore. Then six of the Chartins started rolling out bedrolls and pulling out food from small boxes. Mateo could hear them laughing and talking, but he didn't have his interpreter device so he couldn't understand what they were saying.

Two of them went back to the boat and launched, heading back to the southern continent. Four of the riderless sea dragons lifted turned and began following the boat and shortly after, when the six left behind lay on their bedrolls, confident they were safe, five more dragons, lifted out of the sea and attacked

They swooped in and surrounded the Chartins. Mateo knew, without searching Maya's feelings, that they were extracting revenge for their baby dragons. He watched as the dragons, wings flapping began tearing into the creatures lying on the shore. But when blood and body parts started flying, Mateo turned away and led Maya back toward the island.

He saw that Ian sent the sky riders back to the community and lifted off. He knew he was heading back as well. To give report to those waiting.

CHAPTER 29

Amelia knew that the risk to the community was still high. She knew that the riders were still patrolling day and night. Others were stationed on the islands around the clock, and training with weapons, fists and martial arts continued.

She had put in time learning each of those. She hated every minute of it. But she did it, and Meg told her she was coming along. She put in hours cultivating herbs and helping the healers turn those into medicine.

She knew that every person in the community was worried and frightened and a part of her felt guilty for feeling giddy and happy and in love. She had never thought about making a commitment to another person. Never thought about spending her life with someone and building a family. And now, that seemed to be all she did think about.

Josh was everything she never knew she wanted. He worked hard in the fields, and still put in time with training, and teaching others to fight. He was strong and had a powerful warrior's body. But he was gentle, and kind and he looked at her like she was the most precious thing he'd ever seen. For the first time she felt beautiful and loved and taken care of. And at night when they shared their bed, he let her know how much power she had over him, when he lost control and took her with an almost uncontrollable urgency.

She had taken over the community accounts, and she loved the work. She felt like she had a purpose. And tonight, she was hosting her first dinner party in their home. And maybe they could talk a little bit about the wedding.

It was such a gift to have this group of friends. Meg and Ian, Sarah and Kenji, Quinn and Mateo. She thought this must be what it had been like on Earth. Couples who loved each other and shared dinners and outings with other couples. Well, Ian and Meg weren't there yet, but she saw the looks that passed between them, and she knew it was just a matter of time. She really wanted tonight to be perfect! It was unusual that each of them had the same night off, so they could spend it together.

Amelia had spent the day cleaning the cottage. fluffing pillows, shaking out rugs and setting out pretty little bottles with wildflowers she had picked herself. She made a big salad with vegetables she picked from her own little garden. And had a fruit salad chilling in the fridge with fruit she had picked, washed and arranged in a pretty bowl. Her table was set with her colorful stoneware place settings and a bouquet sat in the middle of the table in a vase she had bartered with one of the community artists for some balm she made for blisters and burns.

She had potatoes with some vegetables roasting together in the oven and had filleted and seasoned some fish with herbs and lemons. She would put those in once everyone started arriving.

She knew Sarah would bring wine, and Ian would bring some ale. She hoped that he would bring his little wooden flute and maybe Mateo would bring his guitar. They could dance and get a little tipsy and just enjoy being together. And maybe forget about the danger lurking across the ocean, for just a little while.

She heard laughter outside and ran to the door to see Sarah and Kenji walking across the meadow with Josh. Molly, who had been grazing in the meadow, went quickly to greet them, and they each took a moment to give her a rub and a kiss on her snout. She had grown so much. And was hardly limping at all. She didn't have the fear in her eyes anymore, and it warmed Amelia's heart to see her greet her friends with welcome and love instead of hiding and cowering like she did those first few weeks. Amelia was starting to have some hope that she might be able to fly. Molly would stretch her wings and run like she was getting up the courage to try.

If it weren't for the Chartins and the threat they held over them, life would be perfect.

When they reached the cottage Amelia welcomed them with a hug, Josh just scooped her up in his arms and gave her a kiss.

"I missed you," he told her.

"You were only gone a few hours."

"I know."

She laughed and he set her down. Sarah was looking around the cottage. "Wow! This place looks amazing, Amelia!. I can't believe how quickly you turned it into a home."

"Thanks. I loved every minute I spent on it." She saw Sarah was carrying two large bottles of wine and led her to the kitchen to put them in the fridge.

"It smells really good in here. And you look really happy, Amelia. So, does Josh. I'm so happy for both of you!"

"Sometimes it feels like a beautiful dream," Amelia said. "But it feels so right, and so normal."

"You're good for him," Sarah told her. "I've known Josh a long time. And I see a difference in him. He seems settled and happy and for the first time it seems like he found his place and his purpose."

Before they could say any more, they heard more voices in the other room and went out to see Quinn and Mateo had arrived followed closely by Meg and Ian.

Ian carried a large jug of ale and Quinn had a basket of bread that she and her grandmother had made that morning. And it looked like Ian had done something different with his hair! It was shorter and instead of standing up in crazy curls, it had been rolled into tight locks. Amelia walked up to him and ran her hand over it. "Ian! Your hair looks amazing! I love what you've done with it!"

He looked over at Meg and she just raised her eyebrows and gave him a smug 'I told you so' look.

They sat at the pretty dining table that Jacob had made and given them as a housewarming gift, set with Amelia's pretty dishes and had dinner. Compliments were given to the chef, and Kenji asked if Amelia could teach Sarah a few things. She elbowed him in the stomach, then laughed. "I'm hopeless," she said. "Thank God for the community kitchen."

They all helped clear the table, and poured glasses of wine and ale, and moved the little party outside where Josh had set up chairs and little tables in their garden behind the cottage. They had a pretty view of the orchards, and the cliffs.

"So, where are you thinking about having the wedding, Amelia?" Quinn asked.

Amelia looked at Josh and smiled. "We thought the cherry orchard would be pretty. It has plenty of room for everyone, and we could set up tents in the field next to it for people to eat and drink and dance, after the ceremony."

"That sounds perfect!" Meg said. "It's a beautiful spot!"

"We don't want to make any final plans until we have this conflict with the Chartins resolved. But we're hoping the blossoms will be in season."

"You have all the time in the world," Ian told her. "I can see you standing in the orchard, with an arch of cherry blossoms over you, saying your vows. It will be a perfect and peaceful day." Ian pulled out his little flute and gave Amelia a wink. He started to play a happy tune. Then suddenly stopped and sat up straight. A second later they saw Molly running to them from the outer field. Darcy, Apollo and Titan flew quickly to join them. They landed together in the field, and each let out a roar. A moment later Yemaya and Leo joined them. They heard the other dragons circling and calling their riders. Then they heard the bell.

"They're coming," Sarah said and squeezed Kenji's hand.

"Everyone needs to get to their stations now!" Ian hollered out over the call of the dragons. He grabbed Meg and gave her a fast hard kiss. "We have a date later. We have unfinished business."

"Damn right we do," Meg said. Then he ran to Darcy, and she went to Leo.

"I love you," Sarah told Kenji, then kissed him. "Be safe." Then she turned and ran to Apollo. Mateo and Quinn ran to their dragons' hand in hand and before they mounted, Quinn grabbed his face and pulled him in for a deep kiss. "Stay safe, don't be a hero and get yourself killed, ok?"

"Ok," he promised. "You too. Stay on Titan." She took a deep breath and nodded.

All of them lifted off, Mateo and Meg to their place in the sea, and the rest to the sky. Josh, Kenji and Amelia were left watching them.

"I've got to get to the ships," Kenji said and ran for the cliffs.

Josh tuned to Amelia and took her in his arms. "I love you. Get Molly and get to the lair."

She nodded and kissed him one more time. "I love you too. Come back to me."

He smiled and ran his fingers down her cheek. "Always."

Then he turned and ran to gather his weapons and meet his team.

Amelia grabbed her bag of supplies from the cottage, then she and Molly ran to Donna's cottage to help her gather what she needed and get to the lair.

Kenji met Jason at the ships, and they started laying out the electrical netting over the grass,

Charlie and a few of the others were handing out the electrical zappers to the men and women chosen to use those. Jacob was at the weapons hut passing out shields, daggers and the extra laser guns they had just finished.

The sky riders split into their groups and took position with their weapons, while the sea dragons and their riders did the same. The children and people chosen to defend them were leading them to the trees and the largest of the dragons' lairs. Medical personnel were already in the other three lairs, setting up supplies for the wounded.

Everyone in the community heard the sound of the ships as they approached.

Ian was posted above the dragons' lair and watched as four ships landed in the field. Two of the ships were replicas of the original ship that crash-landed on the southern continent. The other two he didn't recognize and assumed they were from other planets that had been invaded and stolen. As they started moving out of the ships, Ian saw they were carrying large guns at the ready and had huge machete type swords at their sides. They were moving slowly and looking for any kind of movement. Ian estimated that there were about 200 of them and figured they were just the first scouts. He pulled his scope out and looked toward the south. He saw that they were doing the same at the south end of the field.

They spread out and started moving in all directions away from the ships. When the first of the teams reached the cliff overlooking the community, Ian knew they saw The *Destiny*, *Stonehenge* and *Rapture*, along with all the housing and stores, the community kitchen and the clinic. He prayed that everyone had made it to their hiding places. that those cottages and buildings were all empty, but the Chartins didn't. One of them called out to the others and they started jumping down the cliff toward the city. As they did that, more exited their ships and followed them down. Some remained behind surrounding their ships. Ian felt a sinking in his stomach as he watched them. Those ships were three times the size of theirs. He knew they must hold thousands. And he knew they were outnumbered and outgunned. He took a deep breath and signaled for his riders to fly.

Kenji was in *Stonehenge*, and saw the Chartins jumping off the cliff, heading toward the city. He watched in horror as they just kept coming. There were hundreds of them. He saw some veer off and start looking in the cottages. They would find them all empty, and he hoped they would just keep moving toward the shore. About fifty others were heading towards the ships. He kept his hand on the switch that would light up the electrical net they had set up. He was waiting until all of them entered the area, and once they started getting closer to the ships, he flipped the switch.

He could hear them screaming and smell the burning and knew that most of them would be dead before their bodies hit the ground.

The ships were completely surrounded by the electrical net. And if any managed to get past it, they would have to come from above. The sea riders and their dragons were in the water, just off the shore, and they would be taken out with their weapons as soon as any touched the ship.

Mateo, Meg and the other sea riders were in the water, just on the other side of the ships. They too heard the screaming and knew that Kenji had turned on the net. They each took their laser guns and waited to see if any approached the ships from above. Then they heard the gunfire and the screaming and saw fire breaking out in the city.

Amelia and Donna were in the largest and deepest cave with the children, and the baby dragons. They went deep into the cave so that if any of the little ones cried out, they were less likely to be heard. There were two warriors hidden at the mouth of the cave with weapons to guard them.

There were healers and doctors in the three smaller caves. Standing by for any injured. There were archers in the tree houses watching to make sure no Chartins got through to the caves.

Ian and his riders flew over the Chartins' ship and began shooting at guards. Pax and his riders began doing the same at the other end of the field. The guards on the ground started firing their weapons at the dragons, but it seemed the dragons had a sense about the laser blasts and managed to maneuver around the streams. One by one the guards fell.

Sarah saw Josh and his team in hand to hand combat with some of the Chartins in the town. She signaled Ian, and they broke off and flew to assist in the ground battle. She saw a fire raging in the little furniture store and felt grief and anger. She had been in that shop just yesterday bartering for two rocking chairs for the back porch at the cottage. She flew in low and saw there was no way to shoot without taking a chance of hitting their own people. Ian flew next to her. "Get to Pax and Quinn," he shouted. "Make sure the fields are secure and send any good fighters back to help here."

Before she could respond, she saw him flip his leg over Darcy and jump to the ground. She saw several other riders do the same. She watched in horror as Ian pulled his sword and decapitated a Chartin who was getting ready to strike down one of Jacob's kids.

Ian reached down to give Samuel a hand up, and Darcy grabbed a Chartin coming up behind him with his gun drawn. She engulfed his upper body and started shaking. The Chartin was torn in half and Darcy spat him out and grabbed another, running away.

Sarah and some of the other riders turned and headed back to the cliff to help Pax and Quinn's team at the south side of the field. Then they heard the scream of a dragon, and knew a rider had fallen.

Kenji saw Sarah and Apollo rise up to the cliff, from the window in *Stonehenge* and breathed a sigh of relief. She was safe. For now. He had heard several thumps on top of the ship. He knew that some of the Chartins had made it to the roof, but the sea riders had shot them down, and he saw them fall to the ground and land on the net. If they weren't dead from the shot, they soon were from the electricity.

He hated being stuck in the ship. He wanted to be out with the rest of them fighting these monsters off and sending them to hell. But the net was his baby, and everyone said if adjustments needed to be made, he needed to be the one to do it.

Amelia could hear activity outside the cave, and now that the little ones were settled down and mostly sleeping, she moved to the front of the cave. "Any word on how it's going out there?" she asked one of the guards.

He shook his head. "They've brought in some wounded but didn't stay to say much."

"I'm going to see if they need any help." She jumped to the ledge next to the big cave and entered the smaller cave set up as a medical station.

Beth saw her enter and met her as she walked into the cave.

"How bad?" Amelia asked.

"We only have six in here. They have a few more in the cave next door. Mostly laser wounds from their guns. I don't know about the fourth cave, but Amelia, Jacob was wounded pretty badly. He has burns over most of his body. They set fire to his shop and when he ran to stop them, they threw him into the blaze." Tears came to her eyes, and she shook them away. "We're keeping him comfortable, but I don't know. It's bad."

Amelia nodded and grabbed one of the medical bags she had brought with her when they first arrived. She had set it inside the cave entrance, before going to help with the children. "Where is he?"

Beth pointed to the back of the cave and Amelia found him lying on clean sheets over a cot mattress. His face was unrecognizable, and his body was covered in herbal leaves and bandages. He was struggling to breathe, but he was sleeping through the pain, so she knew they had given him enough medication to keep him comfortable. She sat down next to him. She wanted to reach out and touch him, just to give him some comfort, but was afraid anywhere she touched would cause him pain.

She leaned close to his ear. "I hosted my first dinner party this evening, Jacob. We sat at the dinner table you made for my new cottage and sat out in the garden in the chairs you gave us as an engagement gift. Ian played music on the flute you helped him make when he was a little boy. You are everywhere in this community. Every home, every store, every building. You and your beautiful work will be here long after we are all gone. You are so loved, Jacob. If you can fight to stay, I will help you. But if you need to go, I will be here to help you do that too"

He opened the one eye that wasn't taped shut and looked at her. He smiled and took his last breath.

Amelia let herself grieve for a few minutes. She let the tears fall, and the memories of Jacob fill her. Then she took another sheet and pulled it over him and stood to go and help the others.

Meg and Mateo could hear the battle raging in the city. They looked at each other and no words were needed.

"Shawn," he said. "I need you guys to stay here and keep watch over the ships. I don't think any more are going to try to get to them right now, but if they do, take them down. Brett, Rob and Meg, we need to go see where we can help." Before anyone could say anything, the four riders lifted out of the sea and headed for the city.

Meg saw Ian fighting off a huge Chartin and leapt down from Leo's back to take him out from behind. Leo grabbed another running by and ripped him in half. Ian gave her a nod, and they turned back to back to fight the others closing in on them.

Josh was spent. He lost count of how many of these monsters he had fought. He had burns from the lasers that had skimmed his body, and cuts from the swords they wore.

So, when he saw the four sea riders arrive, and then saw four more coming from the air, he let himself breathe for a moment and say a quick and silent prayer that Amelia was safe. He saw a Chartin running toward him with his machete drawn. He stood and raised his gun, but before he could fire, Leo snatched him up and tore him in half and spat him out. The dragon turned to Josh and gave him a look that said, 'Pull it together man. Get your head back in the game.'

Josh nodded his thanks to Leo and turned to fire at another Chartin fighting Rob at his back.

Amelia stayed with the healers, helping as more and more wounded were brought in. She would occasionally move to the other medical caves, to check and make sure her friends and Josh weren't there.

Sarah watched as Pax, Micha, Alan and Quinn flew toward the battle. She turned to Jessie just as a Chartin came up from the side of the cliff; before she could reach for her weapon he drew his and fired at Jessie. He hit her directly in her stomach, then turned the weapon to Sarah. She started to leap out of the way and felt the heat and excruciating pain of a hit on her right side. Apollo leapt on the Chartin and ripped him apart. She saw him heading back to her and heard Jessie's dragon Sky, screaming in grief just before she lost consciousness.

Amelia left the smaller cave, where they had twelve wounded, and leapt back to the larger one. She heard a dragon's roar in the sky and looked up to see Apollo heading toward the lair. He was carrying Sarah in his front talons, and Amelia felt like her heart just stopped.

He landed on the ledge where Amelia was standing and laid Sarah gently on the ground in front of her, then backed away a little as other medicals came running to take her into the cave.

Amelia looked at Apollo and saw a single tear fall from his eye. "We'll do everything we can to help her, Apollo," she whispered to him. "I promise." Molly jumped to the ledge and stood by Apollo. She leaned her body against him and together they waited.

Mateo saw Ian fall face first after a Chartin hit him on the head from behind. His panic rose, as he realized he would never be able to get to him before the Chartin drew his sword and ended him. He put his head down and ran to tackle the beast about to end the man who had become his best friend. Before he took more than a few steps, he heard what he could only describe as machine gun shots. He hit the ground and looked as the Chartin took multiple shots and fell to the ground. He heard more shots being fired and shouts, calling out for everyone to hit the ground and take cover.

Mateo rolled over to his back and saw a man in full camo and military gear, holding an AK rifle, reach down to offer him a hand. When he raised the visor on his miliary helmet, he saw his brother, Zander.

He looked around and saw dozens of other soldiers either shooting at retreating Chartins or holding them at gunpoint and telling them to put their hands up, in their own language.

Mateo looked at his brother with his mouth hanging open.

Zander grabbed him in a huge tight hug. "Hey, little brother. Sorry we're late."

Josh had pulled himself to the side of the battlefield, he saw that he was near the community kitchen, and there was no fighting there. He thought if he could just make it inside, he could rest for a minute, then he could rejoin the fight. He was losing a lot of blood from multiple wounds, but he was alive. And he was going to stay that way. He was not going to leave Amelia and the life they were building together.

As he reached the entrance to the community kitchen, he heard the sound of gun fire, then what sounded like explosions coming from the upper field. He turned and saw a group of soldiers joining the fight. He let himself fall face first onto the entrance floor of the kitchen. He heard footsteps coming, and prayed Amelia would not grieve too long for him. He knew he was done. There was no way he could fight another one right now. He felt himself being turned over and when he opened his eyes he saw Christov Wagner looking down at him.

"How bad are you hurt, Josh?" Christov asked him.

"Christov? What the hell? Am I dead?"

"Not yet. But you're bleeding every fucking where." He turned his head and shouted, "Medic!"

"What are you doing here man?" Josh asked.

"Saving your ass," Christov said.

Kenji couldn't stay inside any longer. "Charlie!" he hollered. "I'm going out there." He shut down the net. "Once I reach the edge, and get past the net, turn this switch and reignite it."

"Kenji, no!" she said.

"I'm a fucking black belt in Karate," he told her. "I have a taser, and I can't stay here while my friends and my woman are out there fighting!" He opened the hatch to the ship and looked back at her. "Turn the net back on, once I'm clear." He jumped to the ground and started running. He heard the electrical field come back up, once he reached the outer edge, but before he could go any further, he heard a familiar sound of jet engines in the sky. He looked up and saw four ships enter the atmosphere and head toward the landing strip. He raised his hands in the air in a victory fist pump. "Yes!" he yelled and headed toward the battle.

Amelia was standing back letting the medical team work on Sarah, when she heard a sound coming from outside. She backed up toward the mouth of the cave and looked up. She saw four ships flying toward the field. They were exact replicas of *Stonehenge*, *Rapture* and *Destiny*. A sob escaped her, and she moved to Apollo and Molly who were still standing on the ledge, both looking up at the sky. "We're going to be ok now," she told them and threw her arms around Molly's neck and let herself cry with sobs of sorrow and joy.

Zander handed Mateo an AK gun that he had strapped to his back. "Let's round these bastards up and end this."

Mateo took the gun and nodded. He went to Ian first. He kneeled by him and saw a lot of blood on the back of his head. He was afraid to move him but put his hand on his shoulder. He heard him let out a low moan and start to move. Mateo let out the breath that he didn't realize he had been holding.

"I hurt too bad to be dead," Ian said, still lying face down.

Mateo laughed. "Yeah. Not dead."

"Did we win?"

"Yeah. We won. Don't try to move yet. I'm going to get a medic over here."

Ian didn't try to move. He just gave Mateo a thumbs up. "Not going anywhere dude."

When Sarah opened her eyes, she saw Kenji slumped in a chair next to her bedside, sleeping. She turned her head and saw Gaia sitting on the bed beside her. "Gaia?"

"Hello Sarah." Gaia smiled at her.

"Am I dreaming? It doesn't feel like a dream. Are you really here?"

"Yes, sweet girl. I'm here. The battle with the Chartins is over. You're safe now."

"Oh, God. I was hit. I don't remember anything after that. Jessie. Jessie was killed," she wrinkled her brow, trying to remember. "Apollo. He picked me up. I think he killed the monster coming for me."

Kenji, who had heard her voice, stood and went to her. He took her hand. "He got you to Amelia. You're going to be ok."

She nodded. "You're ok?" she asked him.

"Yeah. I am now."

She turned back to Gaia. "How are you here? What happened?"

Before Gaia could answer, she heard a familiar voice. "Hey slacker."

She turned and saw Christov standing in the doorway smiling at her.

"Oh, my God! Christov!" She struggled to sit up, and Kenji put his hand behind her back to help her. Gaia moved off the bed, to make room for Christov. He moved quickly to her and took her gently in a hug.

"Hey, English. You scared us," he told her.

"I can't believe you're here!" she sobbed into his shoulder. "Who else is here?" She turned to Kenji. "Where is everyone else? How many did we lose? What the hell happened?"

Kenji began filling her in.

The community lost 2,162 people during the battle, including Jessie, Jacob, Gill and Micha. Josh was in critical condition, as was Pax and a few others. A few dragons were injured, but none were lost. Ian had a severe head injury, but the healers from the Center were working on him and he was expected to make a full recovery.

Gaia had seen when the Chartin ships watched *The Destiny* approach Asteria. She had been keeping an eye on them for a while. But when she saw what they were planning, she had to intervene. They had technology that they had not earned. She began working on a new passageway from the Center to Asteria.

"But we left the Center over 250 years ago. How are you all still alive. How is it that you don't look any older than when we left?" Sarah asked.

313

"For us, you left 6 years ago," Christov told her. "Time works way different at the Center. Once the passageway was complete, it took us less than eight hours to get here."

"I guess I don't need to understand that," Sarah told him. "I'm just so glad you're here. Who else came with you?"

She learned that Zander and his team all came. The soldiers that had surrendered their weapons all came. Ben and Hank were there too. They would be there soon to check on her. Akemi and her father and children would be coming in a week with another ship of supplies and some gifts for the people of Asteria. Jewel stayed home with her daughter, Eve, the first Earthling born at the Center, and her newborn son Henry.

Pete and Ishaan, along with Akemi's best friend, Jenna, had taken *The Enterprise* and a crew from the Center and were exploring new galaxies, and according to Gaia, having the time of their lives.

"Were the Chartins destroyed?" Sarah asked.

They all turned and looked at Gaia.

After they took the remaining Chartins into custody, they led them back up to the cliff. Gaia told them that she was sending them back to their home planet. She destroyed their ships and would be hunting down any others traveling the universe. She would be sending them all back to Chartin and return any stolen ships back to the planets they stole from. She told them that they would be quarantined on their planet. She would cloak it and put a warning about the dangers to any space travelers in the area. They would be forced to create their own technology and learn to live with the resources they had on their planet. She even stripped them of the metal clothing, swords, shields and guns they had because they were all stolen from others. She had then surrounded them in a white beam of light and shot them up and out of the atmosphere. The small ship they had stolen from Earth would stay on Asteria for their use.

Gaia told them that she was cloaking Asteria as well. There are other, hostile species in the surrounding galaxies, those that were developed and had weapons and ships they had not stolen. But Asteria was peaceful and did not deserve to have their lives threatened by those that are not. So, they would be invisible to any who did not know where to look. And the passageway to the Center would remain open.

When Hank Ranson and Ben Logan slipped into Sarah's room they found laughter, tears, and it seemed everyone was talking at once.

"Hey," Ben said. "No one told me there was a party going on in here."

"Ben!" Sarah shouted. "And Hank, oh my God! It's so good to see you!" They both made their way to Sarah's bedside and gave her hugs and kisses on the cheek.

Gaia slipped out of the room and went into the quiet room next door. She saw Josh sleeping in the bed, and Amelia sitting on a chair she had pulled up to the bedside. She had her head resting on the side of the bed and was holding Josh's hand while she slept.

Gaia tipped her head as she looked at Amelia. She was lovely and Gaia knew she had a gentle and sweet nature. She waved a hand over Amelia's head to send her into a deeper sleep with soft dreams. Then she stepped up to Josh and placed her hand on his forehead.

His eyes fluttered open, and he looked confused when he saw her standing beside him. "Gaia?" he whispered.

She put a finger over her lips to keep him quiet and glanced at Amelia. He looked over and saw her sleeping. Gaia saw his features soften and saw all she needed to see in that glance. When he looked back over to her, she smiled.

"I never had the opportunity to talk with you when you arrived at the Center. I wanted to thank you for all you did, to contribute to the team, and the journey. You are precious to me, Josh, just as much as any of the others. You have the heart of a warrior and the soul of a dreamer. I need you to forgive yourself, as you have been forgiven by all you

315

think you betrayed. I'm so glad you found your place here. You have sweated and bled for this land, and these people. You are a hero and will forever be a child of the Center." Gaia saw tears swell in his eyes. "You are loved and appreciated and safe. And you have my love and gratitude always," she told him.

He shook his head and tried to swallow the lump in his throat. "My father?" Josh asked after a moment.

"Your father is building a life on the moon Kajax. He's adjusting surprisingly well. And this I promise you, Josh, one day, he will think of you and know with all his heart what a strong and brave man you are. And he will be proud."

"I'm a farmer now. And soon I'll be a husband." He glanced over at Amelia who was still sleeping. "I don't know if he'll ever understand what I have here."

"He will be proud Josh. And one day, he'll meet your wife and your children and then, he will understand."

He looked back at Gaia. "Thank you. For everything."

"You have nothing to thank me for. You did it all, Josh. And I can't wait to see what you build here, with this woman. She loves you with her whole heart, as I see you do her. I hope you will invite me to your wedding."

"I was hoping you would perform the ceremony," Josh said with a little laugh.

Gaia embraced him and kissed him on the cheek. "I would be honored!"

As Gaia slipped out of Josh's room, she found Kendra waiting for her in the hall.

"Someone told me they saw you go in there," Kendra said. "I was wondering if I could have a minute of your time?"

"Of course. What can I do for you, Kendra?"

"Can you come with me for a minute?"

Gaia nodded and Kendra started leading her down the hall. She stopped in front of a closed door.

"Kylie, one of our citizens went into labor during the battle. Luckily we were able to get her to the clinic before the child was born. But I'm hoping you can shed a little light on what she gave birth to."

Kendra opened the door and walked in with a smile. Gaia followed closely behind her. She saw an exhausted woman who had obviously been crying, being held by a man with dark hair and eyes.

"Kylie, Lucas, this is Gaia," Kendra said. "I'm going to have her take a look at your baby."

"Gaia!" Kylie breathed out. "Thank goodness! Please, what's wrong with my baby?"

Gaia walked over to where a nurse was cleaning a pretty baby girl with big blue eyes. "She's beautiful," Gaia said loudly enough for her mother to hear. "She appears to be healthy." The nurse turned the baby to show Gaia her back. There were two long gashes running the length of her back just outside of the spine.

"Ah," Gaia said with a smile. "May I?" she asked the nurse. She took the baby and walked with her over to the bed, where were parents were anxiously waiting. "Your baby is just fine," she told them. "How many generations have you been here?"

"We're both seventh generation," Lucas told her.

"Then you're right on schedule." Gaia said. She handed the baby to her mother who held her on her chest to nuzzle her soft little head.

"On schedule for what?" Kylie asked. "What's wrong with her back?"

"Nothing is wrong with her back. She is perfect," Gaia told her. "Congratulations, Kylie and Lucas. You have just given birth to the first true Asterian," She reached out and ran a fingertip softly down the baby's spine, tickling lightly. Suddenly two bright pink and gold wings popped out of the slashes and started fluttering.

"Oh!" Kendra let out a little gasp. "They're beautiful! But Gaia, why does she have wings?"

"Because your planet and her people are evolving."

"Evolving into what?" Lucas asked. "Dragons?"

Gaia laughed. "No, Asterians. What did you decide to call her?"

"Lilly," Lucas said. "After Kylie's Grandmother."

"Well, welcome and blessings on you, Lilly of Asteria," Gaia said and gently felt one of her wings.

"But she's still human, right?" Kylie asked.

Gaia smiled. "No. She's Asterian and I imagine she'll have many more friends with wings, soon."

"Why didn't our son Brax have wings?" Lucas asked.

"Maybe it wasn't his time. Or maybe they just haven't come in yet. Boys often develop slower. How old is he?"

"He just turned two a few weeks ago," Kylie said. "And Lucas, he has that long birthmark on his back."

"I'd keep an eye open for his wings to come," Gaia said with a wink and a last look at little Lilly. "Blessings on your family," she said and left the room.

Kendra scrambled out after her. "Wings? Is there anything we need to know? Is there anything special we need to do for them? To keep them healthy and safe?"

"No, nothing really. Their wings will be retractable, so just make sure the area is kept clean and open. I imagine in another hundred years or so, your people will share the sky with their dragons. I can't wait to see how they build this planet!"

The following day, some of the soldiers and members of Zander's team took the military ship, *Justice*, and returned to the Center through the skyway. Others followed on Kenji's *Victory*. Many of them had families waiting for them and they wanted to let them know they were safe. Others were protectors of worlds and had jobs to get back to. Most of the wounded were healing well and released to return to their homes.

Josh, Ian and Pax were told they had to remain in the clinic a little longer. Their wounds were more extensive, and they each needed more time with the healers. But they were allowed to attend the memorial service for the 2,162 souls lost in the battle with the Chartins.

The bodies of the fallen were burned in a mass pyre, and the dragon riders spread their ashes over the land that they died defending.

Sarah and Kenji hosted Gaia and Ben in their little cottage, now that they had an extra bedroom. And Zander stayed with Mateo in Josh's old room. Hank took up a spot on their couch, while Christov took over Josh's guestroom.

Hank was fascinated with the technology in the cottage. He understood how they got the running water but questioned Kenji on every aspect of the sewer system, and the electricity that was funneled from the ships to allow for lighting, and power for the refrigerators and stoves.

The community started cleaning and rebuilding the following day. Jacob's kids found enough wood from his store to use as a foundation for the new store they would build. Other buildings had been destroyed as well and were already being rebuilt. There were others needing repairs, and everyone pitched in to get that done.

Ben, Hank and Christov stood with Kenji and watched as Sarah approached Apollo the morning she was released from the hospital. The huge dragon lowered his head and bowed to her, and she threw her arms around his neck. She was whispering to him, giving him thanks for saving her life. Then she leapt onto his back, and they lifted off the ground to fly high into the sky.

"Holy crap," Hank said. "That is a sight."

"She's incredible," Christov said.

"She is," Kenji agreed. "We might as well go grab something to drink. They'll be gone a while."

They reluctantly turned from the field and went to meet the others at The Dive.

By the following week, when the *Okinawa* arrived with Akemi and Akemi and Kenji's father Hurato Tanaka, her 9-year-old son Kai and her 14-month-old baby daughter Sage, all the remaining patients had been released and were on the landing pad with hundreds of the community members, waiting to greet them. There were only a few others on board, the pilot, Ryan, and his wife who lived at the Center but was from the Planet Nexla and their two children. 8-year-old daughter Nexi and their son, 5-year-old Paul.

Akemi spotted her husband Zander standing by her brother Kenji and let out a squeal and started running toward them. She had been warned about the light gravity on the planet but wasn't quite prepared how quickly she would reach them. She almost overshot, but Kenji reached his arm out and caught her in a huge hug. Mr. Tanaka walked toward them with a smile holding little Sage in his arms, and Kai's hand in his.

Kenji grabbed his father in a hug, then took the baby. "So, this is my niece. Hi Sage! I'm your uncle Kenji" He nuzzled her, and she grabbed his face and gave him a big open mouthed kiss. He laughed and looked at his nephew. "Hey, Kai. Do you remember me?"

"Yeah. I remember you, uncle." He put his fist out to fist bump his like he saw his father do with friends, and he taught his friends to do at school."

Kenji fist bumped his hand, then grabbed him in a hug too."

Sarah stood back and watched the reunion, then stepped up to hug Akemi. "I've missed you so much!" she told her.

"Oh Sarah! I've missed you too. I have so much to tell you and so many questions to ask about Asteria!"

"I hope you're planning on staying for a while! We can catch up and spend some girl time."

"I think we can stay a while," Akemi said, then looked around. "This is a beautiful place. I'm so sorry you had trouble. But we brought you gifts!"

She took Sarah's hand and turned to go back toward the ships. She stopped when she spotted Josh standing off to the side, with a pretty, blonde woman holding his hand. His other arm was in a splint, and he still had bruising on his face, and a bandage over his left eye. She walked up to him and grabbed him in a hug.

"It's so good to see you, Josh. When we heard about the battle and heard you were badly wounded, I was so worried about you!"

"Hi Akemi. It's really good to see you too." He pulled back and looked at Amelia. "Akemi, I'd like you to meet my fiancé, Amelia."

Akemi looked shocked and looked over to Amelia. "Fiancé? Well, this I did not know! How exciting! Hi Amelia, it's so good to meet you!" She embraced her and Amelia smiled.

"I've heard so much about you, Akemi! It's wonderful to meet you. Welcome to Asteria!"

"Come!" Akemi said. "See what we've brought you!"

When they reached the ship, Zander, Mateo, Christov and some of the others were unloading huge cryotubes.

Ben stepped forward. "We had to create new cryos for these guys."

Christov stopped by where they were standing, started looking around. "I didn't see Breen," he told Akemi.

"She said something came up and she wasn't able to come," Akemi told him. "The kids were disappointed, but she said they'd plan a trip another time."

"What came up?" he asked.

Akemi shrugged. "She didn't say."

He nodded and returned to the ship. A few minutes later he and Hank wheeled out another large tube.

"What the heck is in there? Did you bring us giants?" Josh asked.

Akemi laughed. "Look!" she told him.

Sarah, Josh and Amelia crept closer, and then Josh started laughing.

"Where did you guys get cows?"

"We had DNA stored on a couple of the ships. Cows, Sheep, goats, Chickens. We brought feed for them too, until you can grow your own. But now you will have milk and eggs and wool."

"Wow!" Josh said. "That's freaking awesome!" The farmer he had become felt like jumping up and down.

They now had eight milking cows and a bull. They had twelve chickens and a rooster. There were ten sheep and two rams. They also brought a barrel of butterflies and turned them loose.

Gaia and Ben slipped off to the side of the field to watch the interactions. He put his arm around her shoulder, and she leaned into him.

"This is a great place, Gaia," he told her and kissed her head.

"It is."

"I'm glad you broke your rule and intervened here."

"I told you once, a very long time ago, that if there is a rule I don't like, as long as it harms none, I'll break it."

"Well, thank God for that!" Ben said and scooped her into his arms for a long deep kiss.

Mateo introduced Quinn to his brother, niece and nephew. He took Sage from her father's arms and tossed her into the air. Akemi let out a squeal, when Sage didn't return to Mateo's arms, but just kept going up and up, into the air.

Quinn rolled her eyes at Mateo and jumped to catch the baby and bring her back down.

Sage was laughing and reached for Mateo. "Again unca. Again."

"I don't think so," Akemi said and grabbed the baby from Quinn. "Thank you," she told Quinn.

Quinn smiled. "There is nothing here that will harm your children, Akemi," she told her. "Even their childish uncle."

Mateo rolled his eyes and looked at Kai. "That was so cool! Can you do it with me Uncle Mateo?"

"I have something even better for you Kai. Here, climb on," he turned his back and kneeled down.

Kai climbed on Mateo's back, then he turned to Akemi and smiled. He ran to the ledge and jumped down the cliff.

"Even jumping off a cliff?" Akemi asked and started running to the ledge.
She watched as Mateo and Kai came to a soft landing and looked up. "Come on, Mom!" Kai hollered up at her. "That was so cool!"

Akemi looked at Kenji, her mouth hanging open. Kenji smiled and took Sage from her arms and handed her off to Sarah. He grabbed Akemi's hand. "Come on," he said and pulled her off the ledge. Quinn jumped behind them.

Sarah, Zander and Mr. Tanaka watched as they landed gently on the ground next to Mateo and Kai.

"Ready to jump?" Sarah asked Mr. Tanaka. He nodded hesitantly, and she took his hand. She held Sage close, then they all followed and jumped off the cliff.

"That's crazy!" Akemi said. "What a fun place you have here, guys!"

"You aint seen nothin' yet," Mateo said. "Come on, Kai." He turned and headed toward the shore, with Kai running after him.

The group followed behind. Kenji turned toward Akemi and Zander, walking hand in hand. "If Kai jumping off the cliff worried you, maybe you shouldn't watch this," he told them.

"What? Why?" Akemi asked and started running after her son and brother in law. When she reached the shore, she saw Kai and Mateo standing there. Mateo knelt down next to Kai and was pointing out at the sea. Kai started nodding and jumping up and down. "I see them!" he said, delight in his voice.

Akemi put her hand up to shield her eyes from the sun, and looked out at the sea, where Mateo and Kai were looking and pointing.

Before Akemi could move closer, Kenji grabbed her arm to stop her. "Wait," he told her. "I promise you, nothing here will harm him. He's about to have the experience of a lifetime. Let them be, sister."

It took everything she had to stay in her spot when a huge red dragon appeared and rose from the water.

"This is Yemaya," Mateo told Kai. "But I call her Maya," he moved forward and put his head against hers. Maya looked at Kai and bowed to him.

"Woah," Kai said in a whisper. "She's a real live dragon. Can I touch her?"

"Yeah. She'd like that," Mateo told him.

Kai moved slowly forward and put his hand on her neck. "She's so soft. And she's so pretty! Is she yours, uncle?"

Mateo smiled. "She is mine, and I am hers. Would you like to go for a ride?"

Kai's big brown eyes snapped to Mateo. "Can I? She won't mind?"

"Nah, she likes kids. Take off your shoes, buddy."

Kai kicked off his shoes as did Mateo, then he picked up his nephew and placed him on Maya's back. He jumped up behind him and wrapped an arm around him, then patted Maya and she backed up into the water.

They moved slowly through the water, Kai holding his hands up in the air and laughing.

"I'm going to have to come up with something huge to regain favorite uncle status," Kenji said.

Sarah just patted his arm and hugged little Sage closer as she watched her brother with huge eyes, as he rode a dragon across the sea.

Now that Zander's family was here, Hank moved to the couch at Josh and Amelia's place and Mateo moved into Quinn's tree house.

That evening, they sat out on her back porch, looking over the field. The butterflies that Akemi had released seemed to be making themselves at home in the trees, and Quinn was thrilled to see several on the leaves of her tree. She had little fairy lights lit around the banister of her porch, and as the sun started to set, the lights twinkled on.

"This is really a great place."

"Yeah," Quinn said with a smile. "I imagine, someday, I'll get too old to climb the stairs and I'll need to move into the village, but right now, I can't imagine being anywhere else. I love being so close to the lair. Every night, I sit here, and when Titan turns in, he sends me a roar to let me know he's home."

"I'll get out of your way and move back to my place as soon as Zander and Akemi take the kids back to the center. I appreciate you letting me stay, though."

"You're not in my way, Mateo. I enjoy having you here." She slid over to his lap and straddled him, putting her arms around his neck. "I think I might like it a lot."

"Yeah?" he asked

"Mmmhumm" She leaned in and pulled him toward her for a kiss he felt all the way down to his toes. "So, what if you didn't?" she asked him.

"What if I didn't what?" he asked still recovering from the kiss.

"What if you didn't go back to your place. What if you just stayed here with me?"

"You want me to move in with you?"

Quinn nodded. "I think I'd like to have access to you anytime I want," she said and started nuzzling his neck with kisses.

Mateo smiled and stood up with her still wrapped around him. "I think I might like you having access to me," he said and carried her into the tree house.

A team of builders started working on enclosures for the cows, on the north side of the field. Several of the farmers went to the AROE to learn about the care and needs of the new animals being introduced to the community.

Quinn and her grandmother set up a chicken coop behind her cottage with the supplies brought in from the center including the chicken wire.

Molly was lying near the gazebo watching and huffing in disapproval. She had started visiting Donna during the day while Josh and Amelia were working. "Don't worry, Molly, my girl. I won't forget about you, my darling," Donna told her when she saw her watching the chickens with disdain.

When Mateo came to see how they were doing, Donna let out a sigh of joy when she saw Quinn go into his arms without hesitation. She never thought she'd see the day that her girl would learn to love and be loved. But this man from a strange land broke through her barriers. And the way he looked at Quinn put Donna's heart at peace.

That evening, Donna and Mr. Tanaka were set up on the shore with little Sage and Kai watching the sea dragons. They agreed to keep an eye on the kids while the rest gathered at The Dive for their last night together

Ben looked around the tables that had been pulled together so it felt like they were all joined at one big table. He watched his team, and the people they loved. Josh and his Amelia. Akemi and Zander. Sarah and Kenji. Mateo and Quinn. Meg and Quinn. Christov. Hank and Jewell, who had arrived that morning leaving little Henry and Eve with his parents at The Center. And always his Gaia. He thought about how far they had all come. He missed Ishaan and Pete, like a missing limb. But at least they had communication with *The Enterprise* and were able to talk to them.

Gaia reached over and took his hand with a knowing smile. He brought her hand to his lips and smiled back. They had done it. Delivered humanity from a dying planet and took them to paradise. Whether on Asteria or The Center, or wherever Ishaan and Pete ended up.

Humanity would live on.

Coming Soon

The Center Book 3:
Invasion

Other titles by BLKDOG Publishing for your consideration:

Britannia: The Wall
By Richard Denham & M. J. Trow

THE END OF ROMAN BRITAIN BEGINS.

The story opens in 367 AD. Four soldiers - Justinus, Paternus, Leocadius and Vitalis - are out hunting for food supplies at an outpost of Hadrian's Wall, when the Wall comes under attack.

The four find their fort destroyed, their comrades killed, and Paternus is unable to find his wife and son. As they run south to Eboracum, they realize that this is no ordinary border raid. Ranged against the Romans at the edge of the world are four different peoples, and they have banded together under a mysterious leader who wears a silver mask and uses the name Valentinus - man of Valentia, the turbulent area north of the Wall.

Faced with questions they are hard-pressed to answer, Leocadius blurts out a story that makes the men Heroes of the Wall. Their lives change not only when Valentinus begins his lethal sweep across Britannia but as soon as Leo's lie is out in the world, growing and changing as it goes.

Goblin Market
By Maryanne Coleman

Have you ever wondered what happened to the faeries you used to believe in? They lived at the bottom of the garden and left rings in the grass and sparkling glamour in the air to remind you where they were. But that was then – now you might find them in places you might not think to look. They might be stacking shelves, delivering milk or weighing babies at the clinic. Open your eyes and keep your wits about you and you might see them.

But no one is looking any more and that is hard for a Faerie Queen to bear and Titania has had enough. When Titania stamps her foot, everyone in Faerieland jumps; publicity is what they need. Television, magazines. But that sort of thing is much more the remit of the bad boys of the Unseelie Court, the ones who weave a new kind of magic; the World Wide Web. Here is Puck re-learning how to fly; Leanne the agent who really is a vampire; Oberon's Boys playing cards behind the wainscoting; Black Annis, the bag-lady from Hainault, all gathered in a Restoration comedy that is strictly twenty-first century.

Fade
By Bethan White

There is nothing extraordinary about Chris Rowan. Each day he wakes to the same faces, has the same breakfast, the same commute, the same sort of homes he tries to rent out to unsuspecting tenants.

There is nothing extraordinary about Chris Rowan. That is apart from the black dog that haunts his nightmares and an unexpected encounter with a long forgotten demon from his past. A nudge that will send Chris on his own downward spiral, from which there may be no escape.

There is nothing extraordinary about Chris Rowan...

www.blkdogpublishing.com